THE HUNTED

POLICE SCOTLAND
BOOK 10

ED JAMES

Copyright © 2017 Ed James

The right of Ed James to be identified as the author of this work has been asserted in accordance with the Copyright, Designs and Patents Act 1988. All rights reserved.

No part of this publication may be reproduced, stored in or transmitted into any retrieval system, in any form, or by any means (electronic, mechanical, photocopying, recording or otherwise) without the prior written permission of the publisher. Any person who does any unauthorised act in relation to this publication may be liable to criminal prosecution and civil claims for damages.

This is a work of fiction. Names, characters, businesses, places, events and incidents are either the products of the author's imagination or used in a fictitious manner. Any resemblance to actual persons, living or dead, or actual events is purely coincidental.

Cover design copyright © Ed James

DAY 1

Thursday
12th May

1

HUNTER

DC Craig Hunter slowed the pool car as he approached the roundabout. The wipers cleared a hole in the rain-splatter pattern on the windscreen, almost immediately refilled.

Who'd believe it was May?

Galashiels emerged through the hazy deluge. Typical Scottish town. Could be anywhere — Elgin, Dalkeith, Forfar, Stranraer — but it was in the Borders. Stuck at the top edge of the square of small rugby towns that anyone with half a mind would escape at eighteen and never look back. The weather made it look even worse, sucking the life and colour out of the sky.

One of the new trains was grinding its way back towards Edinburgh, water sluicing down the side windows as it gathered speed. The tracks hid behind a low brick wall, an older one set into steep steps higher up the cliff face, the beige blocks darkened by the rain.

He switched into the right-hand lane and took the old bridge across the Tweed — at least, he thought it was the Tweed — and waited by a grand hotel opposite Farmfoods, the indicator clicking.

DS Chantal Jain sat next to him. Skin tone a barista could spend hours getting coffee to match. Cheekbones that could cut diamond or blunt the sharpest drill. Hunter's boss and didn't she know it.

She rattled the cable hanging out of her phone. 'Bloody thing still isn't charging.' She waved a hand over the road, obscured by the wipers squeaking across the windscreen. 'It's that way.'

'Shite, aye.' Hunter flicked the indicator to the left and set off down a long street. 'Not paying attention.' Old buildings faced off against the sixties police station, three grim storeys of white harling. He turned into the busy car park and settled for the furthest space.

Chantal was already out, snapping her brolly open like it was a police baton. She jogged across the tarmac towards the cop shop.

Hunter turned off the engine and got out into the rain. Even heavier than it looked. He darted through the stair rods and burst in through the front door. His jacket looked like he'd dived into the deep end of a swimming pool.

Chantal shook out her umbrella by the public desk, water spraying in the empty room. 'You're kidding me.'

'Wish I was, doll.' The sergeant perched on a stool, sneering at his computer like it was beneath him. 'All that way and she can't be arsed to turn up. Nightmare, eh?'

Hunter joined Chantal and rested his soaking hands on the desk. 'What's going on?'

'She's not showed up.' Chantal glowered at the desk sergeant, like that'd do any good. 'Have you misplaced her on the system?'

The sergeant swivelled the monitors around to show four empty rooms. 'Just the two here, hen. She's not in either of them.' He chinked the screen. 'And these others are the only places she's allowed. She's not here.'

Hunter clamped his eyes shut. 'Think she's bumped us again?'

'Three times in a week.' Chantal snapped out her umbrella, a fresh mist of water spraying off. 'You'd think she didn't want that dirty raping bastard to go to prison or something.'

What if she's not bumped us, but...

Hunter swallowed hard. 'Tulloch can't have got to her, can he?'

He checked his watch, sweat trickling down his back. 'Supposed to still be at Fort George until about now.'

What if we're wrong?

What if he left the barracks early and headed down here to...

Hunter dug out his phone. 'Aw, shite.'

Five missed calls from Paisley Sanderson.

~

HUNTER TOOK his chance and joined the snake of cars and vans winding down the High Street. Curry house, hairdressers, charity shop. Wetherspoons, pool hall, kiltmaker. He slowed the wipers a notch. 'Is she answering?'

Chantal stared out of the window, a slight shake of her head. 'Still nothing.' She put the phone to her ear. 'Tell me this isn't another one.'

'I'd love to.' Hunter drove on, twisting his fingers against the rubbery steering wheel. Polish shop, taxi firm, corner pub in an old bank building. 'Four victims pulled out, now it looks like another. How's this happening?'

The hills climbed up to surround the town's valley.

'I don't know, Craig.' Chantal looked back at him, eyebrows raised, her lips an O. 'Voicemail.'

'Eight months.' Hunter grunted as he twisted around another bend. 'Twenty cops across half the bloody country, trying to get enough evidence to put one shitebag away.' A financial advisor's office hid amongst the old shopfronts, long since converted into houses. 'He's not getting away with it.'

The McDonald's arches loomed in the distance, the Californian yellow glowing in the grey Scottish sky.

'Ah, shite.' Hunter braked hard, the car skidded. He pulled a sharp left and overshot the turning, almost smacking into a Toyota SUV. He climbed up towards some orange flats overlooking the river valley. 'Maybe you should've driven.'

'You can't navigate for shite. Left, then left again.'

Hunter followed the road around. Victorian houses on both sides, all with dormer roofs, the left-hand side dotted with satellite dishes. He took another left onto a row of modern houses dripping in the rain. Brick ground floors, covered in harling upstairs. He pulled in opposite and killed the engine. 'He's put four women in hospital and kept their mouths shut. We'll put him away and get justice for his victims.'

Chantal got out and jogged across the road. Rain teemed down, soaking her black hair. She knocked on the first door and turned around, holding her jacket above her head.

Hunter joined her in the downpour, the lights flashing as he plipped the pool car. Already felt like his suit had just come out of the washing machine.

Chantal thumped on the door. Nothing.

Hunter took a step back, rain sliding down his shirt collar. A tiny little house, only one window on both floors. Most of the interior would be stairs. Next door was a mirror, followed by another three pairs.

No sound from inside.

A lane ran down the back. Steps led up to a flat at the rear of a main-road house, backing on to this side street.

Chantal knocked again. 'Ms Sanderson, it's DS Jain.' She waited for a few seconds, tapping her foot, then another knock. Nothing again.

Hunter checked his baton was in his belt, his teeth grinding into each other. 'Stay here, I'll check the back. Keep trying her phone.' He marched over to the thin path at the side of the house.

Second-hand curry fumes hung on the air. A small yard lay at the back, a four-square patio that would never get any direct sun. Not that it was a problem today. Two green plastic chairs sat either side of a pile of bricks. Raindrops dotted the water filling an ashtray, submerged cigarette butts up to halfway. No chance of telling if they'd been smoked ten minutes or ten years ago.

Hunter peered in the kitchen window. No immediate signs of life. Lights off, gloomier than a funeral home. The room was like an IKEA catalogue. The kettle had misted the window glass.

Bingo. Someone is in.

Hunter stepped over and tried the back door.

The handle jolted down and the door flew back into the house. A boot lashed out, cracking into Hunter's knee. Something thumped his chest and he tumbled backwards. He reached out, grabbing hold of one of the bricks as he fell.

His hip cracked off the concrete. Crunch.

The ashtray toppled onto his face, covering his suit and trousers in grey water. Burnt ash powdered his face, covered his tongue. He swallowed dirty rainwater, thick lumps getting caught in his throat. He tried to cough it up.

A boot hit him in the side.

Hunter rolled away and swiped out with his leg, trying to sweep.

He missed.

Another boot sparked off his thigh. A hand gripped his wrist and twisted his arm back. His lips kissed the slabs. Hunter wriggled round. 'Stop!'

A hand pressed Hunter's face against the slabs, grit digging into his chin. 'Sean Tulloch, you're under arrest!' Irish accent.

'I'm not Tulloch!' Hunter jerked his head round, getting a nice scratch on his cheek. 'I'm a cop!'

The grip slackened off. 'What?'

Hunter slapped the hand away and rolled over. 'DC Craig Hunter, Sexual Offences Unit.' He reached into his jacket pocket for his warrant card and flashed it.

A lanky cop stood over him, confusion pulsing his bushy eyebrows. He took off his cap, coiled-up curls springing free, the sides shaved to a step. Glamour biceps stretched his standard-issue T-shirt. 'Shite.'

Hunter pushed himself to standing. His kneecap felt like it had swivelled round to the inside. 'Who are you?'

'PC Lenny Warner. How're ye?' Dirty Dubliner accent, hiding out in the Scottish Borders for no obvious reason.

Hunter spat out a cigarette butt. He almost vomited. 'Jesus.'

'You okay?'

'Not really.' Another butt came out. Still tasted like... like a bloody ashtray. 'This is horrible.'

'I'm sorry, I thought you were Tulloch.' Warner was a good few inches taller than Hunter. He looked young, his designer stubble a desperate attempt to add maturity. 'What are you doing here?'

'We're supposed to be interviewing Paisley Sanderson.' Hunter tried to dust off his crotch. Looked like he'd had an accident in a baker's. 'She's one of many long-term domestic abuse cases relating to a Sean William—'

'—Tulloch.' Warner groaned as he put his cap back on. He

thumbed inside the house. 'Yer woman there called us. Said she's got a nasty text from her boyfriend, one Sean Tulloch. Tried calling some cops, but they didn't answer.'

'That's us.' Hunter hadn't seen a squad car. 'You here alone?'

'For now.' Warner pulled the back door open. 'So, can I get you a cup of tea?'

2

CHANTAL

Chantal tipped the boiling water into the pastel-coloured teacups, her phone clamped between her ear and her shoulder. She mashed Hunter's teabag. How the picky bastard liked it. 'Aye, we've got hold of her now.'

Not without Craig making an arse of himself yet again.

Sharon McNeill sighed down the line. 'You had me worried.'

'Tell me about it.' Chantal dumped the first teabag into the grey compost bin on the counter and splashed in milk. 'Shaz, we'll get him, okay?'

'Right, well, let me know if anything happens.' Click.

Chantal pocketed her phone and started going through the cupboards.

Cheap sub-IKEA junk, like the rest of the kitchen.

An animal sanctuary calendar hung off the side of the metallic fridge. May's animal was Pumpkin, a squat donkey with its head stuck into a bucket of carrots. Nothing much filled in on the days. Except…

Today's date had two entries:

11 — APPOINTMENT IN TOWN
2 — SEAN BACK!!!

Something to go on, at least.

She picked up Hunter's tea and her own and headed back through.

Hunter was standing in the hallway, staring into space, his lips twitching. His cheek was scuffed red.

What the hell?

She waved her hand in front of his face. 'Craig, are you okay?'

Hunter blinked hard, then focused on her. He huffed out a breath. 'Is that my tea?'

'What were you doing?'

'Pain management.'

Chantal passed him his cup, milky liquid sloshing over the sides. 'Because that big Irish guy beat you up?'

'Right. Number of times I've had my arse handed to me over the years. Getting battered so often is messing with my head. I need to centre myself again. No big deal.'

∽

CHANTAL SAT ON THE SOFA, almost sending a pile of women's magazines toppling over. She rested her tea on the coffee table and tried to make eye contact.

Paisley Sanderson wasn't having any of it. She cowered on an armchair, the wings slumping at almost the same angle as her shoulders. Her gaze shot around the living room, hazed with smoke, clouding out the thin shaft of light the Roman blinds let in. An ironing board sat face down behind her, an expensive-looking model. PC Warner leaned against the wall near the kitchen door, sipping his tea.

Her focus finally settled on Hunter, standing in front of her. 'You didn't answer the phone!'

Her navy dressing gown was frayed around the wrists, hanging open by the chest, her white top greyed. Pale skin lined her mouth. Her dark-ringed eyes struggling to focus on anyone in the room. She had the same look in her eyes as the other four victims. Felt like Sean Tulloch could home in on something about them, like they were a type. Pick out their weakness from miles away, like an owl would a mouse, swooping down to claim his prey.

Vicious bastard left a trail of battered women, fractured shells, memories of abuse and torture their only souvenirs. Too frightened to speak.

So they needed to keep her talking.

Hunter stood and rubbed at his trousers again, covered in ash. Could smell the cigarette stink from here, as bad as the room. He gave Paisley a smile. 'I was driving. I'm sorry. You did the right thing.'

'Doubting that.' Paisley's shattered nails clawed at the gown, her purple polish cracked and frayed. 'You said you'd protect me from him.'

'And we will.' Hunter stopped short of reaching out to touch her. 'Can I see this text message?'

'Here.' Paisley reached over to the coffee table and picked up a giant Samsung, shiny and new. 'Have a look.' She held it out with a shaking hand.

Hunter took the mobile and checked the display. His eyes shut as he handed the phone to Chantal.

The texts app with that graph-paper background, her messages in yellow, Sean Tulloch's in pale blue. All gushing and lovey-dovey until the last one from him:

NO WHO U SPOKE 2. U R DEAD BITCH.

Shite.

Shite, shite, shite.

Chantal took a sip of tea, trying to stop her hand shaking.

How the hell did Tulloch know we're speaking to her? Who'd blabbed?

And what about the others? Has he only contacted Paisley?

Chantal set her cup down on the coffee table. 'Did you tell him you were talking to us?'

Paisley slumped back in the chair and tugged her dressing gown tight. 'I only spoke to you two because I've had enough of him.'

'Okay, but did you mention us to him?'

Paisley shook her head.

'Anything at all that he could put two and two together over?'

'Nothing.' Paisley nibbled at a thumbnail, a fleck of polish jumping off. 'Sure it's not one of you lot, eh?'

'We have checks and balances in place to protect your identity.' Chantal rested the phone on the unvarnished coffee table. 'We will do everything in our power to make sure you're okay.'

Paisley picked at her index finger with her teeth, a frown crawling over her pale forehead. 'You don't know what he's going to do to me!'

'We do. We're—'

'You don't!' Paisley's hands shot out wide. 'He's going to kill me!'

'Listen to me.' Chantal settled into a crouch in front of her. 'You're not the only one, okay? You're the latest in a long line of women Mr Tulloch has been abusing across Scotland. There are victims in Livingston, Leslie, Edinburgh and Falkirk. There may be more.'

'Shite.' Paisley's eyes clamped shut. 'It's not just me?'

'Far from it.' Chantal smiled, hoping for reassurance. 'He's got a pattern. He finds a fragile woman, charms them, moves in and it's all smashing. Then he starts abusing her, hitting her, tormenting her, frightening her until she's so scared of him she won't tell her family what he's doing to her, let alone the police. Then he leaves her with a final warning and he's on to someone new. Someone like you.'

Paisley patted her cheek, the heavy purple they'd seen a fortnight ago now yellowed. 'So he's done this before?'

'Your statement will bring the story up to date and help secure a prosecution.' Chantal rested a hand on the floor. *The calendar...* 'Now, do you know where he is?'

'He's due back today.' More nibbling at her nails. 'He's got two weeks' leave.' Paisley caressed her jaw, thumb and forefinger wrapping around. Then it clicked, sending spasms of revulsion down Chantal's spine. 'He's coming back from Fort George tonight, getting the train from Inverness to Waverley. Then down to here.' She clicked her jaw again. 'I was meant to be meeting him at the station this afternoon.'

'When?'

'About two. Said he'd call when he got on.'

'Thanks.' Chantal bounced to her feet. 'We'll try to intercept him in Edinburgh before he comes down here.' She snatched up the phone from the table. 'We'll have to take this as evidence.'

'But that's my life—'

'I know it's difficult, but I'll get it back to you by tomorrow, okay?' Chantal flashed a smile as she dropped it into an evidence bag. 'The good news is we can prosecute him for this threat right now. We won't have to wait.' She rattled the bag, smiling at Paisley. 'At least three crimes I can think of, once we've confirmed this came from him.'

Paisley nodded, staring into space. 'Do you want me to meet him at the station?'

'God no.' Chantal shot a finger at Warner by the kitchen door. 'There'll be a uniform presence here as long as it's needed.'

'Right.' Paisley scowled. 'I need my phone back as soon as.'

'Of course.' Chantal walked over to the front door and opened it. 'We'll be back later, okay?'

Paisley gave a tiny nod. 'Okay.'

Blue lights flashed in the street. A squad car purred outside, hopefully it'd add enough presence and keep Tulloch away.

Chantal stepped out of the house and nodded at the female officer behind the wheel, then at Warner. 'Under no circumstances are you to let Paisley out of your sight.'

'I won't.' Warner put his cap back on. 'See that statement, can I do it for you?'

Chantal looked him up and down. 'We need a detective.'

3

HUNTER

Hunter nudged the passenger seat down another notch. Still not right. He cleared his throat again, trying to shift the cigarette butt he wasn't sure was still there or not. Close to vomiting.

He tried calling again. 'Pick up, you daft git.'

Chantal turned left to get back on the A7, the wipers sweeping the heavy rain off the windscreen. She glanced over. 'Elvis still not answering?'

'Probably pulling his wire in the toilet.'

Chantal laughed. 'Charming.'

He pocketed his phone. Bloody jacket was damp from the fight and never-ending Borders rain. Knee still aches.

He cleared his throat. Definitely a fag stuck down there. Another cough and something shifted. 'How did Tulloch find out we were speaking to Paisley?'

She glanced over at him. 'Been wondering that myself.'

Hunter leaned back in the chair and threw some ideas around. Nothing landed where he wanted it. His knee throbbed. 'Maybe one of the other victims blabbed? He could've done this to the other four, as well. You know, scattergun approach.' He stabbed the phone then redialled. 'Either way, we've got a leak.'

Two rings. 'Hunter...' DC Paul Gordon. Elvis. Yawning like he'd just woken up. As ever. 'What's up?'

'You in the office?'

'Been speaking to DI—'

'Right. I need you to speak to the British Transport Police for me.'

Elvis groaned. 'Why?'

'Get them to check if Sean Tulloch was on the nine o'clock train from Inverness to Edinburgh.'

'Hold on a minute.' Computer keys clattered in the background. 'Aye, he's on it.'

Hunter frowned over at Chantal. 'What, how have you done that?'

'I wave my wand and magic happens, Craig my man.' Elvis laughed down the line. 'I've got access to the ScotRail CCTV feed, you dobber. Only reason you lot hired me, right?'

'Knew there had to be one.' Hunter swapped his phone to the other ear and shuffled his notebook out of his soggy suit jacket. He winced as something creaked in his chest. Then his knee throbbed again, giving him that old gag reflex. 'It's definitely him?'

'Oh, aye. I see this Tulloch boy's face when I close my eyes at night thanks to all the skivvy work you've had me doing.' A sigh cut through the office chatter. 'The big bugger got on at Inverness, just before the train pulled off I hasten to add. Chancing it a bit.'

'Right.' The pine-covered hills rolled past. 'Can you get a call out to local uniform to check in with his other victims?'

'What did your last slave die of?'

'Stupid sideburns and a penchant for donuts.' Hunter tried to ignore Chantal's laughter. 'One last thing — DS Jain requests that you meet us at Waverley.'

'What, as in now?'

'Well, as soon as.'

'Christ's sake, man. Jim's been to Krispy Kreme's.'

'Sure you'll be able to munch a couple on the way over.'

'Wanker.' Click.

Hunter pocketed his phone, careful not to damage anything. 'Take it you got the gist of that?'

Chantal nodded. 'You are a wanker.'

∼

Hunter got out of the car. Market Street, down in the depths of Edinburgh's old town. Passengers spilled out of Waverley, a gang of Japanese tourists ran past in translucent raincoats, rain spattering their exposed heads. A coach hissed. Nearby, a pair of confused tourists struggled to get their message across to an idling taxi.

DC Paul Gordon got out of the car in front, munching on something. He stepped in a puddle, oily rainwater splashing up the beige legs of his trousers. His fingers shot out to flash across the air. 'In the name of the wee man.'

Hunter unclicked Chantal's brolly, unable to stop laughing. 'You okay, mate?'

'Like shite I am—' Elvis nodded at Chantal as she dumped the "on official police business" sign on the dashboard, rubbing his triangular sideburns. 'Sarge.'

'Paul.' Chantal looked up and down the street. 'You were supposed to get the Transport cops.'

'Aye, the lad's waiting downstairs.' Elvis clicked his heels like he was a doorman at a nightclub. 'Follow me.' He set off into Waverley, dancing down the steps. 'Oh, before I forget, I checked with those other victims.'

Hunter kept pace with him. 'And?'

'Nobody else's even heard from Tulloch in months. No death threats.'

Hunter stopped and swung around to face Chantal. 'So he's only targeted Paisley?'

'Looks like it.' Elvis smirked. 'Who names their kid Paisley? It's asking for trouble.'

'Constable...' Chantal rolled her eyes at him. 'Can you try and escort us to the BTP office without making yourself look any worse?'

'Aye, soz.' Elvis started off again. Click, click. 'Better name than Ardrossan or Saltcoats, I suppose.'

∼

PC Pete Davies paced around his grotto, a dark little room stinking of stale coffee from the mouldy dregs at the bottom of a mug. No natural light, just the greyscale glare of the computer monitors. He looked like he was born bored, sauntering out of the womb with a yawn. The British Transport Police officer slurped at his paper cup of tea and licked his lips. Again. He rubbed his moustache and tapped at the screens in front of them. Another lick of the lips for good measure. 'So, like I was saying, pal, it's a needle in a haystack.'

Why is everything so bloody difficult with that lot? Hunter rested against a seat back, clawing at the ripped fabric. 'I need to know if Sean Tulloch is still on that train or not.'

'Still?' Davies frowned at Elvis. 'How do you know he's on it in the first place?'

Elvis cleared his throat. 'Got a mate with access to the CCTV feeds.'

'You've got a mate, have you? Lying bastard.' Davies huffed as he waved his hands at the monitors. 'Right, the only problem is, *I* can't access the on-train feed from here.'

Each screen showed live footage of Waverley station at lunchtime. A few people milled around by the announcements board, clutching coffees and pastries.

Davies licked his lips again. 'We usually use these things to back up assaults. Drunk wankers from Prestonpans missing the last train on a Friday night. That kind of thing. Dreading the Cup Final next week.'

Chantal looked ready to launch herself across the room at him. 'Is this you saying you can't help?'

Davies glanced round at Elvis. 'Maybe DC Gordon's *mate* can help.'

Chantal hauled open the door. 'Right, come on.'

Davies held up his hands. 'I'm not being a dick here.'

'Fine.'

'We'll need to hurry, though.' Davies tapped at another screen. 'That train's just left Haymarket.'

Hunter jogged up the stairs then followed Chantal down the narrow corridor. Behind, Davies and a couple of Transport Police officers jog-walked, their red faces indicating they'd fail a fitness test at the warm-up. He frowned at Elvis. 'Elv—' Cough. 'Paul, are our lot still in position?'

'Should be, aye.'

'Can you bloody phone them?'

'Keep your hair on.' Elvis reached into his pocket and almost tripped over.

'Sod this.' Hunter darted down the concourse past the WH Smith. He sprinted through the turnstile, getting a polite nod from the waiting guard.

A squad of local uniform spread out along the platform to the right, stretching off to the tunnels leading to Haymarket. Across the tracks, the other platforms were mostly empty.

Big Jim was strutting around like he was in charge. His shaved head caught the worst of the rain. His suit looked like it was wearing him. He nodded at Elvis.

Hunter spun round. 'Which carriage was Tulloch in?'

Elvis rubbed at his left sideburn as he slowed. He was sucking in breath. 'Erm, the second.'

'Counting from which end?'

'Oh, eh. This end.' Elvis frowned. 'I think.'

A train spluttered out of the tunnel, the dirty yellow front hissing towards them, rain flashing in the headlights.

Hunter jogged partway up the track, trying to gauge the train's braking as it screeched to a halt, the front metres away from him.

'Shite.' Hunter raced down the platform.

The bulk of the uniforms stepped towards the train, blocking the exits. A door further down bleeped open and a guard stepped out. He reached in to fiddle with the controls, but a cop stopped him.

Hunter peered through the second carriage's windows. Two queues merged at the doors. A couple were facing the wrong way, lost in an argument. Empty cans of lager filled some of the tables. An old man stood, letting his walking stick take the strain as he joined the queue.

A pair of hulking giants, both matching Tulloch's description. *Which one is he? Hard to tell when you've never seen the guy in person.*

Hunter locked eyes with Chantal, getting a nod.

The doors hissed open. A small woman with a buggy and two toddlers was first out. Passengers flooded past as she did up her coat in the pissing rain.

The first of the giants stooped below the doorway and stepped onto the platform. A uniform grabbed him and pulled him through the crowd. Chantal headed over towards him.

The second giant slipped out, his hooded head twitching around. He clocked the nearest uniforms and disappeared, lost in the crowd.

Oh, shite.

Hunter took one look at the wheezing Transport cops and made a decision. 'Stop, police!'

Tulloch was on the tracks. He ignored Hunter and bounded across the planks.

Hunter bombed off and followed him into the pit between platforms, easing himself onto the pebbles. The air fizzed with electricity. Bloody thing's live.

Tulloch hauled himself up the other side with military ease.

Hunter stepped across the boards, careful to avoid the tracks, and hefted himself up onto the platform. Took two goes to stand. Bloody knee was still aching.

Tulloch jumped to the next set of tracks and ran towards the main body of the station. His hood kept flapping back but never fell.

Chantal was scowling at Hunter, arms wide. 'Craig, what the hell are you doing?'

He set off across the empty platform, trailing Tulloch along the edge. Tulloch's stride was much longer than Hunter's, but the stones were slowing him down. He reached the end and swung up like a cat.

Hunter grabbed Tulloch as he got up to a crouch and stuck his knee between his shoulder blades. He pulled him to his feet and jerked his right arm up. Something damp splashed on his trousers. Hopefully not Coke.

Tulloch's mid-grey tracksuit bottoms darkened in a patch winding round his leg. A yellow puddle spread out at his feet.

He'd pissed himself. All over Hunter's legs.

Chantal skidded to a halt next to them, frowning at him. 'Craig, you—'

'My name is DC Craig Hunter of Police Scotland.' He tightened the grip on the arm. 'Sean Tulloch, I'm arresting you for threatening and abusive behaviour, you don't—'

'I'm not Sean Tulloch!' Thick Australian accent.

'What?' Hunter let his grip slacken off.

Chantal reached into his pocket and pulled out his wallet. She flipped it open and groaned. 'James Maxwell?'

'That's me.' He grimaced. 'That's hurting, mate!'

Hunter eased off the grip a touch and shrugged at Chantal. 'Is it a fake ID?'

'Not with a Brisbane accent.' Chantal got in Maxwell's face. 'Do you know a Sean Tulloch?'

'What? No!'

'So who were you running from?'

'You lot!' Maxwell tried to glance round at Hunter but didn't make it very far. 'Look, I've got the new series of "Game of Thrones" on a memory stick. Thought you were after that.'

Bloody, bloody hell.

4

CHANTAL

Chantal let Maxwell go and pushed him towards one of Davies's Transport cops.

All that shite for a drive full of some stupid TV show.

She tried to snap herself together. 'So where is Tulloch?'

Hunter frowned at her. He didn't speak. Couldn't speak. He raised his shoulders.

'The other big guy who got off the train is one Keith Brannigan.' Chantal glowered at him. 'Tulloch wasn't on that train, Craig.'

'Bloody hell.' Hunter stepped backwards with a squelch. 'Jesus.'

'And you stink.'

'Craig, Craig, Craig.' Elvis grinned wide. 'You caught some rube with "Tits and Dragons" on a stick. Man...' His nostrils twitched. 'Did he piss all over you?'

Hunter couldn't make eye contact with him. 'You said he was on that train.'

'Aye, he *was*.' Elvis's tongue flicked across his lips. 'Must've got off somewhere between here and Inverness.'

Chantal got between them. 'Paul, I need you and Jenny to get down to Galashiels *now* and take a statement from Paisley Sanderson.'

Elvis's shoulders slumped. 'Don't you want me to help find him, Sarge?'

'You can do both. If Jenny drives, you can muck about on your laptop.' She narrowed her eyes at him. 'I want to know everything Sean Tulloch's done to her. Every little detail. And I want you to compare it to the other victims. Is she different? Is there something we've missed about the others that could get them to talk?'

'But I've got to get away at—'

She put a finger to his lips. 'Paul, her abuser is still at large. Every time Sean Tulloch's back on leave, he knocks seven shades of shite out of her. Exactly like the other four victims. We're going to stop him.'

'Look, it's—'

'You've got three hours overtime tonight, you can go when the statement's done.'

'But, Sarge—'

'But nothing.' Chantal took a step forward, her eyes narrowing further. 'Are you telling me you don't know how to take a statement?'

'No, it's—'

'You're a DC, Paul. You take statements. And I'm your boss, so you take orders from me. Okay?'

Elvis looked away with a glower. 'Right. Fine.'

Hunter clapped him on the shoulder. 'You live in Dalkeith, Paul. Galashiels isn't a million miles from home.'

Elvis's nostrils twitched. 'Have you got any of that piss on me?'

Chantal smirked at Hunter's trousers. 'You'll need to get to Markies for a new fighting suit, Craig.' She started off towards Davies. 'I'll see what I can do about you trespassing on the tracks.'

∼

CHANTAL OVERTOOK a lorry on the inside lane. The wipers struggled to cope as the pool car thundered along the M8, dirty rain spraying across the windscreen.

What a disaster. What an absolute disaster.

Tulloch gave us the slip. He's out there, somewhere. Meaning he knows we're after him. Doesn't it?

She reached over and flicked on the radio.

'—while, Newcastle detectives investigating the disappearance of three-year-old Harry Jack from his home in Alnwick last night believe he might have been taken to Portugal. DI Jonathan Bruce of Northumbria Police had this—'

Chantal snapped it off and glanced over. 'You can thank me, you know?'

'Right.' Hunter rubbed at his new trousers. She could still smell the vague whiff of second-hand piss from him. 'These are far too bloody tight. You can see my balls, can't you?'

'Might stop you chasing the wrong guy next time.' Chantal flicked the indicator left and pulled off onto the slip road for Bathgate. 'I meant that you can thank me for getting you off a charge for trespassing on the tracks.'

Hunter ran a hand over his skinhead, dark dots on his pale Scottish bonce. 'Those Transport cops would have to catch me first.' Another tug at his trousers let out a fresh blast of pee smell. 'So, what's the plan?'

'Get my ovaries chewed by the boss.'

Hunter scowled over at her. 'What did you say?'

'Get my ovaries chewed by the boss.'

'That sounds a bit laboured.'

She groaned. 'Come on, Craig. That's shocking.'

'Well, that wasn't in particularly good taste, given what we're investigating.'

'What?' She sighed. 'Right. Sorry. Force of bloody habit. Something we used to say...' She barged through the roundabout, ignoring the honking Mercedes on the right, and powered up the road at the far side. 'What's your take on Elvis?'

'Worked with him for years, on and off.' Hunter stretched out his trousers, hulking thighs squeezing the fabric. The swell of his bollocks. Too many bloody squats, the vain twat. 'You know he's got his uses when it comes to CCTV.'

Chantal overtook a dawdling bus on the way into town and shivered. 'So, I'm now thinking that Sean Tulloch has *definitely* got wind of our investigation.'

'What, you think he was leading us a merry dance at Waverley?'

'That's what it looks like to me.' Chantal exhaled as she slowed to the thirty limit. 'And I'm worried about Paisley. You've seen what he's done to the others.'

'And I've seen that sort of sick shite before on the beat. And in the army. This isn't my first rodeo, but I'm fed up of it. What men do to these women, treating them like punchbags. I've seen the fallout, I've seen the scars.'

'Craig, we don't know where he is. He could be—'

'Relax. Tulloch can't get at her. That unit are still at Paisley's house and Elvis is taking the statement. Once that's in the bag, we'll prosecute him. He isn't getting away.'

'I wish I shared your optimism.' Chantal pulled into the station car park and parked next to a bottle-green Golf. The rain wasn't making much inroads in the dirt clarted to the back. She let her seatbelt go. 'Right, I'm starving. Do you want anything from the shop before I get a shoeing?'

5

HUNTER

'I've got my piece with me.' Hunter grabbed his bag from the back seat, his sandwich box rattling around inside. Hopefully the contents were still intact.

His mouth watered at the prospect. Goat's cheese and beetroot, with that lovely new rocket he'd been growing in the kitchen.

Chantal checked her handbag's clip. 'Not even a cup of tea?'

Hunter blew air up his face. 'That would be nice. Thanks.'

'Won't be long.' Chantal got out and wandered off into the rain, mobile in hand.

Hunter clunked open his door and got out of the pool car, hit by the sort of west-coast downpour that felt like half of the Atlantic was coming down at once.

A damp figure trudged out of the station's front door, tall and athletic, marching off towards the Golf. Baby's-arse face twisted into a bitter scowl. DS Scott Cullen. He clocked Hunter and the glower deepened.

Hunter smirked. 'You look like someone's caught you shagging their girlfriend.'

'Craig.' Cullen zapped his car and leaned against it. He

exhaled, his breath catching in the nervous laughter. 'Bit close to the bone that, isn't it?'

'If you can't laugh about something...' Hunter shrugged. 'What brings you here?'

'Supposed to be having lunch with Sharon, but she's too busy. Driven all the bloody way out.'

'Hope she's in a better mood than you are.'

'Worse, if anything.' Cullen opened his door and nodded over at Chantal, phone to her ear, waving back at them. 'Cosy little morning with your lover, aye?'

'We're not an item, Scott.'

'Aye, bollocks. I remember when me and your boss started seeing each other. Sneaking around like schoolkids.' He shook his head. 'We should get that pint sometime, Craig. I'll give you some tips.'

Hunter gave him another shrug. 'Name the date.'

Cullen got in the car and the engine roared. He rattled out onto the street, the left brake light knackered.

What a day. You start off thinking you're taking a statement, next thing you know someone's pissing on you.

A black Audi pulled into the car park and stopped by Chantal. An A7 or A8, one of the posh ones. Looked official, too.

The back door clunked open and an army Captain got out. Number two uniform, service dress, olive-green khaki. Royal Scots Dragoon Guards. MP stamped on a black armband, showing off. Medium height, medium build, though his gut pushed his trousers up a size. Cheeky bastard didn't have to wear uniform. Trying to intimidate the civvies.

His simpering gaze settled on Hunter. 'Captain Brian Rollo-Smith.' The sort of accent a braying father would've spent a hundred grand on acquiring at public schools.

Hunter had to fight the urge to salute. 'How can I help, sir?'

'I'm with the Special Investigation Branch. I'm looking for a DI McNeill?'

∼

HUNTER STOPPED by the entry system and swiped. 'Follow me.' Then he marched down the corridor. Felt like being on bloody parade again.

Rollo-Smith frowned at him. 'You're ex-services, aren't you?'

Like it's stamped on my forehead...

'3 Scots, sir.'

'Third Battalion, eh?' Rollo-Smith gave a military nod, short and precise. 'Lance Corporal Craig Hunter, isn't it?'

How did that twat get my name?

Hunter returned the nod with interest. 'That's Detective Constable Craig Hunter now.'

'I see.' A brief flick of the eyebrows ended the chat. Rollo-Smith couldn't bring himself to speak to a lowly Lance Corporal.

Hunter led across the busy office. A box of donuts was half stuffed into the bin, the card and plastic twisted into a knot. He held open a door at the far side. 'DI McNeill's in here, sir.'

Rollo-Smith stuffed his cap under his arm, frowning at Hunter, nostrils twitching. 'Can you smell something?'

For once, the room didn't stink of Pot Noodles and Gregg's sausage rolls. Just donuts. Sickly sweet donuts. And his pissy socks.

Rollo-Smith's aftershave hung in the air. Surprised he could smell pissy socks over it.

Hunter shook his head. 'Nothing unusual, sir.'

'Very well.' Rollo-Smith entered the office without another word.

DI Sharon McNeill sat behind her desk, glaring at her laptop with an expression that could freeze fire. She brushed her dark hair over her pale forehead and folded her arms across her blouse. 'Captain Rollo-Smith, I presume?'

'Inspector.' Rollo-Smith took the seat opposite and rested his cap on the desk. He shifted his sneer towards McNeill and tilted his head at the door. 'I'd prefer we did this alone?'

'I'd rather DC Hunter stayed.' McNeill smiled, though her eyes had missed the memo. She beckoned Hunter in and he sat next to Rollo-Smith. 'I'm honoured by your presence here in sunny Bathgate.'

'Yes well, I was passing, as it were.' Rollo-Smith cleared his throat, trying to maintain the high level of syrup in his voice. 'I must say that I'm used to dealing with a DCI in such matters. However, given your superior is on leave, you will have to suffice in his absence.' He unzipped a document holder and pulled out a notepad. 'Let's start with your failed attempt to apprehend a member of the Armed Forces, mm?'

McNeill held his gaze and exhaled slowly. 'We discussed this on the phone.' She looked away, eyes almost connecting with Hunter's. 'Tulloch wasn't at Waverley.'

'I'm curious as to why you thought your remit, at this juncture, extended to arresting him.' Rollo-Smith scribbled on his pad with a silver ballpoint. 'Have you got additional evidence or intelligence, mm?'

'This operation was purely preventative.' McNeill cracked her knuckles and leaned forward. 'As you well know, these crimes are all civilian in nature and don't relate to any time when Mr Tulloch was—'

'Private Tulloch.'

'—when *Mr* Tulloch was on Ministry of Defence business.' McNeill let it hang in the air like the sweet tang of the donuts. 'As per your agreement with DCI Fletcher, the MoD won't prosecute *Mr* Tulloch until we've had a fair chance to obtain evidence. Then, when he is at Her Majesty's Pleasure, you'll have all the time in the world to conduct your court martial, assuming you get approval from the Home Secretary.'

'I could rip up that agreement, you know?' Rollo-Smith stopped writing and carefully placed his pen down on the pad. 'You haven't produced any concrete evidence to me or my officers.'

'You know full well that we're still collating it.' McNeill waved a hand over at Hunter. 'My DC here was about to obtain a statement from Mr Tulloch's current victim when he was diverted to preventing your officer from—'

'A private isn't an officer.'

'He was trying to murder her.'

'Ah, the threat.' Rollo-Smith swiped at his pad like a grandmaster at a canvas. 'And you have evidence of this, yes?'

'We've taken the mobile into evidence.' McNeill rested her elbows on the desk. 'Now, given what's transpired this morning, do you honestly expect me to sit on my hands while you pontificate?'

Rollo-Smith sat back, forcing a creak from the wood. He

rubbed at his moustache for a few seconds. 'What additional assistance do you need from my officers?'

'We're fine.'

'Fine? Well.' Rollo-Smith picked up his ballpoint and clicked it. 'You say you're fine and yet you don't appear to have Private Tulloch in custody, do you?'

'You should've kept him at Fort George this morning.'

'That is outwith my remit.' Rollo-Smith clapped his document holder shut. 'As you insist on repeatedly telling me, these crimes do not fall within my jurisdiction. Therefore, we are reliant on you capturing him on civilian territory.'

Hunter cleared his throat. 'Have you spoken to him?'

Rollo-Smith looked at him like he was assessing how best to squash a fly. 'Excuse me?'

'I asked, have you spoken to Private Tulloch?'

'Inspector, keep me apprised of any movement on the case.' Rollo-Smith got to his feet with a clicked heel and nodded at McNeill. 'I'll show myself out.' He left them with a slammed door.

McNeill collapsed back into her chair. 'Christ under a patio.' She waved a hand at the door. 'Are all military cops like that?'

'He's typical for the Royal Military Police. Barging in, expecting everyone to take orders. I've never been investigated, ma'am, but I know people who have.'

He couldn't get that look out of his mind. Rollo-Smith sneering at a lowly DC like a drill sergeant would. Thinking he's a bug, so far below him. His fingers started twitching.

He cleared his throat. 'But I gather they're all as bad as that.'

'Great.' McNeill huffed out a breath. 'Well, my afternoon is going to be spent covering up that incident at Waverley.'

Hunter clenched his fists tight. 'I'll accept full responsibility, ma'am. We should've done better diligence on Tulloch. I should've triple-checked he was still on the train.'

'And maybe not trespassed on the rails?'

Hunter looked away. His heart felt like it would jump out of his chest and start attacking McNeill. 'Sorry about that.'

She smiled at him. 'Craig, I know—'

The door burst open and Chantal waltzed in, clutching a brown paper bag. 'Sorry, Shaz, they were out of chicken. Has to be a BLT, I'm afraid.'

Hunter stared down at his hands. His fingers were twitching like he was playing the banjo. He tried to stop them but he just couldn't.

Bloody Rollo-Smith. Twat ignoring me like that. Treating me like an ant.

McNeill tore open her sandwich and bit into it. The hot bacon smell wafted out.

Hunter shut his eyes.

Bacon...

6

Hunter got on the other side of the door and raised his SA80. The air felt like it could burn your skin, even though the sun hid behind the tall buildings around them. He checked down the narrow street. Clear both ways. He gave the nod.

Terry grinned back. 'We'll make a soldier out of you yet, Jock.'

The other lads laughed along.

Hunter couldn't help himself join in. 'Piss off, you Cockney bastard.'

'That's why you love me, big boy.' Terry lifted his rifle and aimed at the door, the wood looking old enough to have been around when they wrote the Bible. He thumped it with his boot. 'Open up!'

No response.

Hunter's nostrils twitched. Bacon. Someone was cooking bacon. He frowned at Terry. 'Can you smell that?'

That pikey oik from Terry's squad joined in the sniffing. Rat-faced arsehole. 'Thought they didn't eat pig here?'

'Supposed to be dirty or something.' Terry nodded, his eyes narrowing on the door. 'Or was it sacred? I can't bloody remember.' He thumped the door again. 'Open up!'

Nothing.

'Right, on my mark.' Terry looked around them, one by one. 'Hunter, you're with me. Rich, Mike, you stand guard here. Nobody in or out. Capiche?'

A couple of nods. Hunter added his.

'Now.' Terry jolted forward and his size elevens crunched into the dark wood. The door flew off rusted hinges and toppled inward. The bacon smell got worse, overpowering. Stinking the place out. A wave of heat burst out of the room, like a bloody sauna with too much water on the coals.

Something clattered inside.

Terry bolted through the open doorway and came to a dead stop, his SA80 on something in the room. 'You filthy bastard!'

Hunter stopped behind him. He almost lost his lunch rations.

A woman lay naked on a table, strapped down at the wrists and ankles. She twisted her face away from them.

'Craig.'

A man in a cloak stood over her, holding a branding iron in a brazier, hissing something in Arabic or Aramaic or bloody Iraqi.

'Craig.'

Then pressed the brand into the woman's face. Smelled like frying bacon.

～

'CRAIG!' Chantal's grip tore deep into Hunter's forearm. 'Are you okay?'

The image of McNeill was swimming in front of him, scowling as she chewed. One of the four of her was, anyway. The bacon smelled worse. Acrid, deep-fried, sharp.

'Sorry.' Hunter shook himself as he stood. 'Haven't eaten all day.' He flashed a polite smile at McNeill and stormed out of the office.

The woman screamed through her gag as—

Fat Jimmy waddled towards him, carrying a tray of Krispy Kreme donuts like it was the Ark of the Covenant. 'See what I've got—'

'Not now.' Hunter barged past and jogged down the corridor. He swiped his card in the reader and pushed the door. Nothing.

The flesh started to sizzle and pop as—

Not now.

NOT BLOODY NOW!

He took a deep breath. The corridor smelled of coffee. No bacon.

He swiped again, slowly this time. Click.

He nudged the door and stepped out of the back entrance into the narrow lane. Blackened bricks on both sides, barely enough for one person to walk down without slicing their arm open. Rain teemed down on his head. He looked up into the sky and shut his eyes. Scottish air filled his lungs, cold and tinged with petrol fumes.

Cigarette smoke.

Curry spices.

Chips.

He slowed his breathing, sucking in through his nostrils.

Ten.

Nine.

Eight.

Seven.

A hand caressed the back of his jacket, sliding up to his neck. 'You okay?'

Hunter couldn't open his eyes. He gulped in more air, tasting her perfume. Sweet and alpine and...

He opened his eyes and grimaced at her. 'Another flashback.'

'Shite.' Chantal leaned back against the opposite wall. 'Thought you were over them?'

'Me too.'

She ran a hand through her hair, fanning it out. 'The bacon triggered it, didn't it?'

'Maybe.'

'I'm sorry, Craig. If I'd known—' Her jaw twitched. 'Look, I had a...' She smiled. 'I know someone who had a smell trigger. Cigar smoke.'

'Cigar smoke?'

'Bit easier to deal with than bacon, I suppose.'

'It's been years since I had a flashback like that. Years. It's not like I go past a greasy spoon or into someone's house and they're frying bacon and it kicks me off to la-la land.'

'This why you're a vegetarian?'

'Partly.'

She tilted her head. 'You have been taking your meds, right?'

Hunter managed a nod. 'Never missed a day.' He huffed out air. Almost felt the Afghan heat on his skin in the pissing rain. The black Audi was on the street. 'I'm thinking it's Rollo-Smith.'

'What do you mean?'

'Years ago.' Hunter swallowed. 'Back in Afghanistan, I had a run-in with one of the monkeys.'

Her smile twisted into a frown. 'Monkeys? You racist prick.'

'Christ no.' Hunter grabbed her arms. 'That's what we called the RMP. The military police.'

'The monkeys?'

'Right. So, I thought this guy was investigating me, turns out it was someone who'd just died on a mission. It was pretty stressful.'

'I can imagine.'

'Doubt you can, but you know. Those guys are brutal. They don't give up.'

'And this was in your flashback?'

'Right.' Hunter huffed out a sigh. 'And another one. I was back in Iraq. With...' He swallowed. 'Terry and a couple of others. We were supposed to find this... cleric, I think he was. The intel said he was training suicide bombers. But we stumbled on his location. Turned out he was also in the habit of torturing and branding women.'

Her eyes bulged and her mouth widened. 'I'm not having a go, but why didn't you tell me about this?'

'Because I blocked it out.' Hunter dug his knuckles into his eye sockets then stretched out. 'This was before Terry, you know...' His mouth was dry as the Iraq air. 'That guy escaped. We found him later, dressed up in the full hijab, burqa thing. We chased him and...'

Her eyebrows jolted upright. 'And then he...?'

'Then he blew himself and Terry up, aye.'

'Christ.'

'Aye.' Hunter sighed. 'Or maybe it's because he's a captain. Those pricks dropped a clanger, you know? Sending us out on that mission.' He rested against the door, arms folded. 'DI McNeill going tonto at me in there didn't exactly help.'

'You knew she can be hardcore, Craig.' Chantal leaned on the wall. 'Sharon's under so much pressure. The new Chief Constable wants results, not convictions falling apart before they get to court.'

'Stats, bloody stats.' Hunter ran his hands over his shaved scalp. The rasp took him closer to his safe place. 'But we got that stoat last year. He's inside.'

'That's one case, Craig. And that was based on your investigation.' Chantal pinched her cheek. 'Look, there's the careerist shit, like Shaz needing our investigations to come to something, for us to stop witnesses dropping off the face of the earth when they're due in court.' She stared down the lane to the thin sliver of car park, brushing damp hair out of her eyes. 'But there's a reason why any of us are in this unit, right? We want to put these raping, abusing scumbags away.'

'Even Elvis. Even fat Jim.'

'Right.'

'I agree with you. This isn't about another one getting away. Sean Tulloch... The damage he can inflict. Again and again. It'll never stop, Chantal. It'll never stop.'

'So, this army guy. Rollo-Smith... Why do people have to have those double-barrelled surnames? What happens to the next generation? Rollo-Smith-Ponsonby-Smythe?'

Hunter barked out a laugh. Then he rubbed his face, trying to scrape the last fragments of the memory away. 'Chantal, we can't trust him. Once we've got enough evidence, they'll pounce and get Tulloch on a court martial before we can arrest him.'

'So, some serial abusing scumbag goes away. Why's that bad?'

'Because Rollo-Smith will try to cover it over. Trouble with them is...' Hunter cleared his throat. 'See if we arrested an American with child porn on his laptop over here, right, we'd send him back there because the sentence is much longer. Right?'

'I suppose.'

'Well, the RMP aren't necessarily interested in justice the same way most investigators are. They've got an agenda. Least that's the way I see it.'

'Right.' Chantal shook her head at him, her forehead knotting. 'You need to—'

Her Airwave blasted out, the sound shrill in the confined space.

She put it to her ear with a sigh. 'Go on, Elvis.' She nodded then jogged off towards the car park. 'Stay with her!'

Hunter sped off after her. 'What's happened?'

Chantal zapped the pool car and hauled the door open. 'Paisley Sanderson's been assaulted.'

7

CHANTAL

Chantal stomped down the corridor.

Another victim. Another woman lying there, battered and bruised at the hands of Sean Tulloch. While we... messed about. Trying to catch him at Waverley as he waltzed in to her flat thirty-odd miles away and assaulted two police officers, then kicked the living shit out of her...

Then what?

Don't even want to think about it.

Chantal swerved past a porter pushing an old man down the corridor, looked inches away from death. She squeezed against the wall, getting a scowl. She powered off.

'Wait!' Hunter grabbed her arm and stopped her. 'You need to calm down before you go in there.'

'Craig...' She glared at him, waiting until he let go. The wheelchair trundled past them. 'I'm calm enough.'

'Bullshit. You're feeling guilty about it, aren't you?'

'Well done. You know how I think.' She gave him a round of applause. 'Now, do you mind?' She turned the corner into the next room. 'Through here, right?'

'Stop!' Dr Helen Yule caught one glance then dragged the curtains shut behind her, groaning. 'I should've guessed you'd both be involved in this. Just like the last time, isn't it? You swan around and leave other people to pick up the pieces.' She held out her long arms like a nightclub bouncer at three in the morning, her stethoscope swaying from her neck. Her glasses slid down, revealing the missing half of her right eyebrow, though couldn't do much for the vertical scar bisecting it. 'I can't let you speak to Ms Sanderson.'

Chantal was almost out of breath. A pair of nurses milled behind them, whispering to each other. 'How is she?'

Yule checked her tablet computer. 'Well, Ms Sanderson has been savagely beaten. Punched and kicked by someone a lot bigger than her.'

'We had a team at her house to protect her.'

'Well, fat lot of good that did.' Yule stepped away from the curtains and swished another one open. 'This is your idea of protection.'

A woman lay on the bed, two nurses milling around her. Chantal recognised her — the cop who turned up at Paisley's flat to assist PC Warner.

'PC Smith here is still to regain consciousness.' Yule tugged the curtain shut. 'Paisley's been talking, which is something. Saying she's sorry, over and over.'

Chantal gestured behind Yule at the curtains. 'We need to speak to Ms Sanderson.'

Yule stared at her for a few seconds. 'Very well.' She raised a finger. 'But this is on the condition that I will terminate any discussion as soon as I deem it harmful to the patient.'

Chantal smiled at her. 'Wouldn't have it any other way.'

∽

PAISLEY LOOKED like she was some computer-generated alien in a *Star Wars* film. Where she wasn't bandaged, her skin was puffed up, red and dark purple. Dried blood mixed with dark brown iodine on her forehead, sliced open. Her lips twitched, but her words were silent.

Chantal perched on the chair next to her. 'Hi, Paisley.'

She closed her good eye, her lips still twitching. 'Sorry.' Louder now, close to hissing. 'Sorry. Sorry.'

'Why are you apologising?'

'Sorry, sorry, sorry.'

'Paisley, who are you apologising to? Is it Sean?'

She glowered at them. 'Your fault.'

'What is, Paisley?'

She waved her hands around her beaten face.

'This is nobody's fault but Sean Tulloch's.'

'Made him angry.' Paisley stared down at her hands. Her right was a claw, seemingly unable to open or close. 'I should've known...'

Chantal clenched her fists. Listen to yourself. *This isn't your fault.* The training — base and generic and empty. Reaching for platitudes when you need to connect with her. Show her you understand. Deeply. Personally. Not just part of the job but trying to fix her life. Trying to stop craven bastards abusing her.

Tears streamed from Paisley's good eye.

Hunter cleared his throat. 'Is it possible that Mr Tulloch knows we're talking to you?'

Paisley waved a hand at her face. 'Did he do this to the others?'

'So it was Sean who attacked you?'

She closed her good eye. 'Who else?'

'As far as we know, Mr Tulloch has only targeted you. Did he say anything?'

Paisley rolled her shoulder. *Losing her...*

'I know how hard this is, okay?' Chantal squeaked the chair forward. 'How about you take us through what happened?'

Paisley sucked in a deep breath. 'I was waiting on those cops of yours to turn up, right? Bored out of my skull cos you've got my phone.' She let out a sigh. 'Then that Irish cop — Lenny? — he hears something out the back, like when you turned up. So he went outside.' She nibbled at her lips and rubbed a stream of tears away. 'Must've got his arse handed to him, cos next thing I know Sean's in the house. The woman cop tried to hit him, but he...' She scrunched up her face. 'He knocked her out. One punch. Then, he's grabbing my hair and... he started hitting me, anyway. Over and over again.'

Chantal let a breath escape slowly. *Jesus. Everything he did to her. The new injuries. This is my fault.*

Hunter scribbled on his notebook. 'What happened next?'

Paisley's good hand bunched into a tight fist. She'd clammed up again.

Chantal glared at Hunter, trying to shut him up. 'Paisley, it's very important that you tell us exactly what happened.' Paisley's sobs filled the gap. 'He hit you a few times. Did he do anything else to you?'

'He left.'

'Immediately?'

'That prick left me on the floor like this.' Paisley waved a hand down her battered body. 'Tore all my clothes off and left me there while he had a bloody shower. Said this wasn't finished.'

Chantal looked over at Hunter, hope spearing her guts, mixing with bitter revulsion. 'Did he rape you, Paisley?'

She ran a finger along the palm of her hand. 'Not this time.'

Jesus. How casually she talked about being violated. Like she was going to the shops.

Hunter sat back with a sigh. 'Then what happened?'

'Someone knocked at the door.' Paisley lay back on the bed and stared up at the ceiling. 'That's when Sean left.' She made walking motions with two of her fingers. 'Waltzed out the back door.'

'Then what happened?'

'That door opened. A dumpy cow and some boy with sidies had turned up.'

Elvis saves the day.

Chantal leaned forward and waited until she locked eye contact with her again. 'Where could Mr Tulloch have gone?'

Paisley scowled at her. 'His mum died five years ago. His old man... Never knew him, eh? Got mates everywhere, but I was never allowed to meet them. Must've been ashamed of me.'

'He's got a lot of things to be ashamed of, Paisley, but you're not one of them.'

∽

'THAT'S NOT GOOD ENOUGH.' Sharon's voice almost frosted up the pool car's speakers as they sped south. 'I need him in custody like *yesterday*.'

'If you'll let me speak?' Chantal scowled over at the stereo. 'Shaz?'

Sharon paused on the line, huffing out breath. 'Right. Go on.'

'We're on our way to her house right now.' Chantal pulled out into the oncoming lane to overtake a tractor. A Focus hurtled towards them, flashing its lights. She saw Hunter gripping the grab handle tight, eyes clamped shut, but casually slipped back into her lane, getting a blaring horn. 'If Tulloch is still in the area, we'll catch him.' She swept round a cream Mini, in and out just like that. Piece of piss. 'And we've got units guarding his previous victims. He's not getting away.'

'Right, well, I'll leave it in your capable hands.'

Chantal gripped the wheel until it hurt her thumbs. 'Anything from Rollo-Smith?'

Sharon left another long pause. 'I'm keeping this latest development from Captain Flashpants for now.'

'Sure that's wise?'

'We'll see.'

'Your funeral. Speak later.' Chantal killed the call and floored it, the needle dancing past ninety. 'What a bloody shambles.'

Hunter let go of the handle. 'Do you want to talk about it?'

'Not really.' Chantal flicked the radio on.

'— Alnwick where Detective Inspector Jonathan Bruce of Northumbria Police has been briefing—'

She snapped it off again and muttered, 'That's all I bloody need.' She settled back in her seat and flashed him a smile. 'Can't believe Elvis saved the day.'

8

HUNTER

Hunter glanced over at Chantal, his grip on the "oh shit" handle turning his knuckles white like he was on a rollercoaster. Or in a troop transport heading to Iraq.

Chantal's eyes tracked the road ahead of them, narrow, her jaw clenched. She swerved into Paisley's street, the brakes squealing as Hunter was thrown over the handbrake.

'Slow down!'

She tore past the squad car and slammed on the brakes, parking between an Astra and a Fiesta. Then got out her mobile.

Bloody hell.

Hunter got out of the car first.

Across the street, PC Warner was trying to unroll a length of crime scene tape across the open front door to Paisley Sanderson's house, while holding the back of his head. He swung around and clocked Hunter's approach. 'How're ye?'

'Any sign of him?'

'Not likely.' Warner snapped off the tape with a penknife and grinned. 'But there was no sign of him when he battered me on the back of the head, either.'

'I saw what Tulloch did to your partner.'

'Fractured skull, according to my sergeant.'

Hunter pointed at the back of Warner's head. 'Should you be on duty?'

'Ach, I'm not sure...' Warner ran his thumb down the tape, looking for the end. 'Prick came at me when I went out the back there.' He flicked the end up with his thumbnail and stuck it to the door frame. 'Tell you one thing, though, Tulloch's a big guy. Huge.'

Chantal barged past them and ducked under the tape. The house was as quiet as a lawyered-up rapist in an interview room.

Hunter swallowed his sigh and followed her inside, straight into the living room.

Paisley's armchair was on its back. Other than that, it was exactly as they'd left it that morning. Like someone hadn't been almost murdered in there.

Elvis stood in the bedroom doorway, rasping at his sideburns. 'Alright?'

Chantal scanned the room again. 'You getting anywhere with finding Tulloch?'

Elvis rubbed his sideburns again. 'Not yet, Sarge.'

'What about the mobile he used to text that death threat?'

'Switched off after he sent it. Not been on since.'

Chantal nodded slowly. 'CCTV?'

'Nowhere with it, Sarge.'

Chantal took a step closer, head tilted to the side, eyebrows raised. 'Are you saying there's none?'

Elvis shrugged. 'Well...'

She pointed towards the street. 'There's a pair of bloody cameras over there!'

'Right.' Elvis finally looked away. 'They won't give me access.'

'Paul, get access to it in the next five minutes or my toe is going right up your arsehole. Am I clear?'

Elvis nodded, eyes flickering. 'Sarge.' He bent down to pick up a laptop bag then made his way outside. Looked like he was about to burst into tears. He picked up one of the green patio chairs and shook off the rain. Then he sat hunched over, tearing at the catches on his bag.

Hunter beckoned Chantal into the bathroom. An all-white

suite edged with nicotine-yellow silicone. 'You might've been a bit hard on him there.'

'He deserves a rocket up his hoop.' Chantal leaned against the doorframe and grimaced. 'This is a bloody disaster. He didn't spot Tulloch getting off the train.'

'Need to keep your pecker up, Sarge.' Hunter winked at her, his knee throbbing. 'But there's something I don't get.'

'Here we go.' Chantal rolled her eyes. 'What is it, oh master detective?'

'Tulloch's a squaddie, right? Been on for a month, maybe more. He comes home for a week's R&R and—'

'—he's had to make do with Madam Palm and her five sisters.' Chantal made a wanker gesture. 'I get it.' She looked back inside the house. 'You're wondering why he didn't rape her when he had the chance?'

'Right.' Hunter frowned. 'Only problem is he had two unconscious cops here. I don't know what he was planning, but…' He stepped through to the living room and gestured for Warner to join them. 'See when you woke up, did you call it in straight away?'

'No, I lay on the ground for a bit.' Warner patted at the back of his skull. 'Not like I had a choice. Felt like my brains were—'

'Yeah, okay. You didn't hear anything?'

'Wait, I heard water running, maybe?' Warner rubbed at his forehead and stared out of the front door. 'But then I blacked out again. And then I called out, you know? I came in and Sally was on the floor in the kitchen, by the cooker. Guy had gone to town on her.' He swallowed hard. 'Yer woman was next to her. Taken her clothes off, you know?' He pointed at the living room carpet. 'Lying right there, moaning.'

'No sign of Tulloch?'

'Not that I saw. That guy with the sidies was knocking at the door.' Warner stepped forward. 'You know he's crying in the garden?'

'Elvis? Doesn't surprise me.' Hunter clicked his tongue a few times. 'So, if he spooked him, that means Tulloch's scarpered. Made sure he got away.'

Warner frowned. 'Not following you.'

'Come with me.' Hunter paced through to the bedroom.

Built-in wardrobes surrounded a small double bed, the stained sheets crumpled up.

Bingo.

A giant holdall lay on the other side. Standard military issue.

Hunter snapped on some gloves and opened it slowly. 'Elvis should've been through this.' He peered inside. Full of dirty washing — underpants and socks, jeans and T-shirts, not the uniform stuff the military support staff would clean.

'I'm Batman!' Elvis stood in the doorway, holding his laptop up like a trophy. His glee hid his red eyes — he had been crying. 'Got the CCTV from the street.'

∼

ELVIS RESTED the laptop on the coffee table like it was a sleeping baby. A dongle hung out of the side of the machine, its blue light pulsing. He thumped the space bar and the video started playing.

The camera caught Paisley Sanderson's house square on, including the side lane and the neighbour. A car pulled up outside, wheeling back to park. BMW 1-series, looked new. A tall, bulky man got out and grabbed a big bag from the passenger seat. He lugged it over to Paisley's house, dropping it and staring down the street. Then he stood there for a few seconds, apparently thinking. Maybe his military training, assessing threats and opportunities.

Hunter tapped the display. 'So he's seen PC Smith's car.'

Elvis frowned. 'Who's PC Smith?'

'The female officer you found with her head caved in.'

Then, on the laptop screen, Tulloch cut down the side lane.

Elvis set it playing at high speed. A couple of cars shot past. Eighteen minutes later, a grey Vauxhall pulled up outside the house, double-parking and blocking the street. Elvis got out and sauntered over, laughing and joking on his mobile. He rattled the front door and waved at the car. The driver got out — DC Jenny Diamond, shuffling over, her gammy leg giving her hassle. Elvis shrugged his shoulders and knocked on the door again.

Tulloch slipped out of the lane and hid behind the wall, waiting. The front door opened a crack. DC Diamond started tapping at her Airwave. Elvis helped Warner to his feet. Then they entered the house.

The BMW's lights flashed. Seconds later, Tulloch dashed over and got in. The car revved off down the street, the camera catching Tulloch putting on his seatbelt.

Chantal snatched the laptop from Elvis and wound the footage back. The grainy figure wrapping the seatbelt around his bulk. She stabbed a finger on the BMW. 'Elvis, your job is to find this car. Now. And don't mess it up.'

'Right, Sarge.' Elvis took the laptop back and perched on the edge of the sofa, his fingers dancing across the keyboard.

Hunter walked back through to the bedroom. 'What do you think?'

Chantal leaned against the doorframe. 'I think Elvis and Jenny are lucky Tulloch didn't brain them as well.

'You're telling me.' Hunter sat on the bed and dug deep into the open kit bag, wading his gloved hands through dirty pants. Something clattered near the bottom. He piled up the grey jockey shorts on one side and shifted the T-shirts until he found it. Hard plastic wrapped in a pair of pants. He eased it out. A small laptop, shiny and silver. 'Jackpot?'

Chantal flashed her eyebrows. 'See if it's any use.'

Hunter opened the lid and it whirred to life, straight into a football management game. Chelsea versus Heart of Midlothian in the Champions League. 'Didn't even need a password.' He marched back through to the living room and held it in front of Elvis. 'Need you to go through this, Paul.'

Elvis didn't look up from his own machine. 'Can't you?'

'Not been forensics trained.'

'I'll get your dry cleaning as well, aye?' Elvis snapped on a pair of blue gloves. 'Nice trousers, by the way.'

Hunter tugged at the thighs and sighed. 'Reckon you can find anything?'

Elvis tapped the screen. 'He's a dirty Jambo bastard. Hearts playing in the Champions League? Bloody science fiction.' His laptop chimed. 'Oh, what's this?' He squinted at it then swivelled it round. 'Here you go. Got a sighting of that car on the ANPR system.'

A grey image showed the city bypass at Sheriffhall, the BMW on the turning from the A7.

Elvis clicked the space bar and the car followed the road west.

Hunter nodded at him. 'Will this take us to him?'

'Let's see.' Elvis hammered the screen until it went to a map. 'Right, he comes off at the far end of the bypass, then he goes along the A8.' He hit another key and the display filled with the car turning off the road towards a roundabout. 'And he takes the airport exit.'

Hunter stared at the shot of the car, a few pine trees in grey. 'Is that it?'

'Just a sec.' Elvis clattered the keys again. 'Shite.'

'What?'

'Well, the bad news is I've lost it.'

'And the good?'

'I lose him going into the Ingliston Park and Ride and he doesn't come back out.'

9

CHANTAL

Chantal overtook another lorry, hitting eighty as she cleared it. The evening rush hour traffic was piling towards them beneath a bright blue sky.

Guts churning. Teeth grinding.

Where the hell is Tulloch? Who is he battering now? Making us look like idiots while he flies around the countryside, silencing his victims.

She hugged the rear of a coach, banking out into the right lane to chance another overtake.

Hunter grabbed the wheel. 'Do you want to calm down?'

Chantal shot him a glare and held it for a few seconds, then looked away, back on the road. She pulled in, sticking to the bus's fifty-five. 'Sorry.'

'This whole thing isn't your fault, you know?'

She clicked her tongue a few times, then swept her hair behind her left ear. 'We should've had more units stationed at her house.'

'We had two uniforms there. And a squad car. Elvis and Jenny Diamond were on their way there, too.'

'Fat lot of good that was.'

'Warner beat the snot out of me. Tulloch destroyed him.'

'I know that. It's my fault Tulloch was able to do that.'

'Look, she's bumped our statement twice in the last week.' Hunter cracked his knuckles and settled back in the seat. 'I hate to be a dick, but she's got to take some responsibility for what's happened.'

Felt like her eyebrows almost hit the sunroof. Did he really say that? She shot him a glare. 'Do you want to take that back?'

'You know what I mean.' Hunter looked away. 'That guy is a craven bastard. I just wish girls like her would stop falling for his patter or whatever it is. I've seen the evil men can do, I wish *they* could.'

Chantal got right up the bus's arse again, swerving out. There was a turning up ahead so she pulled in.

Hunter folded his arms. His suit jacket puckered up around his over-developed biceps. *What was it about men and working out? Him and those bloody kettlebells. Swinging them and pressing them and going on about them all the bloody time.* He glanced over. 'What's with all the silence? Something I've done?'

'Craig...' She sailed past the bus.

'I mean, come on—'

Hunter's Airwave chimed and he checked the display. 'Here we go. The BMW belongs to a Marcus Wearmouth of Harrogate. Reported stolen from a car park in Cupar.'

'So we can do him for that?' Chantal let out a breath. *Small mercies.* 'Anything from the Park and Ride?'

He shook his head. 'Still waiting on a response. Big security incident on Princes Street at lunchtime.'

'Is Tulloch still there?'

Hunter shrugged. 'Elvis has lost him.'

∼

CHANTAL KICKED down to second and powered towards the flashing blue lights. Ingliston Park and Ride sprawled in front of them. Miles of damp tarmac rammed with what looked like half the cars in West Lothian. A glass box with an inward-sloping green roof obscured a tram stop.

The BMW lay diagonally across two electric car charging spaces. A pair of squad cars blocked it in.

She stopped next to it and got out.

A plane roared up into the sky half a mile away, another coming in to land.

Hunter jogged around to her side of the car. 'Are we cool?'

'We're always cool, Craig. Stop being a fanny.' Chantal stomped off, splashing rainwater up the legs of her trousers.

The doors of the first squad car opened. 'Oh, look who it is.' Six foot something of idiot got out, gurning away at Hunter.

'Steve...' Hunter crouched down to look inside the car.

'Oh, it's *Detective* Constable Hunter.' Another uniform joined the first, leaning against the car, like a pair of grinning chimps. Could even be brothers. 'Got the stabilisers off your Chopper yet?'

Hunter winked at them. 'The only chopper round here is the one you were playing with in that car. Steve's, was it?'

Chantal peered inside the BMW while the boys had their fun. Pretty much empty. A black can sat in the middle, WakeyWakey stencilled in green on the side. *Christ, that takes me back.*

She stood up straight and nodded at the simpering arseholes. 'How long have you been here?'

'Five minutes, Sarge. Nobody's been near it.'

'Right.' Chantal opened the handle and reached over to the glove box. Another can of WakeyWakey fell out, sounded full from the thud. Nothing in there that looked like it'd lead them to Tulloch. She shrugged. 'Well, at least Marcus Wearmouth will get his car back in one piece.'

The rain started thumping down again and the uniforms got back in their squad car.

Hunter drummed his fingers on the top of their pool car. 'So where the hell is Tulloch?'

Chantal looked back over at the tram terminal. 'I'm thinking he's got on there.' A tram made its way towards them down the long straight from Edinburgh Park and the Gyle. The next stop was the airport, the last one. 'I hope he's gone into town.'

Hunter hit dial and put his mobile on speaker. 'Elvis, are you getting anywhere with the CCTV?'

'Struggling, mate. The coverage around there is patchier than Big Jim's hair. Like I said, I lost Tulloch as he drove in.'

Hunter stepped closer to Chantal and held up the phone. 'We think he's on the tram. Can you get access?'

'Shite. It's not working.'

Chantal pulled the phone closer. 'So that's a dead end?'

'Aye. Soz.'

Chantal sighed. 'What about that laptop?'

Elvis groaned. 'Not finding much, to be honest. Guy had signed Messi for Hearts on Football Manager, can you believe it?'

She rolled her eyes at Hunter. 'Any emails?'

'Doing that right— Oh, hang on.' Elvis squealed like a little girl. 'I've got something! He's got a flight booked for today.'

Shite.

Chantal stared off in the direction of Edinburgh airport, an orange EasyJet plane swooping up. 'Where to?'

'Flight to Faro in Portugal at half five.'

Chantal checked her watch. Just after five. 'Come on, Craig!' She sprinted off towards the tram trundling into the station. 'We can make it!'

10

HUNTER

The tram door opened and Hunter sploshed through the puddles at the back of the multi-storey car park. He barged an overweight businessman out of the way. 'Police! Coming through!'

Chantal was lagging behind, waving him on.

Hunter stomped across the road and stuck his Airwave to his mouth as a ned blew cigarette smoke in his face. He swallowed it down like the butts and coughed into his radio, 'Elvis, have you got hold of security yet?'

'Aye, look for the big ex-forces knucklehead at the entrance.' Elvis sniffed. 'That's not you, by the way.'

'Very funny. Any update on Tulloch's movements?'

'Aye, entered the airport at five past four.'

Hunter scanned the grey metal doorway and clocked the security goon immediately. 'DC Craig Hunter.' He swapped the Airwave for a flash of his warrant card.

A lump in a suit stood by the entrance, more muscle on his neck than Hunter's thighs. 'Josh Brown, Airport Security.' He buttoned up his suit jacket. 'You need to get to the RobertsAir flight to Faro, right?'

'Is the plane still here?'

'I'm checking. Follow me, sir.' Brown darted off into the airport, his speed belying his huge frame, and took the stairs three at a time.

Hunter swung a hard left at the top and followed him towards the security desk. He weaved around travellers dumping their water bottles and oversize toiletries.

Brown spoke to the operator of the first scanner and opened the door. Hunter let Chantal go first, then followed them down the middle of the security hall. He bombed through the unused lane in the middle, past the two queues winding away from them, the travellers' eyes wide, mouths hanging open.

Brown stopped to open the gate for them, his radio crackling out static. He darted off to the right into the wide departures area, restaurants and shops lining the way. 'Gate fourteen!' He swerved round a stag party already several sheets to the wind.

Hunter raced after him and checked back the way — Chantal was lagging behind. 'Should I wait?'

She waved him on, sucking in air.

Hunter turned back and smacked straight into a tourist. Three pints of beer flew through the air. Hunter tumbled to the floor, landed on his arse with a crunch. He rolled over, lager sluicing down his new trousers.

'What the hell are you playing at?' The red-faced drinker was on top of him, screaming in his face. 'That cost *fifteen* quid!'

'Police!' Chantal hauled the man off him. 'We need to move, sir.'

'—bloody *disgrace!*'

Hunter pushed himself to his feet and something tore. Fresh air hit his thighs. He'd ripped the arse out of these trousers now.

Bloody, bloody hell. No time to worry.

He sprinted off.

Brown slowed by a huge glass window and barked out an order at the ground staff. The gate was quiet. 'You were supposed to keep the sodding plane here!'

Hunter stopped beside him. 'What's happened?'

'See that?' Brown pointed at the window. A plane shot off down the runway, the RobertsAir logo on the side. It floated up into the air and banked to the south. 'That's your flight.'

11

CHANTAL

'Because this shower can't follow orders!' Josh Brown jabbed a finger at the desk. 'I told you to keep him here!'

Chantal caught up with Hunter, chest heaving, reading their disappointment. *No. No, no, no.* She tried to catch her breath. 'He's gone?'

'Looks that way, sweetheart.' Brown shook his head at the disappearing plane. 'Tell you, if I had a rocket on me...'

Hunter was sucking in breath as he leaned against the security desk, his warrant card resting on the top. He reeked of stale beer. 'Can you confirm if Sean Tulloch was on the flight?'

'One second.' The ground staff rep looked Filipino. Her smile betrayed her experience of dealing with angry brutes. 'We relayed the request to the captain and the tower, but it was too late. I can only apologise.'

Brown scowled at her. 'Check the bloody manifest, Deirdre.'

She smiled as she stared at the screen. 'This is going to take a second, I'm afraid.'

Chantal checked her watch. 'The only bloody time a plane takes off on time with me in the airport.'

Brown looked personally offended. 'Happens more often than you'd think.'

'How the hell did he get through security?' Chantal nodded back the way. 'We weren't that far behind him.'

'Oh Christ.' Hunter grimaced. 'His MOD90 card.'

'His what?'

'MOD90. Every serviceman and woman gets one. Lets you bypass passport control.'

Brown's eyes misting over. 'Aye, I remember the days...'

'Excuse me?' The ground rep raised a hand as she looked up. 'I can confirm that Sean Tulloch was in seat 3C.'

Chantal slumped back against the desk. 'Shite.'

∼

CHANTAL SLAMMED the car into the space. The bumper crunched against the police station's wall, grinding hard. She snatched the keys out of the ignition and grabbed at the door handle. Missed it.

Bloody hell. She tore at it again and the door wobbled open.

Hunter reached over and held her arm lightly. 'Slow down.'

She stared at his hand until he let go. 'What are you playing at?'

Hunter's eyes were narrow slits. 'Slow down.'

She brushed him off and pulled the door shut again. 'That filthy, abusive bastard has given us the slip. He's...' She let out a deep sigh, way deeper than she expected. Like the bottom of her guts had exhaled through her mouth. 'We've dropped a bollock here, Craig. He's in bloody Portugal now. He knows we're after him. He's...'

What? What's he going to do?

Run away?

Ignore them and find some other women to abuse?

The police over there are, well. They don't know about him. His history. What he can do.

He locked eyes with her, jaw clenched. 'We'll get him when he comes back.'

'*If* he comes back.'

He held her gaze like he'd held her arm, but she still shook him off. 'Look, if he's gone AWOL, the MOD will get him back. Trust me.'

'I trust you, Craig, but do you trust the chimps or whatever you called them?'

'Monkeys.'

'Well, do you?'

'About as far as you can throw me.'

'I could throw you to Edinburgh about now.'

He laughed then shut his eyes. 'Do I trust them?' He reopened them and stared out of the passenger window. 'No. It's a gamble whether they prosecute him. The guy I know, they just moved him on. He killed a woman in Iraq, but he was with us in Afghanistan. The army's not very popular. War isn't. They'll cover it up if they can.'

'Even if we shout from the rooftops about him?'

Hunter looked down at the footwell. 'Good luck with that.'

'This cock-up's on us, Craig.' She pushed the door to its full width, clunking into the squad Volvo next to them. '*We* let him get away. We need to get him back.'

'We didn't, he—'

'He's been one bloody step ahead of us all the bloody time.' Chantal punched the steering wheel. The horn blared. 'He wasn't at Waverley. Then he got to Paisley while we were chasing our tails. Now he's on the way to *Portugal*.' She crunched the keys in her hand into a tight ball. 'Who says he'll even come back?'

'As long as he stays in NATO territory, he'll—'

'That's not much consolation.' She shut her eyes and gave a gentle nod. 'Come on, let's face the music.' She opened her eyes again. 'You *stink*, by the way.'

12

HUNTER

The slammed door thudded in Hunter's ears. He sniffed the air. Sweat, second-hand piss, stale beer.

And the bitter tang of letting a raping bastard get away like that.

What a pair of amateurs. Pissing about at Waverley while he beats up our witness and two cops into the bargain. Poor Paisley. Turned to hamburger patty by—

Hunter's gut lurched. He swallowed down saliva, tasted more like stomach bile.

Not now.

Not. Now.

Centre yourself. Focus on the here and now.

Bathgate.

2016. Twelfth of May.

Get that breathing under control.

One.

The drone of traffic far away.

Two.

Children shouting and singing a couple of blocks away.

Three.
Four.
An orange Focus next to a silver Astra, sandwiched between two SUVs.
Five.
High-rise towers in the distance, hills behind.
Bathgate.
Bloody Bathgate. Always Bathgate.
Another deep breath and he got out, back to normal. A gust of wind caught the rip in his trousers. *Bloody hell.*
Walk like the lion in his den, nobody will notice.
He marched across the car park and swiped into the side entrance. The corridor reeked of earthy coffee, stale like the giant drum of instant was nearing the end of its life. He pushed through to their office, still buzzing with activity at the back of six.

Elvis was working in the corner, a smirk on his face. 'You've ruined two pairs of breeks in a day. I can almost see your arse from here.'

'You shouldn't be looking.'

'Think there's some standard-issue ones in the store cupboard.'

'Great.' Hunter perched on the edge of the desk, the wood cool against his buttocks. 'Why aren't—'

'Craig!' Elvis battered him with his notebook until he stood up. 'Tell me you're not going commando?'

'Aye, and I didn't wipe up after my last jobby.' Hunter rested against a column. A mug of instant smouldered on the desk, the black surface dotted with undissolved granules. 'Why aren't you still in Galashiels?'

Elvis leaned back with a huff. 'The SOCOs turned up and got us to leave.' He waved his hands across his midden of a desk. 'So here I am, working.' He scratched at his sidies. 'DI McNeill's not impressed. Not one little bit.'

'Your second week and you've pissed her off.'

'It's you and your bird she's raging at, mate.'

'She's not—'

'Aye, aye, keep telling yourself that.' Elvis opened a silver laptop on his desk. 'Look, I'll no doubt get a good dunt of the blame.'

'And you'll deserve every inch of it.'

'Charming bastard.' Elvis held up the laptop from Paisley's house. 'Got something else on this.'

13

CHANTAL

Sharon ran a hand down her face. 'Look, after you let him get on that plane, I—'

Chantal huffed out breath. 'We didn't let—'

Sharon silenced her with a hand. 'I've spoken to the Portuguese police.'

'Whatever. Are they picking him up?'

'Well, they're not accepting my request to arrest Tulloch at Faro airport.'

'What?' Chantal's shoulders slumped. 'Why?'

'Said I've got to go through proper channels.' Sharon let out a groan. 'Which means we'll have to get the PF to get a European Arrest Warrant.' She looked up from her notepad. 'The trouble is, we don't know if he's absconded or just away for a weekend.'

'Elvis wasn't getting anywhere with it.' Chantal slumped back in the chair. 'Problem is, we're nowhere with the evidence against Tulloch. The PF isn't going to buy the whole case yet, is she?'

'She doesn't have to.' Sharon rapped her fingers on the desktop. 'We can do him for the assault and the theft of the BMW. People have been extradited for stealing chickens in Romania.'

Another thunk on the desk. 'The way I see it, we need to fast-track the detailed statements from Paisley Sanderson and the two officers Tulloch assaulted. We've got CCTV evidence of him entering and exiting the property at the time.'

'What about the phone he used to send the threatening text?'

'Tried it. It's not sufficient.'

'Right. Well, all that's going to take time.' Chantal shot to her feet and started pacing the room. 'Meanwhile, Tulloch's doing God knows what in Portugal. If he stops to think for a *second*, he could run. He's in the Algarve. You can get a boat to Spain or Africa pretty easily.' She stopped pacing. 'We need to get out to Portugal and bring him in.'

Sharon wagged a finger at her. 'This isn't like when you went to Southampton last month to take a statement, okay? Arresting someone on foreign soil is a completely different beast.'

'I'm not saying it's the same.' Chantal paused. 'I know it's not.' Time to change tack. 'Look, all I'm saying is, while all that legal stuff's rumbling on, we need to get eyes and ears on Tulloch. Make sure he doesn't flee the EU. Actually arrest him.'

'And you're suggesting you and Craig head over there?' Sharon's eyes lost their humour pretty quickly. 'This isn't a chance for you pair to have a dirty weekend at the taxpayer's expense, okay?'

Chantal laughed, her eyes rolling back in her head. 'You're still on about that?'

'You're still denying it?'

Chantal sat forward and smiled. 'Shaz, we need to get someone on the ground over there. Send Elvis or Jimmy or whoever. Christ, you and Scott could go.'

Sharon's gaze scanned around the ceiling. 'You've been seeing each for nine months, right?'

'Sharon, this is unprofessional.'

'I'm unprofessional?' Sharon tilted her head to the side, eyebrows raised. 'You're the one sneaking around with lover boy—'

'Hypocrite. You and Scott were—'

'Two weeks. And does that mean you're not denying it?'

'Of course I'm denying it.' Chantal planted herself against the chair back. She rubbed a hand along the rough pink fabric. 'Look,

DC Hunter and I are the ones with experience of Tulloch's MO. We know how he thinks.'

'So how did he manage to outfox you today?'

'Because...' Chantal clamped her teeth together. 'All I'm asking for is the chance to bring him in.'

'Bloody hell.' Sharon slumped back in her chair and folded her arms tight like a petulant teenager. Her blouse popped open near the bottom. 'My hands are tied.'

Chantal got up to start pacing around the room again, running her tongue across her teeth. 'So, what, we're just leaving this to the lawyers?'

'There's the MOD.'

Chantal stopped, hands on hips. 'The army cops?'

'Makes sense, doesn't it?' Sharon slouched back further in her chair, the wheel squeaking. 'They've got jurisdiction over there. We don't.'

'Have you spoken to Craig about it?'

'About what?'

'He used to be a soldier. He said something like, if we involve them, they'll take Tulloch for court martial. You won't get to prosecute him for years.'

14

HUNTER

'Cop your whack round this, big boy.' Elvis gave Hunter a sheet of paper. 'Hotel de Sousa.'

Hunter's heart fluttered. *A chance to grab something positive out of this shambles.*

A giant hotel complex, the dull white concrete not even glowing in the bright sun. Loungers in front of a turquoise pool, the sea and coastline stretching behind it. The sort of Mediterranean dump that looked like it belonged in Leith in the heroin days.

'Bet it's even worse in person, man.' Elvis handed him a wad of pages, filled with an email conversation. 'Anyhoo, still haven't found that return ticket.'

'So he's run off?'

'Shite on toast.' Elvis shut his eyes. 'Aye, he could've run away.'

McNeill's office door grunted open and Chantal stomped out, beckoning him over.

'Here we go.' Hunter folded up the pages and set off. 'If I'm not back in an hour, send in a search party.' He wandered over and frowned into the room. 'What's up?'

'So that's how it'll lie.' Hunter shrugged his shoulders. The office stank of cheap perfume, at least masking his own acquired beer and pish musk. 'Rollo-Smith will hop in, arrest Tulloch and take him away. Whether he'll face any form of justice, well your guess is as good as mine.'

McNeill dug her fingers deep into her eyes. 'I've spoken to Rollo-Smith. He said he doesn't think we've got enough evidence to prosecute.'

Hunter frowned at her. 'We don't or they don't?'

'Both.' McNeill picked up a notepad and ran her pen down it. 'He said Tulloch's on fourteen days' leave. He needs to be back on MOD property before they can go after him.'

Hunter nodded at Chantal. 'The problem is that all we've got is a one-way ticket. He might've gone AWOL and the MOD won't know until he doesn't turn up in a fortnight.'

McNeill rested her pad down again. 'So what should I do then, Constable?'

Hunter passed her the first of his sheets of paper. 'This is where Tulloch's going. Five nights booked there.'

McNeill stared at it. 'What a bonny place.' She slid it over to Chantal. 'Have you seen this?'

'Not yet.' Chantal gave him an icy glare. 'We should get over there.'

McNeill shook her head. 'Chantal, I can't sanction you travelling there.'

'We've surely got budget left in the pot for an operation, though. Our team's still two heads short and we've only just taken Elvis on.'

McNeill smirked but didn't say anything.

Chantal coughed. 'Sorry, DC Gordon.'

'It's not that simple.'

Hunter tossed the other pages onto the table. 'Ma'am, with all due respect, you've seen what he's capable of. He's in the Algarve, literally raping and pillaging.'

'Hopefully the local cops will pick him up.'

'This is a shit show.' Chantal settled against a filing cabinet, shaking her head. 'A complete disaster.'

'Sergeant...' McNeill glared at Chantal.

'Tulloch knows how to play us, ma'am.' Hunter waved a hand at the door. 'Look, I've been to Portugal before. The local cops don't care about anything. It's like Mexico.'

'Craig, my hands are tied.'

'Two days.' Chantal shot to her feet, the cabinet behind her rocking back. 'That's all we need. Two days over there. We'll work with the local cops and bring him back. If we don't, you can kick our arses.'

McNeill blew air up her face and stared at the ceiling. 'Your shift's over, Chantal.'

'Is that a yes?'

'Get home.' McNeill sat up straight and adjusted her blouse. 'But leave your phone on.'

Chantal's face lit up. 'Thanks.'

McNeill winked at her. 'And bloody think about telling me the truth, okay?'

'I've *told* you the truth.'

'Aye, right.' McNeill did up an errant button at the bottom of her blouse. 'And Hunter, change your trousers. You're committing an obscene act.'

～

HUNTER LAY BACK, panting hard. He tied up the condom and stuffed it back in the wrapper as Chantal snuggled in close. He pecked her on the forehead. 'I love you.'

She looked up at him, cheeks flushed, eyes cold. 'You know you only say that when you've shot your load up me, right?'

'Shut up.' Hunter tossed the packet on the bedside table. *That wasn't true, was it?* He frowned at her. 'I tell you it all the time.'

She slapped his chest. 'No, you don't.'

'Okay, well I'm sorry. I do love you all the time, not just after I've shot my muck up you.'

She smirked and settled back into his embrace.

Over by the door, Bubble sneaked into the room, her eyes catching the light. She snaked towards the pizza box on the carpet.

Hunter shot her a look. 'Bubble!'

'Miaow.' Another step closer.

'No, Bubble.'

'Miaow?' She was patting the box with her paw.

Hunter hissed at her. 'Get out!'

She hunkered down on all fours, her focus trained on the pizza like she was hunting a rat.

'Bubble!'

'Miaow.' She leapt forward and grabbed a discarded strip of green pepper, then raced out of the room.

'Bloody cat.'

Chantal drilled a fingernail into his chest. 'She's as much of a freaky eater as you are.'

'More so, if that's possible.'

'I like how you can have a conversation with her, though.' More drilling, getting close to really hurting. 'I bet you tell her you love her.'

Hunter reached down and tickled the rough stubble under Chantal's arms.

She squealed out. 'Stop it!'

Hunter let her go and raised his hands. 'See in McNeill's office... She *knows*. We can't keep this a secret any longer.'

'Craig...' She sat back on her heels and bunched up her hair.

'We're at the point now where we're lying to people. To your boss.'

'Craig, come on...'

'You've never said 'I love you' to me, even after I've sho—'

'Craig, you know why.' Chantal clutched her face tight. 'I'm...' She slapped his chest, hard this time. 'You prick.'

'Hey, hey.' He pulled her tight to him and stroked her back. 'It's okay.'

'Craig. Jesus. It's not okay.' She pushed him back, her palms slapping off his flat belly. 'You know the deal. This has to be on my terms.'

'Okay, but tell me you're not ashamed of me.'

'Stop being a twat. This isn't about you.'

'Some of it is, though.'

'Right.' She nudged away from him. 'I'm not ashamed of you and your little willy. Happy?'

Hunter stared at his wilting cock. Not exactly massive, but...

She grabbed hold of it and it slipped through her hands. 'Relax, Craig, I'm just winding you up. It's perfectly adequate.'

'Adequate. Right.' Hunter shrugged at her. 'You've been quiet today.'

'Aye, making a mess of an arrest is something you want to scream from the rooftops. Twat.' She slapped his chest, harder more than playfully. 'Look, Craig, this case is important to me. Should be important to you as well. Instead of chasing our careers in the MIT, we're on this unit to bring pricks like Tulloch to justice. This isn't for us to sit in interviews and take statements, kiss the right arses and get a promotion. This is about stopping what's happening.'

'I know that. You know that.'

'Right.' She snorted. 'Well, if we come out to Sharon, then it's over. There's no room for both of us in the unit. One of us will have to move. Could be you, could be me.'

She's right. Bloody hell. Such a small team with nowhere near enough people.

'It's the most important thing I've ever done in my career.' Hunter smiled at her. 'I'd go if it came down to it.'

'Back to uniform?'

'Right.' Hunter shut his eyes.

Back to uniform. To chasing cats around houses. Scraping smackheads off railway tracks. Dealing with those twats and their endless banter. Sergeant Lauren Reid and her constant griping about how cold it is. Inspector Buchan and his stupid chess bollocks.

This is where I belong. Doing this shit. Making up for everything that's ever happened.

Chantal picked her bra up from the floor. 'The cat's at your pizza again.'

'Bubble!'

She shot off through the flat, like she could fly.

Chantal followed the cat out into the hall, shaking her head.

Well, Hunter, you are a cockblanket...

He reached down and tore off the crust Bubble had been licking. He dropped it on the box. Then the rest of the slice. No appetite for it.

What can I do? How can we keep this a secret? I feel like Lady Chatterley's lover. Sergeant Jain's lover.

So many bloody secrets. All tangled together like cables in a box, no idea which was the one I actually want.

That bloody Taylor Swift song blared out, muffled under a pile of clothes.

'Chantal! Your phone's ringing!'

15

CHANTAL

Chantal flushed the toilet and tugged on her bra. Out in the corridor, Bubble sat on the laminate chewing on some green beans she'd stolen from the pizza. Freaky cat. Freaky owner.

What am I playing at? He's right. Lying to Sharon like that. Daft cow.

What's so wrong with being split up at work? Having someone else to shadow me, him working with another DS.

Nothing.

It's... It's admitting that I'm in a relationship with someone. Someone that I...

Do I love him? Really?

He's nice. Strong, kind, funny. Smart. Sensitive.

It's just... All the shit in my head. Does he deserve that?

He's as bad. Worse. That flashback at lunchtime. Christ, what if it happened during an operation?

'Chantal! Your phone's ringing!'

Here we go.

She jogged through to the bedroom. 'Shite, where is it?' She rummaged around in the heap of clothes. Bubble lying on her trousers as she ratted at the pizza box. She snatched it from under the cat and checked the display. 'It's bloody Sharon.' She put her fingers to her lips and answered it on speaker as she lay on the bed. 'Sorry, Shaz, I was—'

'Shagging Craig?'

'Piss off.' The photo on the caller display was Sharon drunk out of her skull, hoisting a bottle of blue WKD above her head like it was a gold medal. 'Have they got him?'

'Tulloch walked through passport control an hour ago.'

'They didn't arrest him?'

'Saying they need evidence. Caught a load of flak when they arrested a Romanian last year. Turns out he stole two lettuces.'

Chantal collapsed back onto the bed. 'Shaz, this is boll—'

'I know, I know.' Sharon sighed down the line. 'Look, I've got approval for you and lover boy to investigate over there.'

'He's not my—'

'You're on the seven o'clock flight to Faro tomorrow morning. Three nights' accommodation *max*. Ideally less.'

'Thanks, Shaz.' Chantal looked round at Hunter, smiling like she couldn't control it. 'Whose arm did you have to break?'

'You don't want to know.' Sharon's sigh hissed out of the speaker. 'A local detective will meet you at the airport. Inspector João Quaresma. I think that's how you say it.'

'You seem to be the expert.'

'Right, well, I'm sure you'll be able to find Craig and tell him, aye?'

'Aye, funny.' Chantal scowled at the phone. 'I'll call you once we've spoken to this Quaresma guy, okay?'

'Look forward to it.'

'Cheers, Shaz.' Chantal ended the call and got to her feet. 'Glad that wasn't FaceTime.'

Hunter smiled at her as he chomped on a slice of pizza. 'So, you happy now?'

'Happier. Ball's in our court now.' She stepped into her pants and hoisted them up. 'Right. Need to get someone to look after Muffin.'

DAY 2

Friday
13th May

16

HUNTER

Still far too bloody early.

Hunter stared out of the flat window again, yawning as he sipped more tea. Rain battered the glass as the first rays of sun broke through the heavy clouds overhead. Looked like the Biblical flood had hit again. *Now, where did I put my Ark?*

Bubble rubbed against the legs of his jeans, almost tying herself in knots. 'Miaow.'

A dark car pulled to a halt across the street by the park, the diesel engine's throb transmitting to the stone tenement. Chantal got out of the back, lugging a box, and held out her hand to the driver. Five minutes.

Hunter crouched down and tipped a cup of biscuits into Bubble's bowl then into another next to it. He wagged a finger at the cat, her nose twitching. 'You're in charge, okay Bubble?'

'Miaow.'

'Don't let Muffin eat all the food. Okay, Bubble?'

'Miaow.'

The lock twisted. Chantal pushed through the door, her keys dangling from her grasp. Sunglasses propped over her hair, pastel yellow crop top and a flowery skirt. Not clothes for Edinburgh. She lugged the box over and set it down by Bubble. 'Sure this is the right thing to do?'

Bubble sniffed at the cat box.

'It's going to be fine.' Hunter waved at the window and the giant buildings hulking across the main road. 'Murray works at the Scottish Government building. He looks in on Bubble most lunchtimes. Murray'll feed them and change the litter. This'll be the third time they've stayed together and they're both neutered.' He pointed at a beige plug in one of the sockets. 'Anyway, I've put out some of that stuff that chills cats out. They'll be stoned.'

Chantal laughed through an exhale. 'Okay.' She unclipped the box and a monster-sized blonde cat stepped out, regally, like he owned the place. Muffin. He sniffed the air. 'Ma-wow!'

Bubble paced over to him and kissed him on the nose. Then bopped him with a paw. Muffin sat back and licked his front left leg. Bubble backed off, happy that she was in charge.

Chantal crouched down and rubbed her cat under the chin. 'You know, Muffin was litter mates with Sharon's cat, Fluffy. Nobody would take two huge boys, so we split them up.'

Hunter stroked the top of Muffin's head then did the same to Bubble.

A dry run for moving in together. Not that I'd say it out loud.

Chantal hauled herself to her feet. 'Come on, the taxi's waiting.'

∼

LAND SWEPT past out of the window below, France or northern Spain. Lush green tree-covered hills, sparkly blue rivers and roads with tiny cars and lorries, like a children's play set.

Hunter shifted around in his seat, sweat trickling down the back of his jeans. Too bloody hot and drier than Iraq in the height of summer. Not that an Iraqi winter was much better. Another glance up at the air conditioning and Murray's advice rattled around his head — that's where the germs are. Never turn it on.

A row of golfers danced in the aisle, waiting to drain the four breakfast pints they'd downed.

Hunter unfolded his *Argus*. That newspaper smell. The front page was filled with the grinning face of Harry Jack, the missing Northumberland kid who'd shunted all local stories off the front. A photograph of his mother at a press conference, frail and gaunt, desperate.

HARRY MUM: I JUST WANT MY SON BACK

He flicked through the article. Kid disappeared on his way home from school in Alnwick. Small town between Berwick and Newcastle, that bit of England that was quite Scottish. Not that you'd say that to a local.

He showed Chantal the paper. 'You see this?'

She didn't look up from her Kindle. 'Read about it last night. Horrible.'

'That poor woman.' Hunter tapped at the page. 'I can't imagine what she's going through.'

Chantal finally looked up to point at the photo of the mother, her finger landing on the figure next to her. A tired cop in a grey suit. 'I know him. Can't remember his name for the life of me...'

'Where from?'

She went back to her Kindle without a word.

Hunter rested a hand on her thigh. The tiniest grains of stubble dotted her coffee skin. Her knees were tinged with red. 'Sharon could've got us the extra legroom seats.'

She nudged his hand away and shot a nervous look towards the man at the end of their row, hidden behind his *Daily Mail*. 'You might need to lose a few inches.'

He leaned in to whisper. 'Thought I needed to grow another couple?'

'Craig, get over it.'

Right. That easy.

Hunter adjusted himself in the seat again and folded up his paper. 'I'm not sure we should be flying on Friday the thirteenth.'

'What?' An impish grin filled her face. 'Tell me you're not superstitious.'

'Of course I'm not... It's...' Hunter shrugged. 'I don't want to be the one who laughs at it and the plane falls out of the sky.'

'You have flown before, right?'

'Of course I've bloody flown.' Hunter squeezed his arse to the right. *Not good.* Back to the left. *That'll have to do.* 'You don't drive to Iraq or Afghanistan.'

'Oh, shite. Yeah.' She locked her Kindle and stuffed it in the seat rest. 'Look, you could've brought something other than a paper to read. Instead, you're annoying me.'

'I know.' The food trolley clunked behind them, letting one of the waiting golfers past to the toilet. 'Could do with a sleep.'

'So sleep.'

'Maybe.' Daily Mail man was lost in his latest threat to house prices. Hunter put his hand back on her thigh.

'And we're not joining the mile high club.'

'Wasn't going to suggest it.'

The air hostess leaned over to them. Smelled like she'd spent half her salary on perfume, even at duty-free rates. 'Sir, can I get you anything?'

Hunter shook his head. 'I'm fine.'

'Madam?'

'Coffee, please.' Chantal gave her a five euro note. 'Milk, no sugar.'

'Of course.' She handed her two little milk cartons stuffed into a plastic cup. Serviettes and plastic spoons lurked out of the top.

Chantal wrestled her tray table to horizontal and put them down. She took the coffee from the hostess, whose gaze had already switched to Daily Mail man. 'Thanks.'

'We should go on a holiday, Chantal.'

'Okay.' She tore off the lid and blew on the drink, then tipped in both milks. 'When?'

'When you tell Sharon we're an item?'

'Oh, Craig.'

'I'm serious. We're not going to get time off together any other way, are we?'

Chantal took a drink and grimaced.

The stewardess squeezed past a waiting golfer and walked to the front of the plane.

'We'll talk about this later, okay?' Chantal grabbed her Kindle and unlocked it. 'Now, try and get some sleep.'

'Maybe.' Hunter shut his eyes and huffed out a breath.

The plane droned around them.

Chantal slurped at her coffee.

Am I being unreasonable here?
Probably.
She's got her reasons. Solid reasons. Good reasons, the sort you shouldn't mess with. Respect them.
You selfish twat.
Still. Sharon McNeill's her friend. Best friend. They'd been cat shopping together, splitting a pair of cats. Why can't she tell her as a friend? Come to some sort of arrangement?
Sharon had worn similar shoes when started she dating... him. Surely she'd understand?

'Here you go, sir.'

'Thanks.'

The smell of bacon wafted over to him.

Hunter clenched his fists and fought hard against—

17

HUNTER

White noise, everywhere, the RAF transport's propellers droning in the darkness. Cold wind hit Hunter's cheek, distracting him from his teeth rattling.

A few faces lit up in yellow around him. Friends, now. One grinned maniacally at him. 'Lance bloody Corporal Hunter.' Terry lifted the cap off his hip flask and handed it over, the cockney twat grinning away. 'Have a swig of this, you big Scotch poof.'

'Just because you want to shag me doesn't make me a poof.' Hunter reached over, the straps cutting into his shoulders, and raised the flask. 'Slainte!'

Terry scowled at him. 'Slange? What?'

'Slainte. Gaelic or something. But you spell it with a T.' Hunter downed a measure of the whisky, burning the back of his throat. Disgusting. 'What's that?'

Private Dave Mowat sat opposite, smirking away. Twat from Dundee, barely tall enough to enlist. 'Single malt. Like that Sassenach would know any different.'

'It's Dunpender, if you must know, pipsqueak.' Terry took the flask back and necked a good measure. 'Slainte.'

Mowat almost spat at him. 'You're not allowed to say that, you cockney wanker.'

'I can say what I like when I'm drinking your whisky, pipsqueak.'

Terry put the cap back on and hurled the hip flask at Mowat. It clattered off the bulkhead behind and dropped to the floor behind him.

'Watch it!' Mowat craned his neck to look below. 'You'll have dented it!'

'Hardly.' Terry buckled with laughter. 'Get it down you, Hunter's drying up.'

Hunter wiped the whisky from his chin. Started repeating on him. Horrible stuff, but you've got to play along. 'Last decent booze we'll get for a while.'

Terry snarled as he caught the flask, thrown with enough venom to crack a window, if there were any.

Mowat's gaze settled on the flask as Terry passed it back to Hunter. 'You boys looking forward to killing some of these pricks?'

'That's not what we're there for, pipsqueak.' Hunter sucked down more whisky. Felt half pissed already. 'But I'm looking forward to getting back into action, if that's what you mean.' He lobbed the hip flask over. 'Here.'

Mowat caught it and drank in the spirit's aroma. 'You boys were in Kandahar, right?'

'Right.' Hunter gripped the straps tight, the fabric digging into his hands. 'This is supposed to be a breeze compared to that.'

∼

THE AIR WAS FILLED with the stench of burning opium poppies, bitter and dark, catching in the throat. Hunter tightened his mask around his mouth, but the taste and the reek still got through. *Will smell it for weeks.*

The Chinooks roared above them, their propellers lashing the rising sun into a nightclub strobe. Lashkar Gah gleamed in the near distance, the town's lights flickering in the cold desert air.

Hunter rested against the ledge and looked down into the valley immediately below them. A small stone building sat alone. Looked like a goat hut, but there was no sign of any goats. He looked left, then right. Terry and Mowat looked like he felt — nervous, cold and wanting to get back to base. 'You guys okay?'

'Like shit, I am.' Terry hefted up his SA80 and leaned back against the stone wall, older than time itself. 'I've had enough of this bollocks.' He yawned. 'I want a pint of fizz and my bed.'

'Last Afghan tour for us, mate.' Hunter patted his arm. 'Iraq will be a breeze after this.'

'This was supposed to be a piece of piss.' Terry peered through his rifle's sights and swivelled it around the area. 'Where is everyone?'

'This is more like Operation Kitten's Claw than Panther's.' Mowat slipped his goggles up onto his forehead. 'The bloody brass must be loving— SHITE!'

The wall above them puffed up, the air exploding. A rifle report echoed around.

'Get down!' Mowat hauled them both to the stone floor. 'Jesus Christ!'

More gunshots battered the wall, small fragments tipping down.

'Have you got sight of them?' Hunter put his binoculars to his eyes and scanned for insurgents. 'Anything?'

'Not a sausage.'

The wall exploded five, six, seven times, pebbles lashing down on their legs.

Hunter got up to a crouch. 'We need to move.'

'Where do we go?' Mowat rested on his elbows, twisting his head around to Hunter. 'Where the hell do we go, man?'

'That hut.' Hunter nodded into the valley. 'Then down to the bottom.' He slipped his binocs on. Yep, definitely a trail. 'There's a path down there. It's got to lead to the town.'

Mowat shook his head. 'No way, man.'

'Private, we're moving out and that's an order.' Hunter grabbed hold of Mowat's sleeve and hauled him up to standing. Sheer terror in his eyes, frantically dancing around. He let Mowat go. 'Terry, you okay to lead us down?'

'Waiting to be asked.' Terry bombed off along the stone pathway and stopped by the opening ten metres along. Then he swung down and scrambled across the scrubland.

Hunter followed Mowat, his gear rattling as he jogged down towards the shelter.

WOOOSH!

BOOM!

Hunter dived forward and rolled, tumbling arse over tit until his shoulder dug into a rock. He clenched his jaw and focused on the pain, trying to stop himself screaming. Pebbles rained down the slope. Back up the way, a huge hole smoked in the wall they'd been leaning against seconds ago. 'What the hell was that?'

'Rocket!' Mowat stumbled towards him, sliding on the avalanche until he braced himself against a boulder. 'They've got rockets!'

Midway to the bottom, Terry leaned against the stone hut's front walls, puffing and panting. He shifted his rifle around, pointing above them. His free hand beckoned them to move on.

'Come on.' Hunter pulled himself up to standing and jogged. 'Let's go!'

'No!' Mowat hugged the boulder tight. 'I'm not going anywhere!'

'We're sitting ducks here.' Hunter stomped back up and grabbed Mowat's jacket. The little bastard wasn't budging. 'We're moving out, NOW.' Another tug then he started running towards Terry and cut to the other side of the entrance, spinning round to face back up the way, his SA80 aiming up, ready to fire. All one movement. Like he'd been trained to do. Like he knew what he was doing. Like he could cope with this shit.

'Shit!' Mowat bombed towards them, his short legs pounding, and skidded between them into the hut.

Hunter shook his head at Terry and stepped inside. Half of the bottom right wall was open to whatever elements lived here, shards of light crawling across the scrub floor towards Mowat, lying in a heap, groaning.

'Pipsqueak...' Terry joined them inside as gunfire lashed the building. 'You bleeding tit.'

Mowat pushed himself up to his feet. 'Shut up!' He pointed his gun at Terry. 'Shut your face, you cockney arsehole!'

'You what?'

Mowat lifted his rifle to point at Terry's left eye. 'I said, shut up!'

Terry raised his hands. 'Calm down, Pips—'

'Stop calling me that!'

'Stop it!' Hunter stepped between them. 'Dave, you need to calm down, okay?'

'How can I stay calm?' Mowat switched his gun to focus on Hunter. 'They've got rockets!'

Terry held up his hands to Mowat. 'It's okay. We can stay here for a bit. It's cool.'

Mowat nodded slowly. 'Thanks.'

'This place is safe as houses.' Terry waved a gloved hand around the hut. 'Been standing since we were monkeys in the trees, I reckon.'

'I'm not happy about this.' Hunter pointed his rifle back out the door. 'Like he said, they've got rockets and this place is falling apart.'

'No!' Mowat raised his rifle again. 'I'm staying!'

Hunter tapped the wall with the butt of his rifle. 'One lucky strike and this is coming down.'

Terry sucked in air and peered through the hole. Then back in with a grim look on his face. 'He's right, mate.'

Mowat's breathing sped up. 'I'm staying.'

'Dave, we need to move out.' Terry waved down the hill. 'The path at the bottom of the slope will take us into Lashkar Gah. We'll be okay from there.'

'I'm not going. Send a chopper to pick me up.'

Terry looked lost and alone, his barrow boy cool missing. He frowned at Hunter. 'Craig?'

Ranking soldier here, got to show leadership.

Hunter locked eyes with Terry then Mowat. 'We're moving out. No man left behind.'

Mowat threw his rifle on the floor. 'Piss off.'

'Dave.' Hunter settled into a crouch. 'We need to—'

BOOOM!

The ground shook. Hunter tumbled over, landing face first on the scrub. Dirt covered his teeth. He spat it out and rolled his tongue. Then he got to his feet and huffed out breath. 'No questions, okay? We're moving out.'

Mowat eased himself up to standing, shaking his head like he wanted to be back in his mummy's arms.

Don't we all...

Terry leaned against the wall, surveying the ground outside. 'Looks clear this way.' He waved off to the right. 'The rocket came from over there.' Then down to the bottom. 'Those rocks will give us cover when we're on the path.'

Hunter swung around to Mowat. 'You hear that? One last push and we're safe.'

Mowat nodded slowly. 'Okay.'

'On three.' Terry counted on his thumb, then his forefinger. Then his middle finger. 'Go.' He clambered through the hole in the wall and hurtled down the hill, dust billowing up behind him.

Hunter climbed through the gap and jabbed a finger at Mowat. 'Go!' He ran. Much steeper than it looked. He tripped and pushed himself up into a run, unable to do anything but keep going. It levelled out to a shallow bank near the bottom. He almost clattered into Terry.

WOOOSH!

A gust streaked across the sky from the left.

BOOM!

Pebbles and boulders scattered towards them. Hunter had to cover his face and wait. He pulled his arm away and scanned around the path.

Terry kicked away a pile of stones and picked up his rifle. 'You okay, mate?'

'I'm fine. Where's— Shite.'

An SA80 skittered down the scrub towards them, the strap torn in half.

'Where's Mowat?'

A standard-issue boot rolled towards them, blood streaking the dusty ground as it trundled to a halt.

Terry swallowed hard, his eyes shut. 'That's Mowat.'

'What?' Hunter vomited, a half-digested sausage in amongst the carrots and bile. 'Where is he?'

'He's gone, mate. Thin air now.' Terry clapped his arm. 'Come on. We'll have a squad of Taliban on us before we know it.'

Hunter grabbed Terry's fatigues. 'You're not listening to me! Where did—'

∼

THE OFFICE COULD'VE BEEN ANYWHERE. PAINTED concrete blocks, aluminium filing cabinets from floor to ceiling. The only window was open wide to let out the oppressive Afghan heat. In front, a giant desk the size of a family car, neatly ordered by a series of three trays. No computer, just a phone. Cutlery clattered as Captain William Morecambe tucked into a fry-up. A full plate of meat: four sausages, six rashers of bacon, tomato, fried bread, two eggs. It all looked overcooked. The aroma coiled around Hunter's nose, the sweet burnt smell of the bacon.

Morecambe nibbled at the bottom of his lip, then reached up to flatten down his moustache. Then he sliced off some tomato and speared it with a doubled-over rasher of bacon. Left it hovering in front of his lips. 'Lance Corporal, your actions were responsible for the death of a serving member of Her Majesty's Armed Forces.'

Hunter stood to attention, waiting for Morecambe to let him stand at ease. Wasn't happening. So he stared at him, long enough to show he wasn't going to be messed about with, short enough to show some respect. 'My actions were responsible for the safety of myself and Corporal Terence—'

'You lost a soldier, Lance Corporal.' Morecambe finished chewing and stabbed his fork into another rasher.

'My actions were responsible for—'

'Okay, I get it.' Morecambe cut a sausage in half lengthways, the fat dripping out. 'Someone's trained you. Repeat that pat line over and over, eventually I'll give up, right?' He left a space.

Hunter didn't fill it, had no intention of ever speaking again, especially to a monkey like him.

The cutlery clattered against the plate. Morecambe snapped at the Military Police armband on his arm. Bloody Monkeys. 'Lance Corporal, need I remind you which function I work for?'

'You've made that clear, sir. My actions were respons—'

'Enough!' Morecambe's shout echoed around the room, slipped out of the crack in the window. Could hear it in Iraq. Probably hear it in Scotland. 'Your actions impeded the prosecution!'

Hunter scratched at the scar on his cheek. 'What are you talking about?'

'You got in the way of justice, Lance Corporal.'

Hunter's mouth was dry. He looked over at his glass of water. Already drunk it. He cleared his throat. 'I've no idea what you're talking about.'

'Quit it.' Morecambe sat back in his chair with a creak. 'You know perfectly well what I'm talking about.'

'I don't.'

'Lance Corporal, I can squeeze you and squeeze you until you pop. You will admit to—'

'Are you threatening me?'

Morecambe ran his tongue around his teeth. Seemed to find something worth chewing on near the back left. 'Are you telling me you had no inkling of—'

'None. I swear.' Hunter wanted to open the neck of his shirt. He left it. 'What is he supposed to have done?'

Morecambe waved a hand across to the door. 'Get out of my sight.'

'Look, I led myself and Corporal—'

'We're watching you, Hunter.' Morecambe went back to his breakfast, his cutlery chinking off the plate as he cut away at the fried bread. 'Now, clear off.'

'Sir.' Hunter saluted and marched over to the door. One last look at him, hamster cheeks chewing as he chopped up more. The bacon smell everywhere in the room. Then he opened the door and left.

The corridor was baking hot. Hunter took his beret off and stuffed it under his arm, sweat trickling down his back now. That could've gone better.

'He got you too?' Terry was sitting outside the room, fingers splayed, eyebrows raised.

'He got me.' Hunter marched off down the corridor.

Terry caught up with him by the stairwell door. 'What did he say?'

Hunter pushed through the door and let it rattle shut behind them. 'Tried to haul me over the coals, but I kept to the party line.'

'Good man.' Terry grinned. 'Good man.'

Hunter leaned against the wall, bare breeze blocks that had sucked in all the heat. 'He said they're investigating him.'

Terry swallowed, his Adam's apple bobbing up and down.

'You know why, don't you?'

Terry nodded. 'A little birdie told me something.' He scratched at his cheek. 'Said that little bastard killed a woman in Iraq.'

'Iraq?'

'Last tour over there. Local girl. And I mean girl. Fourteen. Shot her when he was pissed.'

Hunter slumped back against the wall. 'You serious?'

'Deadly, mate. They found this girl's body, didn't know it was him did it. Now someone can place him at the scene.'

'He killed someone?'

'Yup. Shitty business, mate.'

'So why was he on duty?'

'You know what they're like.' Terry thumbed behind him. 'Most of what the monkeys get up to is political. If he'd done that back home, he'd be locked up. Out here? They'll cover over anything they can.'

18

CHANTAL

'—Dave go?!' Hunter jolted forward, almost cracking his head off the seat in front. *What the hell?*

Chantal stuffed her Kindle away and twisted round to face Hunter. His eyes were swivelling in his head, not focusing on anything. His breathing was out of control.

The guy next to Chantal looked up from pretending to read his Daily Mail. Bread churned around in his mouth, chewing his roll, his eyes wild. 'Are you okay?'

'We're fine.' Chantal smiled at him as she clutched a hand around Hunter's. *Are we fine? Jesus...* 'Craig, it's okay.'

'Where's...' Hunter was panting hard. 'Where's...' He pinched his nose. 'Shite.'

'Did you have a flashback?'

They were over tall hills now, maybe even mountains. Was it the Pyrenees? Could even see the plane's shadow on the green. The engine droned, the waft of bacon and coffee filling the pressurised air.

Hunter kept his silence.

'Craig, who's Dave?'

'A squad mate.' Hunter swallowed, his breathing still fast. 'In Helmand. Private David Mowat. We were hiding in a hut and a rocket fired into it. He just blew up. Disappeared. I carried his rifle back to base. The only thing left of him was a boot with... with...' Tears filled his eyes.

She tightened her grip, let him focus on it. Centre around it. 'It's okay, Craig, you're safe now.'

Hunter ran a hand across his face. 'What a bloody mess.' He clenched his jaw tight. 'Dave was a bit of a cock at times, but that shouldn't happen to anyone.'

'You poor thing...'

'Christ, and I want you to commit to me?'

'Hey, hey.' She leaned over and kissed his lips. 'It's okay, Craig. You're with me. Okay?'

'It was so real...' Hunter stared over at Daily Mail man as he slapped at his last bite of roll. 'Bloody bacon...'

'So that's definitely the trigger?' She caressed his hand. 'I'm going to get you through this, okay?'

'You don't have to.'

'I want to.' She reached over and ran a hand over his stubbled head. 'That's two flashbacks in two days. Do you need to call Dr Gold when we land?'

'I'm fine, Chantal. I can keep my shit together.' Their neighbour's ears were burning. *What's going through his head?* Hunter leaned over and kissed her cheek. 'Such a bloody mess.'

'We'll get through this, Craig.' She returned the kiss. 'I love you.'

'What?' Hunter frowned. 'You...' He couldn't help but grin. 'Shite.'

'We're fine, Craig.' She wrapped an arm around his and leaned in close. 'I'm here for you.'

Hunter settled back and stroked her cheek. 'Thank God...'

∼

'THANK YOU, MADAM. HAVE A NICE DAY.' The hostess's smile looked chiselled into her face, repeated a hundred times a day. Doubt she ever meant it. The cockpit hissed behind them, radio chatter turned to noise. Another nod. 'And you too, sir.'

Chantal nodded back as she gripped Hunter's hand and stepped down the stairs. Cold air nibbled at her cheeks, wind clawing at her bare legs. Dots of rain turned into big splodges, the sort you saw on the west coast of Scotland.

'Sure we've not landed back in Edinburgh?' Hunter wrapped his coat around his shoulder.

Chantal reached into her bag for a cardigan and groaned. 'Bloody typical.' She clanked down the steps to the bus hissing and droning at the bottom, already half-filled. The distant airport was so far away that it looked like it was in Spain.

She marched across the tarmac and swung inside the bus, wrestling past the old couple hogging the entrance.

Hunter dropped his bag by a pole and grabbed her hand again. 'Glad I wore my jeans.'

'It's supposed to be high twenties later today.'

Hunter shrugged. 'So I'll get some shorts.'

∽

'Craig, come on.' Chantal led him to the end of the queue.

Hunter stabbed something into a text as he walked. Then he clunked his head on the underside of the staircase. 'Ah, you bastard.'

Chantal rubbed at it. 'You idiot.'

The queue ahead of them wound around the bend, then back again. A rope separated the strands as they forked to the three officers manning the passport control. Looked like they were double-checking every single word on the documents.

Hunter rolled his eyes at Chantal. 'Maybe we'll take that holiday somewhere else.'

'Bloody shambles.' She nodded, her fingers clutching her passport. Close to murdering someone.

Next to them, vodka and rum wafted off a stag party, all dressed in multi-colour suits. A man in green and yellow covered in question marks pointed at his wheeled suitcase and hugged a mate. 'Keep an eye on that, Stevie, aye?' Sounded like he was from deepest, darkest Glasgow.

Perfect planning — two planes full of pissed-up Scots heading to a tiny bottleneck.

A young woman stood between the stag party and them, a frown twitching all over her face. Another stag member gave her a theatrical wink. 'Excuse me, sweetheart, will you marry me?'

The guy who'd sat next to them on the plane was level with them in the other queue, though he'd lost his Mail. He shot them a dirty leer.

Chantal thumbed over at him. 'We're in the wrong queue.'

'So are they.' Hunter kicked his bag forward an inch, though it seemed to be more in hope than actual purpose. 'We've not moved for ages.'

She nodded over at them. 'They have.'

'Sure?'

Chantal shrugged out a huff. 'It's too bloody late, anyway.'

'Wish I still had my MOD90.'

Chantal raised her eyebrows. 'You wish you were still a soldier?'

'Being able to breeze through without all this malarkey.'

The girl in front brushed off the leering stag and swung round to them, panic on her face. 'Excuse me, is this the flight to London?' Polish accent, but with some surface cockney.

Chantal patted her on the arm. 'No, sorry.' She pointed to the passport control, grimacing. 'That's Portugal out there.'

'Oh, not again.' She clicked her suitcase handle and started barging her way against the queue. 'Thank you.'

'Poor girl.' Chantal watched her shove her way through shouts of 'Well, excuse me!' towards the staircase back up to Departures. Their flight neighbour was six people ahead of them now. 'Craig, that queue *is* moving.'

Hunter took another look. 'Can we change?'

'Too late.'

'Bloody—'

'Chantal Jain, as I live and breathe.' A man stood in the other queue, hair slicked back over his head. Tall, broad-shouldered and as much eye contact as you could handle. Thick Newcastle accent and every inch the Geordie, he just needed to be topless in some second division away end. Instead, he wore a suit and carried a long overcoat.

What the hell is his name?

Chantal gave him one of her fake smiles. 'Long time no see.'

'Far too long, pet.' He looked over at Hunter, beaming away. 'This your boyfriend?'

Chantal coughed. 'Partner.'

He frowned. 'Police or personal?'

'Police.' Chantal's polite smile returned as she lowered her voice. 'He's my DC. We're on a case.'

'Ah.' He tapped his nose. 'I see.'

She tried to get a look at his boarding pass. His passport. Anything.

Hunter raised his eyebrows at Chantal and held out his hand. 'Craig Hunter. Nice to meet you.'

'DI Jon Bruce.' He returned the grip.

That was it. DI Bruce.

Brucie Bonus. Oh shit, Brucie Boner. Tried to pull Sharon once.

Bruce's queue moved forward, and he stepped a foot away. 'You're coming with me, right?'

Chantal kicked her bag over towards him. 'I forgot.'

'You can't do that!' A red-faced man in jacket and jeans scowled at her. 'There's a bloody queue for a reason!'

'Sorry.' She gave a shrug and joined Bruce.

Hunter hefted up his bag and followed her. Got a smack on the arm. He gave him his policeman glare. 'Sir, you need to back off.'

'Who the hell do you think you are?'

'I'm a police officer.'

'Well, you're on Portuguese soil now, so—'

'Nice to meet you.' Hunter nodded at Bruce. 'So, how do you two know each other?'

'We were on a course down in London together. Few years back, now.' Bruce leered at her. 'Had cracking fun, didn't we?'

Brucie Bonus, indeed. Play your cards right.

Chantal looked him up and down. 'What brings you out here in your fighting suit?'

Bruce looked away, scratching at his chin. 'Running this bloody Harry Jack case.'

'Heard about that on the radio.' Chantal frowned. 'The abduction, right?'

'Yeah. Kid got lifted in Alnwick on Wednesday. Coming home

from school.' Bruce draped his jacket over the other arm. 'As you can imagine, it's got a bit of press interest. Had a couple of sightings of the lad in the Algarve yesterday. Given the *Daily Express* can still cover their front page with Madeleine McCann and the fact the kid's mother is Portuguese...' He raised his hands. 'Voila. The Chief Constable is going apeshit. Half of Northumbria Police are on their way out. Omnishambles.'

Chantal stepped forward. Their previous queue still hadn't moved, not that the stag parties seemed to care. Or notice. 'At least they've got you, Jon.'

Bruce chuckled. 'Tell you, the Chief's brought in three psychics to help. Can you believe it?' He shook his head. 'And we've got sniffer dogs from one of the Yorkshire forces out.'

'Good luck with it.'

'Think we'll need it.' Bruce stepped forward in the queue. 'What are you here for?'

'A serial sex offender has slipped out of the country.'

'Oh, you bastard.' Bruce grimaced. 'Still, not a bad gig here. It's been pissing down in Newcastle all week. Suspect it's the same up in Edinburgh.' He peered back through the terminal building. 'Not that it's much better here.'

'It's worse than in Edinburgh.'

Bruce nodded. 'We should grab a drink sometime, given we're both over here.'

Chantal smiled at him. 'Sounds like a good idea.'

Hunter frowned at her.

Shit, am I doing it again? Playing the single girl too well?
Probably thinks I've been pissing him about until a DI came along.

He cleared his throat. 'Actually—'

Bruce patted Chantal on the arm and nodded at the passport desk. 'You go first, princess.'

19

HUNTER

The officer stared at Hunter's passport, eyes slowly blinking. Felt like he'd been looking at it for five bloody minutes. He spoke into his phone and turned away. Grumbling voices came from the queue behind.

Hunter couldn't see Chantal or that Geordie guy. Bruce or whatever it was. Seedy-looking git. He smiled at the officer. 'Is there a problem?'

He got a raised finger for his trouble.

Hunter picked up his bag again with a sigh. *Don't speak, don't give them any reason to push back.*

'Okay.' The officer put the phone down and handed the passport back with a sniff and a sneer. 'Through you go, sir.'

Hunter closed his passport and sauntered through to the arrivals area.

Bruce was walking away, Chantal ahead of him, talking on her mobile. The smell of cooking meat hung around from the various food stalls.

Hunter clenched his teeth, his fingers starting to dance.

Not now.

Bruce pushed through the door to outside, his case trundling behind him. More than a day's worth of stubble on his chin. Slight tanning around his ring finger, a pale band cutting across the rough hairs.

A gang of pissed-up stags queued by a row of taxis, a couple of them holding coffees.

Roofed walkways outside the airport hid them from the worst of the deluge but left them exposed to the occasional cross blast of tropical wind. To the west, a shaft of sunlight crept out of the grey gloom, lighting up the towers in Faro town centre.

Hunter sighed, his breathing slowing.

'You okay, mate?'

Hunter cleared his throat. 'I'm fine.'

'Okay...' Bruce grinned at Hunter. 'Well, I'm heading into town, so I'll catch you later, aye?'

Hunter glanced at Chantal again, clenching his fingers into a fist. 'I take it Cha— DS Jain's got your number?'

'Sure has.' Bruce hoisted his jacket over his shoulder. 'You pair supposed to be meeting anyone?'

'Inspector João Quaresma?'

'That's one of our contacts. But I've got to meet the local chief of police first.' Bruce's eyes misted over. 'A mate in the West Mercia force was out here a few years back hunting a fugitive, said the locals are useless.'

'I'll bear that in mind.'

Bruce leaned in close, his minty breath mixing with his aftershave. 'What's the story with you and Chantal?'

Hunter clocked the hunger in his eyes, a little twinkle in the baby blue. 'She's my DS.'

'Riiiight.' Bruce's head tilted almost halfway round. 'Tell you, mate, the things I'd bloody do to her...'

Hunter swallowed an exasperated laugh. *Prick.* 'See you around, sir.'

'Right. Yeah.' Bruce looked him up and down then saluted Chantal as he walked off, his jacket hanging from his shoulder.

Chantal hung up her call. 'Thank God he's gone.'

'Old flame?'

'Craig...' She raised her eyebrows and sucked in her cheeks. 'No, he's not.' She glanced back after Bruce, eyes narrowed. 'Not for want of trying on his part. He was more interested in Sharon.' She yawned. 'We did a week-long course in Advanced Interview Techniques. Sharon's DI at the time wanted us to mingle, so a week in Hendon with him and a load of London cops. He was trying it on with all the girls there.'

'Sounds like hell.'

'And then some.' Chantal waved at someone behind Hunter and put on her fake smile again. 'There we go.'

By the taxis, a middle-aged man held up a card with "DS Jane" on it.

Chantal stopped beside him and showed her warrant card. 'DS Chantal Jain.' She thumbed at Hunter. 'This is —'

'I am just taxi!' He held up his hands. 'I'll take you there now.'

20

CHANTAL

Chantal leaned forward, the seatbelt straining and digging into her chest. 'How much longer?'

The driver's head crept around and stale coffee breath swept over her. 'Not long.'

Chantal slumped back in her seat, letting the belt slap back.

I don't even have a number for this Quaresma guy. What an idiot.

The countryside slid past them. Steep hills metres away from the edge of the dual carriageway. Even the rain couldn't dampen the dry soil too much. The road ahead was almost empty, a camper van lurching between the lanes.

Albufeira came into view around a tight bend, a long sprawl down by the twinkling blue sea, caught under the dark grey clouds. No buildings taller than three or four storeys by the looks of it, certainly nothing like back home.

They swept up to a roundabout and the driver hammered the horn, swearing in Portuguese.

Hunter put his phone away. 'So, what's the plan?'

'Grab some of his officers, find Tulloch, arrest him, take him back to dear old Blighty.'

'Sounds so easy.'

The driver slowed to a halt and hit the horn again. 'You see your press, why do they have to come to my country, eh?'

The road was mobbed with journalists, typical Brits abroad too, all holding their mobiles out like Dictaphones. A couple of TV crews swung around, aiming their cameras at the taxi. Gradually, the driver inched through the crowds and pulled into a car park. 'This is what we have to deal with.'

Chantal tried her door but it was locked. The driver got out and opened Hunter's door first. She squeezed out after him.

A man stood waiting on the tarmac. 'Inspector João Quaresma.' He smouldered away, close to burning out. Grey hair heading towards silver, tanned skin fading to yellow, eyes deep in sockets. He wore a three-piece suit and a long jacket. 'Come on. This way.' He had their cases out already. 'Sergeant, do not speak to the press, okay?'

She shrugged. 'Off you go, then.'

Quaresma marched off across the damp concrete mosaic, a shaft of sunlight breaking through the granite clouds and lighting up the station. Concrete pillars held up a brutal rendition of a Greek temple in pale stucco. All hard angles, the top floor about twenty metres wider on each side than the ground. The windows were narrow, designed to block the sun.

Chantal stopped by the front door. *Keep the head, girl. Don't overreact to anything he says.*

Someone grabbed her by the arm. She swung around. A scrawny man with a skinhead, a haunted look, pale flesh hanging off him. Rich McAlpine. 'Hey, Chantal, you got a minute?'

'Been told not to speak to the press, Rich.'

'Come on.' Rich's phone was almost in her face. Twat was recording this. 'Have Police Scotland been called in to assist with the hunt for Harry Jack?'

'No comment.'

'That cos you are?'

'I said, no comment.'

'Come on, Chantal. We're getting soaked here. A little titbit?'

Another reporter joined Rich, the sort of hipster you only used to see in London but were now everywhere. Big beard with twirly handlebar moustache. Shirt buttoned up to his throat.

She smiled at him. 'Rich, I've got nothing to say.'

Rich's mate piped up. 'So what is it, then?' Northern accent. Maybe Manchester.

'No comment.' Chantal grabbed her case and pushed into the station.

Quaresma was standing inside, hands on hips, lips pursed. 'Sergeant, I told you not to speak.'

'They were local to me and DC Hunter. I gave them a no comment.'

'I see.' Quaresma started off towards a set of doors.

Hunter followed her in. 'That wasn't Rich McAlpine, was it?'

'You know him?'

'Aye, shared a flat with Scott Cullen, didn't he?'

'Well, not anymore. But it was him.'

'You didn't say anything?'

She winked at Hunter. 'Not yet.'

∽

JOÃO QUARESMA SAT behind a cheap-looking desk and leaned back, resting his leather boots on the white plastic surface. The room stank of boot polish. No natural light in there, just a bright desk lamp facing them. 'So, you've travelled all this way for Detective Inspector Sharon McNeill.'

'And it looks like a very long way to travel for nothing.' Chantal perched on the chair opposite Quaresma. She trusted it as much as him. She glanced over to Hunter, standing by the door. 'So, have you got Tulloch in custody?'

'You know we haven't.'

Chantal lurched forward, arms flailing wide. 'He's been here since last night.'

Quaresma flashed a grin at her. 'I'm afraid we've got other priorities.'

'A serial domestic abuser running around on your territory isn't a priority?'

'Sergeant, Sergeant, Sergeant. As much as I would love to help you and Detective Inspector Sharon McNeill. And Mr Farmer here.'

'Hunter.'

Quaresma nodded slowly, his teeth bared. 'You are here to hunt this man, yes?'

Hunter shrugged at him. 'We're here to bring him back to our country. That's it.'

'That's it?' Quaresma reached forward and flicked his left trouser leg back down over his boot. 'You're only here to escort this man?'

'I'm sure DI McNeill passed that on?'

'DI McNeill did.'

Chantal butted in. 'And yet you've let him go.'

'Sergeant, if this was the other way round and I was in Scotland looking to bring home a Portuguese national, would you just let me do it?' Quaresma huffed as he flicked the right trouser leg over the boot. 'You would let me take this man or woman back to Portugal?'

'I'd spend a while looking at the evidence you'd sent.' Chantal looked across the empty desk. 'I don't really see you doing that.'

'I have my hands full, I'm afraid. This sort of case requires professional courtesy.'

'Listen, we shared evidence with you yesterday, by fax *and* email, of Sean Tulloch viciously assaulting a woman and two police officers in Scotland. He stole a car, too.'

Quaresma held her gaze for a few seconds, then ran his tongue across his lips. 'Then you shouldn't have let him leave your country, should you?' His grin was helped along by his twinkling eyes. 'You've heard of Harry Jack, yes?'

Chantal's gut plummeted through the soles of her sandals. *Here we go — Brucie Boner strikes back.* She tried to keep her voice level. 'Of course I've heard about him.'

'He is our priority, I'm afraid.' Quaresma's grin lost its spark. 'We had two sightings of this child yesterday. Another three this morning. Is not a coincidence.'

Chantal looked over at Hunter, teeth clenched, and leaned forward. 'Inspector, we're requesting you divert a couple of resources to support our investigation.'

'Sergeant...' Quaresma chuckled as he got to his feet and strolled over to the tiny window, soaked in Scottish-style rain. He leaned back against the frame. 'We have the weight of the news world pressing down on us right now. This morning, six crews from your country landed. This story is even popular in America.'

Chantal folded her arms tight. 'I still don't get why you can't give us an officer or two.'

'The Harry Jack case is our priority. This is my superior's position, I'm afraid.' Quaresma flashed up his eyebrows, the overhead light catching the shards of white in the silver. 'You saw what happened with Madeleine McCann a few years ago, yes?'

'Our case has the potential to—'

'My hands are tied.' Quaresma put his hands together like they were cuffed. 'This is the start of summer season. Busy time for us. Lots of northern Europeans come down here to party. Usually it all ends in tears and we have to pick up the pieces. Many rapes, many fights.'

'So we're on our own?' Chantal shrugged then stood up herself. 'Fine.'

'Not so simple.' Quaresma wagged a finger at her. 'This isn't your country. I can't have you running around doing what you want, yes?'

'Which is why I'm asking for support from you.'

'Sergeant, I have very limited resources. You are being allowed to operate here by my professional courtesy. The very second I hear that you are abusing that, you are on the next plane to Glasgow.'

'Edinburgh.'

'I will send you to London if it gets you out of my country.'

'Inspector, if this was the other way round, we would give you a superintendent to work with, plus a team under him or her. We would work tirelessly to bring your suspect to you.'

'That is not a luxury I have.'

'Have you done *anything*?'

Quaresma stepped forward and opened a desk drawer. He pulled out a paper file and dropped it on the desk. Not exactly thick enough to thump on the wood. 'This is the work we did before our time was reprioritised.' He nudged it across the table.

Chantal tipped the contents onto the desk. Their faxed evidence stapled together. At the back, the sum total of the local police work was five sheets of A4. One was a form, manually typed. Hard to follow the Portuguese, but she could pick out a few phrases. Hotel de Sousa. She flicked through the other pages. One was a photocopy of the guest list. She held it up. 'So, you have confirmed that he is staying there?'

'That is correct.' Quaresma snatched the file back and locked it away in the drawer. 'Now, that is all the assistance you can have until we find Harry Jack. I will make myself clear — you *will* use my men to arrest this Sean Tulloch.' He reached into a desk drawer and scribbled on a small white card. He tossed it over to Chantal's side. 'Call this number when you need to arrest someone.'

'That's it?'

Quaresma smiled at her. 'That is very generous.'

Chantal put the card in her pocket. *Let him have his petty little victory.* 'Can you at least give us a lift?'

∽

CHANTAL STOMPED across the car park, the rain soaking her hair. 'What an arsehole.' She stopped, hands on hips, scanning up and down the four lanes of cars. The press corps were outside the front of the building, huddled together as they listened to someone speaking. She dumped her bag into a puddle. Water splashed up her bare legs. *Shite. Shite, shite, bloody shite.* 'Tell me this is okay, Craig.'

Hunter sighed. 'I wish I could.'

'Here's where my thinking's at. Sean Tulloch is here and we know very little about what he's doing. We know where he's staying. We know he's with some other squaddies on a boys' weekend.'

'Which is my worry.'

She frowned at him. 'What is?'

'Well I've been thinking, maybe, it's not that big a deal. He's a serial abuser, which is a long game. You know the drill. He meets the women, charms them—'

'—moves in and starts booting the living shit out of them.'

'Look, he's here for a few days. Getting drunk, maybe playing some golf, maybe just lying on the beach.' He broke off.

'But?'

'But, he's here with a load of lairy lads. Squaddies. You maybe don't know what they're like, but it's a powder keg of laddish bollocks. They'll be arsing around, daring each other. This place has a big nightclub precinct. What I'm thinking is—'

'—his aggression might escalate?'

'You're finishing my sentences.'

Shite. She huffed out a sigh. 'But you're worrying all this lairy chat will push him to, what, go on a groping spree here?'

'Or worse.'

'We've got to get him, Craig.' She shook her head and scowled over at the building. Looked like Bruce was heading inside, inching his way past the reporters. 'We need help here. We need Quaresma's men to bring him in.'

Hunter stepped closer to her and stuffed his hands in his pockets. 'We're on our own here. The good thing is we work well together. We'll catch him.'

'Assuming he's still at the hotel.' She looked up and down the road. Not that many cars, none looking like taxis. 'Assuming he's even still in the bloody country.' She looked south. 'Africa's what, twenty miles that way?'

'It's that way, aye, but it's a lot further than twenty. At least a hundred.' A horn honked behind them and Hunter swung around.

Finlay Sinclair leaned against a red Fiesta, the car as battered as he now looked. Arms folded across his chest, his muscle tone turned to flab, the beer gut poking out of the bottom of his polo shirt now upgraded to a keg. He stood up tall, hand held out, and winced.

Chantal frowned at Hunter as she hefted up her bag and started across the road. 'You didn't tell me we were meeting him here.'

Hunter shrugged.

Chantal focused on Finlay. 'How did you end up over here?'

'Long story.' Finlay opened the boot of the car and made to pat down Hunter. 'The metal detector find that cucumber wrapped in tinfoil stuffed down your trouser legs, Craig?'

Chantal burst out laughing, like an explosion. 'Good to see you, Fin.'

'And you. Let me take your bags, madam.' Finlay crouched down and lifted up Chantal's suitcase, struggling with it like he was lifting the moon. 'Ah, you bastard.'

Chantal opened the boot to the full extension. 'Back still playing up?'

'Most days, aye.' Finlay dumped the case in next to some work tools. 'Then again, I'm lucky I can even walk after what happened.'

Hunter rested his bag next to Chantal's. 'I've apologised, mate.'

'It's fine. We caught him, and the compo was more than enough to set up a life out here.' Finlay clapped his hands together. 'Now. Where can I take you two lovebirds?'

∽

'Well, I still don't believe you.' Finlay powered along the dual carriageway, completely empty save for an Aldi lorry ahead. 'But that's not my problem, I guess.'

The rain was back in full shower mode, the water sluicing into drains in the central reservation.

Chantal slumped back in the seat. A rogue spring poked into her back. 'Like being back in Edinburgh.'

'Almost.' Hunter was in the back, still struggling to get his seatbelt to close. 'It's two degrees warmer at home.'

'Crazy.' Finlay laughed. 'So, this motorway, right? They spent all that EU money on it and it's a toll road. Loads of them here.' He held the wheel casually, like when he was Hunter's partner, and swerved out into the fast lane. 'I love it. Cuts the journey time in half for a euro. The locals are too tight to pay it. Spoke to this old geezer in the pub the other night ranting and raving about it. He says it's the EU's fault. They built it for the Spanish coming here for the golf. Or something.'

Chantal craned her neck around to see what Hunter was up to. He'd tugged his seatbelt closer to the buckle, still not quite connecting.

'Casual anti-EU ignorance.' Finlay overtook the Aldi lorry, rain spraying up the sides of the car, his wipers going full pelt. 'Not long till the referendum, is it?'

'Christ knows what'll happen if we vote to leave.' Chantal looked over from the passenger seat. 'All the racists will be trying to kick me out.'

Finlay chuckled. 'Aye, daft bastards probably think India is in the EU.'

'Pakistan. Three generations ago. Four, if you count my baby nephew.'

Hunter leaned forward to wedge his head between them. 'Take it you're quite far down the road to drinking yourself to death, then?'

'Getting there.' Finlay waved behind them, grinning. 'I live in Olhão, which is the other way from Faro. Quieter. Earthier. Like being in Elgin or Nairn or something, but with marginally less wind and rain. Feels alive, not just filled with drunk tourists.'

Chantal smirked at him. 'Except you.'

'There is that.' Finlay pulled off onto the slip road. Water sprayed out as they passed under the main carriageway. 'My flat cost twenty grand. And there's a working harbour, so all the fresh fish I can eat. Nice beer, too.'

'So that's how you're medicating?'

'The old back's shite most days.' Finlay started off down a long straight road lined with Mediterranean-style houses in a range of pastel colours. 'It was horrible back in Scotland over the winter there but give me enough heat and Sagres and it's almost bearable.'

Hunter rattled around in the back still. 'As if there's ever enough with you?'

'Ha.' Finlay stopped at some traffic lights, the Fiesta thudding to a stall. 'Bloody hell.'

'Lovely motor, by the way.'

'Aye, piece of shit I bought off a bloke in the boozer.' Finlay got the engine started again on the third go. 'Gets me to the Lidl for my messages and that's about it.'

'I take it this car rattles like a Glaswegian fishing trip afterwards?'

'Nah. The whisky's crap here.' Finlay trundled over the road as the lights changed back to red. 'You two involved in this missing kid case, then?'

'You get another guess.'

Finlay grinned at her. 'So you're over here shagging each other's brains out, or what?'

'What.' Chantal got her phone out of her pocket. 'We're here to pick up a suspect, if you must know.'

'Oh aye? Need any help?'

'Aye, from the local police.' No interesting texts. Family noise in WhatsApp, two from Sharon and a boatload of emails that could wait. She looked up from her mobile. 'You know any local cops?'

'Not had many dealings with them.' Finlay tapped the dashboard. 'Touch wood. Bar chat, you know how it is.'

'Don't I just.' Chantal sighed. 'If this was the other way round, they'd have a superintendent managing them, and a football team under him. Or her.'

'Bloody Wild West here, Chantal.' Finlay hurtled towards a red light. 'It's a tough game for them, you know? The pay's crap and they're under a heap of pressure. Way I hear it, they cut a big chunk of the budget a couple of years ago, let a load of cops go. The ones left are all pissed off.'

'How bent are they?'

'Not sure. Think they just don't give a shite. Fighting a losing battle. Economy's in the toilet. Their focus isn't on controlling the natives.'

Chantal waved at the passing apartment buildings. 'Even here?'

'Even here.' Finlay pulled down a long street.

The mid-blue sea glistened in the distance, dark rain clouds swimming halfway to the horizon. Sun shone down on the buildings, lighting them up from their gloom. Two sprawling hotel complexes sat in a hollow on the left, one marked with purple signage, the other red. A big fence separated them, though only one had access to the beach.

Finlay took a left and pulled up alongside the first hotel. A few tourists mingled about, one old guy had his top off, showing off his disco muscles. 'Here you go.'

Hunter let his seatbelt flop down. 'Cheers, mate. I appreciate it.'

'I'm serious. You guys need a hand?'

Chantal opened her door. 'I can manage my bag, Finlay. It's fine.'

'I mean with this case, whatever you're up to. I'm here if you need me, aye?'

'We'll think about it.' Chantal pinched his cheek between her thumb and forefinger, then waved up at the sky. 'Sun's out. Go and work on that Leith tan.'

CHANTAL FANNED her face with her hands as they stood in the queue. 'Could do with air conditioning in here.'

'It's a bargain hotel, my dear.' Hunter grabbed her hand. 'The sort of place a bunch of squaddies will go for a weekend on the piss. Or all a young couple like us could afford.'

'Or the sort of place Police Scotland's budget will stretch to.'

A mobility scooter whizzed past them, the obese driver looking like he'd melted in the sun. He stopped next to a group by the counter, a man in a Man Utd shirt shouting at the receptionist, ROONEY and 10 on the back. 'But they've stolen money from my boy!'

'*Definitely* not holidaying here...' Chantal kicked her bag along the floor as the queue shifted up. 'Feels like all we've done since this morning is stand in queues.'

'And get belittled by foreign cops.'

She nodded at the scooter. 'Nice seeing Finlay, though. Thought he'd be in a wheelchair.'

'Aye, good old compo. Six-figure payout plus full pension.'

'This is a disgrace.' Rooney stormed off, the mobility scooter whizzing along behind. 'An absolute pigging disgrace! You can keep the EU, see if I care!'

'Here we go.' Chantal sighed as she grabbed her bag and marched up to the desk. 'Got a reservation in the name Jain. That's J-A-I-N.'

'Nice to meet you.' The receptionist had a South Wales accent, seedier than a valley choirboy. The sort of pretty boy who spent his good-looks years twatting about in holiday resorts, shagging anything he could, while he still could. 'I see you're staying for three nights.' He typed, eyes focused on the inset monitor.

Chantal leaned forward, conspiratorial. 'Do you have a Sean Tulloch staying here?'

Eyes still on the screen. 'Is he a friend?'

'My boyfriend's cousin.' Chantal laughed and grabbed Hunter's hand. 'It's supposed to be a surprise.'

'Sorry, my darling. I can't give out that information.' He hit the keys hard. 'You can leave a message for next time he comes to the desk, though?'

So he is here.

'No, it's fine. Element of surprise and all that.'

'Alrighty. Well, I'll need your passports and then we'll be all set.'

Chantal passed them both over and watched him mince to the photocopier. 'What a charmer.'

'As long as it has no effect on you...'

'Like water off a duck's arse.' She leaned forward and twisted the computer screen round. 'Balls, he's locked it.' She shifted it back again.

The receptionist reappeared with their passports. 'There, that's you checked in.' He made a fish-like motion with his hand. 'Your room is through to the right, then up the stairs and again on your right.'

Chantal frowned at him. 'Did you say *room*?'

21

CHANTAL

'Cheeky cow.' Chantal dumped her bag on the double bed in the middle of the room.

A small kitchen lay to the left, a couple of tatty cabinets above a cooker ring and a counter fridge. The balcony door was open, the curtains flapping in the gentle breeze. Across a narrow lane, other apartments looked in, claustrophobically close.

Calling it chintzy would be doing it a favour. Just... horrible.

She collapsed back on the bed and groaned. 'This is Sharon's idea of a joke, isn't it?'

'What, booking one room?' Hunter dropped his bag on the floor and collapsed onto the bed. He pulled her close, burying his head in her stomach. 'It fits our cover story.'

She looked down at him. 'What cover story?'

'Us being a young couple on holiday.' He lifted up her top and kissed her belly. 'Doesn't that sound good?'

She hauled her top back down. 'I'm not in the mood, Craig.'

'Fine.' Hunter held up his hands. 'Sorry.'

'Shite.' Chantal wrapped her arms around him. 'Sorry, I'm being a cow. It's... I want to text Sharon a load of abuse.'

'So do it.'

She reached over for her phone and started tapping at the screen. 'Thanks for arranging our room. Having to pay for the other one out of my own money. You cow.'

'Think she'll check with the hotel?'

Chantal dumped her mobile on the bed. 'Maybe.'

'Our carefully laid plans thrown apart because of one little slip up?' She silenced him with a glare. 'So we're pretending we're not a couple who are pretending to be a couple?'

Chantal couldn't even begin to follow it. 'Whatever, Craig.' She hopped off his knee and hauled her top over her head, a pastel purple shade soaked in sweat. Bloody thing stank now. 'Don't get any ideas.' She grabbed her bag and rummaged deep until she found the right top. 'We've not got any leads, have we?' She pulled it on. *Feels a bit better.* 'It's not like Tulloch's playing baccarat at the local casino and all we need to do is—'

Her mobile blasted out Taylor Swift again. *Bollocks.*

She rolled over the bed and grabbed it. Sharon. *Even more bollocks.* She stabbed the answer button with a sigh. 'Hi, Shaz.'

'Morning, Chantal. I take it you meant what you typed?'

'Of course I meant it.' She lay back and kicked off her sandals. Her feet started breathing again. 'Wouldn't have texted it if I didn't.'

'So, you and Craig in one room, eh? There'll be a bolster you can put between you. Top and tail, aye?'

'Piss off.'

Sharon laughed. 'Have you really booked another room?'

'What do you think?'

'I think you joined the mile high club on the way over and, right now, he's got his fingers right—'

'I'm warning you.'

'—king you moan with delight?'

'No, stop it.' Chantal lay back on the bed. Could fall asleep here. 'Was there a reason for the call? Like, any progress at your end?'

'Nothing much. I take it you've spoken to your contact?'

'Fat lot of good that was. He didn't even *try* and arrest Tulloch.'

Hunter's phone blared out that drill noise. Chantal glanced down the bed at him, twatting about on his mobile. She scowled and pointed at the balcony.

22

HUNTER

Hunter walked over and wrestled the door fully open, hitting answer. 'Morning, Elvis.'

His lips slapped down the line like he was chewing something. 'How's sunny Portugal, mate?'

Hunter sat on the chair in the shade. The sun was finally out, boiling off the rain, but it missed their gloomy apartment. 'Better than Bathgate. Just.' He got up and leaned against the railing with his free hand. Damp and cold. A couple made their way down the path below, arm in arm. Sunglasses, flip-flops, shorts, sunburnt arms and necks. 'What's up?'

'Eh, calling in a bet. Fat Jimmy says you'll have him in custody. I've got a tenner on you not having a scooby where he is.'

Hunter let his breath out slowly. 'We're nowhere near anything.'

'Ya dancer.' Elvis's hand covered the mouthpiece, but Hunter could still hear, 'Wanker! That's ten quid you owe me!'

Pair of arseholes.

Hunter took in the place as he waited for Elvis to deal with the pressing issues.

Which room was Tulloch's? Any of them? Was he even here?

And how the hell were they going to catch him? Now we're here, we don't have a plan. Getting here was enough of an ordeal, finding the bastard... Another kettle of fish entirely. Barrel of beer. Stack of hay. Take your pick.

Then again, someone like Tulloch will stick out like a sore thumb.

The old couple passed below him now, each step looking like it took momentous effort.

They might've seen Tulloch and a bunch of squaddies. They might know where he is. Then again, they might not. Tulloch could be hiding out he—

'Nice one, mate.' Elvis's lips slapped again. Like he could only eat when talking to Hunter. 'Can always rely on you to make an arse of things.'

Hunter gripped the railing tighter. *If that was Elvis's neck...* 'Have you taken Paisley's statement yet?'

'Doc won't let us.'

'Seriously?'

'I'm not messing about. Me and that Jenny bird were down at the hospital this morning. Jenny's a piece of work, I tell you. Anyway, doctor wouldn't let us in. "Paisley's not up to answering questions, blah blah blah". Stupid mare.'

'And you took that for an answer?'

'I'm not you, Robocop. I don't go in there all guns blazing.'

Don't rise to it...

Hunter rested back against the door, his T-shirt bunching up around his arms. 'What about Tulloch's laptop?'

'Aye, well, I've got round to it now.' Elvis yawned. 'There's a ton of emails between Tulloch and one Gordon Brownlee of Muirhouse in Edinburgh.'

'Any form on him?'

'Nothing major, but that doesn't mean he's not a dodgy bastard.' Elvis clacked at keys in the background. Almost like the lazy sod was only running the PNC check now. 'Ex-squaddie, by the looks of things.'

Hunter sucked in the fresh air. 'Send me a photo, would you?'

'It'll cost me a bloody fortune.'

'So? Expense it.'

Elvis paused on the line. 'Right, aye. I'll fire it through the now.'

'Cheers. Catch you later.' Hunter killed the call and waited for the message to arrive. He grabbed the railing and leaned forward until he was in the sun.

The warm heated up his hair and neck. Not bad at all. Must be low twenties. Nothing like the baking heat in the Middle East. Tolerable. Maybe southern Spain would be good for a holiday. Málaga, Nerja, somewhere like—

His mobile chirruped. He leaned back into the shade and checked it.

Two photo messages.

The first was Gordon Brownlee in full uniform. 3 Scots, for certain. Big lad, typical squaddie — trim, dead-eye stare like he could stab you in the guts without thinking. His left ear looked like it'd been sliced off and reattached by an amateur, hanging a couple of inches below the right.

The other photo was Brownlee in Germany, holding up a full stein of foaming lager, wearing comedy lederhosen and plastic breasts. Classic Schoolbook shot. Wide grin, but the same dead eyes and wonky ears.

The things we see on duty. Hunter caught sight of himself in the patio doors. His arms weren't looking too bad. Nice shape to the shoulders. Still too much of a gut. Always the last thing to go.

Inside, Chantal was sitting on the bed, staring at her phone. She looked up and smiled. 'Bloody cow knew exactly what she was doing.'

'Don't rise to it.' Hunter held up his phone. 'Anyway, in other news, Elvis might've found our baccarat game.' He walked back through and handed her his mobile. 'This is Gordon Brownlee, looks like one of Tulloch's mates.'

'Good effort.' Chantal stared at the screen, like she was sucking in his life story from the two photos. She rested it on the bed and lay back, her hair splaying across the pillow. 'So what's the plan then, Constable?'

'Here's what I'm thinking.' Hunter picked up his phone and stared at Brownlee's dead eyes. 'This lot are boozers on a piss-up. They'll start with a few here, check out if the hotel's up to snuff. Mostly, it'll be old duffers on their holidays, but sometimes it's full of stag and hen parties, and it's the cheapest for drinks. Total carnage, basically.'

'Spoken from experience.'

Hunter raised an eyebrow. 'Anyway, given Mr Quaresma's not playing ball, we're going to have to do some undercover work.' He stared at Brownlee's photos again, then over at Chantal again. 'That Keith Brannigan who got away at Waverley is supposed to be here. There are others, too.' He locked the phone and tossed it onto the bed. 'So, we're on our first holiday together. A young couple in love. Let's hit the bar and see who knows anything about Gordon Brownlee or Sean Tulloch, shall we?'

∼

Hunter bit into the falafel burger and chewed slowly. He swallowed it down with a glug of Sagres, the lager bitter and cold. *Lovely.* He leaned back and soaked up the sun.

The bar area was walled on three sides, but enough sun crawled in. Already felt like it was burning Hunter's peely-wally skin. *Need to rub some suntan lotion on.* The wooden walls could do with a lick of paint.

Hunter took another mouthful. 'Didn't know how hungry I was.'

'Me neither.' Chantal cut her hamburger open, the meat still a touch pink inside, hipster-style. She ate it, anyway. 'That's a good burger.'

At least she hadn't added the bacon. 'Glad to hear it.' Hunter's stomach gargled around the food. Another bite, his eyes watering. 'Don't see any pissed squaddies, though.'

She nodded behind him. 'That lot might have.'

A hen party sat at the far end. All ages from late teens to sixties, though mostly in their twenties. Screaming and shouting and dancing and downing shots. Sounded like an unholy mix of Scousers and Brummies. A waif of a girl appeared with a tray of shots, getting a roar of applause and laughter.

'Christ, that takes me back.' Chantal put her burger down in a pool of liquid fat, shaking her head at them. She finished her wine, the glass still frosted. 'I was here on a hen weekend a few years ago.'

'This hotel?'

Chantal thumbed back up the hill. 'Makes this place look five star.' She scowled. 'Me and Sharon and a load of our old mates from uniform. A few from Turnbull's CID team. You know Angela Caldwell, don't you?'

Hunter shook his head.

'Anyway, it was complete carnage.' She took another bite of her burger then smirked. 'The chief bridesmaid got knocked up by a barman.'

'You're kidding?'

'Wish I was.' Chantal dipped a chip in spilt ketchup. 'Had to get an abortion. Poor Geraldine.'

'Geraldine Fox?' Hunter frowned, swallowing down another mouthful. 'Seriously?'

Chantal shut her eyes. 'Shite, do you know her?'

'Me and Cullen worked with her up in St Leonards, few years back.'

'Aw, shite.' Chantal's cheeks flushed, not all from the wine. 'Don't tell anyone, okay?'

Hunter zipped up his lips. 'Secret's safe with me.'

She wrapped her fingers around her empty glass and squinted into the sun. 'Back at the room, you said stuff about the bar tactics. Finding the best place to drink. Take it you've done this before?'

'I've never knocked up a barmaid. Or DC Fox.'

'Aye, very good.' Another bite of burger, twirling her finger at the hen party. 'But you have been here?'

'Came to Portugal in my army days.' Hunter sipped some lager, barely tasting it. 'That's early on, like. We were based up at Fort George near Inverness. Got a fortnight's leave so a group of us booked cheap flights from Edinburgh.' He swallowed, his nostrils twitching. 'Like what Tulloch and his mates are doing.'

She narrowed her eyes at him, holding the burger in mid-air. A big dod of fat dribbled onto the plate.

'Anyway, we turn up at a place like this, all tanked up from a couple of litres of Captain Morgan's someone bought in duty-free.' Hunter pushed his burger away, smearing minty yoghurt over the plate. 'Worse luck. Turned out a bunch of officers were staying down the corridor from us. Out here on a stag. And one of them knew two of our lads, so they ordered us to join in their session.

Trust me, you've not lived until you've seen an army captain invite everyone to his room for— Well. I'll leave it there.'

'Jesus.' Chantal's burger fell onto her plate. 'Did you?'

'Of course I didn't.' Hunter picked out a lump of falafel and popped it into his mouth. 'Made myself sick. My mate Terry took me back to our room. Win, win.'

'Terry's the one—'

'Aye.' Hunter pressed the burger into his plate, bits of chickpea tumbling out. 'Him.'

'Is that why you're getting all these flashbacks?'

Hunter took another drink, his pint glass below halfway now, and wiped his lips. 'Maybe.'

'You should've said.'

'Look, I don't know what it's like with your PTSD, but mine doesn't say to me "Oh, hey Craig, I'm going to do your head in every time someone eats a bacon roll," or something like that. It's all random shit until I figure out the trigger.'

'I've not had that many flashbacks.'

Hunter nodded slowly. 'Then you're lucky.'

'Well, I'm sorry anyway.' She grabbed her glass and got to her feet. 'Finish that pint, we've got a cover to maintain. We're supposed to be getting arseholed in the sun then shagging each other's brains out.' She gave him a dirty wink then walked over to the bar.

23

CHANTAL

Chantal stopped by the door and let the skinny girl go first. 'Cheers, chuck.' Her Black Country accent cut through the afternoon sunshine.

'My little Chucka!'

Chantal froze, clenching her jaw. She stared around the hotel bar. A gang of wild women at the far side were singing along to someone's mobile, that slushy One Direction song. A coach pulled up by the entrance. Two men with their tops off wandered past, T-shirts on their shoulders, burnt skin close to blistering.

The girl was carrying a tray of shot glasses filled with pale blue liquid. 'You okay, chuck?'

Chantal swallowed bile. 'I'm fine.'

'You look like you've seen a ghost.'

'I'm okay.'

'I'm Bekah, by the way.'

'Chantal.'

'Listen, do you want to do a shot with us?'

Chantal had another scan of the bar area. *Still no likely suspects in the hunt for Tulloch. Maybe Bekah or her mates had spoken to*

Tulloch or his crew. She nodded without a backwards glance at Hunter. 'Aye, go on.'

Bekah led over and set the tray down. 'Here we go, girls!' She took a glass and handed Chantal another. Pale blue shit, way more than a standard measure. Probably stronger. 'Here you go, chuck!'

Chucka... Jesus.

Chantal tried to cover her grimace with a smile. 'Cheers.'

The group folded around them, pushing Chantal and Bekah to the back. One climbed onto a table and raised her glass. 'Here's for Amy!'

'Wahey!' Bekah necked her shot.

Chantal waited until she shut her eyes in recoil then tossed hers over her shoulder. She stuck her tongue out and gagged. 'What the hell was that?'

'I've no idea.' Bekah leaned in close and burped out citrusy breath. 'I asked the barman for the strongest stuff they had.'

'Nice one!' Chantal gritted her teeth. *This is hell. Hell, hell, hell.* 'So how well do you know the hen?'

'She's my cousin.' Bekah's accent sucked the genuine emotion out. 'We're from near Stoke.'

'Edinburgh.'

'Is that Scotland?' Bekah waited for a nod. 'You don't look local.'

Chantal laughed. 'Born and bred there.'

'Get lots of your lot round our way. My best mate Mina, her parents are from Pakistan. Do you know her?'

'I know a Mina but not one from Stoke.' *This is a mistake.* 'When did you come out here?'

'Since Wednesday night. We fly back on Sunday. Having a great time. I don't want to leave!'

Chantal nodded slowly. She caught a glimpse of Hunter on his own, fiddling with his mobile. The hotel bar was busy, full of people who might've seen Tulloch, and he was texting someone. She smiled at Bekah. 'So, what's the chat like round the bar here?'

'The chat?' Bekah bellowed with laughter. Poor girl was way more pissed than she should be at half twelve. 'I *love* your accent!'

'I mean, is this a good place for a laugh?'

'Yeah. Totally. Yesterday, we got chatting to these—'

'Come on!' Someone came back from the bar, carrying yet

another tray of shots, her mouth stretched out way beyond a grin. 'Here we go, ladies!'

Bekah raced over and grabbed two glasses. She bounced back like a spring deer and handed one to Chantal.

She took it, her heart sinking deep into her chest.

Bekah threw her shot down her throat. 'Come on, Chantal. Let's get some more in!' Then she hopped off to the bar.

24

HUNTER

Hunter sipped at the pint, now flat and tasteless, and huffed out a breath. A quarter of it left. *Just as well I didn't down it when Chantal asked me to.*

Across the other side of the hotel bar area, Chantal was laughing at some no-doubt dirty joke. Looked like she'd been caning it with them all morning, rather than only joining in twenty minutes ago.

The waif next to her handed her a glass. Blink and you'd miss it, but it looked like the shot went right over Chantal's shoulder.

That's my girl.

No new messages on his phone. Heat burnt his neck as the sun crawled around to inflict its worst. The rainwater was half-dried now, could almost see it hissing away, the ozone tang was real, though. Like doing a paper round first thing in the morning, before everyone was up.

Early lunchtime boozers. How many of them would merge into all-day session boozers?

At the next table, a guy in his forties lay back in his chair soaking up the fresh sun. Tattoos, shaved head, tat-shop Ray-Ban clones. Maroon T-shirt with a little fish logo. Wiry hair poking out of his pale blue shorts. A red rose climbed up his arm from the wrist.

A squaddie of some sort.

Hmm...

Hunter finished the dregs of his pint and got up to stretch, bright light bouncing off the glasses. 'Excuse me, mate?'

He lifted up his shades, his eyes barely open. 'What's that?'

'Could you watch these seats for me?'

'No worry, mate.' Northern accent. Manchester. Maybe Liverpool or anywhere between.

'Cheers.' Hunter padded inside the bar, avoiding checking out another roar of laughter from the hen party. Even though the doors to the outside were open, it was cool inside. Not just the shade, industrial air conditioning. Took a while for his eyes to adjust to the light. Long marble bar, a tattooed guy sitting at the far end, lost in his mobile.

Hunter nodded at the barman. 'Two pints of Sagres, please.'

'Coming up, sir.' The barman flipped on the taps over two glasses. Short dark hair, designer stubble but sulking like a teenager walking around a supermarket with his mum. He stared at the glasses as they slowly filled with lager.

Hunter reached into his pocket and unfolded a sheet of paper. He placed it on the bar. 'Do you recog— Sorry, do you know this man?'

The barman huffed out a sigh as he flipped off both taps. 'Listen, my friend, we've already had police officers asking about Harry Jack.'

Hunter gave a warm smile. 'This isn't about Harry.' He tapped the photo again. 'Have a look.'

The barman gave the tiniest glance at the photograph and shook his head slowly. 'Sorry.'

'Big guy.' Hunter put his hand a few inches above his head. 'Accent like mine.'

'You see so many people here, my friend.' The barman dumped both glasses on the bar, the handles facing out. 'Six euro.' A little nod at another customer.

'Cheers.' Hunter's mobile rattled in his pocket. A text from Finlay:

SERIOUSLY MATE! NEED ANY HELP?

Hunter pocketed his phone and handed over a ten euro note. 'Keep the change.'

'Thank you, sir.' A smile sparked on the barman's face. 'I'll watch for that man.'

'Cheers, boss.' Hunter carried the glasses by the handles and stepped out of the way as Chantal and a couple of the hens danced their way into the bar.

Chantal's eyes didn't get the memo to smile. Looked every inch as bored as Hunter.

He went back outside into the blinding light and put one beer on his table, one on his neighbour's. 'Thanks for that, mate.'

The neighbour slid his shades down his nose, frowning at the fizzing beer. 'What's that for?'

'Looking after my seat.' Hunter sat down and took a big gulp. Cold and crisp. *Lovely.* He rubbed at his wrist.

Chantal skipped out of the bar following the skinny girl.

His neighbour frowned over the top of his shades. 'Come on, die young? What the hell does that mean?'

Hunter held up his right wrist, showing his tattoo. 'It's an army thing, mate.'

His neighbour shifted his chair, almost sparking fire from the slabs as he ground the legs forward. He offered a hairy hand. 'Ricky.'

Hunter shook it, getting the old masonic thumb press for his troubles. 'Craig.'

'So, are you a squaddie?'

'Ex.' Hunter almost winced. *Shite. Keep up the bloody cover. Can't say you're a cop, you daft bastard.* 'I'm in private security now.' He took another sip of beer. 'You?'

'Still in, mate.' Ricky's eyes glazed over, like he wasn't in southern Portugal any more. 'Corporal. Just back from Syria. *Brutal*, mate, brutal.'

Hunter nodded. 'Worse than Kandahar?'

'You see action there?'

Another sip, the lump in Hunter's throat almost throbbing. 'Two Afghan tours plus one in Iraq. Trouble with Syria is the bloody Russians. I swear. In Afghanistan and Iraq, it was us against the bad guys. Too much pissing about in Syria, mate.'

'Shitty business, innit?' Ricky settled into his pint, clearing half in one long gulp. 'Worst way to make a living. If I had my time again, I'd pay attention at school.' He grinned. 'I'd actually *go*.' He bellowed out a laugh.

'Know what you mean.' Hunter toyed with showing him the photo. 'Seen a few squaddies round here, though.'

'Can't bloody get away from them.' Another gulp of lager, then Ricky's expression darkened. 'Tell you, though. Got chatting to a bunch of lads yesterday evening. Matt, Matty, something like that and his mate. Big prick. Thought he was something. Sean or something.'

Hunter drank some beer, his pulse racing. 'Aye?'

'Pair of pricks were pretending to be squaddies. Can you believe it? Cheeky bastards. Thought it would impress the birds or something.'

Hunter looked around the place. The walls seemed a good twenty metres or so further away than when they'd started drinking. 'This was here?'

'Yeah, right here.' Ricky drilled a finger into the table and snarled into his pint. 'Said they'd been in Kandahar, but the story didn't stack up. I kept prodding at it, finding gaping holes.'

'Did they look the part?'

'Well, they was big lads. Taller than even you. Muscly, you know?' Another gulp. 'But it's all disco muscles with these lads, right? Think they're in the Premiership.' He started lifting his arms like he was raising dumbbells. 'Like that in front of the mirror for hours, mate.' He scowled, darkness clouding his eyes. 'I'm all about functional strength. Press-ups and kettlebells. All a man needs.'

'What do you sling?'

'Sixteen kilo. You?'

'Just gone up to a pair of twenty-four kilos.'

'Hardcore.'

'Yeah, until I drop one on my living room floor late at night.'

'Tell me about it, mate. Twenty-four's a lot.' Ricky went back to his beer. 'This pair of pricks. Matty and Sean.'

'Sean?'

'Sean. Like that Bond actor.' Ricky snarled. 'Wankers. If I see them again… I swear.' He wrapped his fingers round the beer glass like it was a neck.

Hunter took another sip and nodded. *So Sean Tulloch was here, then. Just, where?*

He pushed the glass away from harm, a vain attempt to slow down. 'You reckon they were pretending to be squaddies?'

'Right. Makes me sick.' Another drink and Ricky didn't have much beer left. He eyed Hunter. 'Take it you're not lying?'

Hunter laughed. 'I've got the PTSD to show for it, mate.'

'Right, yeah.' Ricky's stubbly eyebrows flicked up, a stray spike arcing its own way. 'Don't believe in it myself, but there you go.'

'It's real, believe me. So these blokes, do you want to—'

Ricky shook his head, his eyes screwed tight behind his shades. 'Trust me, you don't want to get involved. I had a word in their ears and they pissed off, sharpish.'

Tulloch pissing off at a warning? That doesn't sound like him.

Then again, he knows the police are investigating him. Doesn't want to get into any scrapes out here. The one crime the locals would actually crack down on is good old street fighting, unfettered by the Marquess of Queensberry rules.

If Tulloch is smart, he'll keep his hands in his pockets. A very big if.

Hunter took another sip of beer. 'Have you seen them today?'

'If I had, they'd be in hospital.' It looked like Ricky meant it.

25

CHANTAL

Chantal dumped the glass on the table and wiped her chin like she'd downed that shot.
Playing the odds here. Going to get caught sooner or later.
Their group was thinning out a bit but still at least twenty strong. No sign of them moving on from the hotel bar, either. *Maybe this is where all the action is?*
She leaned forward to pick up her wine, sunlight bouncing off the glass. 'So, you were saying about last night?'
Bekah looked like she was going to be sick. She licked her lips a few times and stuck her tongue out. 'Yeah, there were these lads here. Big strapping sorts, you know?' She puffed up her cheeks. 'A couple of them were Scotch, like you. One of them kept asking me about my fanny. Can you believe it?'
'I can believe anything.' Chantal grinned at her, hoping it looked genuine enough. 'Did you say they were squaddies?'
'My brother's in the army. They acted like him, the bunch of wankers.'
'I'm looking for a friend of my boyfriend's. Did you meet anyone called—'

Another roar went up and a woman appeared with another tray. A bottle of some spirit lay on its side. Chunky and dark. *Shite, it's Jägermeister. Nasty.* The glasses were way bigger than single shot glasses. The woman started tipping out measures, the size that a drunk aunt would give at Christmas, though not in the Jain household.

Bekah snatched up two glasses and handed one to Chantal. 'Here you go!'

Chantal took the glass. Sickly drink sloshed over the side, running down her fingers. *Horrible stuff.*

The woman who'd bought the bottle joined them. Early forties, dyed blonde hair and a crop top twenty years too young for her. She thrust out her hand. 'I'm Kerry.' Sounded Manc. When she smiled, her face lined like old leather. 'You with the hen party?'

Chantal shook her head. 'Bekah here grabbed me.'

'Right, right.' Kerry linked arms at the left elbow and Bekah took the right. 'Here we go, girls!'

No getting out of this one. Chantal downed the shooter and hissed. *Disgusting.* She put the glass down.

26

HUNTER

Ricky dumped the fresh pints on the table. 'Here you go, sunshine.'

'Cheers, boss.' Hunter was still halfway through his previous pint. *Don't let them stack up, you stupid bastard. Feeling it, already.*

He checked over the other side of the bar area, shielding his eyes from the sun. Chantal was lost in a hen party in full flow. *Seriously hope she's getting something other than pissed.*

He touched the beer to his lips. 'So what are you doing over here, then? Holiday?'

'On a month off, mate.' Ricky pushed his shades up. 'After the shit I've seen over in Syria, I thought I'd treat the wife to a nice little trip for my fortieth.' Looked at least five years too late for his fortieth. 'Supposed to be me and her but she's off with those bloody hens, getting sloshed.' Ricky slammed the old glass upside down, like some sort of Viking. 'Only thing is, our bloody son's at home on his Jack Jones.'

Hunter frowned. 'How old is he?'

'Little bugger's eighteen.' Ricky growled at his empty glass, like that would refill it. 'House'll be a bloody bomb site by the time we get back.' He lifted the fresh beer by the handle. 'You?'

'First holiday with my girlfriend.' Hunter waved over at Chantal as she took a fresh shot glass. He got a wave before she started talking to another woman, much older than the waif who'd grabbed her.

Ricky smacked Hunter's arm. 'Jeez, mate! You're punching above your weight there, aren't you?'

'Don't say that to her.' Hunter rubbed at his arm. Stung like a bastard.

Ricky aimed his finger like a handgun over towards Chantal. 'See that bird she's chatting to?' He was pointing at two — the young waif and a short woman in her mid-forties, blonde hair and a smile halfway to a snarl. 'That's me wife. Kerry.' His eyes misted over. 'She's me best mate, man. Best thing in my life.'

'I know the feeling.'

Ricky locked eyes with Hunter. 'Do you?' The deep intensity of the mad squaddie, trying to peer into the recesses of your soul, pull out any doubt over the statement, any lies. 'Do you?'

Hunter nodded over at them. 'That's how I feel about Chantal.'

Ricky cupped his hands around his mouth. 'Oy! Get over here, you bitch!'

His wife rolled her eyes at Chantal and shouted back. 'You'll have to come here, you daft bastard!'

'No, you come here!'

27

CHANTAL

Kerry topped up Chantal's glass again. 'Here you!'
'You're crazy!' Bekah held hers out, hungry for more.
'Don't talk to my husband about how crazy I am!' Kerry joined in the countdown. 'Five! Four! Three! Two! One!'

They linked their arms into Chantal's and yanked them up, locking eyes with her. No choice but to down the drink. Fire burned in her throat. Felt like she was going to vomit. She pulled her arms free, then dropped the glass on the nearest table. 'That's horrible.'

'Thanks for that, love.' Kerry bellowed with laughter. 'I bought that.'

'I mean, it's too much. And I usually have it with Red Bull.'

'Bloody place has run out already.' Kerry tutted. 'Can you believe it?' She tapped at her watch. 'Not even one o'clock and there's no Red Bull!'

'It's rubbish.' Bekah burped into her hand, looking like she was going to be reacquainted with her lunch. If she'd even had any. 'You're not with us, are you?'

'I am now!' Kerry bellowed with laughter. 'No, I'm here with my husband.' She nodded over to the other side. 'See that bald bastard with that— oooh, he's lovely.'

Chantal clocked the object of her affections. 'That's my boyfriend.'

Kerry's eyebrows flashed up and down. 'What I wouldn't give for...' She gave him another long stare then grabbed her bust. 'Do you like my boobs? Got them for my fortieth. Me husband paid for them. They're smashing, aren't they?' They barely moved when she shook them. The skin on her chest was stretched tight.

Bekah couldn't take her eyes off them. 'Can I have a feel?'

'On you go, love.'

Bekah bit her lip as she honked the left breast. 'Wow.' She stared down at her flat chest. 'I've thought about getting some tits.'

'Best thing I've done.' Kerry nodded at Chantal. 'Do you want a feel?'

'I'm good.'

'Yeah, pair of tits like you've got.' Kerry shook her head. 'Wait till you have kids, love, then you'll want to see what these are all about.' She gave them another wiggle. 'So, you're not with this lot, then?'

'It's mine and Craig's first holiday together.'

'Aw, that's lovely.'

'Aye, well. This is when I get to see how bad his personal hygiene really is, right?'

Kerry slapped her on the arm as she roared with laughter. 'Don't you live together?'

'Not yet.'

Kerry leaned over for the bottle and tipped a dribble into her glass. 'Oh, Christ, it's all gone!'

Chantal smiled at Bekah. 'So, did you meet anyone called Sean?'

Bekah was struggling to keep both eyes open at the same time. 'Didn't get any names, sorry. They were lovely, though.'

'Who was?' Kerry sipped the spirit.

'I'm looking for a friend of Craig's.' Chantal nodded over the way. 'Supposed to be a surprise, but we can't find him. Can you believe it?'

'Right, right.' Kerry tapped her nose.

Bekah coughed into her hand and swallowed something down. 'We're going to a club soon, if you want to come?'

Chantal flashed up her watch. 'It's two o'clock.'

'Is it? Well, we want to dance. Then we can come back for a siesta and hit it later. We were out till six this morning.' Bekah stuck her arm in the air, fist clenched. 'Whooo!'

'You're mental.' Kerry's husband shouted something over at her. She bellowed something back. No idea what it was.

Chantal leaned in to Bekah. 'Have you seen any of those squaddie lads?'

Bekah was too far gone. Fast train to Partyville, stopping at Dance-floor Snog and Kebab Central, terminating at Hold My Hair While I Spew.

Kerry nibbled at her lip and rested her head on Chantal's shoulder. 'Here, this lot are getting too crazy.' Sickly shot breath. 'It's still happy hour, do you want to get some booze and head back to our fellas?'

'Come on.' She patted Bekah on the shoulder and whispered into her ear. 'Go and get yourself some sleep.'

Bekah staggered backwards, then took a few seconds to turn before sidling off, the hand on the wall the only thing keeping her upright. Kerry grabbed Chantal's hand and pulled her inside.

The barman smiled at them. 'What can I get you?'

28

HUNTER

Hunter checked his watch. Not even three and the beer was hitting him like a round from an SA80. *Need to slow down.* 'So, what have you got planned, then?'

'Nothing much, to be honest with you.' Ricky pointed over to the bar. 'Oh, here we go.'

Chantal appeared in the doorway, the bright sunshine glinting off her sunglasses, her black hair sucking it in. She walked over and put a tray down on the table. Four pints and a bottle of fizzy white wine with two glasses. 'It's happy hour, so this will save you boys a couple of trips.'

Ricky grabbed a beer by the handle. 'Cheers, darling.' He held out a hand. 'I'm Ricky, by the way.'

'I've heard all about you.' Chantal sat next to Hunter and pecked him on the lips. 'I'm Chantal.' Then she poured out some wine.

Kerry joined them, carrying a smaller tray with eight small glasses filled with black liquid. 'Now, before you get stuck into that, have a go of this.'

Chantal handed Hunter a pair of them.

Jesus... He took a sniff. 'Is this Sambuca?'

'Black Sambuca.' Kerry raised her glass, sunlight twinkling on the frosting. 'After three! One, two, three!' She threw the first one back.

Hunter watched Ricky do the same. He tossed his over his shoulder, slaking the baked lawn behind them. 'Urgh. Not had that in years.'

Ricky slammed his glass, toppling over Hunter's and Chantal's. 'Lovely stuff!'

Kerry sat on Ricky's lap, wriggling around suggestively. 'Those crazy Scotch boys yesterday were drinking it. Haven't done this since our honeymoon, have we?'

'Not in years.' Ricky took the first of his pints below the halfway mark in one gulp. 'I love the lager here. No messing about.' He wiped the foam off his lips with the hair on his right arm. 'I was telling Craig about those Scotch pricks.'

'Bunch of wankers.' Kerry picked up her wine glass and nudged one over to Chantal. She settled back, wiggling on Ricky's lap. 'Fighting and wrestling and showing off.' She sipped at the fizz. 'One of them kept taking his top off and flexing.' She thumbed at the hen girls, their numbers now depleted. 'Started flirting with him. Matty his name was, or something.'

Ricky held up his glass. 'Disco muscles.'

'Sounds like a twat.' Hunter sipped at his beer. He was way behind now. *How can I pass a pint to Ricky without him noticing?*

Kerry swirled wine round in her glass. 'Then this boy pulled his shorts really low. You could see he'd shaved off his pubes.' She cackled. 'So this girl, yeah? She reached down and grabbed his cock then shouted out about how small it was.' She rested her arm against Chantal as if to steady herself. 'He pissed off sharpish, I swear.'

'Bunch of punks.' Ricky finished his pint in another mouthful. 'Not like you or me, Craig.' He reached over for another beer and chinked it off the one in Hunter's hand. 'Not like you and me, mate.'

'Damn right.' Hunter took another sip of beer and looked around. 'So what happened to them?'

'Trust me, mate, you don't want to have anything to do with them.'

Hunter set his glass down on the table and pointed at Chantal while he burped. 'We're supposed to be meeting some mates out here. Sounds like that bunch of clowns might be them.'

Ricky picked up his second beer, flexing his bicep as he drank. 'Whoever they are, they took a lesson and cleared off. Think they went to some bars up the road there.' He waved off behind the complex, the way they'd come into town. 'If those arsewipes are your mates, then...'

'My mates are officers.' Hunter gulped down more beer, burning his gut. 'Not that they're much better.'

'Tell me about it.'

'Wondering if they knew them.' Chantal sipped her wine. 'You haven't seen them since?'

'No way. Not after he gave them what for!' Kerry handed her a shot, then passed one to Hunter. 'Anyway, drink up, boys and girls!'

Hunter's stomach lurched as he sniffed the booze. 'Here goes. One, two, three.' Over the shoulder again.

Kerry washed hers back with some fizz, clearing her glass in one go. 'Crazy stuff, that.' She got up from Ricky's lap and sat next to Chantal. 'So, you got any plans while you're over here?'

Ricky leaned in close to Hunter, sickly Sambuca breath washing over his face. 'She's the love of my life.' He sucked down half of his pint. 'Me best mate, I swear. Hope you get something like that with your Paki bird.'

Hunter sat back and folded his arms. 'Come on, that's not cool.'

Ricky frowned. 'What, she's not a Paki?'

'It's not a nice word, is it?'

'Right, yeah. Sorry.' Ricky stared into the depths of his beer. 'I don't mean anything by it, mate. I'm just saying, I hope you've got something like what we've got with your bird, yeah?'

Hunter looked over at Chantal, braying with laughter at something Kerry had said. 'I think we might do. It's still early days, but...' He shrugged, unsure what he meant. 'I love her.'

'That's all you need, mate.' Ricky gripped his shoulder tight, like he was trying to compress it into diamond. 'All you need.' He finished his pint, leaving a thin layer of slop at the bottom. 'Right, come on, you bitch, let's get back to our room.'

Kerry looked over. 'What did you say, you wanker?'

'I said, let's get back to our room, you bitch.' Ricky got up and stretched out so his T-shirt rode up. His stomach was criss-crossed with scars. Knife wounds. 'It's your birthday, you daft cow.' He gave her a dirty leer. 'Don't want you getting smashed before I get the chance to smash your back doors in, do I?'

'You mean, you still want to be able to get it up?'

'You cheeky bitch. I've got three Viagra with me' Ricky bellowed with laughter and grabbed Hunter's shoulder like it was a walking stick. 'Come on, then.'

'Right. You can have the rest of this.' Kerry chinked a fake nail off the wine bottle. She necked her glass and got up. Then she leaned in and whispered something to Chantal, before planting a kiss on Ricky's cheek. 'Come on, Rambo.'

Ricky put an arm around her waist then set off. 'See you, Craig. See you, Charmaine.'

'She's called Sharon, you daft sod.' Kerry shook her head as they walked deep into the bar, heading for reception.

Chantal pushed her glass away and collapsed back into her chair with a groan. 'Oh, thank God that's over.'

Hunter surveyed the carnage. A pint and a half and two-thirds of a bottle of wine left. So many empties. 'You okay?'

'I feel like I'm going to be sick.'

'You sure?'

She winked at him. 'I'll be fine as long as you hold my hair.'

Hunter pushed his beer into the middle of the table and waved over at the dregs of the hen party, just two older women flirting with two middle-aged men. 'So, Mrs Bond, did you get anything from your mission?'

'Alcohol poisoning.' Chantal yawned. 'You?'

'Lover man had a run-in with some fake squaddies.' Hunter peered around to see Kerry pinching Ricky's arse through his shorts as they walked away. 'Only, they weren't fake. It was Tulloch and his mates.'

'You're sure?'

'Pretty sure.'

The barman appeared, looking harassed and tired. 'Thank God happy hour is over.'

'Like that every day?'

'This is quiet compared to most.' The barman arranged the drinks on a tray. 'Listen, can I see that photo again?'

Hunter frowned as he got out his mobile. His heart started thumping that little bit harder than when he was dealing with Ricky. He held it up. 'You recognise him?'

'I remember. He kicked up a stink about a bottle of spirits last night. Your friend? His name is Sean Tulloch, yes?'

∼

HUNTER HELD Chantal's hand as they walked, warm and tight in his grip. The sun felt too bright, the cars too fast. 'I hate lunchtime drinking.'

She gave his hand a squeeze. 'I love it.'

'Not when we're supposed to be working, though.' Hunter checked both ways down the side street. Two, three, four, five times. 'Come on.' He led her across.

'Where are we going?'

Hunter stopped on the other side and burped into his hand. 'Bloody lager.' He cleared his throat. 'Right, I'm putting two and two together, so bear with me. The barman identified Tulloch. Ricky and Kerry were drinking with squaddies called Sean and Matty.'

'So?'

'They came up this way for a drink.'

The road curved around to the left, climbing the hill. No sign of any bars on the way up so far. A fat man marched out of a chemist's on the right, lugging a wheeled suitcase behind him. A condom machine was mounted on the outside wall. Over the road, a row of bars sat back from the road, the distance filled with empty patio.

The beer swilling in his guts, the booze in his veins surging to his brain.

She marched off towards the first bar.

'Chantal!' Hunter grabbed her arm and pulled her back.

A lorry trundled past, rattling the concrete beneath their feet.

'Remember how pissed you are.'

29

CHANTAL

Chantal swayed up the street, adrenaline fighting with the booze in her guts. *Those shots on a mostly empty stomach. Stupid.*

The bar seemed to be called CHEAP AND CHEERFUL. And it looked anything but cheerful. A two-storey affair with a large veranda in the shade. Deep house music boomed from inside, the sheer volume undoing any chill in the sounds.

Chantal pushed through the door and clicked across to sit on a stool. She leaned against the bar, using it to steady herself.

Hunter joined her, perching on an adjacent stool. Felt as pissed as she looked.

A barman stood in the doorway to the back room, rubbing a towel deep into a yard glass, a long tube shrinking from a pint-sized opening to a narrow stem, ending in a ball. 'Luisa!'

A woman appeared from the far side of the pub and walked across. The light from the floor-to-ceiling windows silhouetted her tiny frame, barely five foot, but black-coffee-and-cigarettes skinny. She flipped the bar up and went to the other side. Seemed to take a week inspecting them. Her olive skin was almost as dark as

Chantal's, just a few shades lighter. Her dark black hair was tied back, darker than her blouse and trousers. She nodded at them then turned the music down. 'Afternoon. What can I get you?' Her Portuguese accent was cut with Essex, could almost taste the Thames estuary on the air.

Chantal leaned forward and yawned into her hand. 'Do you do coffee?'

'You name it, love.' Luisa pointed at a menu. 'Americano, latté, Nescafé.'

'Two Americanos, please. Not too much water in mine.'

'You got it.' Luisa turned round and fiddled with knobs on the hulking coffee machine. It started hissing and growling.

Behind her, the barman rested the yard down on the back wall and eyed them like they were going to rob the till.

Chantal's yawn widened as her eyes closed. 'God, I'm so pissed.'

Hunter frowned. 'But I saw you tossing the shots?'

'Not all of them.' Chantal drummed her fingers on the bar. 'That couple are lunatics.'

'Seen their type so many times.' Hunter caught her yawn, covering his mouth with a fist. 'Marry at sixteen, seventeen, have kids by twenty, then they're stuck into that life. Guy must've enlisted in his teens and he's still a Corporal. Cannon fodder.'

Luisa passed a steaming mug of coffee to Chantal. Dark, thick liquid halfway up the sides. Then she put a small metal jug of milk next to her mug. The coffee smelled bitter, like…

Chantal swallowed hard. *No, it didn't.*

'Thanks.' She tipped the milk in and reached into her bag for her phone. 'Wondering if you could help us.'

Luisa rested Hunter's coffee down in front of him, frowning.

'We're police officers from Scotland.'

Luisa refilled the milk from a UHT carton. 'So, I don't have to help you, right?'

'Your funeral.'

'Listen, I told the other lot who came in, I saw what I saw. I don't know anything else?'

The barman was scowling at Luisa, but she couldn't see him.

Chantal wrapped her hands around the hot coffee. 'But you saw something.'

'This kid with a guy. Walking down the promenade from the old town.'

What? Chantal frowned. 'What are you talking about?'

'Harry Jack.' Luisa's gaze shot between them. 'That's why you're here, isn't it?'

Chantal shook her head. 'Something else.'

The barman got between them. 'Luisa, can you check the ladies' toilet has been cleaned?'

Her forehead knotted then she set off across the bar.

Chantal smiled at the barman. 'Why did you stop her talking to us?'

'We've had enough of that today. Bad for business.'

'There's a child missing.'

'I know, but Luisa only saw something. She's not involved. Listen, if people think children disappear here, nobody comes. Is bad for business.'

'Can you help us, then?'

'What with?'

Chantal got out her phone and flashed up a photo of Sean Tulloch. 'Have you seen this guy?'

The barman shifted his glare between them but didn't speak.

Chantal put a fifty euro note on the bar.

He couldn't take his eyes off the cash.

Chantal took a sip of coffee. Tasted rank, but it might lead back to sobriety. Or gut rot. She snatched up the money before the barman took it.

'Last night. He was in here.' The barman rested against the other side, fingers splayed on the dark fake granite. 'We had karaoke.'

'What time was this?'

'Be about eleven, maybe midnight?'

Hunter's nod confirmed her thinking — it tallied with the story so far.

Tulloch flew out from Edinburgh, landed at the back of eight. Taxi over here, out on the sauce in the hotel, where Ricky threatened him. Then up here to sample the nearby bars.

Chantal focused on the barman again and pointed at the photo. 'It was this man?'

'He did a song. It was...' The barman clapped his hands

together. 'Come, I show you.' He lifted up the bar partition and smiled. 'My name is José.'

'Chantal and Craig.' She grabbed her coffee and got to her feet.

José led them through to the back room, stacked floor-to-ceiling with bottles of beer on one side, wine on the other, a thin column of spirits in the middle.

José pointed at a greyscale monitor, the screen split in four. One display showed outside, two of the bar area, one by the toilets. Luisa shook her head as she mopped at something. Hunter's back was visible at the bar in another shot.

José grabbed a remote and wound the footage back to 23:00 the previous night. The place was jumping, every table full. A load of drinkers, laughing and joking. José was working the bar with two women and another two men, tossing bottles around like they were in that shitty Tom Cruise film.

The bottom left screen showed a stage area near the back, where a girl bellowed into a microphone. Then Sean Tulloch stepped across the veranda outside.

Chantal waved at José. 'Freeze.'

He rewound back until Tulloch was halfway over. Tall and big, grinning like the devil at the crossroads, offering a sweet deal for your soul. He was next to a mate, similarly sized, laughing at something.

Chantal tapped at the screen. 'Can you print it?'

'Of course.' José hit a button on the keyboard and a printer started grinding up behind the beer stack.

'Thanks.' Chantal rested against the first pillar of wine. 'Play it on.'

'Okay.' Tulloch and his mates entered in fast forward. One of them went to the bar and chatted to Luisa, seemed to go on for a few minutes. In the foreground, Tulloch and the other lump were scanning the room. He started speaking to a woman wearing a bridal veil, getting a laugh from her, head thrown back. Then she slapped him. Tulloch spat at her then walked across the room towards the karaoke guy, a middle-aged man in a bright shirt and waistcoat. He leaned in and spoke to him, getting a nod in response.

A few seconds later, the woman gave the mic back and Tulloch snatched it out of the karaoke guy's hands. He jabbed a finger in karaoke guy's face and got an open-palmed gesture back. Then Tulloch started singing something, his mates at the bar laughing.

Chantal tapped a nail on the screen. 'What was he singing?'

José clicked his fingers a few times then jabbed his finger in the air. 'Hall and Oates? "The Private Eyes"?'

'Guy's got taste.' Chantal shook her head at him then at the monitor. 'Oh God.'

On the screen, Tulloch had pulled his trousers down and was waving his penis around.

Chantal's eyes bulged. 'Well, that's a big one, alright.'

José rolled his eyes at her. 'I've seen bigger.'

The three barmen, including José, raced across to the stage, one of them pushing Tulloch over. He tried to fight but stumbled. Out of his box.

José hauled him to his feet and escorted him out of the front of the bar. He pulled Tulloch's trousers up and helped him with his belt.

'I had to help him.'

'Bet you did.' Chantal grabbed the controls and wound it forward.

Tulloch's mates necked their shots and left the bar. José stayed with Tulloch, stopping him getting back in.

Hunter cleared his throat. 'What were you saying to him?'

'He was talking about his girlfriend. She likes the big cock, he said.'

'That was it?'

José flicked his eyebrows. 'That was it.'

'Do you know where they went?'

'Sorry.' José reached down to a printer and handed Chantal prints of Tulloch and his mates. 'This is all I have.'

Chantal smiled as she took the pages and gave him the fifty. She didn't let go and gave him a business card. 'You call me if he comes back, okay?'

∼

CHANTAL STROLLED ACROSS THE BAR. A couple were sitting in the window now, smiling as they sipped at sparkling white wine.

Luisa was leaning against the door, arms folded. She took

Chantal's empty coffee cup, her lip curled. 'Did you get what you wanted?'

Chantal nodded. 'Why didn't he want you talking to us?'

'You heard him. It's bad for business, isn't it?'

'That child was kidnapped in England?'

'So? You think he knows anything but where his next blow job's coming from?' Luisa scowled over at the bar.

Chantal unfolded the printed pages and pointed at the photo of a big thug talking to Luisa. 'Looks like you know this man.'

Luisa smiled at the photo. 'He had a thick accent. I couldn't understand it. He was after a Crazy Vimto, but I didn't know what it was.'

'Did you get him one?'

Luisa shook her head. 'Port and vodka added to a bottle of blue WKD.'

30

HUNTER

Hunter walked down the road, hands in pockets rubbing against his keycard. The street leading down to the hotel was quiet, just an idling taxi belching out fumes. The sun beat down hard, like it was begging forgiveness for all the earlier rain, light flaring across the sea, dappling in the afternoon sky. No clouds, just the deepest blue.

A few girls sat in one of the gardens lining the road, stretching out on the lawns as they passed around a bottle of vodka.

The vaguest whiff of weed on the breeze, mixing with coffee and food smells. Mostly cheese and herbs, the tang of tomato sauce. No meat, thank God.

Hunter stopped on the corner heading towards their apartment. 'What exactly did you mean about Tulloch's cock?'

Chantal gave him that look, rolling her eyes and shaking her head. 'You *saw* it, right?'

'It?' Hunter sighed as a coach pulled past them. 'Looked like two to me.'

'You need to stop worrying, okay?' She laughed as she stroked his arm. 'I know what I like, Craig. I've had a huge guy before and it's not much fun, believe me.'

A huge *guy?*

Hunter scowled at her. 'Look, it's—'

The bus hissed to a stop over by the entrance. A gang of pissed blokes started jumping out, roaring with laughter and shouting at each other. Big lads. Bloody squaddies.

'Hold that cock.' Hunter squinted at one of them. 'I meant "thought".' Wonky ears, dead eyes. He got out his phone and checked the photos Elvis had sent over. 'That guy looks very much like Gordon Brownlee.'

Chantal frowned over. 'Tulloch's mate?'

'Certainly matches the description.' Hunter flicked through the rest of them. 'No sign of Tulloch, though.' He put his mobile away. 'Want to have a wander over and chance it?'

'Got a better idea.'

31

CHANTAL

Chantal marched over to the apartments lining the road and stopped by the second from last. Four girls lay on the grass, groaning as they sipped wine from teacups. 'Bekah, how's it going?'

'Chantal!' She bounced to her feet, almost rising above the fence. Christ knows where she got the energy from. She was lobster red — must've fallen asleep in the garden. 'We lost you, chuck. What happened?'

Chantal smiled at her. 'Had to get a coffee. Too much...' She made the drinky-drinky motion with her hand. She looked around. A couple of the other girls from the bar lay on the grass, sipping vodka from the bottle. 'Thought you were going clubbing?'

'We fell asleep.' Bekah rubbed a hand down her arm and winced. 'So what's new?'

Chantal coughed. 'Going to get some drinks in the bar, if you fancy it?'

'Do I ever!' Bekah vaulted the fence and landed without a sound. She held out a hand to Hunter, like a fairy-tale princess expecting it to be kissed. 'I'm Bekah. Take it you're Craig?'

Hunter didn't look like he knew what he was doing. He smiled and wrapped her hand inside his paw. 'That's me.'

'Lover boy.' Bekah leered at Chantal. 'Heard a lot about you, chuck.'

Chucka...

Chantal grimaced.

'Have you?' Hunter's eyebrows looked out of his control. 'All good, I hope.'

'The best!' Bekah skipped towards reception, the throng of squaddies parting like the Red Sea, most of them checking her out.

Chantal grabbed Hunter's hand. 'Go to the bar. I'm using her as bait.'

~

WELL, this isn't going to plan.

Chantal leaned back in the chair and took another dry sip of rosé, head thumping.

The tables near them were filled with older people, enjoying the sun. Not exactly dignified as they tucked into cheap Portuguese booze. Still no sign of Tulloch's crew, either.

The hen party sipped white wine instead of shooters. The bar staff still hadn't cleared away the bottles of empty spirits lying on their sides.

Bekah leaned forward, her face crumpling with angst. 'So, my boyfriend, right? All he wants is a quick shag and that's it. It's, like, boring?'

Still going on about her boyfriend back home being rubbish in bed. *He's a teenager, it's how they are, love.*

The way she was leaning in to Hunter...

Chantal took a proper sip of wine. Felt a bit better. 'And have you talked to him about it?'

'Talk? He doesn't listen! Do you know what I mean, chuck?'

Chantal gritted her teeth. If she says that one more time... 'I know what you mean.' She winked at Hunter. Poor guy looked like he wanted to die.

'Here we go, boys!' One of the squaddies from the bus sauntered out into the sunshine, dirty Scottish accent and he didn't care who knew it. Tray full of fizzing beer, shades on the top of his head, shorts and T-shirt, his skin salmon pink where it wasn't tattoo black. 'This is the game!' He put the tray down and started chucking some tables together, pushing the chairs into place around them. Enough for about twenty or so.

Bekah hadn't even noticed, but the lads spotted her. She leaned in close to Chantal. 'And he won't even go down on me.'

32

HUNTER

Hunter sipped another millimetre height of beer. Still loads left. The new squaddies were livening the place up, but he didn't recognise any of them. Certainly no Brownlee or Tulloch.

Bekah was doing his nut in. So much banality in one skinny body. Fat Jim back at the station always went on about young girls, the dirty old bastard, but Hunter couldn't see the appeal. Old enough to be her father and he wasn't even thirty-five.

She said something he didn't catch.

Chantal looked like she was struggling to keep a straight face. She leaned forward. 'Do you, you know?' She stuck her tongue in her cheek.

'All the bloody time, Chantal.' Bekah sipped at her Breezer like it was a formula bottle. 'All the bloody time.'

Save me from tedious chat...

They were surrounded by hens slowing down and stags speeding up. Behind enemy lines. Getting rat-arsed with a hen party. *Getting bloody nowhere, while Tulloch was...*

What?

Back home he was abusing women who consented, at least up to a point. Paisley had agreed to have sex with him. When she withdrew that consent was another matter.

Out here, though, rabid stags would be firing into pissed teens like Bekah, consent at the back of their minds.

Hunter necked a couple of inches of beer, then swirled it round, trying to get some head to foam up. Then he sank the rest. 'I'll get another round in.'

Chantal clasped his hand and let it go as she tucked into her wine. 'G&T for me.'

Bekah swayed in the sunshine, waving her bottle in the air. 'Another Bacardi Breezer!'

'Two ticks.' Hunter huffed up to his feet and walked inside, dumping his empty glass on the bar.

The barman gave him a sly nod as he poured out three pints simultaneously. Looked like he'd lost the will to live, if he'd ever had it.

Bloody knee is still sore from that tussle in Galashiels. Feels like a million miles away. And it is.

Hunter checked his phone for messages. Two from Finlay. He pocketed it and rested against the bar. Still nothing from Elvis about those other bloody squaddies.

The barman pushed three beers over to the customer to Hunter's right. 'Ten euro fifty.'

'Here you go.' The lumbering hulk of muscle dumped a note and a coin on the bar. He picked up the pints in pyramid formation and gave Hunter a nod.

Gordon Brownlee.

If you opened the dictionary at squaddie, it would show a picture of Brownlee. Thick cranium, mouth hanging open, beady little eyes keeping an eye on the foaming pints. Had a bit of a twitch every so often, just when you thought it had stopped. The wonky ears were less obvious in real life, but the eyes... The eyes...

Hunter blocked him off. 'Here, do I know you?'

Brownlee scowled at him. 'Doubt it, mate.' He pushed past him into the sunshine.

The barman tapped him on the shoulder, eyes wide. 'Sir?'

'What's up?'

'I've got that beer you ordered?'

∼

Hunter clattered the tray down on the table. Nobody looked up except Chantal.

Gordon Brownlee was sitting next to Bekah. He'd lost two of his pints and it looked like he'd need reinforcements soon. In the time he'd been at the bar, the squaddies' table had filled up and spilled out in their direction. 'Aye, of course it's a hard life.'

Bekah was purring at him. She tossed her hair back. 'So do you miss your wife?'

'Hardly.' Brownlee bellowed out a laugh. 'I'm not married yet!'

Hunter sat between Brownlee and Chantal and distributed the drinks.

Chantal pounced on Bekah, whispering in her ear. She got a giggle.

Hunter cleared his throat and frowned at Brownlee. 'It's Gordon, isn't it?'

He shifted his gaze from Bekah's bare thighs up to Hunter, squinting at the sunlight. 'Look, I don't know you, mate. Piss off.'

'Craig Hunter.' He held out a hand. 'You were in Kandahar, right?'

'Not for very long, mate.' Brownlee supped at his beer. 'I don't recognise you.'

'You still serving?'

Brownlee settled back. Slightly more comfortable, the ice beginning to thaw. 'For my sins, aye.'

'You know a Sean Tulloch?'

'Big Sean... What a guy.' Brownlee bellowed out more laughter. 'You know him?'

'Served with him in Kandahar. He with you?'

Brownlee reached over and tapped someone on the back. 'Matty?'

Matty could've passed for Sean Tulloch's brother. Same height and bulk, his twinkly eyes twisted by booze, coke and God knows what else, puffing on a cigar like he was some Hollywood big shot. He had his top off, cupping a hand around his bicep as he flexed.

Bloody squaddies on R&R. 'All right, mate?' Throaty Leeds accent. 'What's up?'

'Boy here says he knows Sean fae Kandahar.'

'Yeah?' Matty looked him up and down. 'What squad were you in?'

'3 Scots.' Hunter smiled at him, kept eye contact. 'Stationed at Fort George. You?'

Matty picked up a pint and sucked down a third in one go. 'Parachute.'

'Still in?'

A slight nod. 'Thinking of giving it up, though.' Matty swivelled his chair round. 'My year's notice is up in May. Thinking of moving out here.'

'Sounds ideal.'

'It is, mate.' Matty sank some more, his eyes still not quite buying what Hunter was selling. 'What about you?'

'Jacked it back in 2010. Doing private security now, for my sins.' Hunter drank some more of his own pint, trying to spin out the lie rather than inventing too much. Matty wasn't biting. 'Been out in Syria for six months.'

'Yeah?'

'Worse than Kandahar, I swear, but I'm a step removed from the front line, you know?'

Matty punched Brownlee on the shoulder. Hard enough to make noise. 'We met some bloke who's been over there, didn't we?'

'Aye, last night.' Brownlee clinked his fingers off the glass. 'Not a very nice guy, either. Older punter. Cracked in the head. Being in the army that long'll make you go that way, right?'

Chantal sashayed past them to the toilet, arm in arm with Bekah.

Matty whistled through his teeth. 'That your bird, mate?'

Hunter nodded as he sipped more beer. 'Love of my life.'

'Talk about punching above your weight.'

'You're not the first to say that.'

Matty cackled with laugher. 'You're a six at best, right. I'd say she's a nine. At least.' He thwacked Brownlee on the arm. 'What'd you give her, Gogs?'

He looked resigned to this shit. 'I'd give her one.'

Matty rocked back with laughter. 'These boys... I tell you,

mate...' He puffed on the cigar and stifled a cough. 'You're sound, you are. Not like that prick last night. Wouldn't believe we were squaddies!'

'What a wanker.' Hunter drank some more beer. Felt like he was drowning. Maybe now was the time to close the deal. 'So, is Sean around?'

'Was. God knows where he is now, mate.' Matty took another puff of the cigar. 'We was away shark fishing, not that we saw any. A few boys jumped out of the coach back in the old town. Supposed to be meeting them later but they could get lost in a toilet, you know?'

'Only too well.' Hunter wrapped his fingers round his beer glass. 'Tell you what would be a laugh. What about if I meet up with you boys later. It'll wind Sean right up. You know he hates spiders, aye?'

Brownlee was scowling at him. 'Spiders? Piss off.'

Hunter flicked up his eyebrows. 'I'll get a load of plastic ones from one of those tat shops and we can throw them at him.'

'Tell you what'd be hilarious!' Matty fell about laughing. 'Sticking them up his arse!'

Brownlee rolled his eyes. 'Always the arse play with you, Matty.'

'Funny as hell, though, mate. Shove a plastic spider right up his hole.' Matty downed the last of his beer. 'Supposed to be going for dinner down the Strip tonight. Back of eight, I think. Same place we were in last night, if they'll let us in. The biggest steak you've ever seen, mate. And five euros!'

Hunter's gut churned at the thought. 'Sounds brilliant.'

'First one on the left as you hit it from this end. Can't remember the name.'

'Cool.' Hunter got to his feet and nodded. 'See you later, aye?' He offered a fist to bump.

'Sure thing, mate.' Matty obliged. 'Later.'

Brownlee gave him a salute. 'Later.'

Hunter marched off to the bar. Bekah was getting served, though Christ knows how anyone could even think about giving her more booze, the state she was in. Could barely stand up.

He gripped Chantal's arm. 'Come on, I've got something.'

Chantal nodded at him, then patted Bekah's shoulder. 'Think it's time you had a little siesta, miss.'

'You two inviting me back to your room, are you?' Bekah tried for a saucy wink, but she couldn't control either eye.

'Hardly.' Hunter flagged down a passing hen from that party and whispered in her ear, 'Think you should get her tucked up in bed.'

33

CHANTAL

Chantal opened the apartment door and stomped across the tiles. Struggling to not just lie on the bed and fall asleep. She pulled the doors wide and sat on the chair, knees pointing inwards. 'I don't see how this gets us anywhere.'

'We've got a likely location.' Hunter joined her outside and dumped his phone on the table. 'The circle's closing around him.'

'Still feels like a very big one.'

'Speaking of which...'

'Craig, drop it.' Chantal slurped down more coffee. Could barely taste it. 'You're a one-track record.'

'Right.' He didn't look like it was settled. *Coming up next, more of Craig Hunter's perceived penile inadequacy.* 'That Bekah girl, think she'll be okay?'

'I hope so. She needs to get some sleep.' She finished the coffee, the black sludge finally hitting her tongue. 'She's desperate for a shag. I almost thought she wanted to—'

Hunter's mobile blasted out the drill again. Set Chantal's teeth on edge. Finlay Sinclair's ugly mug gurned out of a drunken photo taken on a night out.

'Bloody hell.' Hunter turned it over and covered the speaker. 'Finlay keeps pestering me. I forgot how clingy he is.'

'So tell him to piss off.'

Hunter held up the mobile and turned the ringer down a bit. 'Wish I'd not got in touch with him now.' The phone stopped ringing. 'So you think I should text him?'

'Whatever, as long as you get rid of him.'

Hunter hammered at the screen. 'What were you saying about that Bekah girl?'

'Nothing.'

Hunter put his phone down again. 'Come on, I know it's not nothing.'

Chantal pushed out a sigh. 'Okay, I thought she was—'

'—YOU STUPID BITCH!'

Crash. Thump. Tinkle.

'WHAT ARE YOU—'

Screech. 'I HATE YOU!'

'Oh, shite.' Chantal jolted to her feet and dashed over to the railing. 'What's going on?' She squinted hard. Over the small lane, one of the ground-floor apartment doors hung open, the curtains flapping in the breeze.

A suitcase sconed off the French doors and rolled across the patio, shirts and pants tumbling out. Ricky appeared in the doorway. 'LOOK WHAT YOU'VE DONE NOW, YOU STUPID BITCH!' He bent down and started scooping up his clothes.

Chantal pushed away from the rail. 'We need to sort this out!'

34

HUNTER

Hunter used the plant pots to vault over the picket fence. He landed on the lane and jogged towards the apartment.
Take it slowly, man. You're half-cut.
'STOP CALLING ME A BITCH!' Kerry booted Ricky on the arse and he tumbled forwards. 'YOU FAT PRICK! CAN'T EVEN GET A HARD-ON ANY MORE, YOU PISS ARTIST!'
'SHUT YOUR MOUTH!'
'NO, YOU SHUT— AH!' Kerry fell backwards, cracking her head off the door. 'YOU *BASTARD!*'
'Stop!' Hunter walked forward, arms outstretched. 'Stop!'
Ricky was on all fours, rubbing at a gash on his cheek. He narrowed his eyes at Hunter. 'What's your problem, mate?'
'Calm down.'
Ricky pushed himself up to his feet. 'You want to make something of this, do you?'
Hunter clambered over their fence and landed in their patio.
'You want to stick that big Scotch beak in, though, don't you?'

Ricky spat at him, thick gobbets splattering Hunter's cheek. 'You think you're something, do you?'

Kerry appeared in the doorway again. 'I'M GOING TO KILL YOU!'

'PISS OFF, YOU STUPID BITCH!' Ricky sneered at her, his head butting the air. Then back at Hunter. 'You want to take me on, mate, you'll regret it.'

'It's okay.' Hunter stood slightly back, his fists clenched and in position. 'Calm down and it'll all be cool.'

'You hear what that bitch said to me? See what she *did*?' Ricky picked up his suitcase and hurled it at Kerry, cracking off her head. 'Did you?'

Chantal scrambled over the fence and stopped dead.

'You can piss off and all, you Paki bitch!' Ricky lunged for Chantal.

Hunter stepped forward to block him. Ricky darted left and clawed a hand at Hunter's throat. He pushed hard, pinning him to the side wall.

'Get off him!' Chantal scratched at Ricky's hands. 'Stop it!'

'I'll hurt you next!' Ricky batted at her with his free hand, just missing her.

Hunter dug his chin down into his chest, piling pressure on Ricky's thumb. He gripped his right hand around Ricky's wrist and jerked it down, smashing his attackers nose with his left. 'You don't hit women!' He swivelled his hips to the right and thrust out with his left hand again, cracking Ricky's chin. 'You don't hit women!' He jerked up his knee and cracked Ricky's groin, sending him tumbling to the ground. 'You don't hit women!'

'Stop!' Kerry stood in the doorway, wielding a bread knife. 'Get away from my husband!'

'Craig...' Chantal tugged at his hand, pulling him away. 'Come on.'

Hunter sucked in a deep breath. 'You need to think about divorcing this idiot.'

'You can piss off, you Scotch twat!' Kerry slashed the knife through the air, nowhere near hurting anyone but herself. 'I love my husband!'

Hunter shook his head and helped Chantal over the fence,

eyes trained on Ricky as he groaned on the lawn. Could barely breathe. Felt like his throat was half the usual size.

'Stop!' A male voice came from the direction of the bar.

Hunter swung round, wary of putting his back to Ricky. 'Aw, shite.'

Inspector João Quaresma marched towards them, flanked by a pair of brutish uniformed officers. 'Stop right there!'

35

CHANTAL

All we bloody need...

'He's all yours, officer.' Chantal pointed back the way then put her hands up. Act innocent, don't give them a decision to make. 'He was going to kill her.' She leaned in close to whisper, 'Keep our cover.'

Quaresma peered over at Ricky.

Kerry was crouching by her husband, still brandishing her knife. 'Keep the hell away from us!'

'Typical British behaviour.' Quaresma waved for the two uniforms next to him to take over. 'Leve-os de volta para a esquadra.'

The bigger of the two nodded, then smiled at Kerry. 'Madam, give me the knife.'

Kerry dropped it on the patio and hugged her husband tight. 'I love you, Ricky.'

'These two...' Quaresma started off down the lane back towards reception. 'We got a call and I was driving past. On my way to something of critical importance. This call made me think of you two.'

'It's a coincidence.' Chantal rubbed at her arm, a rash puckering the flesh halfway up. 'We intervened to stop him killing her. Ended up the other way round.'

Quaresma rolled a tongue over his lips. 'Mr Hunter, from what I saw, you assaulted a foreign national on my territory.'

Hunter's turn to raise his hands. 'Completely self-defence.' He rubbed a hand across his throat, already turning purple. 'He went for me. Grabbed me. I took him down.'

Quaresma narrowed his eyes at Chantal. 'Sergeant, we agreed that you get my approval *first*, yes?'

'This wasn't an—'

'No questions, no exceptions.' Quaresma stopped by a squad car next to an Audi. 'Mr Hunter, do I have your word?'

Hunter bowed his head. 'You've got my word.'

'And you, Ms Jain?'

'We'll call you next time.'

'Then we have an understanding.' Quaresma grinned at Hunter, his face lighting up like a little kid at Christmas. 'Was that Krav Maga?'

Hunter lifted a shoulder. 'I know a bit.'

'A bit?' Quaresma laughed. 'You should be in the UFC!'

'Hardly.'

Quaresma's face darkened again. Prick could change like the wind. He waved at the uniforms as they led Ricky and Kerry to the car. 'We're going to put the fear of God into these two.'

Ricky snarled at them as the cops forced him into the back. 'You pair of wankers!'

Chantal caught Quaresma's door as he opened it. 'Look, we've got some intel on Tulloch's whereabouts.'

Quaresma stood up tall with a huff, his eyes tracing the car's route up to the main road. The glint was gone from his eyes. 'I'm listening.'

'We believe he's down the Strip.'

'Sergeant.' Quaresma waved his hand around the area. 'Stick to these parts, please. Much safer for you and your partner.'

'But Tulloch's not here.'

Quaresma licked his lips again. 'Keep yourselves to yourselves. Tomorrow, I give you some men.'

'Tomorrow's not good enough.'

'Tomorrow is good enough, my friend.' Quaresma put his fists up in the air and grinned at Hunter. 'Just don't fight me, eh?'

'We need to get him tonight.' Hunter folded his arms, his biceps bulging. 'He might be gone tomorrow.'

'Listen to me.' Quaresma rested a hand on Hunter's back and one on Chantal's. 'My friends, we have a high-profile case from your country already. That is my priority. Until we find the boy.'

Chantal shrugged off his hand. 'So what you're saying is, if I go to the press with our case, you'll give us some support?'

Quaresma held her gaze, his eyes full of ice. 'You are very funny.' He opened the car door wide. 'You keep to this area, okay?'

'Fine.'

Quaresma got into the black Audi and gunned the engine. A final wave and the car tore up the hill to the main road.

Chantal folded her arms, her right hand playing with the rash. 'What a disaster.'

'Look, we saved her life.' Hunter wrapped his arms around her and kissed her on the head. 'They'll prosecute him for that. One wife-beating arsehole off the street is a result.'

'Sounded like she gave as good as she got.' She collapsed into Hunter's embrace, her back against this stomach, and let out a monster sigh. 'Jesus, I'm so pissed.'

Hunter kneaded her shoulders. 'You've done very well, Mrs Bond.'

'*Ms* Bond, thank you very much.' Chantal stared at the road. Quaresma's Audi droned away into the distance, louder than the rest of the traffic. 'That clown's just getting in the bloody way.' She waved up at the main street, the karaoke bar out of view. 'Meanwhile, Tulloch's in this town, up to shenanigans. We need to get him.'

'You heard what Quaresma said.'

She reached round to wink at him. 'He likes you. We should use that.'

'Not sure how.' Hunter gripped her shoulder where it hurt the most. *Heaven...*

Chantal sorted out her hair, smoothing it down. 'This is above our pay grades.'

CHANTAL STABBED a finger on her screen and stuck it on speaker. She laid it on the bed between them. Then huffed out air. *Here we go...*

The light outside was dimming to an early evening glow. Way earlier than in Scotland, but the heat was still there, still hotter than the warmest Scottish day.

'Afternoon, Chantal.' Could almost hear Sharon's grin down the line. 'Just left the beach, have you?'

'Hardly.' Chantal yawned into her fist and blinked hard a few times. *How many more coffees can I drink?* Another yawn hit her in the face. 'We've been working hard.'

'You're slurring, you daft mare.' Sharon sighed down the line. 'Tell me you've not been drinking since you got there?'

'It's our cover, Shaz.' Chantal picked up the phone and scowled at it. 'Did you get my text?'

'Aye, something about a possible location on Tulloch blah blah blah. And a cock block? What?'

'Quaresma, our liaison, is blocking any progress. We know where Tulloch's going to be tonight. He won't give us any officers. So, any suggestions?'

Sharon sighed then left a pause. Sounded like someone shouted 'She was over eighteen!' in the background. 'Like we discussed, we have to progress through the local cops.'

'Quaresma isn't playing ball. This missing kid's taking up all their time and we... had an incident.'

A deeper sigh crackled the speaker. 'Christ on a moped, what have you done now?'

'Some knuckle-dragging squaddie was battering his wife. We stopped him.' She flashed Hunter a wink. 'We should try and claim credit for it.'

'You've got no jurisdiction over there, Chantal.'

Chantal stabbed a finger in the air. 'Quaresma isn't helping us at all. In fact, he's told us to stick to the hotel area.'

'Which is where Tulloch is, right?'

'He's a mile away, tops.'

The line went silent again. The same voice shouted 'Eighteen!'

Hunter got up and started pacing the room.

'Right, I'll speak to his superiors, see if I can chivvy things along.' Another Sharon sigh. 'But you need to listen to what

Quaresma says, okay? I don't want you messing this up because you've pissed him off.'

Chantal rolled her eyes. 'Like I would.'

'Did you say this guy was a squaddie?'

'From Manchester or something.' Chantal tried to fend off another yawn. 'We've met a few soldiers here. Seems to be armed forces week off.'

'Right. Well, it's been all quiet from Rollo-Smith. Not sure that's a good thing.'

'So, how do you want us to progress?'

'How's your double bed?'

'Aye, very funny.' Chantal shook her head at the phone. 'Sort out Quaresma, okay?' She ended the call and tossed her mobile on the bed. 'Christ's sake.'

The bed squeaked as Hunter knelt behind her and started rubbing her shoulders again. 'Think she'll get anywhere with Quaresma's bosses?'

Right, yes. There. Her head collapsed forward. 'I think it'll just piss him off.'

'Isn't that what we want?'

She tried to shrug but it didn't happen. 'Maybe.'

Hunter kissed her neck and slid her bra strap down from her left shoulder. 'So, what do you want to do?'

'A little lie down wouldn't go amiss.'

'I'm with you there.' Hunter slid the right side down and kissed her neck again, still hitting the right spots on the massage. 'Then?'

'Then we'll get something to eat. I'm thinking we should head down the Strip.'

'Nothing to stop us going for a walk, is there?'

'Nothing.' Chantal swung round and kissed him hard on the mouth, bashing against his teeth, her tongue wrestling against his. 'Get one of those condoms, then.'

∽

CHANTAL'S HAND clamped round Hunter's, warm and tight, as they walked down the street. The sun was low on the horizon, but the air was still hot. Her boozy haze was replaced with a nice feeling in her gut. 'This must be what happiness feels like.' She put her head to his shoulder and wrapped her arm round his torso. 'I love you, Craig.'

'You only say that after you've got your way with me.'

Chantal pinched his side as they walked on. 'Very funny.'

The wide street joined a crossroads. Busy neon led to the right, a deep bass drum thud booming out. A couple of lap dancing clubs were across the other side, right next to three cash machines.

She waved a hand over the road. 'Think Tulloch might've gone in there?'

Hunter tossed his head from side to side. 'Someone like Tulloch would rather not pay for it.'

'Maybe. Maybe not.' Chantal clenched her jaw. 'You see what he did to the four victims before Paisley. What they went through at his hands, made them too scared to talk to us. It doesn't come down to paying for it, he takes what he wants and screw the consequences. We need to get him, Craig.'

'We will.' Hunter led her over to the crossroads. 'So I guess this is the Strip, then?'

A long avenue crawled down a gradual hill, kinking slightly then twisting back to the left. Like the high street of any small Scottish town, but instead of butchers, bakers and post offices, every door was a bar or club. Flashing neon, hissing dry ice, thumping house music. Men and women outside handing out flyers. A steady stream of boozers traipsed down, grouped by gender, shouting and laughing.

Hunter looked over at her. 'You ready for this?'

Chantal sucked in a deep breath. She pointed to the right. A two-storey Irish pub that looked like a saloon in a Western. A staircase led up the side to a steak restaurant. 'Was that where Tulloch was going?'

'Maybe.' Hunter scowled at her. 'But. Steak?'

'Shite, I didn't think.' She rubbed his arm through his shirt. 'We can sit and watch.'

'It's fine.' He started up the steps. 'I think Matty said first on the right.'

'You told me left.'

'Did I? Shite.'

'Come on.' She grabbed his hand and squeezed, hauling him across the road.

El Rancho Steak House. A single floor and long, with an olive climbing up the stucco front.

Hunter stopped. 'Another steakhouse?'

Chantal took a look inside. No sign of Tulloch or the other two. Brownlee and Matty. She glanced at the placard outside and chapped her knuckle off it. 'Look, it's mostly pizza and pasta.'

'Now we're talking.' Hunter scanned down the menu. 'You sure you're okay about missing out on a steak?'

'I'll be fine. Already had a big portion of meat.'

'Hardly big...'

'You know what I mean.' She tried to lead him in, but he held back.

Hunter let out a groan. 'What self-respecting pizza place doesn't have a banana topping?'

Chantal tightened her grip and pulled him by the hand, waiting by the front desk.

The restaurant was pretty big. A few tables for couples ran along the windows with long benches stretching from front to back, like a school canteen. Stag and hen parties all dicking about. Selfie central. Twenty-odd blokes filled a bench to the far wall. Halfway up, some of them were turned to chat up the hen party behind them. The nearest men looked like they were still asleep, no doubt the result of a hardcore Thursday night. Evening meal of the living dead. Someone shouted out 'Pintman!', whatever that meant, whoever that was.

Chantal folded her arms. 'No sign of Tulloch or his mates.'

'The night's still young.'

A waiter flounced over to them and grinned at Chantal. 'Table for two?'

She nodded. 'Could we get one away from everything?'

'Sure thing, my sweet.' The waiter led over to a series of tables on the side and pulled out a chair.

Chantal took the seat facing back the way. 'Thanks.'

The waiter brandished two menus. 'Can I get you something to drink? Wine? Beer? Cocktail?'

Chantal sighed as she flipped hers over. 'A bottle of the Rioja, please.'

'Sure thing.' The waiter sauntered off past the bedlam, rolling his eyes. One of the lads was dancing on a table, throwing Marty

McFly air-guitar shapes to a Guns 'n Roses track pumping out of the stereo.

Hunter reached a hand over the table. 'A whole bottle?'

'Sod it. We've got to blend in, right?' Her phone rattled the table top and she groaned. 'Bollocks, it's Sharon.'

36

HUNTER

'Well, take it.' Hunter pulled the menu close to him. Looked like it was mostly barbecued meat. Can't even see the bloody pasta. 'You can't do a speakerphone call in a place like this.'

'Back in a sec.' Chantal snatched up her mobile and headed outside.

Hunter flipped the menu over. Pizza and pasta. *Right, good.*

He glanced at his phone. More texts from Finlay. *Give it up, mate.*

He rubbed at his throat. Still hurt from Ricky's clawing, but maybe back down to seven out of ten. Maybe.

The menu was a hard choice. Usually best to just go for the margherita. More cheese and less messing about.

Maybe worth asking for a banana?

The waiter came back with a bottle of wine and a frown. 'Has madam left, sir?'

'Had to take a call.'

'I see.' The waiter rested the bottle in front of Hunter. He twatted about with a knife, tearing at the foil, instead of yanking it off like any self-respecting barbarian would. Then he plunged a corkscrew in with a wide smile. 'Are you both drinking, yes?'

'Aye, we are.' Hunter unlocked his phone and found the photos. He held it up to the waiter. 'Do you recognise any of these men?'

The waiter splashed wine into Hunter's glass and frowned at the photos, as he slowly flicked through.

Hunter picked up the glass for a sniff and sip. Passable, though not a Rioja.

The waiter's eyes bulged at one picture. Tulloch. 'How is the wine, sir?'

'It's fine.' Hunter slid the glass back. 'So, do you recognise him?'

The waiter poured some wine into Chantal's glass. 'This man was in last night. Loud and drunk.'

'I take it that's not out of character for here?'

The waiter rolled his eyes at the excess behind him. 'You see what we have to contend with every night.' He tipped some plonk into Hunter's glass, filling it up, then rested the bottle in the middle of the table. 'I take it you are police.'

'From Scotland, aye.' Hunter took another sip of the sour wine. 'Have they been in tonight?'

'They would not be allowed in.' He puckered his lips. 'Shall I come back when madam has returned?'

'Please.' Hunter stared at the menu again. 'Hang on, can I get banana and mushroom on a pizza?'

'Well, of course. Whatever sir desires.' The waiter flounced off.

Another two men and three hens were up on one of the long tables, playing air guitar to that Bryan Adams song.

'Bloody hell.' Chantal slumped down in her chair and gulped down some wine. 'Bloody hell.'

'That good?'

She pinged a finger on her wine glass, letting it ring. 'Sharon didn't get anywhere with Quaresma's boss.' Another drink. 'We still have to go through him if we need any assistance.' She fanned her hair out. 'And, of course, we've pissed them off now.'

Last thing we need. 'Well, the good news is they were in here last night.'

'Tulloch?'

'And company. They won't get back in, though.'

'Shite. So we're wasting our time?'

The waiter reappeared with his hands clasped. 'Are you ready to order, madam?'

37

CHANTAL

Chantal sipped at her wine, her cheeks flushing from all the booze. Still tasted like diluted balsamic. *Why the hell did Craig accept it?*

Hunter nibbled at the crust of his pizza. Looked disgusting. Tomato and cheese and banana. The mushrooms looked canned. *Hate mushrooms.*

He finished chewing and pushed his plate away. 'That wasn't bad at all.'

'I'll take your word for it.' Chantal dug into the last layer of her lasagne. Red meaty mush. *Not even sure it's beef.* 'This is minging.'

'Looks okay to me. Apart from, you know, the meat.'

'They had a veggie option.'

Hunter took a sip of wine. 'So, what do—'

'There you are!' Finlay Sinclair was marching across the tiles towards them. 'Knew I'd find you here!'

What the hell?

Has Craig been texting him? Asking him to help out?

Hunter got up and got in Finlay's face. 'Fancy seeing you here.'

'What? I'm meeting a pal for a drink.' Finlay leaned back against an empty bench, still encrusted with second-hand food. The stag party had left with their air guitars.

Finlay beamed at Chantal. 'Evening.'

She tried to smile, but the rage must've twisted into a snarl. 'Evening.'

Hunter was smiling, looked as forced as hers felt. 'Mate, you're not a cop anymore.'

'I want to help.' As Finlay stood, his back clicked like a seatbelt. 'I know the area.'

'You live the other side of Faro.'

Finlay put on a puppy-dog face, his eyes sagging. 'Look, let me—'

'Finlay.' Chantal got up and dusted off the shoulders of his polo shirt. 'I appreciate it, but this is for Craig and me, okay?'

Finlay did a petulant teenager stomp. 'Come on...'

Chantal pushed her plate away. 'The local cop isn't impressed with us and, well, I don't want you getting caught up in this. Might get you in some trouble. And you have to live here.' She flashed a grin at him. 'Look, the local cops are supposed to be helping us tomorrow. Could maybe use your help making sure they're not bullshitting us.'

Finlay nodded. 'Cool.' He rubbed a hand across his face. 'Cool. What time?'

'Probably best that we phone you.'

'Then I'll wait for the call. Let's do that.'

Chantal smiled again and patted his back. 'Now, we've got something to get on with, so...' She tapped her nose. 'Aye?'

'Aye.' Finlay beamed at them and strolled off out of the restaurant, his back ramrod straight.

Hunter sat again and drained his glass. 'Thanks for the save.'

'Have you been goading him?'

'I swear I haven't.'

Chantal waved over at the waiter and held up forty euros. She got a saucy wink in return. 'Come on, lover boy.' She left the rest of her glass of vinegar and set off out of the restaurant. 'Before Finlay comes back.'

CHANTAL GRIPPED Hunter's hand tight and led down the hill. The rubbery tang of hot dogs belched out of a small van parked at the side of the road. A queue wound back across the street, blocking the traffic.

Hunter's eyes were almost rolling back in his head.

'Jesus, are you alright?'

His lips twitched. 'I'm... trying to centre myself.'

'What, why?'

'That van.' Hunter ran a hand across his nose. 'The smell. It's...'

She tightened her grip. 'Craig, it's okay.'

Hunter shut his eyes, clamped them tight, his forehead knotting. 'I'm getting better at it.'

She gave his hand a pulse. 'Good.'

He reopened them, smiling. 'Thanks.' Then he frowned.

Matty and Gordon Brownlee leaned against a bar's window, munching on hot dogs. Matty waved at Hunter. 'Alright, mate. You seen Sean yet?'

'Not yet.' Hunter beamed at them. 'Getting the spiders now.'

Matty finished chewing some hot dog. 'We'll shove them right up his arse!'

Brownlee bunched up his wrapper, shaking his head. He tapped on the glass. 'Supposed to be meeting him in here, if you're ready?'

'See you inside, yeah?' Matty followed Brownlee into the bar.

Chantal scowled at him. 'Craig, what are you up to?'

'Finding Tulloch. Far as I'm aware, he doesn't know anything about us. Who we are, that we're cops.'

'But he'll start to smell a rat if you say you served with him.'

'I'll say it's John Tulloch. The important thing is we'll know where he is. Then I can call Quaresma and we can get out of this godforsaken place.'

Chantal stared into the bar. Matty was shouting an order at the bar staff and waving euros around. 'Come on, then.'

Hunter led her inside. The bar was hot, sticky sweat trickling down the walls. Old-school house pumped out of giant speakers, genuine Detroit sounds not mid-nineties Balearic dross.

Chantal stopped by the bar, a two-deep queue around it, and smiled at Matty. 'Sean here?'

He shook his head. 'Nobody's seen him, love.'

She stared at Hunter. *This isn't the right move. Need to regroup and replan.*

'Here.' Matty handed her a pint glass of dark red liquid. Then another. 'Get stuck in!'

'What are you playing at?' Hunter was in her ear. 'We need to go.'

'This is your fault not mine.' She took a drink. Bloody did taste like Vimto. She flashed a smile at Matty. 'Cheers!'

Hunter took one and started sipping at it.

'Chantal!' Bekah wrapped her arms round her, vomit breath crawling over her skin. 'Chantal!'

Chantal had to stop her drink from spilling. 'How are you doing?'

'I'm on it! Whoo!' Bekah jumped in the air, barely took any effort to lift off.

Matty gave Bekah a good going over with his eyes. He took a gulp from a pint glass. 'Alright?'

She held out her hand. 'I'm Bekah!'

'Matty.' He offered her a drink from his glass. She slurped it down. 'How's my girl?'

'Starving!' Bekah leaned against Chantal, barely any weight at all. 'Anywhere good to eat round here?'

'Me and Gogsy here just had a hot dog from that van. Lovely.'

'You had a big sausage, did you?' Bekah swapped Chantal for Matty, resting one hand on his arm, the other on his stomach. She started running her hand around the edge of his shorts. 'Bet there's a big one in your pants.'

'Massive, love.'

Bekah hauled his shorts down to his knees. Matty's cock was half-erect, barely two inches long.

'Piss off!' Matty pushed her over and stormed off out of the bar.

'Shite.' Brownlee downed his Crazy Vimto. 'Now look what you've done.'

The crowd around them were laughing. More than a few girls from Bekah's hen party, all wagging their pinkies.

Chantal leaned in to whisper in Hunter's ear. 'Craig, that was a normal-sized cock.'

He scowled at her. 'Hardly.'

'I doubt you've seen many cocks in your life, have you? You've watched too much porn. Those aren't real knobs.' She grabbed his groin. 'There's nothing wrong with yours, okay?'

38

HUNTER

Hunter trotted after Chantal, almost losing her in the throng of boozers marching down the Strip.
Gangs dressed in uniforms — superheroes, wrestlers, Star Wars characters, Australians.
Gangs in jeans and shirts.
The next-door bar had spilled out onto the street, stags necking bottles of Grolsch and eyeing up the passing women. No sign of Tulloch in there, either.
Hunter stopped in the street and rubbed at his eyes. 'We're stuck in bloody Groundhog Day here. I've no idea what time it is, other than night. That daytime boozing is messing with my head.'
'It's twisted my melon, as well.' Chantal leaned her head on his shoulder. 'I can barely remember why we're here, other than I keep seeing Paisley's battered face when I close my eyes.'
'I know what you mean.' He grabbed her hand and led her down the street, walking past a 5D cinema. *Whatever that means.*
A big lump of holiday apartments sat across the road, set back like they were keeping away from the bacchanalian excess.

A blue light flashed down the side street by the apartments, too far away to be the neon of a bar or club.

Two armed police officers guarded a side entrance. Black polo shirts, maybe even navy. Baseball cap, black boots and trousers with a holster hanging off.

Hunter clasped Chantal's hand and stopped her. 'Something's going on down there.' He nodded at the officers and started off down the street.

The street widened out into a small square. Police officers leaned against their cars, arms folded, looking bored. Quaresma was marching around, shouting instructions in Portuguese.

The first officer sniffed, taking his eyes off a hen party across the road. 'Is your apartment down here?'

'I'm police.' Hunter flashed his warrant card. 'What's going on?'

'I need you to move on, sir.'

'We need to speak to Inspector Quaresma.'

Chantal slapped his hand away. 'Craig, we should go.'

The officer smiled at Hunter. 'You should listen to your girlfriend here.'

DI Bruce followed him. Didn't look good, whatever it was.

Hunter nodded over at him. 'Is this about Harry Jack?'

'Move on, sir.'

'Come on, Craig.' Chantal pulsed Hunter's hand and led him away.

'Chantal!' Bruce was jogging towards them, his coat flapping behind him. 'Look, we're two skulls down and this lot have given us intel on a sighting at the arse end of town. We need to run a raid. Can you help?'

39

CHANTAL

Chantal sat back in the passenger seat. Booze swilled in her guts and veins. *Doesn't feel like the right thing to do, but it might curry favour with Quaresma, so...*

Bruce tore through night-time Albufeira, heading away from the clubs and pubs towards a residential area. Houses set back from the road, blocks of flats hugging it. The occasional shop or café. Street lighting was optional, clearly.

Hunter was in the back seat, tapping away at his mobile. Better not be texting Finlay. He pocketed it and leaned forward. 'So, what, you've got a sighting of this kid?'

'All we've got, mate.' Bruce turned right at a roundabout, blasting down an empty road. The satnav on his dashboard pointed a blue line towards a street more than a mile away. 'This whole thing started out because someone called us, saying they saw the kid. Recognised him from their Sun or Mirror or whatever. Trouble is, she spoke to the papers as well. So, we're here chasing our tails while all hell breaks loose. Absolute nightmare.'

'Does she work at a bar?'

Bruce craned his neck round to glare at Hunter. 'How the hell did you know that?'

'Coincidence.'

'Right, well. Aye, she does.' Bruce tugged at his collar and powered down the road. 'We had a word with her earlier. Stupid cow should've kept her mouth shut. Couldn't back it up. Kid might not even bloody be in the country anymore.'

Chantal waved ahead, the white lines dancing around in her vision. 'So where are we going?'

'Someone else called us up tonight. We thought it was another one of those things, you know? Sighting that came to nothing. But we raided a flat off that hellhole where you were. Found this woman hiding in the bath. She said she'd seen Harry out this way. Then we got another call, right? Same story, saw the kid near this house. Could even describe him, wearing the same clothes as when he got taken. Gave us an address.'

'Which is where we're heading?'

'Right.' Bruce sighed. 'Aye.' He cleared his throat. 'Look, I asked you pair to help because it might ingratiate you with our chum Quaresma.' He tossed over a pack of gum. 'But chew that, for Christ's sake. Pair of you smell like a brewery.'

40

HUNTER

'Go, go, go!'

Hunter burst into the house and clattered up the stairs. A pair of uniforms stormed into the living room. He grabbed hold of the wooden banister to keep him upright as he climbed. He tripped and went flying, cracking his head against Chantal's leg. Pushed her over on the landing, the carpet bunching up around her hands. 'Watch it!'

Bruce was standing over them, face red with fury. 'What are you playing at?'

Hunter helped Chantal up. 'Caught my footing on the carpet there.'

'Get up, you pair of arseholes!'

Hunter followed Bruce over. Two doors led off. The first was a bathroom. One of Bruce's plainclothes was hovering over the bathtub, shaking her head. 'Not in here, guv.'

'Right.' Bruce stood one side of the other door, holding up a finger. Then two, then three with a nod at Hunter. 'Go!'

Hunter tried the handle. Locked. He shouldered the door and tumbled into a bedroom. The curtains twitched. He charged over and pulled them open. The window was locked from the inside, the key still in.

'Out you come.' Bruce was kneeling on the bed.

Three pairs of hands appeared, including one child's. A man raised himself up to standing. Looked English from his weak chin. Maybe French or German, but certainly not Portuguese.

Then he helped up a woman. Looked local, dark hair and olive skin. She shook her head. 'No, no, no.'

'Out you come, Harry.' Bruce reached and lifted up a small child, kicking and screaming.

Blonde hair, blue eyes. Wearing pink.

Not Harry Jack.

41

CHANTAL

Bruce pulled up down the street from the Strip. He killed the engine and sighed. 'Tell you, Chantal, I thought that'd be my ticket out of here, but no.'

'I'm disappointed in you, Jon.' Chantal spat her gum into a tissue and stuck it in the ashtray. The car reeked of cheap cigarettes and that hideous aftershave Bruce wore. 'A seasoned DI like you shouldn't have any hope left.'

Bruce laughed. 'Must be all the sun here, or something.'

'Right, well, make sure Quaresma hears about us helping.'

'Almost breaking your necks on the stairs.' He shook his head. 'I swear.'

'That wasn't my—'

CRACK.

Behind Bruce, two faces beamed in. Rich McAlpine and his hipster mate. Bruce wound down the window. 'Evening, lads. Do you need someone to wipe your arses or something?'

Rich nodded at Chantal. 'Wonder if you wanted to answer some questions about that raid.'

'What raid?'

'Don't be a fanny. Me and Liam know what's been going on. You found him, didn't you?'

Bruce wound up the window. 'Pair of pricks.' He smiled at Chantal. 'You fancy getting a drink later?'

She yawned. 'Going to get an early night. Maybe tomorrow?'

'Right. Tomorrow.' Bruce got out of the car and grabbed Rich and his mate by the arm. 'Come on, lads, let's go for a coffee and you tell me what you know.' He plipped the locks and led them off.

Hunter appeared from the other side of the car. 'You're going for a drink with him?'

'You feel threatened?'

'Hardly.' Hunter chuckled, but it didn't look like he meant it. 'So what's the plan?'

'We've lost the scent of Tulloch and his mates.' She started walking towards the thump and flash of the Strip, yawning into her fist. 'Let's see if we can pick it up.'

42

'So, where the bloody hell is he?' Chantal stood at a crossroads, hands on hips.

More of the Strip crawled up the hill, but it looked more like accommodation than drinking dens. Grimy old bars lined the side streets to the left and right. A golf tee-shaped building loomed up, lit up in blue from below.

'I don't fancy our chances up there, Craig.' She swivelled round. Flashing blue lights burst out at the top of the hill behind them.

Hunter shrugged at her. 'I think we should retrace our steps.' He stuffed his hands in his pockets. 'There are at least four clubs we only glanced into. They could've been on the dance floor or doing coke in the toilets. Anything.'

'We can't miss a group of twenty squaddies.'

'Maybe Tulloch and his mates haven't met up yet, or they've branched off into smaller groups.'

Made sense.
Made almost perfect sense.

She glanced at her watch. *After ten. Christ.*

Tulloch isn't here. One last sweep and that's it.

'Come on, then.' She grabbed Hunter's hand and paced off up the street, swerving between two groups, one dressed in old football kits, the others as Native Americans and not very tastefully at that.

'You okay?'

'I need a drink.' Chantal stopped by a bar and folded her arms. Bar Shooters. Classy as hell. A middle-aged man stood outside, dressed as a pirate. That or Captain Morgan from the rum bottle. He was handing out vouchers to passing piss artists, his eyes empty, like each voucher was a little bit of his soul. Two men in Fitch T-shirts pulled him in for a photo.

Outside the bar next door, a fat man in a polo shirt sucked on a cigarette then proceeded to vomit on a window.

Chantal took two vouchers from the pirate. 'Did we try in here, Craig?'

'It looked empty earlier.'

'That's no, then. Come on.' Chantal entered the bar, stretching deep into the building, longer than she expected. Two fat men strutted on the dance floor, gyrating to some two-step like they were kids.

A bar filled most of the front, decorated like a desert island with coconut trees and bamboo, a hen party stood beside it, getting their free shooters. The barman poured out of an unmarked bottle. God knows what it was. Meths. Ethanol.

Chantal handed over her vouchers to the barman.

'Cheers, princess.' Essex boy, spiky blond hair and a vest with torn-off sleeves. 'Coming right up.' He tipped the unlabelled spirit into glasses.

Chantal took them with a smile and gave one to Hunter. She sniffed the drink. Had a citrus tang to it. *Toilet Duck, maybe?* She downed her shot and grimaced. 'That's... Wow.'

Hunter took a sip of his. 'I'm not drinking that.'

'Go on, you big jessie.'

'Come on...'

She raised her eyebrows, trying a bit of peer pressure. 'Got to keep up the cover.'

'Sod it.' Hunter threw it back. 'Jesus.' He gagged, like Ricky was still grabbing his throat.

A gaggle of women in pink piled in through the door, a middle-aged one waving her free shot voucher. 'Woo!'

The music turned up a notch, the off-kilter beat rattling her fillings. Typical Scottish diet growing up. Too many sweets.

Hunter leaned in to whisper into her ear. 'When did music get shit?'

Chantal started swaying to the beat. 'I like two-step.'

'This is just... Ugh.'

'Wow!' Bekah, the skinny girl from the hotel bar, wrapped her arms around Chantal. 'Oh, this is so cool!'

Shite, the state of her. She should be in bed.

43

HUNTER

Hunter stepped away from Chantal and Bekah. *Wasted. Someone needs to keep an eye on her.*

The dance floor filled up with a group of lads. One wore full Highland gear, a dangling foam cock hanging below the line of his kilt. Completely out of his skull.

Hunter walked outside, his throat burning. Either from being strangled or the turps he'd necked.

Captain Morgan was still handing out vouchers. People were taking, but nobody was buying.

Hunter smiled at him and held up his phone, showing the photo of Tulloch. 'Have you seen this man tonight?'

A gang staggered towards him, dressed as Australians in outback gear, corks dangling from their hats. One took a voucher and tripped over. He hit the ground at the pirate's feet, scratching at the ground for his voucher.

'Have you seen him?'

The pirate shrugged. 'I've seen a lot of things, my friend, but I try to forget them.'

Chantal stepped outside, her forehead creased. 'Good news. Ish. Bekah's lot stayed with Matty and Brownlee. They've seen Tulloch tonight.'

44

CHANTAL

Chantal left him behind, chatting to Captain Morgan. Footsteps rattled up behind her. 'We should call Quaresma.' Hunter, trying to grab hold of her wrist.

Chantal stopped and trailed a couple walking arm in arm on the other side of the road. 'Jesus, can you see that?'

Hunter frowned over. 'What?'

'It's Ricky and Kerry!'

'How the hell—' He started across the road.

Chantal grabbed his arm and stopped him. 'Come on, Craig.'

Hunter let them go.

Kerry swung round and scowled at them. 'Here you, you Paki bitch!'

Chantal clenched her fists. 'Say that again.'

Ricky took one look at Hunter and knew he was beaten. 'Come on, love. She's not worth it.'

'She's a dirty bitch!' Kerry spat at them. 'Go back to your own country!'

'You're in Portugal, you daft cow.' Chantal's heart thudded. Like all those pricks at school. Everyone who spat on her dad's shop.

Everyone who put shit through their letterbox. Like that lecturer at uni who tried it on and got knocked back. Like any stupid scumbag she picked up as a cop. 'And Scotland is my country!'

She let them go down the Strip.

Hunter grabbed her and pulled her into a tight hug. 'It's okay.'

'It's far from okay.' She shrugged him off and sighed. 'Right, let's get Tulloch.' She barged round a group of women guarding a girl vomiting on the street. 'She said they're over here.'

Mambo thudded out into the night, enough neon to light up the sky. A bar in the middle, ad hoc dancing and drinking all around it. Just inside the door, a woman who looked about twelve danced with a man who looked about forty.

Over the other side of the bar, two of the guys from the hotel were drinking and chatting to two blonde women, both of them struggling to stand up. Matty and another beefcake, similarly big. Not Brownlee, but not far off.

And between them, perched on a stool, Sean Tulloch.

At bloody last.

He got up. Six and a half foot of muscle and rage. Looked bigger in the flesh. Thick muscle padded his shoulders, a tight shirt showed off his physique. What no photo could get across was how the light caught his eyes, almost sparkling. Mischief and danger hidden in his grin, suggestive of something worth risking.

45

HUNTER

'Come on.' Hunter stomped off towards Tulloch. He felt Chantal grabbing his shirt, pulling him back.

'Wait. I'm calling Quaresma.'

'Fine.' Hunter kept his eyes on his target.

Tulloch stood between that Matty guy and another lump of gristle, chatting to an older woman, dark haired. Another couple of girls lingered around. Tulloch's target tried to stand up from the stool but fell over. Her eyes were rolling back in her head. Tulloch picked her up and plied her with another sip from a tall glass.

'Shite.' Hunter shut his eyes. 'Do you see that?' He got out his mobile and called Quaresma. Two rings and it went to voicemail. 'Cheeky bastard's bounced it.' He redialled.

Didn't even ring. Quaresma breathed hard into the receiver. 'What is it, Constable?'

'We've got sight of our target.' Hunter locked eyes with Chantal. 'We need two or three of your officers to secure him.'

'This is going to have to wait.' Quaresma was out of breath, panting into his phone. 'We're in the middle of a complicated operation. Tomorrow, as agreed.'

Click.

Hunter pocketed his mobile. Tulloch's hands were snaking all over the woman. 'Looks like we're on our own.'

Chantal stared at Tulloch, shaking her head, nostrils flaring. 'He's not getting away with this.'

'We should tail him. Keep an eye on him until—'

Tulloch shoved the woman's hand down the front of his shorts and snogged her.

'Sod this.' Chantal barged into the bar, separating the child-woman and her sugar daddy, and made straight for them.

Hunter followed her in, getting a grunt from sugar daddy.

Tulloch towered over Chantal. 'What's up, princess?' He grabbed his crotch. 'You want a portion, do you? Never had a Paki before—'

Chantal scratched at her eyebrow. 'What do you think you're doing?'

'There's enough of my knob to go around.'

Chantal gritted her teeth. 'Paisley Sanderson sends her—'

'Shite!' Tulloch pushed the woman into Chantal. She tumbled across the dance floor. Tulloch lurched forward and cracked Hunter with a punch to his left cheek.

Stung like a bastard. Hunter windmilled his arms as he staggered backwards. He bumped into someone and hit the deck in a heap, landing in stale beer and sticky cocktails. Somebody landed on him, squeezing the wind out like an accordion.

Then the heel of a flip-flop cracked into his side and Tulloch barged through the dance floor.

Hunter freed himself from the man on top of him and pushed himself to his feet in one go.

No sign of Matty or the other squaddie.

Chantal lay prone under a pair of bar stools.

Hunter grabbed her under the armpits and pulled her up. 'Are you okay?'

She nodded and rubbed at her chin. 'I'll look after this lot. Go get him!'

Hunter followed the parting of the crowd. The Strip thronged with drinkers up and down the hill. Walking, always walking.

Across the road, Tulloch cut down the lane where Quaresma had been earlier. *No sign of any police.*

Hunter darted over the Strip and tried to pick up speed, a spearing pain digging into his side. Felt like he'd cracked a rib or something.

Tulloch had slowed to a jog, his flip-flops going shlup-shlup-shlup. No doubt thought he'd got away from them.

Hunter hurtled into the back of him and pushed him over. Tulloch twisted to the side as he rolled.

Hunter landed on the ground, cracking his knee off it. Pain seared up his leg, up his left side.

Tulloch was on his feet already, scanning around the area. 'Who the hell are you?' He moved back slightly and lifted his hands, one foot forward getting into the basic stance.

Hunter pulled himself up to a sitting position and flipped up to standing. He stepped into the pose, trying to ignore the burning pain in his knee, trying to give the immediate area a once-over. No obvious danger. 'I know what you were up to in there.'

Tulloch was bouncing on the balls of his feet. 'You jealous, you big poof?' He lurched forward and launched a punch at Hunter's head. Missed by miles.

Hunter got a punch to his gut as he followed through. Then Tulloch pushed him against the wall. Another missed punch, hitting brick. Tulloch yelped. Hunter deflected another blow and smacked Tulloch on the chest. He crunched his knee into Tulloch's groin and pushed away from the wall, then stepped back into the stance.

Tulloch shot backwards into his pose. Then jolted forward and lashed out with his left fist. Then feinted right and crunched a rising knee.

Hunter tried to parry it with his hands but staggered back.

Tulloch jabbed at Hunter three times, each blow rattling the bones in Hunter's forearm. Fists darting towards his hands, blocking his face.

Footsteps thundered from behind.

Hunter blocked another blow and backed away from Tulloch. He glanced behind him.

Tulloch got a shot into his left knee.

Hunter tumbled over, cracking his shoulder off the ground.

Another kick hit his back.

Footsteps raced away. Shlup-shlup-shlup.

Another blow hit Hunter's spine. Felt like it'd shifted his kidneys a few inches. Hunter lashed out with his feet and smacked his sole off something. The crunch of a cheek. Something metallic clanged off the ground.

He tried to spring to his feet. His knee wasn't having it. He did a quick scan of the area.

Tulloch was gone.

'You're a nosy bastard!' Ricky was staggering towards Hunter, holding a length of metal pipe over his head. 'That was between me and my wife!' He swung it down, aiming for Hunter's skull.

Hunter kicked up with both feet bending back the fingers of Ricky's left hand. The pipe clattered to the ground and rolled away.

Now!

Hunter pushed up to his knees and jumped low at Ricky. He caught his legs and pushed him back into the wall.

Hunter tore his knee into Ricky's gut and lashed a fist into his face, then grabbed hold of his throat. He looked around, his heart pounding. His breathing sounded distant, like someone else's. Blood pumped in his ears, poured into his mouth from somewhere.

The pipe rolled down the lane. A man stopped at the end and looked their way, then walked off.

No sign of Tulloch.

No sign of anyone else, either.

He tightened the grip around Ricky's throat.

'Pare!' A voice roared out from the right. 'Stop!'

Hunter spun back towards the Strip.

A local cop stood a few metres in from the main drag, his rifle trained on Hunter. 'Get off him.'

Hunter raised his hands. 'You need to arrest this guy.' He kicked at the pipe. 'He threw that at my head!'

Quaresma appeared alongside the cop, shaking his head. 'Constable, Constable, Constable.'

46

CHANTAL

Chantal gasped out her breath. Felt like a cracked rib and a load of bruising. She tried to sit up, but her chest screamed out. Probably hadn't cracked the rib, but it still hurt. The dance floor had pretty much emptied, the sight of two big lads fighting enough to send everyone fleeing.

The two girls swayed around next to her, nowhere near controlling their movements. One blonde, one dark-haired. Both skinny.

The blonde girl opened her left eye and tried to focus. 'Where's Sean?'

A tall woman wandered over, head tilted to the side. 'I'm the bar manager.' West Country accent. 'What's going on?'

'I'm a police officer.' Chantal couldn't find her warrant card. 'These women have had their drinks spiked.'

'What can I do to help?'

'Call the police.'

'Sure thing.' The manager disappeared through the crowd of rubberneckers.

Chantal hefted the stools upright and rested them against the wall. Much heavier than they looked. 'Sit here.' She helped the first woman onto the seat, like a small child or an old lady. 'Take your time.'

'I love him.' Both eyes clamped shut. 'I looooove him.'

Chantal rested a hand on her shoulder to stabilise her. 'What are your names?'

Dark-hair burped, eyes shut. 'I'm Nora.' A melodic rasp, Belfast by the sounds of it. 'This is me cousin, Siobhan.' She patted blondie on the back. 'Have you seen Heather?'

'Not for aaaaages.' Siobhan wobbled around on the stool. 'Where's Matty? He's *lovely*.'

'Nora, I need you to focus, okay?' Chantal looked around the place for the drinks Tulloch had been forcing on them. Some crumpled plastic cups and a big puddle. A cleaner swept his mop through the liquid.

Shite.

The bar crowd were all outside, looking back in. The manager waved over, her hand in a telephone shape, then gave a thumbs up.

'Where's Sean?' Nora opened her eyes, but her pupils were swimming around. 'He's got a massive wanger.'

Chantal held her shoulders. 'Can you understand me? Sean spiked your drinks.'

'Whaaaat?' Nora's head lolled forward. 'He's *lovely*. He bought us cocktails! They're *lovely*!'

Getting bloody nowhere.

Someone grabbed Chantal's arm. 'Step away, miss.'

She swung round.

Two uniformed police officers, one male, one female, both armed. The female officer stepped forward. Lantern jaw. 'What's going on?'

Chantal looked at the two girls. Barely in their twenties. She had to hold Nora tight. 'Their drinks have been spiked.'

The uniform stared at her partner. 'One second.' The uniform stepped away and spoke into her radio.

Chantal smiled at the girls, though only one of their four eyes was open. 'It's going to be okay.'

Keep telling yourself that...

'Okay, madam.' The uniform was back, her jaw set even squarer. 'My partner is going to take them to the hospital.'

'I'm going with them.'

The uniform shook her head. 'That's not going to happen. I've to take you to the station.'

47

HUNTER

Quaresma thundered down the single carriageway, the patchy street lighting not exactly giving a clear view of their route. Palm trees lined the road, not quite blocking out a brilliant white monstrosity hulking on the left. It looked like it'd been built upside down.

Hunter was in the back, cracking his knuckles. He stretched out his knee and got a different timbre of crack. Felt about twice the size of the other one. His arms were peppered with tiny burns where Tulloch had punched him. Felt like he needed a new back.

The car smelled new, like the leather seats were fresh from the tannery. Local radio droned out at a low volume, loud enough to make out that it was people speaking, just not which language.

Hunter got a click from somewhere in his ribs. He pressed a bruising hand to it, red welts rising up his forearm. 'I said, where's DS Jain?'

'I heard you.' Quaresma swung right through a tight gap into a car park next to the white building. He slammed into a space by a bare brick wall and killed the engine. Then he sat there, drumming his thumbs off the steering wheel. 'Get out.'

Hunter tried the door and it clicked open. The pale grey mosaic glinted in the street lighting. Bloody stuff was everywhere. He leaned against the Audi's roof. 'I can't see her.'

'Constable, come with me.' Quaresma waited for Hunter to shut his door before plipping the locks, then he marched over to the station. He held the front door, breathing slowly. 'Inside.'

Hunter shook his head and stood his ground. 'What happens if I go in there?'

Quaresma rolled his tongue across his teeth. 'Get inside, Constable.'

'You've not arrested me or anything, so...'

A squad car trundled to a halt nearby. The officer with the rifle got out and opened the back door. Ricky seemed to take a week getting out. He scowled over at Hunter, then burped into his hand.

'Come with me.' Quaresma marched inside.

Hunter followed him in. Couldn't even be bothered to shrug.

The station was quiet, a bored desk sergeant in full uniform sticking his nose into a local newspaper. Harry Jack's cherubic face stared out of the front, haunted and lost, like the kid was already missing when the photo was taken.

Quaresma nodded at him as they passed and put his hand on a metal door handle. Looked gloomy inside, but not a cell. 'In here.'

Hunter stopped on the tiles, a few metres away from the door. 'This isn't a cell, so what is it?'

'Come with me.' Quaresma rolled his tongue over his lips. 'Now!' He grabbed Hunter's arm and tugged him into the room.

48

CHANTAL

Lantern jaw held a door open for Chantal. 'You wait in here.'

The room was spartan at best. Bare white walls, functional desks. Only one window in the room, six vertical slices of glass lit up sodium yellow from outside. The place was quieter than the grave, just the occasional drone of a passing car. A vehicle thundered past and screeched to a halt somewhere nearby.

Not the time to argue.

Chantal sat at the desk. Everything ached. 'Are those girls okay?'

'They're on the way to the hospital.'

'My partner, Craig Hunter. Do you know where he is?'

'I can't say.'

'Have you got him?'

'That's not for me to say.' She shut the door and left Chantal alone.

This is a disaster. Where the hell is Craig?

Tulloch is at large. Has Craig caught him? Has Tulloch got Craig?

And no sign of Matty or the other big lump. Three against one... Craig would be heavily outgunned.

The only good thing is stopping Tulloch raping someone. Focus on Nora and Siobhan. Watch what you drink, girls. Trust will cost you dear...

She dialled Hunter's phone. Still nothing, just voicemail. 'Craig, I'm at the station. Call me when you hear this.' She started tapping a message to Sharon:

TROUBLE BREWING HERE. CALL ME.

The door clicked open and she looked up. DI Jon Bruce walked in, a cheeky grin on his face. 'Evening.'

Chantal slumped back. 'Jon. What's going on?'

Bruce sat on the edge of the table, far too close to her. Brucie Boner, indeed. 'I was in the area. Quaresma called me, told me I was needed here. So here I am. We were responding to a sighting on the Strip.'

'Do you know where Craig is?'

Bruce shook his head. 'Didn't even get the kid, either. Another false alarm.' He adjusted his cufflinks, big spangly things. 'Starting to doubt he's still here.'

'Think you'll find him?'

'Doesn't matter what I think.' Bruce shot her a wink. 'Now, what trouble have you got yourself into?'

She huffed out breath. 'We found him, Jon. The guy we're after. Spiking drinks, by the looks of it. She was in no position to consent.'

'One of those cases, eh?' Bruce got up and started pacing the room, just like he did when he gave a training course. Working up a flow, or whatever he called it. Looked so artificial. 'From what I gather, your boyfriend's in the shit.'

'He's not my boyfriend.'

'Sure about that?' Bruce's eyebrow pinched up. 'Sharing a room, aren't you?'

'Craig's a gentleman. He's on the sofa.'

'Right, right.' Bruce rubbed at the rogue eyebrow, like that was the only control he had over it. 'All I know is Craig got into a scuffle with someone.'

'Tulloch?'

'No idea, Chantal. Way Quaresma said it, he'll get done for fighting. Affray or God knows what they call it here. Maybe breach of the peace.'

'He was doing his job.'

'Not sure our mutual friend sees it that way.'

'He can take a running—'

'Here we go.' Bruce moved over to the window and sat against the sill.

The door opened and Quaresma stepped inside. Hunter followed him in, his head low.

'Craig!' Chantal wanted to wrap him in a hug but stayed sitting. 'Are you okay?'

Quaresma clapped Hunter's shoulder. 'He is fine.' He sat behind the desk and shrugged off his long jacket. 'But this is my country and you two keep on popping up.'

Chantal narrowed her eyes at Quaresma. 'We had Tulloch.'

'By breaching protocol.' Quaresma undid his tie and loosened it off. 'We had an agreement.' He pointed a bony finger at her. 'You were told to wait.'

'We called you and—'

'Sergeant.' Quaresma gripped the edge of the desk, his eyebrow cocked. 'I told you no! Tomorrow, yes?' He left a pause, but she wasn't going to fill it. 'You've ruined our operation! People like you—'

'People like me?' Chantal tilted her head to the side. 'You want to be careful what you're saying.' She nodded over at Bruce in the window. 'You've got witnesses here.'

'I don't mean the colour of your skin or wherever you're from, Sergeant.' Quaresma lowered his head, shrouding his eyes under heavy brows. 'I mean the attitude you've been raised with. You Brits think you can steamroller in here and do whatever you want, like you own the place.'

'You know what happened in that bar, right?' Chantal sat back in her seat, arms folded. 'Sean Tulloch spiked that girl's drinks. He was going to rape her.'

'And those girls are now in hospital, where they are being looked after at my government's expense.'

'I think you'll find that our government pays your country for that.' Chantal scowled at him. 'But it would be better if you had someone in custody for it, wouldn't it?'

Quaresma held her gaze, rubbing his fingers together, then glanced over at Bruce. 'We're going have to let Richard Smith go.'

Hunter frowned at him. 'Who?'

'The man you attacked on the street? The man you attacked at your hotel?'

'What?' Hunter raised his hands in the air. 'Why are you letting him go?'

'Because you assaulted him, Mr Hunter.'

'He attacked me when I was—'

'Mr Hunter!'

'—to arrest a suspect in multiple—'

'Mr Hunter!'

'—which you don't seem to be bothered to do anything—'

'ENOUGH!' Quaresma's voice rattled around the small room. He pulled out a sheet of paper and jotted a note on it. 'I have to keep reminding you whose soil you're on.'

Chantal got between them, waving her hands to try and calm the situation. 'Look, Craig and I prevented Tulloch raping that girl.'

Quaresma gave them mock applause. 'Well done.'

What the hell is he playing at? 'You are going to arrest him, right?'

'Sergeant, you need to learn to keep your hands to yourself. Especially when you're in someone else's country.'

'He tried to *rape* one of those girls.'

'I see it happen every night here. What can I do?'

'You can start by arresting him.'

'This is my country!' Quaresma thumped his desk, eyes drilling into Chantal. 'I run this operation. Not you. Not him. *Me*. This is how we play it.'

'Look, this is your chance to bring Tulloch in.'

'We agreed to meet tomorrow morning.' Quaresma dropped his pen on the desk. 'Given your inability to understand time and instructions, perhaps I will keep you here overnight? Nice comfortable cell for two, ah?'

Bruce cleared his throat and waited for Quaresma to look over again. 'João, let them go.'

'Excuse me?'

'We've got to get on with investigating that sighting of Harry.' Bruce gave a slow sigh. 'You agree with that, right?'

Quaresma sat back in his chair and snorted. 'Fine.' He jabbed a finger at Chantal then Hunter. 'We're going to be busy all night. I shall meet you at two o'clock tomorrow. Here. No deviation from that, okay?'

Second-class citizens...

'Okay, fine.' Chantal scraped her chair across the tiles and got up. 'Can we get a lift back to our hotel?'

Quaresma shook his head, chuckling. 'It's only a few kilometres walk.'

Hunter glowered at him. 'This is taking the piss a bit.'

'Listen, my friend, you've assaulted someone. Ricky is leaving the country. This is your last warning.'

∽

CHANTAL STOMPED along the side of the dual carriageway. 'Are you sure it's this way?'

'Think so.' Hunter checked his phone again. 'Still looks like the right way. Should end up at the Strip. Might be able to get a cab from there.'

'The Strip?' Chantal stopped and stuck her hands on her hips. 'Jesus, Craig.'

'All roads seem to lead there.' Hunter pocketed his mobile. 'I could call Finlay.'

'Don't.' She leaned against the wall of a house. 'Bloody hell.'

Hunter was still checking up and down the road, like that'd do anything. He looked over at her. 'You want to talk about this?'

She let her shoulders slump. 'No.'

'Sure?'

A taxi whizzed towards them. Hunter held out a hand and got a shrug in response.

Chantal sat on the kerb, her feet pressing down on the asphalt. 'I lost you. I'd no idea what happened to you.'

'I got seven shades of shite kicked out of me.'

'You could've died, Craig.'

'Takes a lot more—'

'Shut up.' She shook her head at him. 'You can't fight people all the time, you know? Especially three of them.'

'It was only Tulloch. Ricky must've seen me and...' He shrugged.

'Craig, Tulloch's bigger than you. At least as strong. You stupid bastard.'

Another taxi flew past.

'I don't get what Quaresma's playing at here.'

'Craig.'

'Look, sorry. But we did stop those girls being raped.'

'As harsh as this sounds, I don't give a shit about those girls if you're lying dead somewhere.'

He grinned. 'So you do love me?'

Prick. She looked away. 'Piss off.'

'Sorry. I... Look, I'll try and keep the head, okay?'

'No, you *will* keep the head.' She wiped away a tear. 'If you want me to commit to you, it cuts both ways. I almost shat myself with worry, Craig.'

'Right.' He looked lost. Another glance at a passing taxi then he looked back at her. 'So, what are we going to do?'

'Wait for Quaresma.'

'Like I said, I don't *get* him.'

'He's in a bad situation. No resources, trying to maintain law and order in the Wild West. Then the world's press descends here looking for that kid.'

'Along with your Geordie boyfriend.'

She fixed him with a steely glare. 'Craig...'

'Sorry. But I know what you mean. Quaresma's up against it. Maybe our agenda isn't quite meshing with his.'

Chantal leaned forward. 'So, we go back to Scotland with our tails between our legs?'

Hunter stared at her then he turned away. 'I'm trying to be positive.'

'I understand. It's...' She bit at her lip. 'Craig, we're... nowhere.'

'Well, that's great, because I've had the living shit kicked out of me and I'm glad my efforts have been so successful.'

'Stop being a drama queen.'

'Look, I'm black and blue all over.' Hunter stood over her. 'I narrowly avoided getting brained with a steel pipe.'

She looked up at him again. 'You okay?'

'I'll live.' Hunter held out a hand and winched her up. She let him. 'Look, Quaresma's not going to help us, is he?'

'I doubt it.'

'So, we need to track down Tulloch and bring him in when Quaresma's ready.'

Chantal took his hand. 'Which is exactly what's pissed him off.'

'I'll try and keep the martial arts to a minimum.'

'Well, that'll be a start.' She almost laughed. Almost. 'But, we're back to square one. We've no idea where Tulloch is.'

'Not quite.' Hunter shrugged. 'He's staying at our hotel complex, right?'

A taxi swung round the bend, its yellow light on.

Hunter stepped out and flagged it down. 'Someone's got to have seen him.'

49

HUNTER

There was a light on in Ricky and Kerry's apartment. No shouting or screaming.
If that pipe had connected... Can't believe Quaresma let the bastard go.
Hunter huffed out a sigh. *Jesus, just ignore them.*
They were in the small garden between apartment buildings.
Chantal whisper-shouted at him. 'I can hear something.'
Hunter listened closely. Deadly quiet, except for a TV booming out from the far side of the quad. Traffic droned past. Could almost hear the bass-drum din of the Strip from here.
But there was something weird. A sort of moaning sound.
He frowned at her, not that she could see him in the darkness. 'What is it?'
'It's over there.' Chantal pointed into the pitch black, right in the middle where the lights failed to cover. 'Come on.'
Hunter flashed on his phone's torch. *What the hell is it? A victim of Tulloch's, moaning as she wakes up? Hotel security after Tulloch assaulted them?*
He shone a light on a patch of ground. Something moved,

something fast. He stepped closer. It jumped towards him. He stumbled away. 'What the hell is that?'

Chantal squinted into the light then let out a groan of her own. 'Frogs.'

'Frogs?'

'Yes, Craig. Frogs.'

Looked like a spring, water pouring out at the top. Dark green foliage surrounded a tree. Tiny little frogs jumped up and down in a pool, making a hell of a racket this close up. 'Well, that's a result, I suppose.'

Hunter switched off his torch. 'What are we going to do, then?'

Chantal shrugged. 'Start again tomorrow.' She looked over at the bar area. 'Night cap?'

'Night cap.'

∽

HUNTER STARED into the fizzing lager, the glass pretty much exactly half empty.

'You okay?' Chantal's fingers were cupped around her glass, just a splodge of red at the bottom.

Hunter took a swig. *Still tastes like shite. Horrible stuff.* 'I saw that Ricky twat. Well, a light on in their room.'

She grabbed his hands, her fingers warm and soft. 'You stopped him murdering his wife.'

'I merely delayed it.' He broke his hands free. 'It's his fault Tulloch got away. He went after me with a length of pipe. If he'd cracked me over the head...'

'Shite.' Chantal shut her eyes and sighed. 'Craig, you need to stop getting into those situations.'

'You told me to go after Tulloch.'

'Did I?' She screwed up her eyes. 'I'm sorry. Look, you almost got him.'

'Almost got brained.' Hunter battled through his revulsion and finished the beer in one long gulp. 'I met my match. Tulloch does Krav Maga, too. And he's got power behind all that... evil. We need to watch what we're doing with him.'

'What, so we let Quaresma deal with him?'

'Of course.' Hunter grabbed their glasses and got to his feet. 'Right, one last drink before bed?'

She gave a tiny nod.

Hunter walked over to the bar. The place was quiet, just a crowd of older people winding down. He smiled at the barman. 'Two glasses of whatever the red is.'

'Rioja, my friend.' The barman unscrewed a bottle and poured some wine into a waiting glass.

Hunter nodded and leaned in close. 'Has our friend been back?'

The barman tipped the last of the wine in and reached behind him for a fresh bottle. He twisted the cap off and topped up Chantal's glass. 'Not tonight.' He started pouring into Hunter's. 'A couple of his friends were in earlier, causing chaos.'

'What sort of chaos?'

'All the same shit as earlier. Dancing on the tables. Taking their tops off. The security man had a word with them and they left.'

'Did you see where they went?'

'Sadly not.' He pushed the glasses over the bar. 'Seven euro.'

Hunter gave him a ten. 'Keep an eye out for them, okay?'

The barman gave him a nod.

Hunter collected the glasses and headed back to the table. 'Here you go.'

'Thanks.' She sniffed at her drink, frowning. 'Look, I was thinking. This shit about us being in the closet. How much does it mean to you?'

'At least as much as you. Why?'

'Well... I don't know. Back a few years ago, when Scott Cullen caught that serial killer... Well, he wasn't really a serial killer, but the press said he was.' She nibbled at her bottom lip. 'Scott and Sharon got together then. He ended up in hospital or something. Anyway, they started seeing each other. Two weeks later, they told their boss. Cullen got shifted to this total prick DS, I got shifted to Sharon.'

'So you did well out of it?'

Chantal shrugged. 'I've got my sergeant stripes now.'

'So, what are you saying?'

'That, I don't know.' Another shrug, her lips and forehead

twisted. 'Maybe it wouldn't be the worst thing. I could go back to the MIT, you could keep doing this.'

'This is important to you, though, right?'

'Of course it is.' She wrapped her fingers round her glass. 'What we do in this unit is important to me. You're important to me. I don't know what to do.'

'Well, we need another solution, then.' Hunter took a sip. Peppery and sweeter than he expected. 'Not bad.'

'You drinking wine is a weird sight.'

He took another sip, much better. 'When I was fifteen, I used to down a couple of bottles to get pissed before we went out.'

'Classy.'

'I'm a proud Porty boy.'

'Aye, and you haven't changed.' A big hand clapped him on the back. 'You twat.'

Finlay, gurning at them, his eyebrows dancing. *Bloody hell.*

Hunter swivelled round to face him. How much had he heard? 'What are you doing here?'

'Passing through, thought I might find you here.'

'Fin, I told you. There's nothing for you.'

'Get over yourself, Hunter. Took a lady out for dinner.'

Chantal frowned at him. 'Thought you were married?'

'Aye, was.' Finlay sat between them, twisting his car keys in his fingers. 'Mary chucked me out a few years back. Took me to the cleaners, too. Just as well we didn't have kids, I tell you.'

'Can I get you a drink, Fin?' Chantal took a sip of her wine. 'Look like you need it?'

'I'm driving.'

'Right. Sorry.'

'Wanted to see how you love birds were doing?'

'We're fine.' Hunter narrowed his eyes. 'And we're not—'

'I get it.' Finlay gripped Hunter's shoulder right where it bloody hurt. 'Your secret's safe with me.' He tapped his nose.

Chantal cleared her throat. 'So, this date?'

'Aye, not so good.' Finlay ran a hand over his chin. 'Maybe she thought the same about me, who knows?' He got to his feet. 'Look, if you need any help, I'm more than willing to step in, okay?'

'It's noted.' Hunter raised his glass. 'Safe drive back to Olhão.'

'Aye, see you Chantal.' Finlay waddled off, his straight-backed gait even worse than before.

'What a guy.'

'Sounds like he's bored, Craig.'

'Maybe he is. We can't use him, though.'

DAY 3

*Saturday
14th May*

50

HUNTER

'Gnnnnaawwww.'
 Sunlight burst through Hunter's eyelids.
 Head thumping. Mouth dry. Dying for a piss.
Shite, how many did we have in the hotel bar last night?
'Gnnnnaawwww.'
Christ, what is that sound? Like a chainsaw.
Hunter opened his eyes and turned over.
Chantal faced him, her hair plastered across her face, naked. The duvet kicked off her side of the bed. She hissed in air then snored it out. 'Gnnnnaawwww.'
Hunter wiggled the mattress and she snorted a couple of times.
'Gnnnnaawwww.'
Bloody hell. This isn't getting us anywhere.
He got out of bed. His phone was plugged in by the kettle. *Least I had the presence of mind to charge it.* He grabbed it and padded through to the bathroom. As he pissed, he tried checking his messages. Not a bad job, either, all in the pan.
10.04.

How did it get to that time?
Hunter sat on the lid. Didn't flush in case that woke Chantal.
'Gnnnnaawwww.'
Nothing would wake Chantal.
He flicked through the texts. Four from Finlay *after* him turning up in the bar. Desperate, much?
One from Murray:

CATS BOTH FINE. SUCH A CUTE COUPLE, ACTUALLY. LIKE YOU AND CHANTAL.

There was a photo. Bubble had let Muffin sleep next to her on her giant bed, far too big for a skinny little cat. The poor boy lay on the edge, though.
Hunter tapped out a reply:

THANKS FOR DOING THAT. THEY LOOK HAPPY.

The one person he'd trusted with the news. The one person not on the bloody job. His bloody brother.
'Gnnnnaawwww.'
A text flashed up. Elvis:

LYING BASTARD! KNOW YOUR SHAGGING HER.

Shite. Shite, balls, bastard.
Hunter replied:

THAT'S SHITE, MATE. WE'RE NOT.

He sent it and sat back against the cistern, rattling the porcelain.
'Gnnnnaawwww.'
Here they were, able to act like the couple they were because of the cover, and it felt right. And they'd bloody blown it. Back to uniform. Back to—
Bzzz.
Another text from Elvis:

QUIT LYING, DUDE. FIN TOLD ME.

Shite on a hamster wheel. Bastard. Stupid bastard.
Back to a squad car, chasing scumbags, responding to calls. Back to Steve and Dave. Fat Keith and his constant moans about his motor.
'Gnnnn— Craig?'
Do I tell her?
Of course I tell her. This is our problem. Not mine, not hers. Ours.
Hunter locked his phone and walked back through, his feet slapping off the cold tiles.

Chantal was squinting at him, her hair sticking up at all angles. 'What time is it?'

Hunter knelt on the edge of the bed. 'It's gone ten.'

She slumped back in the bed and dug her palms into her eyes sockets. 'We've slept in. Great.' She yawned. 'Think it was that early flight yesterday?'

'That or the amount of booze we put away.' Hunter held up his phone, showing the picture of the cats. 'See how well they're getting on?'

She smirked at it. 'They look so cute. Poor Muffin.'

'He's about twice the size of Bubble.'

'Like you and me.' Chantal snuggled into him and he eased himself back down on the worst mattress in the world. She rested her head on his chest. 'How much did we drink last night?'

'Not much, in the end.'

'Feels like a lot.' She brushed her hair out of her face and yawned again. 'Do you think Tulloch's run off?'

'Could've done.' The curtains flapped in the breeze, giving a glimpse of the bright day outside. 'Might still be here.' He ran a hand through her hair, stopping when he got to a knot. 'Chantal, I need to—'

'So what's the plan, Craig?' She swatted his hand away. 'We've got to meet your fan club at two. Right?'

Hunter put his phone away and lay back on his pillow, pulling her in close. 'Aye, but, look—'

'We should try picking up Tulloch's trail.' She batted his chest. 'Can't believe you let me sleep in.'

'Can't believe you got leathered.' Hunter kissed her forehead.

She smelled of broken biscuits. 'See this stuff about keeping us a secret?'

'Shh.' She put a finger to his lip. 'I'm hungry. Time for food. And coffee. Then we'll talk.'

'This is serious.' Hunter unlocked his mobile. 'Finlay overheard us. He's told Elvis.'

51

CHANTAL

Chantal slammed the door behind her and checked it was locked. Then again.

Can't believe we've been so bloody stupid. All that time, all that sneaking around, only for Finlay bloody Sinclair to find out. One careless moment and one of them was going to be booted away.

Back to the MIT. Working with Cullen, working for Methven. Bain, Stuart Murray, Simon bloody Buxton.

Hunter's shoulder were slumping as he walked ahead of her.

The MIT would be better than what was in store for him. They'd chucked him out before, weren't likely to take him back.

So it wasn't a choice.

She caught up with him and wrapped her hand round his, letting him lead her away. 'Craig, look, I'll take the heat, okay? I'll go back to the MIT. You can stay.'

'I appreciate it, but I don't think we'll get a say in it.' Hunter couldn't look at her as they climbed down the stairs. 'How's Sharon going to feel finding out from bloody Elvis?'

Chantal stared at the marble, sparks of light bouncing off.

He's right. I should phone her. Now. Tell her. Come out and...

What if he hadn't told her? What if he wasn't going to?

She let go of his hand and sped up towards the staircase leading to the restaurant area, a long balcony above the bar.

My head's not in the game yet. I need to think this through.

Too many variables. Too many things in play. What ifs like you wouldn't believe, stacked on top of each other. Hard to figure out who knew what and who'd do what armed with that information.

Hunter caught her by the bottom of the stairs, grabbing her hand. 'Can we go somewhere else?'

Chantal spun round and locked her arms across her chest, stretching her vest top at the sides. 'What? I'm *starving* and I need coff—'

Hunter glanced up the staircase. 'The bacon?'

'Isn't it just cold meats and cheese and stuff?'

Hunter's nostrils twitched. 'Well, someone's cooking the cold meat, then.'

She rolled her eyes and stared up at the sky. *Well played, girl.* 'Right.'

'Come on, Chantal. I don't want—'

She bounced down the step and kissed him on the lips. 'It's fine. We'll go somewhere else.' She grabbed his hand and led him away. 'But you need to sort it out.'

Hunter let go of her hand. 'I *just* need to sort that pesky PTSD shite out?' He shook his head at her, real anger in his eyes. 'You're pissed off because you can't have your bloody coffee. If I have another flashback... I can't believe you.'

Chantal shut her eyes. *Selfish bloody cow. This is when he's at his lowest and you're... Jesus.*

'Craig, I'm sorry.' She pressed her thumb against his palm, caressing it. 'You'll manage. Okay? I'll help you.' She stopped on the slabs in the full morning glare. 'And I'm being a total cow. I'm sorry. This shite with Elvis is doing my head in.'

He pulled her tight. 'It'll be alright.'

She pushed her head into his chest. He tightened the hug around her. She looked up at him. 'Do you think I should call—'

'Excuse me?' A woman stepped down the staircase, frowning at them. Blonde hair tied back tight. One of the girls Tulloch and Matty were forcing themselves on in that club. Nora, was it? She shivered in the sunshine. 'Chantal, isn't it?'

'Hi, Nora. Are you okay?'

'Breakfast has stopped serving, by the way.' She thumbed behind her. 'One of the bars up there serves a fry-up all day. That's where I'm heading.' She narrowed her eyes at them. 'You were in the club last night, weren't you?'

'Someone was spiking your drinks. I helped you.'

'Right.' Nora's shoulders collapsed back. 'Did you catch him, then?'

'He got away.'

'Jesus.'

'We're doing all we can to catch him.' Chantal rubbed Nora's arm. 'Did you go to hospital?'

Nora nodded. 'We got out at three.' She flicked up her eyebrows. 'I didn't know why the hell I was there. The cops are useless out here.' She nibbled at a painted nail, a crack forming in the purple sheen. 'You're cops, right?'

'Edinburgh.' Chantal coughed. 'Well, Police Scotland, but yes. We're cops. Sexual Offences Unit.'

'Are you after one of those guys?'

'Can't really tell you that.'

'Well, I hope you can't really cut his balls off.'

Chantal laughed and rubbed her arm again. 'Did they get anything they can use?'

'Wouldn't tell us.'

'Have you got the name of any local police officers?'

'Elena something or other.' Nora grabbed Chantal's hand. 'It's the big one, isn't it? Sean?'

'I can't say.'

Nora tilted her head to the side. 'Tell me. Please.'

'I'm sorry.'

'*You're* sorry?' Nora screwed up her face and scowled at Hunter, then back at Chantal. 'I...' She nibbled at her bottom lip. 'Look, are you after him or not?'

Hunter stepped forward and craned his neck low. 'We're here to bring him in.'

'What's he done?'

'He's a serial abuser of women. His latest victim is in Edinburgh Royal Infirmary right now.'

'Ah, shit.' More nibbling as her face pinched tight. 'Look, what he tried to do to us last night...'

'What?'

'Come with me.'

～

NORA PUT her keycard in the lock and it clicked open. She twisted the handle and stopped. 'Shit, I don't...'

'Come on, Nora, it's fine.' Chantal leaned against the door frame. 'We're trained in this sort of thing. Okay?'

'Okay.' Nora opened the door and led inside.

The apartment was bigger than theirs and faced due south, the sun belting in. One of the curtains was drawn across the patio door, shielding the room from the light. No signs of life.

Nora sat on the bed and prodded a mound of duvet. 'Heather?'

Nothing.

Nora nibbled at her lip. She shook her head and stabbed a finger into the mound. 'Come on, you. Get up!'

Nothing.

She shook the duvet and pulled it off. Nobody was underneath. 'Shite.'

Chantal looked over at Hunter, looking as worried as she felt. 'Where is she?'

'I don't...' Nora rubbed at her face. 'I don't know.'

'No idea?'

Nora shrugged. 'I can't think. Sorry.'

'It's natural if you've had your drink spiked.' Chantal gave her some space, let her settle down. 'Take us through this from the start. Who is Heather?'

'She's me cousin.' Nora sniffed, couldn't keep her focus away from the floor for longer than a second. 'We're here on another cousin's hen weekend. Flew over here on Thursday night, typical first night blues. Got hammered on the flight over, then we hit the Strip. Last time I remember seeing Heather was her chatting to that big lad in the bar.'

Hunter crouched down and showed her a CCTV screengrab. 'Was it him?'

'Sean...' She caressed it then her face twisted into a snarl. 'That's him.'

'And he raped her?'

A slight nod of her head. 'I think so.' Nora went over to the sink and poured herself a glass of water. She downed it, liquid sluicing down her hand. 'She's... Look. She didn't come out with us last night. Didn't speak to me all day. I thought she was too hungover, but... Some of the girls got chatting to those lads again. Sean just started on me, you know? I thought he was lovely, but...'

'But you think he raped her?'

'Well, I don't *know*, but I think so.'

'Come on, Nora. You *think so*?'

'She sort of said something, then she just stopped.' Nora tapped something in her phone and set it down. 'She clammed up. But...' She refilled the glass and held it in front of her face. 'Seeing you... It made me think.'

Had enough of this.

Chantal stepped over to the kitchen area. 'Let me get this clear. You don't have any idea whether she was attacked or not?'

'All I know is, she was chatting to this Sean guy the other night.' She put the glass down with a thud. 'Then she's in this state. I mean, come on. After what he tried to do to me and—'

Her phone rattled on the counter. She picked it up. 'I know where she is.'

52

HUNTER

Nora stood on the golden sand, her left hand shielding her eyes from the sun. 'There she is!' She started jogging towards a bridge leading to the sea. Metal handholds around wide wooden slats leading out to a pier. A woman sat halfway along, facing away from them, crouched down, rocking back and forth.

Hunter set off after her, trudging across the dry sand, much slower than he'd like. He clambered over the walkway's edge and slowed down as he approached.

Nora stood over the woman, rubbing her shoulder. She smiled at Hunter. 'Heather, these guys are cops.'

Dark hair, her lined face was blurred by smudged make-up. She wore a skirt, her handbag lying next to some Ugg boots. She looked up at Hunter and scowled. 'Nora!'

'Heather.' Nora flashed her a smile. 'These guys are from Scotland. They're looking for Sean.'

Heather looked over at them, suspicion knotting her forehead.

Hunter squatted down between the cousins, giving a warm smile. 'Heather, can I get you anything?'

She looked up at him, her eyes hiding behind her fringe. 'Who the hell are you?'

'I know what's happened to you.'

'Do you? Do you really?' Heather hauled herself up to standing. 'How the *hell* can you know what's happened to me, eh?'

'Your cousin told—'

'Get away from me!' Heather pushed Hunter.

He stayed rock solid, still squatting. 'It's okay, we know how you feel. You need to express that anger.'

'Get away from me!'

'Look, I'm a police officer. We're trying—'

'Piss off!'

'—to arrest Sean Tulloch.'

'Piss off!' Heather frowned at him. 'You don't say his name to me! Piss off!' She slapped him across the cheek.

Stung hard, like she'd taken a couple of layers of skin off. He kept his hands at his side, tried to control his breathing. 'Heather, we know you were drinking with Sean Tulloch on Thursday night.'

'Piss off!' She stepped forward, one arm raised to slap again. Nora grabbed her arm, pulling it down to her side.

'Did he buy you a drink?'

Heather disappeared under her hands, hiding her face and her eyes from them. 'I'm not talking to any of you. Piss off away from me!' She reached down and grabbed her handbag. Only caught one of the handles. The contents spilled over the sandy boardwalk. 'Oh, now look what you've made me do!' She bent down and started stuffing tampons, paracetamol and her purse back in the bag.

Nora's jaw clenched as she crouched down next to her. 'Heather, he spiked my drink last night.'

Heather looked up, frowning. Half the contents of her bag still lay on the sand. 'He what?'

'That Sean spiked mine and Siobhan's drink.' Nora thumbed at Heather. 'After he raped you.'

Heather collapsed back against the railings. 'Nora, will you keep your mouth shut?'

Hunter crouched between them. 'Heather, my name—'

'Leave me alone!' Heather shifted away from him. 'Piss off!'

'My name is DC Craig Hunter.' He got his warrant card out and held it to her. Her eyes widened as she looked at it. 'And this is DS Chantal Jain. We work for Police Scotland's Sexual Offences Unit.' He took his ID back. Then he showed his phone, the photo of Tulloch on the screen. 'This is the man you were drinking with, isn't it?'

'Heather!' Nora snatched the phone off him and waved it in her cousin's face. 'This is Sean! He spiked my drink as well!'

A tide of wind blew across the sand towards them, spiralling as it hit the walkway.

Heather stared at the phone for a few seconds. 'It could be him, I suppose.'

Sean Tulloch's twinkling eyes glared out of the screen, hiding the menace and evil.

I wish we'd arrested him back in Scotland. I wish he'd not been able to do what he's done to these women.

'I can only imagine how you feel right now. All the anger and rage and hate for yourself. It's natural. But it's not right. Sean Tulloch has a history of domestic violence against women. His latest victim is in hospital back in Edinburgh, fighting for her life.'

Heather leaned into Nora, shutting her eyes.

Chantal rested on the supports. 'What happened, Heather?'

Heather looked at Nora for a few seconds, then shut her eyes again. 'I don't remember.'

Hunter let the cool sea breeze hit his skin. His stomach growled. 'Heather, I know this is difficult, but it'd help us if you could tell us what you do remember.' He left a pause, waiting for her nod. He smiled at her. 'Nora said you're here on a hen weekend. Is that right?'

Heather ran a hand through her hair, sweeping it back. 'Look, I don't remember too much. We were down that Strip thing on Thursday night. Dancing and drinking, you know how it is.' She pressed the heels of her palms deep into her eye sockets. 'I feel so *stupid*.'

'Heather, this isn't your fault.' Hunter crouched down to eye level. 'Okay? None of this is your fault.'

Heather nodded but it didn't look like she believed it. 'I got speaking to this fella in one of the bars.' She scratched at her wrists, the flesh scored from her nails. 'Look, I got divorced last year. Not had a lot of luck with men since.' She stabbed a finger at the phone, still couldn't look up. 'This guy was charming. Lovely fella. Gorgeous eyes. Lovely smile. He asked if I wanted a drink. So I said, make it a double.'

Hunter got to his feet, leaving her some space but she wasn't filling it. 'Did he get you a drink?'

'Bacardi and Diet Coke.' She swallowed hard. 'I can still taste it. I can still see it fizzing away when I close my eyes.' She scratched at her wrist again. 'If only I'd not...'

'Heather, it's okay.' Nora was trying to stop Heather from scratching herself. 'You need to tell them what happened.'

'What happened?' Heather pushed herself up to her feet and got in Hunter's face, covering him in sour vomit breath. 'I woke up with him shagging me!' Spit flecked in the air, covered his cheeks and dribbled down her chin. 'And he was hurting me!'

Chantal smiled, looking like she was trying to act calm. 'This was in his bed, right?'

'Right.' Heather started pacing along the planks. 'Arsehole had taken me to his room. Some taxi bastard must have let him do that! The state I was in!' She wiped her bare arm across her nose. 'Sean fell asleep and I left. I got back to our room early. Late, whatever. Like five, six. Can't remember. It was still dark outside. I felt so disgusted with myself I just stayed in the room yesterday.' She cracked her hand off the walkway support, the metal ringing. 'And his cock... It hurt like... I'm so sore. Had to take eight ibuprofen...' She slumped back against the handrails. 'I've been pissing blood. It's like having me period.'

Hunter couldn't speak.

'Okay.' Chantal nodded at Hunter. 'We need to get you to the local police, Heather. Have you had a shower since the attack?'

'I had a bath last night.'

Another chance to stop Tulloch slipped through our grasp. All their bloody fears about him, his blood lust escalated by the leery atmosphere of a bunch of squaddies out on the lash. Heather was the cost of that.

Not arresting him in Inverness when he went for the train.

Not catching him at the airport.

Quaresma not arresting him when he landed.

Ricky battering Hunter and letting Tulloch escape.

Heather's anger turning in on herself because Tulloch wasn't behind bars.

Chantal held her glare. 'We're going to catch him and prosecute him for what he's done to you. Were there any witnesses?'

'Of course there wasn't.' Heather stared off towards the beach. Tears seeped out of the sides of her eyes, slicking down her cheekbones. 'Wait. There was someone in the other bed.'

Shite, what?

'I can only like see snatches, but I think...' Heather brushed away some tears. 'I think his mate was there. While this bastard raped me. He was there the whole time!'

Hunter reached into his pocket for his phone and a photo of Matty. 'Was it him?'

Heather shook her head. 'Smaller.'

Hunter found one from the CCTV, Gordon Brownlee lurking at the bar. 'Him?'

'Maybe. I remember him from the bar. He had these funny ears. They weren't the same height on his head.'

'Did he have sex with you as well?'

Heather shook her head again. 'He... was there. Watching. Prick might've been wanking.'

'Okay.' Hunter pocketed his phone. 'We're going to find him, okay? We'll arrest Sean and he'll do time for what he's done to you.'

'Look, I don't want any trouble.' Heather ran a finger across the marks she'd made on her arms. Dark bruises circled her wrists like watch straps. 'He... He's a big man. I don't...'

Hunter clenched his fists and scanned the area. 'Heather, we're going to make sure he can never do this again. We'll make sure he's punished for what he's done to you.' The beach was getting busy, though the cool breeze was picking up. He frowned at her. 'You said it happened in his room?'

∽

Hunter stopped dead and groaned. Could bloody see his and Chantal's apartment from Tulloch's, not even twenty metres away. He leaned back against the wall and dialled Quaresma's number, listening to it ring and ring. No answer. So he redialled.

Quaresma moaned into his phone. 'Yes?'

'It's Craig Hunter. I need you—'

'I can see it's you, Hunter.' Quaresma sighed. 'Two o'clock.'

'I need you to get some officers out here to enter a property.'

A pause on the line. 'And I told you, two o'clock.'

Hunter looked over at Chantal, her left arm wheeling as she spoke to McNeill on the phone. 'Tulloch has raped a woman.'

Quaresma gasped. 'What?'

'A Northern Irish woman. Look, we need your men to enter the premises and collect evidence.'

'Two o'clock.'

Click.

What the hell?

Hunter stared at his mobile. *He bloody hung up on me!*

53

CHANTAL

'Look, Sharon, we'll dig into it.' Chantal wheeled away from Tulloch's room, leaving Hunter to guard it. *What happened in there, what Heather went through at Tulloch's hands. Using his physical bulk to make sure he got his way, using his penis as a weapon.* 'It's likely he's raped this woman. It's on Portuguese territory, so our chum'll have to—'

Hunter scowled at her.

Chantal covered her mouthpiece. 'What?'

'He hung up on me.'

'Is he sending anyone?'

'Don't think so. Just said "two o'clock".'

Chantal stared at him, her jaw clenched tight, and put her phone to her ear. 'Right, Shaz, we need to escalate this. He's still dicking Craig about.'

'Well, I'm not promising anything.' Sharon sounded worn out. 'But leave it with me.'

'We need approval now.'

'Chantal, I said leave it with me, okay. Look, Elvis wants to speak to me. I've got to go.'

Don't need a million guesses to work out what that's about. Not the right time to tell her.

'Right.' Chantal pocketed her phone and stared at the door for a second. 'Craig, we can't. Any defence team worth their salt will—'

'I know. We'll have a little peek.' Hunter twisted the handle. 'Bloody thing's unlocked.'

Chantal snorted. 'You make Scott Cullen look professional.'

'Tell me to stop, then.' Hunter wiped his T-shirt on the handle and nudged the door open wide with his trainer. 'Can you hear that? Sounds like there's someone in there.'

'Go on.' She nodded and Hunter stepped into the room. She kept an eye on the door then entered it herself.

Gordon Brownlee was Tulloch's roommate. No sign of either of them, or anyone.

The bathroom door was ajar. Smelled like an open sewer mixed with mint shower gel. Didn't look like the toilet was working. Dirty bastards were just shitting on shit and paper.

In the main room, Hunter was over by the kettle, rummaging through a pile of stuff. 'Bloody nothing here.'

A little camera case sat to the side. Chantal opened it and pulled out the contents. Then held something up to show Hunter. 'Is this Tulloch's MOD90?'

He took a glance and nodded. 'He should be a bit more careful.' He got out his mobile and snapped a photo. 'Must think he's invincible.'

Chantal squatted down near a plastic shopping bag. A pair of jeans, some shorts and T-shirts. 'Looks like he's bought this lot here.' She padded over to Gordon Brownlee's side of the room. Neat piles of clothes, a trolley suitcase, coins ordered by denomination. Much less chaotic.

'Shite.'

She swung round.

Hunter held up the jeans, gripping them with a towel. A brown pill bottle poked out of the back pocket. He shook it out and Chantal picked it up between a pair of teaspoons, her tongue sticking out with the effort. A silhouetted image of a man, side on, standing up and penetrating a woman bending forward in front of him.

"HEAVEN"
(THE ORIGINAL U.S.A.)
GHB
PURE ECSTACY

Blood boiled in Chantal's veins. A smoking gun against Tulloch.

But... Jesus. That's how the guy thought.

Didn't explain how someone like Paisley could fall for his charms without chemical assistance.

She couldn't take her eyes off the logo. A bloody typo on the bottle, too. *Ecstasy, you raping arseholes.* 'How the hell did he get that into the country?'

'Maybe bought it here.' Hunter shrugged the pills back into the jeans, then dropped them back on the bag. 'Come on, we can't be here.'

Chantal followed him back out into the courtyard. 'Did you find anything that points to where he is?'

'Sweet FA.'

She hit dial and put her phone to her ear.

'Sergeant.' Quaresma gave a massive sigh. 'I told your partner, two o'clock.'

'Listen, we've reason to believe there is direct evidence supporting the rape allegation.'

Quaresma's sigh was even bigger this time. 'What?'

'We believe Tulloch had some Rohypnol.'

'Wait there.' Click.

Chantal pocketed her phone. 'He's sending someone over.'

'Finally.' Hunter huffed out a breath. 'So we're guarding it until they get here?'

'You got a better plan?'

Hunter shrugged. 'Brownlee isn't here.'

'So?'

'So, assume he comes back and sees us here. He must know we're cops by now. He'll tell Tulloch and he'll piss off out of here.'

'Assuming he's not gone already.'

'You want to take that chance?'

She grabbed his shoulder. 'Right, go over to the bar and see if they're there, okay? Then wait out front, while I guard here. There's only one way up. If you see him, warn me, okay?'

54

HUNTER

Hunter leaned against the front wall of the hotel and put his phone to his ear, listening to it ring. The bar was heaving now, not even noon and the shots were out. *Typical Brits abroad. Must make the rest of the EU so proud of us. Maybe a vote to leave in next month's referendum would spare the continent the worst of our behaviour. Doubt it. Probably make it worse.*

Chantal answered the phone. He couldn't see her from there. 'Room's still empty, Craig. Any sign of the cops?'

'Not yet. Negative on Brownlee, too.' Hunter looked up and down the street. No police cars, just the occasional taxi winding past the row of coaches. 'Five minutes and Quaresma's getting another call.'

'Better go.' Click.

Hunter pocketed his phone. *Bloody Quaresma.*

A Mercedes taxi pulled up and a man stepped out, jacket and jeans, his black shoes gleaming in the sunlight. Looked totally out of place with the sagging bodies tucking in at the bar. The driver lugged out a set of golf clubs and he trundled them inside, the passenger strolling ahead of him.

'Wa-haaaay!'

Four topless men wobbled about the bar area, half muscle, half flab. They downed drinks then tossed plastic shot glasses in the air, raining down on a middle-aged couple tucking into a bottle of red.

Too polite to say anything, their ears going the same colour as their Rioja.

Gordon Brownlee left the bar, carrying another tray of shots, blinking in the glare as he set the drinks down on the table.

Hunter took another look around. No cars approaching. Not much drone from the main road. He scanned through Brownlee's mates — Tulloch and Matty weren't there.

There was a third guy while Tulloch was spiking that girl's drinks... Where was he?

He tapped out a text to Chantal:

GOT GORDON BROWNLEE AT BAR. GOING TO APPROACH.

Then he thought about whether to actually go through with it.

Sod it, here goes. Another check of the road and he walked over to lean across the fence. 'Hey, Gordon?'

Brownlee gave a nod back and toasted him. 'Alright, mate.' Clearly didn't recognise him. Matty and Tulloch hadn't passed on anything about them. He downed the shot and strolled over, lugging a pint. 'What's up?'

'Tried catching up with Sean last night, but I couldn't find him.' Hunter shrugged his shoulders. 'Seen him today?'

Brownlee shielded his eyes from the sun. 'Not since first thing.'

Hunter nodded slowly. 'You're rooming with him, right?'

Brownlee squinted at him. 'Aye.' Could almost see the cogs whirring through his eyes. He got up and leaned on the fence, almost face-to-face with Hunter. 'You seem in an awful big hurry to see big Sean.'

'Fly back home tomorrow and I've not seen the prick. Not seen him in ages.'

'Right. Aye, well, he crawled back into the room in the wee small hours, you know?'

So where the hell is he?

Hunter flashed a grin. 'Still a shagger, eh?'

'Tell me about it. Not that I can talk.' Brownlee laughed. 'Out at the tits till the back of four.'

Hunter gave him a conspiratorial wink. 'Which one did you go to?'

'First one at the crossing. Classy place.' Brownlee gulped at his lager and bared his teeth. 'Anyhoo, Sean'll still be with Matty.' He shook his head. 'Dirty big bastard was up in my room at eight this morning, off his tits. Said he'd got back at six but couldn't sleep. Got hold of some sniff, probably. Sean perked up and they started tucking into it.'

'Why didn't you go with them?'

'I was pretending I was asleep. Those two pricks snorting coke and dancing to tartan techno on Sean's phone. Then big Geordie Keith pitched up with a bottle of voddie.' He took a swig of lager. Looked like it wasn't settling very easily. 'They went off to the pub at half eight, no sign of them since, likes.' He checked his watch. 'They'll head back soon for a kip, I reckon.'

A spear of pain stung Hunter's gut.

Chantal was up at the room. Three huge squaddies against her.

You stupid bastard.

55

CHANTAL

Chantal stood outside their room, eyes trained on Tulloch's door, phone against her ear. 'Still no sign of them, Shaz.' She did another scan. Bloody nothing. 'Craig went to wait by the bar. Not heard from him.'

'Well, there's nothing I can do, Chantal.' Sharon sounded like she was out and about, wind rustling leaves. 'Sorry.'

'Thought you'd like to know.'

'I've got better things to do on my day off than this shite. Not that I'm getting any time off.'

Chantal's phone buzzed with a text. She didn't check it. 'Sorry, but— Shite.'

A man was approaching Tulloch's room, swaying about as he staggered. Absolutely shit-faced. Carrying a chemist's bag. Christ knows what was in it. He leaned his head against the door frame and knocked. 'Gogs!'

Gogs?

Gordon?

Shite, he was looking for Gordon Brownlee.

'I've got to go.' She killed the call and pocketed her phone.

'Gogs! Come on, mate! Party's getting started!' Sounded like a Newcastle accent. He swung back round and faced her. *Shite.* It was the third guy from the bar last night. The third drink spiker. He locked eyes with her but looked right through. 'Right, get your cock away, you big poof, I'm coming in!'

The evidence! Shite!

Chantal darted across the quad towards him. 'Here, mate.'

His hand rested on the door. He gave her the up and down, stopping to linger on her boobs. 'What's up, sweetheart?'

'Gordon was looking for you?'

'Aye?' He pawed at the door, swaying. 'Thought he was here. Was this morning, anyway.'

'I was supposed to be meeting him and Sean at the hotel bar.'

He frowned. 'Who're you?'

'Jane.' She stood far enough away and held out a hand.

He lunged forward and reached out to kiss her hand. 'Pleasure to meet you, Jane.' He burped out vodka fumes. 'I'm Keith.'

'I've got to change my knickers.' Chantal winked at him. 'Gordon's getting a round in.'

'I was going to get a kip, but...' Keith leered at her. 'Bugger it, I'll see you over there, pet!'

56

HUNTER

Need to get away... Hunter nodded at Brownlee, sweat trickling down his forehead. Far too bloody hot, the sun felt Iraq strong. 'What bar do you reckon they're in?'

Brownlee took another swig of lager. 'Any. All.'

'Cheers, dude.' Hunter set off.

He bumped into a big lump of gristle and rugby. Eyes like holes in the snow, if they were deep red. Stank of neat vodka. 'Alreet, Gogs, how's it gannin', mate?' Thick Geordie accent.

'Keith, my man.' Brownlee slapped his arm. Looked like it took a layer of sunburnt skin off. 'You met Craig? He served with Sean in Kandahar.'

Keith eyed Hunter, gave him an ocular pat-down. 'Aye?'

Shite.

Tulloch's other accomplice from the bar last night.

Hunter nodded, struggling to keep his breath under control. 'We did Operation Diablo Reach Back. Must be 2006?'

'2006?' Keith straightened up, twisting his head to the side. 'You sure Sean was there?'

Hunter's guts churned. He grinned. 'He was just a pup.'

'Little virgin back then.' Keith held out his hand. 'Keith Brannigan.' He burped vodka fumes.

'Craig Hunter.'

Brownlee sank the last of his pint. 'Craig was asking after Sean.'

'Keep clear of that wanker.' Keith opened a chemist's paper bag and took out some eye drops. He dropped some into his left eye and blinked hard and fast. 'Had me contacts in two nights on a row. Feels like I'm going blind, man.'

'You seen Sean?'

'I tell you, I was seeing two of him after last night.' Keith squirted into the other eye. Then another squirt. 'Went up to that bar on the corner for breakfast. Cheap something or other. Matty bought a bottle of absinthe over the counter.' He belched. 'We finished it.'

Brownlee reached back for another pint of lager. 'After that voddie?'

'You keeping a tab, Gogs?'

'Not me.'

Hunter thumbed behind them. 'Sean still up there?'

'Nah, mate.' Keith scowled at Brownlee. 'You know what Sean's like. Fired into the waitress in there, chatting her up till her shift ended. Bought her a drink, then she started doing shots of absinthe with us.'

Tulloch plus women plus alcohol means trouble.

Hunter nodded slowly. 'Did he get lucky?'

'Bird was all over him, man.' Keith put his eye drops back in the bag and blinked hard. 'I'm broken.' He rubbed his thumbs deep into his eyes. 'Either of you got any Valium?'

'Clean out.' Hunter did a fake pat-down and huffed out air. 'I'll maybe take a walk up there. Might surprise him.'

Keith nodded, but his eyes were all over the tray of pints on the table behind.

'Right, I'll see you around.'

'Not so bloody fast.' Keith grabbed hold of Hunter's T-shirt and glowered at him. He scowled at Brownlee. 'Gogs, who is this prick?'

Brownlee opened his eyes wide. 'Said he's a mate of Sean's.'

Keith stepped forward, looming over Hunter. 'Who are you?'

Take him down now? That'll just make him clam up.

Hunter caught a flash of white from the left, over Keith's hulking shoulder. 'Tell me where he is and I'll be on my way.'

Keith took another handful of Hunter's shirt. 'Who the hell are you, mate?'

Hunter got in Keith's face. 'Where is he?'

Booze breath swept across Hunter's face. 'Piss off.'

Hunter gripped his wrist and twisted through, pinning it to Keith's back. 'Where is he?' He jerked it up. 'Tell me!'

'Sir.' A uniform tried to wrest Keith away. The lantern-jawed woman from the previous night. Didn't seem to recognise any of them.

Keith didn't budge.

'Sir, step away from him.'

Hunter tightened the grip.

'He's gone to a bird's flat!'

The cop pushed Hunter back. 'Get off him!'

Hunter let go. 'Which flat?'

'Up at that bar! Cheap and something!'

57

CHANTAL

Chantal scanned around the area. *Still no bloody cops. Still no sign of Tulloch or Matty. Or Brownlee. So many squaddies, all up to their necks in it.*
She fished out her phone. Nothing from Hunter since...
That text. She checked the message again.

GOT GORDON BROWNLEE AT BAR. GOING TO APPROACH.

And she'd just sent Keith down there.
She jogged off towards the bar. No sign of Hunter. A police car sat on the road, the blue lights flashing.
A horn blared and a black Audi pulled up next to her. Quaresma got out, stretching out his long coat. 'Sergeant.'
A stark choice — preserve the evidence or help Craig?
Chantal held up her hands. 'We've got something.' She started walking. 'This way.'
Quaresma followed her. 'What is it?'
'We need you to secure the room.' She stopped by the room

and pointed into it. 'We have some intel that he's got some GHB in there. Date rape drugs.'

Quaresma nibbled at his lips. 'And you think this supports the accusation last night?'

'It'll add to the girls' statements.'

Quaresma looked away.

She grabbed his coat. 'You have taken statements?'

'Not yet.'

Chantal sucked in a deep breath. 'Tulloch has raped someone on your territory. Why aren't you arresting him?'

Quaresma's eyes shifted in the sockets. 'Sergeant, we are—'

'Sir!' Behind Quaresma, a female uniformed officer pulled Hunter down the pavement. Lantern-jawed and focused. 'We have situation.'

Quaresma marched over and grabbed Hunter by the lapels. 'What do you think you are doing, Constable?'

Hunter nodded at Chantal then pointed up at the main road. 'I know where Tulloch is!'

58

HUNTER

Hunter swung round, fists clenched. *Tulloch isn't getting away this time, no random assaults, no saved-by-the-bell bullshit. Just him in cuffs, heading back to Scotland.*

The bar's veranda was rammed with early boozers. José the barman was clearing up a beer pitcher from the nearest table, frowning at a man in black jeans and a Slipknot hoodie holding a support column and vomiting into a heap in the corner.

Hunter bounded up the steps and grabbed José. Sweat and stale lager mixed with the acidic sick stink. 'Has Sean Tulloch been here?'

José looked over at Quaresma's Audi. Then gave a tight nod. 'He was here.'

'You didn't think to call me, like we agreed?'

'Sorry.'

'Was he talking to a barmaid?'

'Luisa.' José nodded. 'Get on like the house on fire.'

'Where did they go?'

José pointed to the side. 'Third one along, top floor.'

An alleyway ran past the bar, lined with lock-up garages, a stone wall about thirty metres back.

Quaresma joined them. 'Do we have him?'

'Not yet.' Hunter stamped down the steps and beckoned for the uniforms to follow them down the lane. Tall blocks of flats loomed up past the garages. Third one along, top floor. Looked like holiday apartments.

Hunter jogged down the street and climbed the steps to the front door. 'This one here.'

Quaresma joined him on the veranda and grabbed his wrist. 'This is on your head, my friend.' He nodded at him then tried the door handle. 'Okay. I lead, remember?'

'Absolutely.' Hunter held up his hands and stepped back.

The first uniform piled in, leaving the second on guard.

Hunter followed Quaresma in and powered up the stairs to the third floor. Three doors.

Bollocks.

Quaresma scowled at him. 'Which one?'

Hunter put his ear to the first. Quiet as the grave. Then he moved over to the middle door. Muffled screams came from inside. 'Here.'

'Stand back.' Quaresma waited for Hunter to comply and knocked on the door. 'Esta é a polícia. Abrir!'

No response.

Another knock. 'This is the police. Open up!'

Again, nothing.

'We enter now!' Quaresma twirled his fingers at the uniform. 'Quebre a porta!'

The local cop stepped back and launched himself at the door shoulder first. It toppled into the flat and the uniform tumbled in after it. He rolled out of the way.

Quaresma was in first, Hunter following.

Sunlight streamed into the hallway from a kitchen lounge area, misted by something that smelled a lot like skunk.

The scream was louder, came from a closed door to the right.

Quaresma tugged it open.

Tulloch was on the bed, naked. He held his hand over a woman's mouth, thrusting hard and fast. 'You like that, don't you?'

59

CHANTAL

'What's your name?' Chantal stood by Tulloch's apartment door, guarding entry.
Hope that Craig's getting somewhere with whatever bullshit he's up to.
The lantern-jawed uniform worked her way around the room, her blue gloves almost strobing in the sunlight. 'Elena.'
'Nice to meet you, Elena.' Chantal looked back out into the quad. A pair of lads in jeans ran towards the stairs carrying a giant inflatable dolphin. *Pair of wankers.* 'You find anything?'
'This.' Elena held up the bottle of GHB. Her male partner noted it down on a clipboard. She bared her teeth. 'Dirty man who is sleeping here.'
Chantal exhaled like it was the first time she'd seen it. 'That's disgusting.'
'We see this a lot.' Elena shook the bottle and popped it into an evidence bag. 'Your men come here and make women have sex with them.'
'I work in a sexual offences unit back home.'
A smile flashed across Elena's face. 'That is good.'

'When we can put someone away, aye.' Chantal waved around the room. 'The man who stays here, he's wanted for—'

'Hoy!' The voice came from behind Chantal. A hand grabbed her shoulder and yanked her back.

She stumbled over and landed on her side. Crunched her hip against the mosaic.

Gordon Brownlee stood over her. 'What the hell are you doing in my room?'

Chantal pushed herself up to a crab position, ready to kick out. 'We're searching it.'

'Aye, have you got a warrant?'

Elena appeared in the doorway. 'I don't need one.'

'Shit.' Brownlee's eyes darted around. *Prick's going to make a run for it.*

Chantal swept out with her left leg and jabbed her heel into his shin.

Brownlee fell backwards and cracked his head off the wall. He landed on Chantal, squeezed all the air out of her lungs. Somehow, he got a punch into her side. Then her stomach.

'Enough!' Elena lashed out with her baton and clattered it off Brownlee's skull. He slumped down, knocked out.

Chantal pushed him off and eased herself up with Elena's hand. 'Thanks for the save.'

'Is not a problem.' She prodded Brownlee with her baton. 'Are you okay?'

'Maybe.' Chantal caught her breath. Her gut felt like it was on fire. 'I'll heal in time.'

Elena held up the bag. 'Drug is maybe his?'

Chantal ran the logic through and got a better idea. She took Elena's cuffs and wrapped them round Brownlee's wrist. 'He's a witness to a rape.'

60

HUNTER

Hunter stepped into the room. 'Stop!'

Tulloch swung round and clocked him, clocked the local cops too. 'Shite!' He pulled out of the girl and darted off to the side. The condom barely went halfway up his penis. 'Piss off!'

Quaresma jumped forward and grabbed Tulloch by the throat. 'Mr Tulloch, come with me.'

The girl hauled the duvet over her, curling into a tight ball. Luisa Oliveira, the barmaid they spoke to the previous afternoon.

Tulloch struggled back against Quaresma, wriggling around.

Quaresma pulled Tulloch's arm round his back. 'You. Are. Coming. With. Me!'

Tulloch rolled forward across the bed and let Quaresma cuff him. 'This is bullshit.'

The girl darted out of the bedroom, heading for the bathroom.

Hunter stood over the bed, wanting to crack Tulloch in the back of the head, smother him in the pillow. Instead, he cleared his throat. 'Sean Tulloch, once you're back at the police station, I'm going to place you under arrest.'

Tulloch's face was pressed against the duvet. He still managed to shoot a glare at Hunter. 'You're a *cop?*'

'You're coming back to Scotland with me.'

'What for?' Quaresma flipped Tulloch over and helped him to his feet, his half-swollen penis flapping around. 'You want a portion of my ten-inch cock, eh?'

'You're not my type.'

'I've seen your type. Dirty little Paki bitch, eh?'

Hunter took one look around the room. *Kick Tulloch in the balls. Make him scream like a pig. Lash out again and again, keep kicking until Tulloch was a eunuch. Until he couldn't get an erection. Until he didn't have a cock.*

Quaresma yanked Tulloch to his feet. 'Enough!'

61

The car park was a lot quieter than the last time, barely recognisable. Hunter couldn't spot any of the reporters. They'd either gone home after no news or were just off drinking somewhere. The white building was blinding in the sunshine. Two uniformed cops stood by the entrance, arguing with angry tourists.

Chantal was standing by a squad car, scowling as a female officer helped Gordon Brownlee out of the back.

What the hell is he doing here?

Hunter opened the door and tried to get out.

Quaresma grabbed his wrist. 'You're not playing ball, Constable.'

Hunter brushed him away. 'You need to start letting us do our jobs.'

'Your job is working with me.' Quaresma waved at the squad car next to them. Two local cops helped Tulloch out of the back. Their black uniforms and hats sucked in the sunlight. Tulloch's shorts and T-shirt seemed to glow. 'I saw in your eyes what you wanted to do to him.'

'Someone should've done that a long time ago.' Hunter got out into the baking heat. Much worse this side of town, this far from the beach.

Another squad car pulled up. Looked like it had Tulloch's

latest victim in the back, though her hair shrouded her face. *Luisa, is that her name?*

Chantal stood there and nodded. 'You okay?'

Hunter wanted to rush over and grab her, then hold her tight. But stayed at a distance. 'Almost.'

She frowned at him. 'What's up?'

'I'll tell you later.' Hunter folded his arms and leaned back against Quaresma's car. 'What's the plan?'

Quaresma rested his hands on top of the Audi. Bloody asbestos fingers. He nodded over at the car next to them. 'I am going to interview Luisa. This *supposed* victim of Mr Tulloch.'

'Supposed?' Hunter scowled at him. 'You saw him raping her.'

'I saw sexual intercourse, Mr Hunter. Whether it was consensual, we shall identify.'

'It was rape.' Hunter rubbed at his cheek. Felt like it was on bloody fire. 'Look, I want to interview Tulloch.'

'If I let, you will leave?'

'Of course.'

Quaresma shrugged. 'Be my guest.'

'You want to join me?'

'It will be recorded.' Quaresma clapped Chantal's shoulder. 'Your sergeant and I will have a word with Luisa, yes? See if we can get the truth from her.'

I wanted to take him back to Scotland. Now. The next flight out of Faro. I'd settle for Newcastle, Glasgow, Prestwick.

But he's committed a crime here. He should go away for that.

Quaresma nodded slowly as he jabbed a finger at Hunter's sternum. 'When we get the European Arrest Warrant through. Until then, Mr Tulloch will stay here.' He gave Chantal a wink. 'Come on, Sergeant, let's see how the masters in Scotland do it, yes?' He marched off across the dusty mosaic.

Hunter glared at him as he went. 'Tell me there's no point in arguing with him.'

'There's none, Craig. Play it through and see how it all looks at the end.'

'Right.' He frowned at Chantal. 'Why's Brownlee here?'

'Well, he assaulted me for starters.' She switched her glare to Quaresma. 'And he's a witness to Tulloch raping Heather Latimer yesterday morning.' She flapped a hand over at the building as Quaresma entered. 'If this goes tits up, we can fall back on that.'

'Where is Heather?'

'I wasn't allowed to accompany her in.' Chantal huffed out a sigh. 'No authority. Usual shit.' She sighed again. 'The good news is that Jon Bruce seems to have authority and he's giving her a lift here.'

~

THE STANDARD of interview room in the Algarve wasn't what Hunter was used to. A battered table, four seats. The only recording equipment was a CCTV camera looming overhead, its red light pulsing like a Terminator.

The female cop, Elena, sat next to him in her full uniform, focusing on the interview.

Tulloch was opposite them, leaning back in his chair to stretch out the maroon HARVARD shirt he wore. He gave Elena his full attention, his gleaming eyes trained on her. 'So, do you fancy a drink? After this is over, we'll go somewhere, I'll get you a nice steak or something?'

She looked away.

Hunter felt that pang of spent energy in his muscles. A slight ache.

Tulloch was finally here, under lock and key. Secure. Unable to rape anyone else. It'll be even better when he's on the plane, heading for a nice, warm cell in Edinburgh.

Hunter glanced up at the camera, no idea who was at the other end. Quaresma said it was recording, but... 'Can you state for the record that you do not wish to have a lawyer represent you?'

Tulloch kept his focus on Elena, running a tongue over his lips. 'Told you pal, I don't need a lawyer. You've got hee-haw on me.'

'Right.' Hunter sat back in his chair. 'Mr Tulloch, I need you to outline your movements today, if you don't mind?'

'I don't need to speak to you, do I?'

Hunter rested on his elbows. 'You know why you're here, right?'

Tulloch smirked at him. 'Because you fancy me?'

Keep calm. Keep calm.

Hunter leaned back and cracked his knuckles. 'Why do you think we picked you up in that apartment?'

Another leer at Elena. 'To check out my penis?'

Hunter cracked his knuckles, popping them in the sockets, trying to keep the rage from his face. 'You were sexually assaulting a woman. Luisa Oliveira.'

'Never done nothing to anyone in that flat except make sweet, sweet love to Luisa.' Tulloch drilled his gaze into Elena. Strong as she seemed, she couldn't help but look away. 'Pretty sure he's after me, don't you think?'

Elena jerked her chair back, scraping it across the floor, and thumbed at the door. 'Mr Tulloch, you were sexually assaulting Luisa Oliveira, weren't you?'

Tulloch tilted his head to the side, giving her the full matinee idol look. 'You think that's what happened, do you?'

'You put GHB in her drink.' Elena held up an evidence bag containing the tub of pills. 'And then you *raped* her.'

Tulloch frowned at the bag. 'That's not mine.'

'We found it in a pair of your jeans.'

Tulloch smacked his lips together. 'See if I spiked this lassie's drinks, how come you've got the drugs, not me?'

'Because you took some pills with you.' Elena rested the bag down on the table and started smoothing out the plastic. 'You're stupid, but you're not going to carry that bottle with you, are you?'

'Listen, this guy here is a lying bastard.' Tulloch nodded slowly at her. 'He's trying to fit me up for God knows what reason. Tell you, though, I bet you'd be pretty hot in a bikini.'

Elena's cheeks flushed. 'You...'

This is all I bloody need.

Hunter leaned forward, distracting Tulloch from his prey. 'Did you use GHB on Luisa Oliveira?'

'No, I never.' Tulloch slumped back in his chair, his hairy hands clasping his bald knees. 'Never used it on anyone.'

'She's undergoing a blood test, so I'd advise against lying.'

Tulloch just laughed.

Hunter set out the photos of Tulloch and his mates in the bar. 'On Friday morning, you raped one Heather Latimer.'

'Here we go.' Tulloch shuffled through the photos. 'Take it

you've kept the shots of me with the python out in that bar for your collection, aye?'

Hunter put another photo down on the table and prodded it. 'You raped her yesterday morning.'

'Just another lassie who wanted my portion, mate.' Tulloch started drumming on his knees, grinning. 'Sure you don't get what I'm saying here?'

Hunter banged the table. 'You raped her.'

Tulloch grinned at Hunter. 'This is hilarious.'

'As well as Heather Latimer, you raped Luisa Oliveira, didn't you?'

Tulloch was still ignoring Hunter, eyes trained on Elena.

Hunter leaned back in the chair. *Need to turn the tables somehow, anyhow. Fight fire with fire. Just... how?*

Tulloch rested his arms on the table. 'So, I'm thinking that as soon as you let me out of here, we go get a drink?'

Elena smiled at him. 'You're staying here.'

'Listen, darling.' Tulloch thumbed over at Hunter, his eyes twinkling in the spotlights. 'Whatever he's telling you, it's bullshit, okay? I've not raped anyone. And this prick thinks he's all smart, but he's jealous of me.'

Elena tapped at her page, keeping her focus away from Tulloch. 'You raped Luisa Oliveira, didn't you?'

'This again...' Tulloch shook his head at her. 'Luisa consented to everything we did. She wanted more. Like a wild horse, I swear.'

Hunter waved at Elena to stop. 'It didn't look like it to me.'

'Aye?' Tulloch shuffled his chair to the side. 'The lassie was drinking with us. Then she wanted a length of pipe.'

'You were raping her.'

'No, mate. She was gagging for it. You know how the song goes.' Tulloch ran his fingers down the bulge on his shorts again. 'She wanted every inch of my love.'

'You raped her.'

'I never. Now, why don't you piss off out of here. Leave me and Elena to get better acquainted while you check with Luisa what actually happened, eh?'

62

CHANTAL

Luisa rubbed at her bare arms, gooseflesh puckering the skin all the way down to her elbows. Her ponytail was gone, her hair hanging loose around her shoulders.
Chantal shuddered as well. The interview room was freezing, the air conditioning turned up to make it feel like Christmas in Lapland. She got up and started walking around, passing behind Quaresma, sitting there with a stupid look on his face, like this was all such a laugh. 'So, let's go back to the start, shall we? You were working at the bar, correct?'
Luisa nodded. 'We had some breakfasts, but they left.' She nibbled at her nails. 'Then John walked in.'
'John?'
'John.' Luisa frowned, then cradled her head in her hands. 'Sean.'
Chantal leaned across Quaresma to reach into an evidence pouch on the desk. She got out a photo of Tulloch. 'Is this him?'
'That's him.' Luisa snatched the photo off and ran a finger across Tulloch's face. 'That's him.'
'Was he on his own?'

'He was with Matty.'

Chantal frowned at her. 'You know Matty?'

Luisa cleared her throat and stroked the photo again. 'He's been in before.' She rested it on the table. 'There was someone else. Keith, maybe?' She shrugged. 'But he left. His eyes were stinging.'

'How did they seem?'

'Typical tourists. Drunk at ten o'clock in the morning.'

'Did you serve them anything?'

Luisa nodded. 'A bottle of absinthe.'

'A bottle of spirits at that time?'

'It happens.' Another shrug. 'Cheaper for them, we get lot of money. And they stay there, buy food. Maybe.'

'And did they?'

She looked away. 'No.'

'So, the three of them sat around and tucked into the bottle of absinthe?'

'They drank about a quarter of it by the time—' She ran a hand through her hair. Clammed up.

Chantal tilted her head to the side. 'By what time?'

Luisa nibbled at her bottom lip. 'In off-season, the boss lets us go early. We can drink with customers. Sean let me have a drink.'

'Did he try and put anything in your drink?'

'What?'

'Like a drug?'

'Hardly.' Luisa shook her head. 'I like him. I said I lived close. We went to my apartment.'

'Just like that?'

'Like what? I liked him.' She shrugged. 'Well, he's my type.'

A chill shot up Chantal's spine. 'You chose to go?'

'Yeah?' Luisa chewed at more of her lip. 'I like him. We were kissing each other on the stairs.'

'Did you consent to having sex with Mr Tulloch?'

'Yes.' Her expression darkened and she waved a hand at Quaresma. 'Then he pulled him out of me.'

Quaresma levered himself up to standing and buttoned up his long coat. 'Sergeant, we should have a chat.'

63

HUNTER

Hunter leaned back into the tiny window space and rested his arms on the concrete. 'Mr Brownlee, I need to go through your movements on Thursday night.'

'We've been through this in detail.' Brownlee scowled back at him. 'What's the point in her writing this down if you keep asking me to repeat it, eh?'

Elena was sitting opposite Brownlee.

Nice to have someone working for me for once. Someone who wasn't Elvis.

'You said you were drinking at a bar near the hotel, then down the Strip.' Hunter pressed his arms against the cool wall. 'What was the name of the bar?'

Brownlee exhaled slowly through his nostrils, his focus locked on the desk. 'Something like Cheap and Cheerful.'

'And you were doing karaoke in there?'

'Sean was. That shite he always does.' Brownlee smirked. 'Hall and Oates.'

'And you said you left?'

Brownlee looked up. 'Aye.'

'You weren't thrown out?'

'Sean was.' Brownlee scratched at his neck, lobster red around the T-shirt collar. 'Like I told you, we went back to the hotel to meet up with some of the other boys. Then we headed down the Strip.'

Hunter nodded slowly, leaving space for Brownlee to swim in. 'Where did you end up?'

'Couldn't tell you.'

'Wouldn't be Mambo, would it?'

Brownlee shrugged. 'Take your word for it.'

'That's where you...' Hunter leaned over Elena's shoulder to read her notes. In bloody Portuguese. He coughed. 'Where you met the "Irish birds".'

'Well, aye, but I didn't call them "birds". It's demeaning. Ladies, I think I said.'

Hunter almost laughed. Caught himself in time. 'Did you chat to any of them?'

'No.'

'Did Sean chat up any of these girls?'

'No.'

Hunter pulled out a photo of Heather Latimer. 'What about her?'

Brownlee took it and stared at it. He flapped it in the air, like he was weighing up the decision to tell the truth or not. 'Never seen her in my life.'

'Sure about that?'

Brownlee put the photo back on the table. 'Don't recognise her.'

Hunter held it up and gave Brownlee one last look. 'So, what happened next?'

'Some of the boys were heading off to the ti—' Brownlee coughed and cleared his throat. 'They were heading to a lap dancing bar.'

'And did you go?'

'Not my scene, dude.'

'You told me earlier that you were at "the tits" till four.'

Brownlee let out a deep sigh. 'Fine. I was in there. Had a few dances. Then I went back to my crib.'

'Which you share with Sean Tulloch?'

'Well the room, aye.'

Hunter got out the bottle of pills. 'Have you ever seen this?'

Brownlee raised his hands. 'Nothing to do with me.'

Elena put down her pen. 'We found that in your hotel room, Mr Brownlee.'

'Well, it's not mine. Sorry.'

Hunter rested it on the table. 'Is it Sean Tulloch's?'

'Never seen it in my puff, pal.'

Hunter passed the pills to Elena. 'So, you got back to your room and you went to sleep, right?'

'That's what I told you.'

'When did you wake up?'

'In time for breakfast. Always make sure I have a proper breakfast, you know? Sets you up for the day.'

'Was Mr Tulloch in the room when you roused yourself?'

'Might've been. Can't remember. Had a stinking hangover. All I could think about was coffee and bacon.'

Hunter grimaced. 'And was he alone?'

'Look, pal, I can't even remember if he was there, let alone whether he'd pulled.'

'Heather Latimer wasn't there, was she?' Hunter tapped the photo.

Brownlee didn't even look at it. 'What is this?' He threw it over his shoulder. 'I never saw the girl.'

'Ms Latimer says you were looking at her as Mr Tulloch raped her.'

'Not me.'

'Staring at her while he—'

'Not me, pal. Must've been in a different room. Have you spoken to Matty?'

'She identified you from a photograph. You're pretty distinct, you know that?'

Brownlee rubbed at his ears. 'Shut up.'

Hunter snorted out a sigh. 'What sort of person lies there watching someone being raped?'

'You tell me.'

'Sean raped that girl. You saw him do it. If you had an ounce of human decency, you'd tell us what happened.'

Brownlee sat there and folded his arms. 'You're getting nothing more out of me.'

'You let her be raped. Just lay there, playing with yourself.'

'You've got my statement.' Brownlee pushed his chair back and got up. 'Now, if you don't mind? I'm supposed to be on holiday.'

64

CHANTAL

Quaresma led Chantal down a long corridor and opened a door at the end, holding it for her.

Classic ID parade. A room with a wide window running down the side, looking onto another one. Two women stood silhouetted against it, a local female uniform, and Heather Latimer.

Chantal followed Quaresma over, stopping behind them.

Heather nodded at her, though her eyebrows were squashed together.

Five giants loomed behind the glass, Tulloch fourth from the left.

'Ms Latimer, thanks for your assistance.' Quaresma licked his lips slowly. 'Now I know how difficult this must be, but can you identify your attacker?'

Heather huffed out a breath and shrugged. 'Sorry.'

'You can take your time.' Quaresma gave her his full smarmy charm bottled in a smile. 'Do you recognise any of them?'

'They all seem familiar.' Heather blinked hard like she needed some glasses. 'It's... I can't remember. That stuff they put in my drink.'

Chantal let out a groan. *Shite.*

Heather turned round and frowned at Quaresma. 'Sorry.'

Chantal tried a smile, but it wasn't happening. 'You don't recognise any of them?'

Heather took another look. Long, slow, one by one. Focusing hard, her fingers twitching. She settled on Tulloch and locked eyes with him. He snorted. Then she shook her head. 'Sorry.'

'It's okay. Take your time, if you need it.' Chantal wanted to shake her. Grab her by the shoulders and make her point at Tulloch. 'One more—'

'Ms Latimer, you can leave now.' Quaresma smiled at the uniform. 'My colleague will show you out.'

Heather followed the uniform out of the room, her head bowed.

'This isn't the way to do it.' Chantal glowered at Quaresma. 'We use a system called VIPER at home. It's proven to give better results by not letting the suspect see—'

'You're not at home, Sergeant.' Quaresma got in her face, blowing coffee breath over her. 'This is how we do things here.'

65

HUNTER

Quaresma held the door for them. Hunter followed Chantal in and slumped in the corner.

The observation suite was a broom cupboard filled with a big computer monitor, the display split in four, the bottom half empty. Tulloch was in the top-left, Luisa top-right.

'Then we have no choice.' Quaresma hauled himself up to standing. 'Elena, please let Mr Tulloch go.'

'What?' Hunter's gaze darted around the room, his heart thudding. 'You can't let him go!'

Quaresma folded his arms and lowered his eyes. 'Constable, we don't have any grounds to hold him. Therefore, we are letting him go.' He waved a hand at Elena. 'Now.'

She left the room.

'This is complete bullshit!'

'I can't keep him here, Constable. He hasn't committed any crime in this country.'

Hunter held his gaze for a few seconds until Quaresma looked away. 'He *raped* someone.'

'We haven't got any evidence of assault on Ms Latimer. Your witness isn't testifying and there's no proof that the GHB found in Mr Tulloch's room was even used, let alone to rape any of these women.'

'That's your fault.' Hunter's voice felt hoarse, sounded like it was a million miles away. 'If you'd—'

'Constable, we had an agreement to discuss this operation at fourteen hundred hours today. It's not even thirteen hundred now.' Quaresma held up his watch, the gold glinting in the light like an Aztec pyramid. 'I was going to allocate two of my officers to you, but not now. I won't be disrespected like this. If you move on him, I will arrest you.'

'What's your problem?' Hunter locked eyes with him. 'Are you getting a backhander from someone?'

'Excuse me?'

'Every step of the way, you've blocked us. Our suspect landed here, what, forty hours ago? You could've arrested him and sent him back to Scotland. Or you could've kept him in a holding cell until we got here yesterday morning. But no, you've let him run wild, raping.'

'Constable, I know your country. I worked there. It is a degenerate land filled with people of low morals. Men like this Sean Tulloch are everywhere in Scotland.'

'I can't believe I'm hearing this.' Hunter started pacing the small room. 'Is this your official position?'

'Listen to me, Constable. My priority is decided by my superiors. Harry Jack takes, how you say, precedence. An innocent child, abducted from his home and taken here against his will. Your Mr Tulloch, well, these women are complicit in the crimes, aren't they? They come here, drink us dry, and can't say no because of their lifestyle. Then they expect us to prosecute? That is not justice, that is a farce.'

Chantal stepped forward, almost going head to head with him, then she walked over to the door. 'I need to speak to your superiors.'

'You're going to, how do you say, grass to teacher, yes?' Quaresma tried the smile on Hunter. 'Your DI McNeill has attempted that manoeuvre already, Sergeant. My superiors are uncomfortable with the actions of you and Constable Hunter.' He nibbled at his bottom lip. 'You should consider going home, yes?'

Hunter almost put his hand through the screen, stopping to jab a finger at Tulloch. 'He's coming back to Scotland with us.'

Quaresma tucked his thumbs through the loops on his trousers. *Three steps and I could break both fingers.* 'Mr Hunter, I can and will arrest you for assaulting your friend Ricky.'

Chantal stomped back over, her fists clenched. 'Look, we've got Tulloch for five serious long-term sexual abuse cases back home, plus a violent assault, then assaulting two cops. If you let him go, then it's on your head.'

'I can't spare the manpower. We've had a sighting of Harry Jack in Vilamoura.'

Hunter looked into his eyes, searching deep for the lie. 'Is that the truth?'

'Are you accusing me of lying to you now?' Quaresma laughed. 'We have not received the promised European Arrest Warrant. Even if I could arrest him, I can't pass him to you.'

Chantal shook her head at him. 'Why are you being as obstructive as possible?'

'Listen to me, I have to manage my resources very carefully. If you were an inspector, maybe you'd understand.'

'Look, if you won't release him to us, then you need to keep him here until we can come to an agreement.'

Quaresma puckered his lips. 'In this country, I can't detain a suspect without charge.'

This is going to the dogs and fast. How the hell do I get him back onside?

Hunter cleared his throat. 'Can you at least take a detailed statement of Tulloch's movements over the last few days, then?'

Quaresma held his arms wide, shaking his head. 'That won't happen.'

66

HUNTER

Hunter leaned back against DI Bruce's car and let the sun burn his skin. 'How come we don't get a hire car?'

'Because we're not special, Craig.' Chantal stuffed her hands in her pockets.

Hunter felt ready to kill Quaresma, or raid the police station and kill Tulloch with his bare hands. She just stood there, an ice queen in the baking heat.

'But I suppose I'd better call Sharon and let her know the great news.' She shuffled away towards the shade.'

Hunter got out his mobile. Two texts, the first from Finlay:

I GET THE MESSAGE, MATE. CALL ME IF YOU NEED ME.

When is that going to be likely?

And a photo from Murray, Muffin lying on Hunter's bed, Bubble standing over him, paw in the air.

FIGHTING LIKE YOU AND CHANTAL!

He's never bloody seen us fight. Not getting into it, slamming doors.

'You filthy bastard!' Matty was tearing across the car park towards Hunter, fists clenched, fury in his eyes. 'You pig bastard!'

Hunter got himself into the basic stance, ready to fight. 'Unless you want to tell us all about Sean Tulloch, I suggest—'

'Piss off!' Matty stabbed a finger at the police station. 'I've just been inside doing an ID parade! You stupid prick!'

'Come on. Hit me. Go on.'

Matty moved his head close, almost touching. 'You're not worth it.' He stormed off, heading away from the station's entrance.

Hunter settled back against the car and folded his arms. Blood thudding in his ears.

Should I take him up on his threat? Go and batter him?

DI Bruce leered as he approached. He thumbed over at Chantal, wheeling around at the other side of the car park. 'Updating the boss?'

'That's right.' Hunter put his phone away. 'Getting a kicking.'

'Typical. This place is a shambles, I swear.' Bruce shook his head at the building. 'So, are you two an item?'

Hunter gave him a long look. 'Surprised to see you here what with that sighting of Harry Jack.'

Bruce's head twisted to the side, his forehead pulsing to some unheard rhythm. 'What did you say?'

'Quaresma said they had a sighting of him in Villa something.'

'Vilamoura?'

Hunter shrugged again. Felt like it was becoming a habit. 'Maybe.'

'That cheeky bastard!' Bruce stormed off towards the police station, kicking up clouds of sand from the pebbles. The door rattled as he battered his way inside.

Not a happy man.

Hunter stared at his phone as another text from Finlay popped up.

Maybe it's time.

67

CHANTAL

Chantal stomped across the car park, her phone tight to her ear. *What an absolute joke.* 'What's up, Shaz?'

'It's a nightmare here.' Sharon's sigh hissed out of the speaker. 'DI Fletcher's been on the bloody phone every hour, talking about coming back off holiday and taking over.'

'Shite.'

'Aye. And then some. Over a year's work on this bloody case so that scumbag can walk?' Another sigh. 'And to top it all off, I've had Inspector Quaresma's superior on the phone.'

'Already?'

'Already. I don't know what you two have been up to, but there's no option but to return home.'

Chantal scowled over at Hunter. 'We've got Tulloch. We—'

'Chantal, no.' Sharon's breath rattled against the microphone. 'The Portuguese are giving us no quarter here. I need you and Craig out of the country.'

'They've got Tulloch and—'

'Chantal!'

'—when they let him go, we can—'

'Chantal, will you just bloody listen to me?' Sharon paused. In the background, a door clunked shut. 'If you pick Tulloch up from the station or anywhere else, they will arrest you. Doing a Bruce Lee impression and barging in on Tulloch having consensual sex with a local didn't impress them.'

'Craig acted accordingly in both cases.' Chantal shrugged an apology at nobody. 'Look, we need that arrest warrant.'

'Not going to happen this week.'

Chantal shook her head. 'So we're giving up?'

'We're never going to give up. This is one of our highest priority cases, okay?' Sharon paused again. 'But I'm going to have to go cap in hand to Rollo-Smith, okay?' She let it hang there, hissing in the sun. 'The MOD can bring Tulloch back to this country.'

'That sounds exactly like giving up.'

'Do you think I'm pissing about back here? I've been in meetings all weekend while you've been drinking.'

'If Rollo-Smith gets him, you better wave goodbye to any prosecution from us.'

'Let's hope it doesn't come to that. Meanwhile, Paisley is finally well enough to let Elvis and Jenny take a statement from her. He assaulted two cops, too. We're close to getting a full statement on Tulloch. While it's going to shit out there, another two days and we'll have a complete story to take to the Procurator Fiscal. The noose is tightening. Okay?'

Chantal shoved her free hand deep into her pockets. 'If anyone remembers their story when Tulloch gets out of military prison.'

'Come on, Chantal.' Sharon sounded battered and bruised. 'I'm trying my hardest here.'

'That's what it's about, isn't it? Statistics? We're letting a rapist out of our sight. Do you know what—'

'Chantal, enough!' Sharon paused. 'You're booked on the half eight from Faro to Edinburgh. Your passes are with the airline. Make sure you're at the airport by seven.'

68

HUNTER

'So that's us knackered.' Chantal rested her head on Hunter's shoulder, her hair flopping against his neck. She blew air over her face, giving him a backdraught of sweet suntan lotion. 'Tell me there's something we can do.'

Was there? Hunter couldn't even think. They had Tulloch in custody, had witnesses against fresh crimes and...

And it all falls away to shite.

Hunter pulled her closer, wrapping his arm around her. 'The only thing I can think is Rollo-Smith will be days getting out here.'

'I wanted good news.'

'Sorry.'

'Rollo-Smith will be on the next flight out, won't he?'

'Maybe.' Hunter shrugged again. *Feel like I don't know anything.* 'But the military can be bloody slow. If they're getting wind of him having drugs, then maybe. The blowback on them could be pretty bad if he rapes and kills someone.'

'This isn't good enough.' She pushed away from him and pointed at a grid of thin windows overlooking the car park. 'Meanwhile, Quaresma will let that scumbag out and he'll go on raping women. Or he'll disappear into thin air.' She folded her arms and leaned back against Bruce's hire car with a thud. 'I hate this bloody job at times.'

'Tell me about it.' Hunter drummed his hands on the top of the car. 'We've got Tulloch pinned down.'

'For now.'

'Aye, for now. But we know he'll get let out.' Hunter stopped drumming and rasped a hand across his stubble. 'So, what we need is to keep an eye on him.'

'What, you're saying we ignore Sharon and stay here?'

'If we do that, Quaresma'll arrest me.'

'You honestly think so?'

'Put it this way, I'm looking around for a drill and screws to try and tighten up the shoogly peg my coat's on.'

'So, what then?'

'I've got an idea.'

'I'm all ears.'

Something clattered behind them.

DI Bruce stomped out of the front door, charging across the car park towards them.

Hunter nodded at Bruce. 'Can you try and persuade him to get one of his lot to keep a tail on Tulloch?'

'That's your idea?'

'He's got resource and nothing to do with it. Tell him he's involved in Harry Jack's disappearance?'

'Craig, I can't lie...'

Hunter marched across to meet him. 'How did it go?'

Bruce stopped a few metres away, shaking his head, jaw clenched tight. 'Have you pair got anything on Quaresma? Any dodgy behaviour. Vague suspicions that he's up to something. Anything.'

'He's pissed off with us for trying to do his job for him.'

'But he's not done anything that wrong yet?'

'No, why?'

'He had another sighting of Harry in Vilamoura this morning.' Bruce's jaw clenched tight as he swung round to glare at the police station, not that he could see Quaresma through any of the tiny windows. 'It's not far from here, but he's kept us out of the bloody loop. Didn't tell me or my team.'

'Was it Harry?'

'That's not the point.' Bruce unlocked his car and pulled his hand away from the hot door. 'Came to nothing, like everything around here.'

Chantal folded her arms. 'Sounds like you're in the same level of shit as us.'

Bruce frowned at her. 'Isn't that what you've been doing to him?'

'Maybe.' Chantal shrugged at him. 'I don't like it, though. We've been ordered to head back to Scotland tonight.'

Bruce opened his car door. 'Well in that case, do you guys fancy a crafty lunchtime pint?'

Chantal nodded. 'Thought you'd never ask.'

Hunter smiled at Bruce. 'I'll leave you to catch up, if it's all the same.'

69

CHANTAL

Chantal sat outside a bar on the main drag through Albufeira's old town. Close enough to the sea for the bitter salt tang but far enough to avoid too many smoking Brits getting tanked up. The town stretched out ahead of them, white stucco buildings climbing the hill, harsh cliffs edging the sea. Behind, a wide beach was squeezed back by the high tide, hardly any sunbathers, despite the heat. Still too early in the season for that.

Bruce was at the bar, paying. *Can still just walk away.*
Bloody Craig dumping me in this.
She picked up her phone. Still nothing from him.
Bruce came outside and dumped two full pints on the table, the lager's head fizzing away.
Chantal sat back in her chair and sipped the cold beer. 'Nice place this.'
'Not bad.' Bruce gulped down his lager like he hadn't drunk anything all day. 'Much better than where you're staying, Chantal, let me tell you that.' He swallowed more beer, his eyes misting over. 'I love it here. Used to bring the kids in the summer for a fort-

night. Every year. Sometimes get a week at half-term in October.' He smirked. 'And then there's the golf trips with the boys.'

Chantal clutched the handle of her glass, ready to drink. 'You any good?'

'That's not the point.' Bruce tore open a bag of crisps. One of those continental brands that looked like the British ones, but with a different name. 'Help yourself.'

Chantal grabbed a handful and shovelled them down. 'Haven't eaten all day.' She nodded as she chewed, the vinegar tang biting her gums. 'Been hard at it since we got up.'

'You caught him, though, that's a good thing.' Bruce ate a crisp, daintily like someone's gran. 'Just because the wheels of justice don't turn very quickly, doesn't mean you haven't done great.'

'Doesn't feel great.' Chantal looked over at the bar's door and fiddled with the tie on her shorts. A couple of knuckle-dragging mouth-breathers kept leering at her. 'Great would be sitting at the airport, escorting that raping bastard home.'

'Just saying, you and Craig caught that scumbag.' Bruce's gaze stayed on her hand as she munched through the crisps. 'You've done well, pet.'

'He's going to slip through our grasp, though.' Chantal finished her crisps and took a gulp of lager, giving herself a beer moustache. 'God, I needed that.'

Bruce reached over and wiped the foam off. 'You missed a bit.'

She pushed his hand away with a glare. 'Can't believe we're getting kicked back to Scotland.'

Bruce shuffled the crisp bag round to her. 'Two-bit operation here, Chantal. Calling them cowboys doesn't do it justice.'

She took another and chewed slowly, her forehead creasing. 'Any chance you can get a tail on him?'

'With our resources?' Bruce laughed. 'No chance. If we get caught doing that, it'll be all over the papers, too.'

'That might not be a bad thing.' Chantal took another sip of beer. 'Your case isn't short of profile in the media, which means it's all Quaresma seems to bother about.'

'Aye, to the detriment of my work. That prick wants all the glory for himself.'

'We could play to that.'

'Chantal...' Bruce bellowed out a laugh, then downed the rest of his pint. 'Right, after the morning I've had, I'm having another. What about you?'

Chantal's glass was below halfway. 'Aye, go on.'

'I'll get more crisps.' Bruce got up and went inside, leaving the door hanging open.

Chantal took another crisp. Bloody starving. She picked up her phone and dialled Hunter. Took him an age to answer.

'Hey, lover, how are you doing?' Sounded like he'd taken four MDMA.

'I'm okay. Wallowing in my grief here. What about you?'

'Still waiting.'

'On Tulloch?'

'He's still inside.' Hunter sighed down the line. 'Do you want to get some food?'

'Too pissed off to eat properly, Craig.' Chantal took another angry drink of beer, her teeth chapping off the glass. 'Right now, I want to get so drunk they don't let me on the plane. Then I can stay here and catch that bastard.'

'You want to face Quaresma's wrath again?'

'We should be tailing him.'

'Have you got Bruce to bite yet?'

'No resource. Press profile. You name it.'

Hunter's sigh hissed down the line. 'What's to stop me just happening to walk back to the apartments the same way as Tulloch?'

Chantal took a drink of beer. 'Nothing, I suppose.'

'Look, I've got to go, okay?'

'Is Tulloch—'

Click.

Bloody hell. Should never have left him up there. Bloody superhero twat is going to get himself killed.

Chantal finished her beer in one gulp. Felt like a spider crawled up her spine. She hit it when it reached her shoulder. Only problem was it went both ways at the top and snaked down both arms.

Bloody hell.

'Think that rain will get us?'

Chantal swung round, the spider on her neck scurrying off. 'What rain?'

Bruce was clattering through the small door. 'That rain.'

A giant storm cloud hovered over the sea, dirtying the turquoise a dark grey. A British pub sat opposite, advertising "real beer!" and "Proper English fry-ups!". The sunburnt skinheads drinking inside seemed to enjoy it anyway. Older, though, not the sort to go raping their way down the Strip.

'Nah, it's a sea storm.' Chantal pushed her empty glass away on the table.

Bruce handed her a fresh pint, foam dripping off the side, and tipped four bags of crisps on the table. 'Time to forget about the case, okay?'

She hauled the beer over and snatched a pink bag of prawn cocktail. 'You're sure you can't get a tail on Tulloch?'

Bruce's chair squeaked as he collapsed into it. 'No dice.'

'Even if you get intel suggesting that he's involved in the disappearance of Harry Jacks?'

'Don't be so bloody stupid.' He waved a finger at her. 'Anyway, my place isn't too far from here, if you fancy a little wander?'

70

HUNTER

A red Fiesta van pulled up a few spaces away. Hunter stretched out. His back was starting to ache from all that sitting. The section of wall he'd been on was covered in a damp patch from his sweaty arse. It evaporated in seconds.

The police station was still quiet. No sign of Tulloch getting out. No sign of Quaresma or Elena or any of the other cops.

Finlay Sinclair got out of the Fiesta and grabbed Hunter into a bear hug. 'Amigo!'

'Fin.' Hunter patted him on the back and broke off. 'Thanks for meeting up, mate.'

'No worries, jabroni. No worries.' Finlay took a look around the place, like he was assessing some Leith crime scene. 'So what's the deal?'

'Chantal and I are heading home tonight.'

'And...?'

'What do you mean "and"?'

Finlay whistled through his teeth. 'There's always something with you, dude.'

'That's it.'

'Aye, bollocks.' Finlay raised a finger in the air. 'Before I forget...' He reached into the car and groaned, his hand going to his back. 'Oh, you bastard.' He straightened up and handed a paper bag to Hunter. 'Got this for you.'

'You okay?'

Finlay pushed at his spine until something clicked. 'That's it.' He opened his watering eyes and waved a hand at the bag. 'Open it, then.'

Hunter peered inside. A plastic container absolutely rammed with salad. A thin burrito lay on the top, almost an afterthought. 'I don't know what to say, that looks... Wow.'

'Don't mention it.' Finlay took greater care getting a second bag out. He leaned back against the car and pulled out a chunky tortilla unadorned by anything except a drizzle of chilli oil. 'Enjoy it, dude.' He bit into the fajita and chewed with his mouth open, his lips slapping together.

'I've been craving vegetables since we got here.' Hunter ate a forkful of salad, crunchy in a way you didn't get in Scotland. 'This is more fruit and veg than you eat in a month.'

'Try a year.'

You can take the boy out of Dalkeith...

Finlay looked at Hunter's food. 'They didn't have any banana or goat's cheese, though, you freak. Still eat that poof food?'

'Don't know what you're missing.'

Finlay laughed, his tortilla poised over his mouth. 'Weirdo.' He picked up his fajita and bit into it. 'Ah, that's the bambers.'

'Remember that Met DI who was up for a bit a few years back, would only ever eat a burrito?'

'God, aye.' Finlay chomped with his mouth open. 'What was his name again?'

Hunter shrugged. 'Can't remember.'

'Whatever. Had a bit of a darkness behind his eyes, that one.' Finlay flashed up his eyebrows. 'So, how's the case, then?'

'Like I said, mate, they're sending us home.'

'Meaning you got the punk you were after?'

'Sort of.'

'Always a grey area with you, right?' Finlay's lips slapped

together as he laughed. 'And another part is why we're meeting in a police station car park.'

'It's a long story and...' Hunter bit into the burrito. Felt like his tongue was on fire. 'Christ. I need some asbestos for my mouth.' He got the bottle of water out of the bag and slurped it down. 'Ah.'

'Too hot for you, jabroni?' Finlay wiped his chin and a dod of chicken fell back in the box. He picked it up and ate it. 'Saw some stuff on the news earlier. That kid from Geordieland was supposed to be in Vilamoura. Was that you guys?'

'Not us, but I know about it. Like our case, it's gone to shite, mate.'

Finlay chuckled as he plucked a pepper out of his fajita and set it aside. 'Usual story, then?'

'Aye. Usual.'

'You are boning her, aren't you?'

Hunter put a finger to his lip. 'Don't ask, don't tell.'

Finlay shrugged. 'I can't force you to talk to me, dude.'

Hunter finished chewing a mouthful of burrito. 'We're an item, yes.'

'And DI McNeill doesn't know?'

Hunter sighed. 'She suspects, but we haven't come clean.'

'Very unprofessional.' Finlay's eyebrows shot up. 'Not like you, Hunter.'

'It's not at my insistence.'

Finlay shut his tray. 'Do you want my advice?'

'Not really.'

'Well, I'll give you it anyway. Don't lie. And don't get caught out in a lie.'

'Like I said, it's not at my insistence. It's complicated.' Hunter picked up some olives from the salad. 'Look, mate, about your back. I'm sor—'

Finlay waved him away like an old lady trying to pay for tea and scones. 'Forget it, dude. It's old news.'

'I mean it. It's my fault you went upstairs in that house and...' Hunter held up the olives, the green surface glistening in the light. 'And he did that to you.'

Finlay leaned forward with a sickening crunch. 'It's cool, dude. I'm fine.' He waved at the sunshine, away from the cloud. 'I'm enjoying my life out here.'

'It shouldn't have happened.'

'But it did. I mean, if it hadn't, I'd be stuck in a squad car with Dave or Steve, getting a shoeing off Lauren every five minutes. You want that?'

'Suppose I've saved Lauren a lot of hassle.' Hunter bit into his burrito. Couldn't taste a thing. 'I don't know what I'm trying to say.' He swallowed it down. 'How bad is your back?'

'It's fine, jabroni.' Finlay finished off his fajita, leaving a pile of green and red peppers in his box. 'The only downside is I'm bored shitless out here.'

'What about drinking yourself to death?'

'Even that gets old.' Finlay closed the box and dumped it back in the bag. 'I mean it's fine and everything, but once you get over the novelty, it's just another place, right? You see the same bams all year round except when they go back home for a bit. Doctors appointments for their hearts, trying to see the kids that don't speak to them anymore, that kind of thing. Getting more lively now the tourists are rocking up. Not that we get many of them in Olhão, mind.'

'But you're bored?'

'Like you wouldn't believe. Didn't you get that from my texts?'

'Oh, I got it.' Hunter bit into his burrito and chewed slowly. 'How would you like to help me out?'

~

HUNTER PACED along the main street, the hordes of tourists making way for him. He had to swerve past an old man who stopped in front of him to inspect a menu, wiry hair coiling out of his flip flops.

'—Paula's bloody wedding. Can you imagine?' Chantal was still outside the bar, though a parasol blocked the sun from her and Bruce. The table was full of empties, a load of crisp packets rammed into a glass.

Inside the bar, a group of Scots stood near a telly showing the Celtic-Rangers match, though they were shouting abuse at each other rather than focusing on the football. And not very good-natured abuse at that.

Chantal got up and wrapped a hug round Hunter. 'I've missed you.'

'I've only been an hour and a half.' Hunter pulled her tight. So pissed she didn't care who saw them. Didn't care who Bruce knew in Scotland. 'Who's Paula?'

She collapsed into a chair and clutched Hunter's hand like it was the last thing she'd ever hold. 'Never mind.'

Hunter rolled his eyes. 'No. Who?'

'It's just...'

Bruce ran his tongue over his lips and raised his glass. 'The old truth serum, mate. Chantal's been talking to me. I know what's going on.'

'That's more than I do.'

She whacked him on the arm. 'Hoy.'

Bruce finished his pint then grinned. 'Another round?'

'I'll have one.' Hunter took her hand in his again.

She nodded. 'Nothing for me, though. Christ.' She coughed into her hand once Bruce had gone inside. 'God, lager makes me so bloated.'

'So why are you drinking it, then?'

She lifted a shoulder. 'That sleazy bastard has been hitting on me.'

'Bruce?'

'Brucie bloody Boner.'

Hunter got to his feet. 'I'm going to smash his face in.'

'Craig, drop it, okay?' Chantal burped into her hand. 'He's scared of you.' She tried to clear her throat but stopped short. 'Cat's out of the bag with bloody Elvis anyway.' She shrugged again. 'How's Finlay?'

Hunter couldn't stop his eyebrows shooting up. 'How do you know it was him I was meeting?'

She tapped her nose. 'I just do.'

'Right.' Hunter pulled his seat closer to her. 'You know how he is.'

'What was he after?'

'Food and the pleasure of my company.' Hunter started shifting the empties to the next table. 'This wedding. Whose is it?'

'Paula Zabinski.'

'Oh, I know her.' Hunter nodded. 'Not well enough to get invited to her wedding, dear.'

Chantal raised her eyebrows. 'Dear?'

'You know what I mean. Worked on the beat with her.' Hunter drummed his thumbs on the metal table. 'Is this a new thing?'

'Craig...' She waved her hands around the air, didn't seem to be aiming anywhere in particular. 'Can't we just enjoy this?'

'Fine.' Hunter sat back and pulled his sunglasses off his head. 'Here comes lover boy.'

Another thwack on the arm. 'Piss off.'

Bruce dumped the beer on the table. 'What did I miss?'

Chantal smirked. 'Nothing.'

'My ears were burning. Come on, what's going on?'

Hunter took one of the pints and had a sip. He stared at his beer, the fizz in his gut tasting worse than the cheapest Portuguese lager. 'There's a serial sex offender in the police station and he'll get out soon.'

'You think that's bad?' Bruce thumped down in a seat and cracked his knee off a chair, almost knocking the pints over. 'We were working till four this morning. The locals had another false sighting of the kid at seven, so I had to get out of my pit on three hours sleep.'

'Like being back on shift.'

'Tell me about it.' Bruce tore into a bag of crisps. 'The bellends here don't know how to do subtle. Guns and dogs and God knows what else.' He crunched a crisp, swallowing it down. 'Spent the rest of the morning interviewing mum and dad, proving they were the kid's parents.' He sipped his beer again. 'Tell you what, though, Quaresma was pissed off at your little Wrestlemania on that street last night. Almost put our obbo at risk.'

'Thought you were long gone by then?'

'We were still waiting on a warrant. The courts are a bit slower than back home. Like most things out here, it was all a waste of time.' Bruce reached into his pockets for some more bags of crisps and tossed them on the table. 'I don't feel so guilty about having a pint after the shifts I've put in on this case.'

Chantal swirled her lager around her glass, the beer fizzing up to the top. 'I'm with you there.'

Bruce tore open a crisp bag along the seam and splayed it on the table. 'We've got the *Express*, the *Mail*, the *Sun* all auditing what we're up to. The *London Post* and the *Edinburgh Argus* too, God knows why. On a bloody jolly, the lot of them.'

'Think you'll find him?'

'I don't.' Bruce stared deep into Hunter's eyes, almost into his soul. 'I think he's long gone.' He took another sip and rocked forward on his chair. 'My lads are monitoring every flight out of this country and most out of Spain. We've got all the shipping manifests. I recommended to my superintendent that we head back home.'

'And?'

'The cogs are still grinding in Newcastle.' Bruce picked up a crisp and ate it carefully, his forehead knotting. 'Not that the locals help.'

'You think they're bent?'

'Well, I find ineptitude hard to swallow at the best of times.' Bruce yawned. 'Christ, I need my bed.' Another yawn, threatening to engulf him. 'Better make this the last. I'd offer you a lift, but...' He held up his glass.

'We can walk.' Chantal supped her beer. 'We need to check out soon, anyway.'

'You guys know the way to your hotel?' Bruce pointed back down the street. 'Follow the beach round to the path, then follow the yellow brick road.' He gave them a wink. 'Couple of secluded spots if you want to—'

'Right.' Chantal rolled her eyes and got to her feet. 'I get the idea.'

∽

THE DAMP SAND stuck to Hunter's feet as he walked, the drier stuff grinding against his soles. The sun burnt his neck, the sea breeze cooling it. Chantal's hand was soft in his. Life was good.

Except for the serial abuser not facing trial. Not in custody. Free to reoffend whenever he got out.

'You're right, Craig.' Chantal led them inland towards a craggy rock, following the path. 'It'd be nice to go on a proper holiday.'

'Not here, but aye. We should.' Hunter dropped his trainers on the sand and stepped into them again. He took his T-shirt off and stuffed it into his shorts' pocket. That's better. 'How about after this wedding?'

Chantal let his hand go. 'Craig...'

'What's going on?'

'Look, it's difficult. You know her, right?'

'Used to. Kind of lost touch.'

'Well. She's a mate.' Chantal tucked her hair behind her ear. 'The problem is she's worked for Scott Cullen for a year or something and he's going.'

Everything clicked into place.

Hunter nodded. 'So Sharon will be there?'

'Right.'

Hunter put his hand on his hips. 'So we should come out.'

'Craig, it's not that simple.'

'Come on. Either I am your boyfriend or I'm not. None of this grey area shite.'

She narrowed her eyes at him, her steely glare cutting through to his marrow. 'You accepted this when you started shagging me.'

'I know but... Chantal, we need to move on.' Hunter grabbed her shoulders, his fingers tightening around them. 'Maybe it's time we move in together.'

She brushed his hands away. 'You think you know me well enough?'

'I trust you. I love you. What else is there?'

'It's...'

'Come on.' He put his hands back. 'What's stopping you committing?'

'I don't know.'

'Is it because we've been lying to people for months now?'

'Part of it.'

'Well, we can say we got together out here. One thing led to another and...'

She grabbed his hands. 'I'll think about it, okay?'

'I'm serious, Chantal. You know I'm crazy about you, it's too difficult for us to keep this a secret. And I don't even know why we are.'

'I'll bloody think about it!' She stomped off towards the rocky path, sand clouding up behind her.

Bloody child.

He jogged after her. 'Look, this has got to stop. You're acting like a teenager. I've been making allowances for months. This is...' He threw his hands up in the air. 'Sod it, I don't need this drama. I don't deserve to feel like an embarrassment.'

'You're not an *embarrassment*.'

'Right, well you're making me feel like one. You owe it to our relationship to stand up and say we're in love with each other.'

'Craig...'

'What?'

'Look, it's just—'

'Just *what*? Sod it, I'll go back to uniform. I just want you to be *honest* about us.'

She kicked a stone along the road. An elderly couple crossed the street to avoid them. 'It's not that easy.'

'I should never have agreed to this charade.'

She stormed off down the road, head low, fists clenched.

'Chantal, wait!'

She wasn't slowing down. Speeding up if anything.

Bloody hell. He jogged off after her.

Rain started hammering down on them, splashing off his bare torso.

71

CHANTAL

'Craig, just shut up.' Chantal stopped outside their apartment and put her hand to her head. *Why can't he stop? For once?*

She got out her card, almost dropping her wallet in the process. 'Look, I said I'll think about it, that doesn't mean on the walk home, okay?'

'Fine, whatever.' Didn't look it. He was sulking, his bottom lip sticking out.

Chantal swiped through the door and stopped dead. 'Shite.'

The place was a mess. Clothes lay all over the floor. The bed was pulled apart, the two mattresses they'd pushed together were now bunched up against two of the walls, the bases upturned.

～

'This isn't happening...' Chantal scanned around the carnage. Their clothes were all mixed together, the toiletries stuffed into the kitchen sink, the washbags turned inside out.

Her case was on the kitchen floor, filled with water. Just a bra left inside.

Hunter's was next to it, soaked through. Empty.

'Craig.' Chantal tapped the lockbox under the TV. 'What's the code?'

Hunter was still standing in the doorway. '1776.'

She entered it and twisted the lock. Their passports were still inside. She let out a sigh of relief. 'Some good news, at least.'

Hunter snatched his off her and put it in his back pocket. 'This can't be Tulloch. He's still at the station.'

'How do you know that?'

Hunter shrugged. *Cheeky bastard is hiding something.* 'We need to get to the bottom of this. Come on.'

'I'm staying here, Craig.' Chantal got out her phone and dialled Quaresma's number.

72

HUNTER

'You don't understand.' Hunter leaned across the reception desk and kept his voice low. 'I'm a police officer.' He slid his warrant card across. 'Is there any way you can expedite this?'

The receptionist scanned across the card, his eyes flaring. Same Welsh guy as when they checked in, the one who flirted with Chantal. He passed it back. 'I see, sir.'

'I need to access your CCTV footage to see who's been in our room.'

'Give me a second, sir.' He tottered off behind the giant cheese plant.

Hunter grabbed his phone and redialled Finlay for the sixteenth bloody time.

'Yo.' Sounded like Mansun playing in the background. "Wide Open Space." Like it was 1997.

'Finally.' Hunter turned to scan the reception area. 'Been calling for the last five minutes. Where have you been?'

'Sat right outside the police station, amigo. Had my phone on mute. Only noticed the now.'

A middle-aged American sidled up to the next desk and gave it the full, 'Howdy, y'all?'

Hunter leaned forward, trying to follow where the receptionist had gone. 'Is Tulloch still there?'

The background music twisted down a few notches. 'He's still inside.'

'You're sure?'

'Fifty million percent, dude. I can see both exits from here.'

'You've not pissed off to get a sandwich or anything?'

'After that monster fajita?'

'What about going to the toilet?'

'After that monster fajita?'

Hunter frowned. Didn't even make sense. 'What about a drink or a paper?'

'Got a load of bottled water in the boot for when I go on a long drive.' Sounded like he took a swig, as if on cue. 'Listen, I recognised a guy from the pub. Paolo, he's a cop. He checked for me and Tulloch's still inside.'

'You could've opened with that.'

'Where's the fun in that?'

The receptionist wandered back round, followed by a knuckle-dragging brute who could've played rugby for Portugal.

'Right, Fin, I'll catch you later. Call me the second you hear.'

'Will do, jab—'

Hunter killed the call and pocketed the phone, giving the receptionist a wide grin.

'Sir, Pepé here is the head of security.' The receptionist ran a hand down the muscle ball's arm, thicker than his waist. Looked like he spent all day with a pair of dumb bells in front of the mirror rather than looking at CCTV. 'He'll be able to help you.'

'Come with me, sir.' Pepé spoke in the most brutal English, all clipped vowels and hardened consonants. He pulled up the partition and guided Hunter through, past the cheese plant. 'You are police?'

'Based near Edinburgh in Scotland.'

'Ah, Edinburgh.' Pepé opened a door behind a photocopier machine. 'Beautiful city. I play rugby there many year ago.'

Hunter entered the office, plusher than the standard of the rooms, anyway. A glass desk ran along the far wall, with a laptop plugged into a giant TV mounted on top. 'Did he tell you what happened?'

'Is not uncommon.'

'I need to see the CCTV for the area outside our room.'

'Kevin told me.' Pepé sat behind the desk, almost blocking the TV, and twisted his neck until it cracked. 'Unfortunately, Mr Hunter, we do not have CCTV covering those rooms.'

Hunter gritted his teeth. 'None?'

'Sorry, sir. That block is only two years old and we haven't had approval to install the system. Very high cost.'

Looked a lot older than two years. 'What about the entrances?'

Pepé waved a hand back towards the door. 'There is one by the reception.'

Hunter peered round to look at the TV. It showed the bar area from the roadside, with a thin sliver of beach and the next hotel. Gordon Brownlee and a couple of the other squaddies were there, but no sign of Tulloch or Matty.

Hunter tapped at another camera, pointing to what looked like their apartment block. 'What about that one?'

'Is not recording.'

Hunter shut his eyes and clenched his teeth. 'You're joking.'

'Dummy camera. Sorry. Is standard practice.'

'Do you have staff?'

Pepé's thick forehead creased. 'I have a bo staff, yes.'

'I meant people working for you.'

'There's me.' Pepé patted the side of the TV. 'This replaces my men.'

'And you've not seen anyone suspicious by our room?'

'Sorry.'

73

CHANTAL

'You need to send someone right away.' Chantal stood in the doorway, scanning up and down the path outside their apartment. No movement in Tulloch's flat. She leaned against the wall instead. 'This is serious.'

Quaresma sighed down the line. 'Sergeant, I thought you were leaving?'

'We're trying to, but someone has turned over our room.'

His snort turned into laughter. 'And you think it is Mr Tulloch?'

'Tell me it's not.'

'He has only just been released.'

'You've let him go?'

Another sigh. 'If your paperwork was—'

'You!'

Chantal swung round to look behind her.

Nora O'Meara was powering towards her, face puckered tight. She stopped and looked her up and down. 'This is your fault!'

'I've got to go. Send some officers now.' Chantal killed the call. 'Nora, what's—'

'You bitch!' Nora slapped her palm off Chantal's shoulder. 'I believed you!'

Chantal pushed the next slap away, a thud rocking though her phone, sending a dull shockwave down her arm. 'Stop hitting me!'

Nora held up her hand for another go then let it drop. She pointed over at their apartment. 'My cousin's just got back from the police station. Do you know what they did to her?'

Something I can bloody report, I hope.

'I spoke to Heather when I was there.' Chantal smiled, trying to disarm Nora. 'She was giving evidence, wasn't she?'

'Not like you'd think.' Nora squinted at her. 'They don't believe she was raped. Hauled her over the coals for it. Made her speak to that Sean boy.'

'What?' Chantal rubbed her hair out of her face. Still felt half pissed. 'That shouldn't have happened.'

'Well it did.' Nora raised her hand again. 'And it's all you—'

'I'm warning you.' Chantal gave Nora her fierce police officer stare, waiting for her arm to flop back again. 'How is Heather?'

'How do you bloody think? She's blaming herself for what happened.'

'Christ.' Chantal ran a hand across her forehead.

Running in there, trying to force everything through without understanding the ground rules. The caveman attitudes of the local cops. How hard it is to get anything done.

'I hope you're happy with yourself.' Nora brushed her hair away from her face. 'I've been in our apartment all afternoon, waiting for her. Then she called me and…'

'How bad is it?'

'I'm a psychiatric nurse. I've seen worse, but not much. Heather's not in a good way. Catatonic.' Nora stepped forward. 'Aren't you going to do something about it?'

'We'll report it to our local liaison.'

'I bet you bloody will.' Nora's eyes widened as she looked into their room. 'What happened here?'

Chantal glanced behind her. 'Someone's raided it.'

'Oh, Jesus.' She simpered at Chantal. 'Sean?'

Chantal rubbed the back of her hand along her mouth. She pointed back down the lane. 'Your room looks out on this bit. Did you see anything near ours?'

'Not that I can think of.' Nora shook her head, tears flooding her eyes. 'Wait a second. I saw him, when I went out for a bottle of water. That guy. The big one from Leeds, I think.'

'Matty?'

Nora clicked her fingers. 'That's him.'

Chantal glanced back at the room next door to Tulloch's. Nobody there.

When was the last time I saw him? Craig had a run-in with some of them, but not Matty.

'What was he doing?'

'Well, he was sort of sitting near your room. Reading a paper.'

'Anyone else with him?'

'Not that I saw.'

'Thanks.' Chantal nodded at Nora. 'I'll speak to my boss and —' Her phone blared out. Hunter.

74

HUNTER

Hunter stepped out into the blazing sunlight and swivelled his shades over his eyes.
Bloody amateurs.
Slow down. Think things through.
Hunter glanced over at the bar area. Gordon Brownlee and his mates were settling into a more leisurely pace of drinking, sipping their pints slowly.
What do they know? Was one of them in the room?
He got a scowl from Brownlee as the big lump Keith joined him, looking like he'd found his Valium.
So Brownlee had been released. How long till Tulloch was out?

∽

Hunter ran a hand across his forehead. 'Matty?'
'Matty.' Chantal was pouting at him. 'We need to find him.'
'I've got an idea.' Hunter stomped off away from her, his feet squelching on the damp mosaic tiles, and sidled up to the bar area.

Big Keith's eyes lit up as he caught sight of Hunter, his nostrils twitching. He was smoking a cigar, sucking deep on the brown leather. 'Gogs, can you smell bacon?'

Don't mention bacon...

Hunter stopped, the partition separating them. *Not now.*

He stared around them, the bar filled with lairy lads lying in the sun, drinking lager. The sounds of the pool, splashing and giggling and roars of laughter. Distant traffic. The smell of cigarette smoke and diesel belching out of a coach.

'Definitely some pork-based product.' Gordon Brownlee took another sip of beer. 'Maybe ham?'

Keith smirked. 'Or spam?'

'This isn't the time for this sort of shit.' Hunter checked the wall. Easy enough to jump over. Get high enough and crack Keith in the face as he landed, then settle in on Brownlee. His other two mates looked a bit handy, though.

He rested against the partition. 'I need to speak to Matty Ibbetson.'

'Oh aye?' Brownlee nodded slowly. 'Oink don't know where he is.' He frowned at Keith. 'Have you seen ham?'

Keith took another suck on his cigar. 'Might be in a pigpen.'

'I don't have time for—'

'Piss off, you pig bastard.' Brownlee shook his head as he got up. 'You can't come over here and expect us to help you.' He jabbed a finger at him, inches away from Hunter's nose. 'You arrested Sean, took me into the cop shop and now you're after Matty. When's it Big Keith's turn?'

Hunter stood up tall. Felt like he needed a few more feet to intimidate this lot. Not just a bunch of neds in Newhaven. 'Someone's raided our room and I'd—'

Brownlee stuck out his bottom lip and ran his finger over it. 'Aw, diddums.'

I could batter you into next—

Hunter's phone blasted out. He narrowed his eyes at Brownlee, then at Keith. 'This is serious. Where is he?'

Brownlee flicked him the Vs. 'Piss off, pig.'

Hunter glared at Keith then started smiling. 'I'll piss off, alright. But when I get home, I'll get in touch with the cops where you live. A little bit of stop and search every day. Maybe some accidental police violence when you resist arrest on some false charge. Every day.'

Keith scowled at him. 'You can't do that.'

'You live in Muirhouse, don't you?' Hunter nodded at Brownlee. 'Much easier to call in favours for you.'

Brownlee collapsed back into a chair, his face white.

'See you around.' Hunter walked off, checking his phone. Missed call from Finlay.

Shite.

He stuck it to his ear and scanned around, looking for a red Fiesta. 'What's up?'

Finlay's engine roared in the background. 'Been trying to call you, dude!'

'Sorry, something's come up.'

'Aye, well, I need a bit of a hand, jabroni.' The engine's roar turned to a squeal. 'Tulloch got out two minutes ago and a car picked him up. I'm following them right now.'

Hunter spun around. No signs of any new arrivals since the last scan. 'Where are you?'

'They're not far from where you're— Shite.' A squeal of brakes. 'They've stopped outside a bar. Just up from your hotel.'

'What?' Hunter started jogging up the slope away from the bar area. 'It's definitely Tulloch?'

'Aye, he's just got out of the car. And what the—?'

'What's going on?'

'Shite, he's gone down a lane at the side.'

Hunter sped up, his gut lurching. 'Is it the Cheap and Cheerful?'

'Aye, it is. Why?'

'That means he's going back to Luisa's apartment to finish the job.'

75

CHANTAL

Chantal caught up with Hunter by the main road as a bus thundered towards them. Could almost feel the ground rumbling through her sandals. 'You got him?'

He had his phone clamped to his ear. 'Going to voicemail, as per bloody usual.'

'Bloody hell.' She jogged along the road then darted through a gap in traffic. 'Are you leaving a message?'

'That's the fifth one.' Hunter followed her over the road as cars hissed past behind. 'What's the plan?'

Chantal stopped to look around. The lane at the side of Cheap and Cheerful was empty and quiet, but that didn't prove anything. 'We need to wait for Quaresma, Craig.'

'He let Tulloch go.'

'We still need to play by the rules.' Her phone blasted out. Quaresma. 'Here we go.' She answered it. 'We need—'

'Whatever you're about to say, Sergeant, save it.' Quaresma paused. Sounded like he was driving. 'Leave my country or I will arrest you and Constable Hunter. If he calls me one more time, I will—'

'You've let Tulloch go.' She stopped, hand on hip. 'Why?'

'Sergeant, I let Mr Tulloch go because he's not a suspect of any crimes in my country.'

Hunter stomped up the steps towards the bar manager, shouting the odds at him.

Chantal grimaced. Not the time to argue the toss. 'Look, we need some support here. He's gone back to Luisa Oliveira's apartment.'

'Their sex had consent.' Quaresma's voice hissed down the line. 'If you or Mr Hunter assault him again, I will arrest you.'

'Two men.'

'Get on the plane, Sergeant.'

Click.

Shite.

Chantal pocketed her phone and shook her head at Hunter as he stomped back down to her level. 'No dice.' She motioned behind him. 'What were you doing up there?'

'Having a go at our friend José the barman for not calling me when Tulloch showed up this morning.'

'Great, that's all we need.'

Hunter shrugged. 'We're screwed, aren't we?'

Chantal got out of the way of a red Fiesta as it barrelled towards her, the windows wound down. 'That's pretty much the size of it.'

'Size of what?' Finlay poked his tanned head out. 'Your wanger, Hunter?'

'I'm not in the mood.' Hunter crouched down next to the car. 'Where did he go?'

Finlay waved over at the bar. 'Down that alley.'

Chantal stared down the lane again. Tulloch was down there, doing God knows what to Luisa.

Chantal dug the heels of her hands into her eye sockets.

If we go in there, Quaresma will go apeshit.

But if we don't...

Footsteps rattled nearby.

'Shite!'

She opened her eyes again.

Finlay was staring at her, his eyes widening.

Tulloch was running right at her. He stepped into a right hook and punched Chantal on the cheek. She tumbled backwards over the bonnet of Finlay's car and cracked her head off the windscreen.

76

HUNTER

'No!' Hunter raced down the steps towards Finlay's car. Chantal rolled back over the car, her head crunching off the windscreen in a sickening thud. She toppled off the far side.

Hunter vaulted at Tulloch, hauling him face first onto the concrete. He dropped his knee on Tulloch's back. 'You don't hit women!'

Tulloch twisted to the left and threw Hunter off, his hip crunching against the edge of the pavement. Tulloch lashed out with his feet, thudding his boots into Hunter's fists.

Tulloch was up and driving both feet at Hunter's thighs, pushing him back against the car. Tulloch kicked Hunter in the balls. 'That's for earlier, you prick!'

White light burst in Hunter's eyes. White noise in his ears. He couldn't breathe. Just pain. Everywhere. His stomach. His arse. His balls felt like lava. He doubled over on the pavement and spat out vomit. The smell of stale piss and beer, warm concrete against his cheek.

A hand rested on Hunter's side. 'Christ, jabroni.'

Hunter opened his eyes. Finlay. 'Where is he?'

Finlay helped Hunter up. 'You okay?'

Hunter leaned against Finlay's car, sucking in deep breaths. Needles dug deep into his scrotum, felt like he'd pierced both bollocks. 'Have you got him?'

'I'm making sure you're okay, dude.'

Hunter cupped his balls. Couldn't feel anything other than nuclear fire.

Finlay got back into his car and tore off down the street.

Hunter rolled to his knees and tried to stand up. Felt like his balls were in his stomach.

Chantal was sitting by the side of the road, staring into space, dabbing at the back of her head. Her face was puffing up already, thickening around her left eye.

He stepped over to her and held out a hand to help her up. 'You okay?'

She stumbled back against the wall, blood trickling down the back of her neck, dyeing her shirt. 'Jesus.'

Behind them, the bar staff were out on the veranda with a couple of punters, looking on.

Finlay's car was stopped at traffic lights, Tulloch's army boots clopping away towards the beach.

He's getting away.

Hunter waved the barman over. 'Stay with her!'

∽

HUNTER THUNDERED ALONG THE STREET, his feet skidding on the downward slope. His balls were still on fire, but Tulloch wasn't getting away.

Not this time.

A long coach turning left blocked the junction up ahead. Couldn't see Tulloch or Finlay past it.

He slipped between two idling cars and waited for a gap to open up in the oncoming traffic, to weave round the back of the coach.

The street leading to the beach bent round at the end, where they'd walked back from the old town that afternoon. Tourists strolled hand in hand, pausing to frown back the way.

Further down the street, Finlay's Fiesta was pulled in by a backstreet strip bar, the neon sign dull in the daylight.

A couple were peering inside.

Hunter bombed over to the car and barged them out of the way. 'Police!' He checked inside.

No sign of Tulloch or Finlay.

Shite.

He stood tall, hands on hips, searching the area. No sign of them. No sign of anyone except bloody tourists.

No, wait. There.

Finlay's straight-backed run, weaving through a group of tourists towards the beach.

'Finlay! Wait!' Hunter pushed off from the car and started sprinting after him. 'WAIT!'

Crack.

Hunter stumbled to the ground, his shoulder feeling like it'd been pulled right out of the socket. Pain flowered in his skull. He almost hit the parked cars. His forehead was on fire.

What the—?

Matty Ibbetson stood over him, swinging brass knuckles round his pinkie. 'Alright, mate?' He took a dirty suck on a cigar, then tossed it into the gutter with another twirl of the brass.

Hunter touched his temple. Blood trickled over his fingers.

Matty put the knucks back on and lashed out. Hunter blocked the blow with his hands. The metal dug into his flesh and tore his wrist open. A searing pain ran up his arms.

Matty followed up with a boot to the side. Right where Tulloch had caught him earlier. Another kick in the ribs. 'Keep him here!' Then he was off, sprinting towards the beach.

Hunter opened his eyes again and tried to push up to standing. A meaty paw battered him back down.

Big Keith stood over him, brandishing a knife, the blade glinting in the sunlight. 'Up you get, wanker.'

Hunter pushed himself up to all fours. Then he brought himself slowly to his feet, hands raised. 'You won't get away with this.'

'I don't give a shit.' Keith lashed the knife towards him, half-arsed, teasing him. 'I'm going to gut you like a pig!'

Hunter jumped forward and clapped both fists into Keith's

wrist. He gripped it with his left and swung his right fist round, punching through Keith's jaw.

Caught a tooth right in the open wound. Pain shot up his arm.

He lashed out again, smacking Keith in the middle of his nose. And again. Then he stuck the head on and pushed him back against Finlay's car. He grabbed him by the ears and rammed his head against the bonnet. Twice, three times.

The giant tumbled over. Out cold.

Hunter stood there, panting, fire burning his hands, his sides, his ribs. His balls. Blood covered his face.

'No!' A shout boomed out from the beach.

'Shite.' Hunter loped off towards the sound, blood pouring out of his wounds, filling his eye socket. He wiped it away and tried to sprint on, but his legs weren't shifting fast enough.

The path twisted across the rocks heading for the golden sand. No sign of anyone, just the shine off a pair of brass knuckles lying in a rock pool.

Hunter slowed to a walk.

The tide was pushing out, leaving a stretch of damp beach exposed to the sun.

'No!' The shout battered around the walls of rock.

Hunter sped up but had to skid to a halt at a wide plateau a few steps down.

Tulloch and Finlay were squaring up at the edge of the rocks. Tulloch was jerking forward, throwing fake punches and laughing. Toying with him.

Finlay locked eyes with Hunter. He was heavily outgunned and he knew it.

Matty roared towards them. Finlay saw it too late, twisting round as Matty barged into him. Finlay's arms windmilled backwards across the rocks. He tripped and skidded. Then he disappeared off the side.

Matty stumbled and fell to his knees, panting between barked laughter. 'That's how you do it, mate!'

Tulloch raced across the path towards the beach, Matty following him down.

Hunter sprinted over and stopped at the edge.

Finlay lay on his back on the sand, moaning, face covered in blood.

77

CHANTAL

Chantal leaned against the red Fiesta and rubbed at her head. Black blood still flecked off her fingers. She dialled Hunter's number again. Still no answer.

Where the hell are they?

A few tourists gawped, hiding behind their hands. Some looked down from their balconies, shielding their eyes from the sun. Three dark-skinned girls stood outside the lap dancing bar, squinting at her.

'NOOOOOO!'

The scream came from round the bend. The beach.

Chantal stumbled across the path towards the sound. No sign of Hunter. 'Craig!' She skittered over the paving until it became rocks. 'Craig!'

Two men ran along the wet sand away from her, chased by a small dog. A game of football was kicking off back towards the old town.

Hunter was over by the edge of the cliffs, in a daze.

'Craig!' She bounced forward and grabbed hold of him, pulling him into a tight hug, away from the edge. 'Come here!'

Hunter settled into the hug. 'He's... Finlay...'

'What?' She let go. 'What did you say?'

'Finlay! He's killed him!' Hunter swallowed hard. 'He's killed Finlay.'

'What? Who has?'

'Matty!' Hunter looked around, confusion creasing his forehead. 'Where's Matty?'

Chantal grabbed his shoulders and tried to get him to lock eyes with her. She shook him. 'Where's Finlay?'

Hunter pointed down, off the rocks.

She stepped over to the edge. Finlay lay on the rocks below, coughing and huffing, his cracked body contorted.

'Go!' Chantal put her phone to her ear and followed him down the path. It rang and rang.

Some gritty Portuguese erupted from the speaker. 'Boa tarde.'

'I need urgent medical attention to the Praia da Oura beach.' Chantal dropped down the path to the sands. 'We're at the road leading from the street by the Hotel de Sousa to...'

Hunter was kneeling next to Finlay.

He coughed, spitting blood down his chin. Crimson soaked his shirt. He looked up at Hunter, his eyes struggling to focus. 'Did we get him?'

~

THE PARAMEDIC NUDGED Hunter back but couldn't sever the hand hold. 'Let go!'

Chantal tried to pull him back. but Hunter held on tighter. *He can be a stubborn bastard.*

Finlay's eyes were still open, swivelling around in his head. They closed again.

Hunter slapped his face, making his eyes jerk open again. 'We need to keep his eyes open.'

The paramedic took a handful of Hunter's T-shirt. 'Sir, let go.'

'Keep him alive!'

'I'm trying, sir.' The paramedic pushed the trolley towards the ambulance and started winching it up.

Chantal wrapped her arms around Hunter, half in affection, half trying to control him. 'He's going to be okay...' She worked her way round to cuddle him from the front, blocking his path to the ambulance. 'This isn't our battle anymore.'

Hunter's nostrils flared. Didn't look under control. 'He's got to stay alive.'

The ambulance's back door slammed and the engine sparked into life.

'We'll get Matty for this.'

'It's not enough.' Hunter collapsed into her embrace. 'It's nowhere near enough. If we'd had Ibbetson and Tulloch, Finlay would still be... would still...' He rested his head on her shoulder. He touched the back of her head. 'Shite. He got you as well, didn't he?'

She brushed his hand away. 'I'm fine.'

'Are you sure?'

Chantal rubbed at the back of her head. 'He got lucky.' The blue lights of the ambulance shone ahead of them.

Hunter sighed and looked down at the blonde sand, already covered in dirty footprints. 'We should've stopped this.'

She grabbed his hand tight. 'It's not your fault.'

'How isn't it?' Hunter shot her a glare. 'Lightning striking twice... Of course this is my bloody fault.'

Another grip of his hand, trying to send a pulse into it. 'If it's anyone's fault, it's mine. I'm the ranking officer at the crime scene. If anyone should've stopped what happened to Finlay, it's me. Okay?'

'I brought him into this, got him doing that PI shit. If wasn't for me, he'd be drinking heavily somewhere...' He swallowed again. 'It should've been me.'

'What?'

'It should've been me fighting them, not Finlay. I'm trained to. Fin wasn't.'

'They're both big guys, Craig.'

Hunter shrugged. 'So am I.'

'Craig, Tulloch got lucky. Two against one. His mate turned up and joined in.'

Hunter's head darted around. 'Where's Keith?'

'What?'

'Keith attacked me. He had a knife.'

Chantal followed his gaze. The tourists were giving statements to some local uniform. No sign of any of Tulloch's crew. She grabbed his hand and pulsed it again. 'They'll catch Tulloch and Ibbetson. Quaresma will do them for what's happened.'

Fire burnt deep in his eyes. 'We need to get Tulloch.'

'Craig…'

He's right.

But how?

A lone figure stood in the blinding sunshine by a black Audi. Quaresma, smoothing down a stray spike of grey hair.

'Come on.' Chantal led him away from the flashing lights and the reversing ambulance.

Quaresma raised his eyebrows at their approach. 'Sergeant, this is not good.'

Chantal jabbed a finger into his chest. 'You should've kept Sean Tulloch in custody.'

Quaresma grabbed her finger and swallowed a sigh. 'Do we need to go over this again?'

'Tulloch was heading back to Luisa's apartment.' Chantal thumbed back up the way. 'What do you think he was going to do there?'

Quaresma leaned back against his car and clicked his tongue a few times. 'You had this Finlay Sinclair follow him, didn't you?'

'I'm not answering that.' Chantal folded her arms. 'I suggest you find Tulloch.'

Quaresma ran his tongue over his teeth, his eyes flicking between Chantal and Hunter. 'Because of your unlawful actions, I now have a murder case on top of everything else.'

Hunter's eyes bulged. 'Murder?'

'Well, I doubt Mr Sinclair is going to pull through.' Quaresma turned to watch the ambulance trundle up the road, giving a blast of siren to clear the way. 'My priority is in prosecuting whoever did this.'

'It was Matthew Ibbetson.'

Quaresma looked away. 'We have officers out searching for him.'

'And Tulloch?'

'We will ensure whoever did this spends a good portion of the rest of his life in a jail.'

Chantal shook her head. 'Glad you take something seriously.'

'Excuse me?'

'Nothing.' She shrugged, the energy seeping out of her body.

'Tell me you've got Keith?'

'Keith?' Quaresma frowned into space then nodded slowly. He thumbed behind him. 'We've got a record of Keith Brannigan saying someone assaulted him.'

'Assaulted *him*?' Hunter got between them. '*He* attacked *me*. With a knife!'

Chantal cleared her throat. 'Keith attacked Craig after Sean Tulloch assaulted me. Matty Ibbetson attacked Craig then... then pushed Finlay off the edge. You need to prosecute him for that, at least.'

Quaresma let out a deep sigh. 'Sergeant, before you leave my country, I need some statements from you and Mr Hunter.'

78

HUNTER

Hunter walked up the road towards the hotel, for the last time, leading Chantal by the hand. *Two minutes in a room with Matty. That's all I need.*

She let out a sigh. 'I need to call Sharon.'

'She'll tell us to head home.'

'You don't think we should?'

Hunter raised his shoulders. 'I don't think it's— Wait a sec.' He jogged over to the bar, his trainers squeaking as he ran.

'Craig!'

The bar was pretty empty now, just a load of older punters sinking pre-dinner drinks. A few of the Irish hens sat nursing hangovers and glasses of wine at the other side. An old couple nearby were staring at Hunter, giving him the up and down.

No sign of Tulloch or any of that crowd.

Hunter craned his neck to look around. Then he slumped back against the fence. 'Shite.'

Chantal caught up with him. 'What the hell are you doing?'

'They're not here.'

'Who? Tulloch? Hardly.' She scowled at him. 'You honestly expected them to be here, waiting for you?'

Hunter clenched his fists. 'I need to find them. They can't—'

'Craig. Stop.' She grabbed his arms. 'You need to focus.'

'They... they've killed Finlay.'

'We don't know that.'

'He's broken and...'

'Come on, I need to speak to Sharon, okay?' She pointed at her matted clothes. 'And we can't walk around looking like this, can we?'

79

CHANTAL

'Sharon, we can't leave it like this.' Chantal paced towards their apartment, gripping her phone for grim death. 'Tulloch's still at—'

'We've got no choice here.' Sharon sighed down the line. Office chatter rattled in the background. 'Chantal, I told you and Craig to get back here. My orders still stand.'

Chantal stopped by their door. Tulloch's room was right there. Not twenty metres away. 'We need to—'

'Just stop!' Sharon's voice echoed around in the background. More donut chatter cut in. 'I should never have agreed to this in the first place. First, Craig assaults Tulloch. Next, he's involved in a failed arrest. Now someone's *dead* because you got him tailing Tulloch!'

'He's not dead.'

'Yet.'

'Shaz, Tulloch's on the run now. He's desperate and at his weakest.' Chantal slid her hair behind her ear. Blood cracked on her temple. 'He's raped someone and assaulted God knows how many, and now he's involved in what's happened to Finlay.'

'Wait, Finlay? It was Finlay bloody Sinclair?' Sharon sighed again. Someone asked if she wanted a coffee. They didn't get a reply. 'What was he doing there?'

Chantal glanced over at Hunter, like a cry for help. He unlocked their door and went inside. She followed him in. The place was still a mess. 'Helping us.'

'What? Why?'

'Because we asked him.'

A door slammed and the office chatter died. 'You're still checked in for that flight. Get on it.'

Chantal sat on the edge of the bed. 'Just one more day, Shaz. That's all we need.'

'No. Quaresma's people will track down Tulloch. Failing that, it's Rollo-Smith's remit.'

'What?'

'Listen to me, Quaresma's people have locked down Tulloch's room and he's on a no-fly list, okay? He's not getting out of the country. You are.'

'Shaz...'

'Chantal, I need you back here so I can pour boiling oil on the pair of you. Get to the airport.' Sharon paused. 'And I mean it this time. Okay?'

Chantal looked over at Hunter, eyebrows raised. Looked like he wanted do anything but head back to Scotland.

What was the right move? Stay and fight?

The RMP would win. Tulloch would escape justice for what he's done. His victims wouldn't be able to heal their suffering.

Hunter jolted to his feet and reached for the phone.

Here we bloody go...

Chantal glared at him, trying to get him to shut up. 'We've seen what he's done with our own eyes. One woman raped, another plied with spiked drinks. What happened with Luisa, I don't know. I think it's another attempted rape. We need to make sure he pays for these crimes and all the crimes back home. We can't just go home.'

Sharon was quiet for a few seconds. Office chatter boomed out loud as before. 'I expect you on that plane.'

Chantal let her head fall. 'We'll be on that flight.'

'Good.'

Click.

'Bloody hell...' Chantal tossed the phone onto the bed. Hunter was over by the window, staring out.

She started stripping off her clothes, bloody and soaked with sweat. Her hair was matted solid. She padded through to the shower and turned on the water. It burst out, a tepid trickle. Within seconds, it heated up and shot out in a torrent. She stepped under the spray and worked the water into the wound on her head, cleaning it. Her feet were covered in red water, starting to fill the bathtub. The shampoo stung as she lathered it into the wound.

All this pain and agony and we don't have Tulloch.

Finlay is lying in hospital, his life in the balance, and Tulloch is... What? Where the hell is he?

HUNTER

The shower's white noise hissed through the apartment. Hunter sat on the balcony, scanning around for any movement outside. Like he was on an operation again, hunting insurgents. Looking for enemy combatants.

Just...

He checked his phone. No news on Finlay.

Won't even get a chance to visit him in hospital. Poor guy was alone, nobody to see him.

Maybe calling Mary would be a good idea, let her know, at least. Maybe she'd come out here. And what? See her broken ex-husband? At least give her the choice.

His phone flashed up. Elvis. He stabbed the screen. 'Finally...'

'Craig, I heard about Finlay.'

How? Bloody Quaresma banging those jungle drums.

'Right... He'll pull through.'

'Sure?'

Hunter didn't reply.

Down the line, horse-racing commentary blared out of a TV

speaker somewhere. Elvis was in the bookies, as per bloody usual. 'You still in Portugal, mate?'

'Why?'

'Well, DI McNeill told me to pick you up from the airport, bring you straight back here.'

Hunter stopped at the top of the stairs and shut his eyes. 'Did she now?'

'Tell me about it. Hell of a day I've had. Just getting my piece now, mate.'

'In the bookies?'

'That's a problem?'

Not the time to get into it.

Hunter swapped his phone to the other hand. 'Have you got anything on Tulloch?'

'Like what?'

'Where he is?'

'No, mate. We're monitoring all the airports. Nothing's pinged up. Fat Jimmy's calling round on repeat. Nobody under that name has travelled.'

'What about under another name?'

'Very good. Got his photo and description with all the airlines. They're checking that, too. Tulloch's a pretty unique fella, hard to miss. Already stopped some giant psychopath from getting on a flight from Faro. Turned out the boy was Polish, lives in Edinburgh.'

'What about the other end?'

'Craig, he's on a no-fly list. Drop it.'

'Right. Keep me posted, okay?' Hunter killed the call and pocketed his phone. He leaned back in the creaking chair and put his feet up, let the sun attack his skin.

What to do, what to do...

Get on that plane? Go home, tail between our legs?

Stay and fight?

CHANTAL

Chantal twisted the handle to cold and let the freezing water blast her head, her shoulders, her back, her bruised arse. Her breath slipped out in a rapid pant. Then she twisted the shower off and grabbed a towel, wrapping it around her hair.

She snatched Hunter's towel and started drying herself off.

All that time preparing a case and it goes to shite so quickly. All that work, for nothing.

She wrapped the towel round her body.

Finlay lying in a hospital bed, dying because of her.

She walked back through and fished out the only clean clothes that hadn't been soaked. Black top, black skirt.

Should just wear a white flag.

She hauled on her underwear then tugged the skirt up.

Hunter was out on the balcony, tapping his phone off his hands, usually a bad sign. All that thinking going on inside that skull. He'd changed into shorts and a T-shirt, finally looking like the Scotsman abroad. *Filthy sod hadn't showered.* 'That call didn't sound like it went well.'

She hauled her top on and sat on the edge of the bed. 'We're leaving.'

He scowled at her. 'So that's it? We're flying back?'

'Like we have a choice.' Chantal stared out of the window. Dark clouds billowed in off the sea, like a fortnight in Ullapool. Two rainbows arced through the sky, the sun still bright in the foreground. 'Is there anything else we can do?'

Hunter shrugged. 'We can stay here.'

'And wait for Quaresma to arrest you.' Chantal put her feet into her sandals and tightened the grips. 'You saw what he was like at the crime scene.' She paced over to him, resting her head on his shoulders. He flinched away, so she kissed it instead. Both of them, battered and bruised, for no benefit. 'We don't have a Plan B, do we?'

'I'm all out of ideas.' Hunter pushed away. 'It'd be nice to stay here for a couple more nights. I'm so tired I could do with lying on the beach.'

'Sipping wine and reading.' She wrapped him in a hug. 'A nice red from the—'

Across the quad, Tulloch's door burst open and Captain Brian Rollo-Smith stormed out, shaking his head.

Chantal grabbed Hunter's hand. 'That looks like a Plan B to me.'

82

HUNTER

Hunter stomped across the paving towards Tulloch's room, his knee cracking as he walked. 'Captain!'

Rollo-Smith stood outside, ramrod straight, chatting to a local uniformed officer. He spun round and frowned at them. 'Lance Corporal Hunter.' Then he rolled his eyes. 'You're still in the country, I see.'

'Just leaving. Surprised to see you, though.'

Rollo-Smith gestured for the uniform to leave them. 'I need to visit the scene of Private Tulloch's alleged crime.' He paused as Chantal arrived. 'The rape.'

'Which one?'

Rollo-Smith scowled at Chantal. 'There has been more than one?'

'Two that we know of. And he's party to an attempted murder.'

'Let's take a step back, shall we?' Rollo-Smith got out a small notebook and a black pen with brass fittings. 'You're suggesting Private Tulloch has been on some sort of crime spree in the Algarve?'

'It's not a suggestion.' Hunter shoved his hands in his pockets, grabbing his keys and his wallet. 'Speak to Inspector Quaresma.'

Rollo-Smith nodded slowly. 'I have an appointment with the good Inspector soon.'

'He likes his appointments.' Hunter glanced inside the room. Nothing much going on in there, just a uniformed officer looking bored. 'Why are you really here?'

'Due diligence.'

'And have you got anything?'

Rollo-Smith shrugged. 'This room has been cleared out.'

Hunter pointed into the room. 'Heather Latimer was raped in there. Her blood toxicology will show he laced her drinks with that GHB.'

'You're sure of this?'

'Again, ask Quaresma.'

'Of course.' Rollo-Smith rubbed his gleaming forehead. 'Listen, do you know if anyone's done a full forensic analysis of this room?'

Hunter nodded at the uniform in the room. 'Can't you ask him?'

'He's my chaperone, Lance Corporal.'

'What?' Hunter's gut lurched. 'Hasn't he been guarding?'

'He met me at Faro half an hour ago and brought me straight here.'

'Shite.' Hunter barged past him into the room, blood thudding in his ears. The stupid bastards had left the place unattended.

Meaning Tulloch can get back in here and...

Hunter raced over and picked up the pile of stuff by the kettle. The camera case was gone. 'You stupid bastards.'

Chantal stopped next to him. 'What's up?'

Hunter grimaced. 'Tulloch's passport and MOD90 have gone.' He scowled at Rollo-Smith. 'You need to—'

'I will not take orders from you.'

'This is all your fault, you know that?'

'Excuse me?'

'You've dropped a bollock here.' Hunter stepped forward. 'If you'd been on the ball, we'd have Sean Tulloch in custody. Paisley Sanderson wouldn't be in hospital. Heather Latimer wouldn't have been raped. Finlay Sinclair wouldn't be fighting for his life!'

Rollo-Smith grabbed his wrists and locked his thumbs. 'Listen, sonny, I'm a Captain. You were a Lance Corporal before your discharge.'

'Discharge? You cheeky bastard.' Hunter shook him off. 'You've got no power over me. I don't even have to call you "sir".'

'Of course you don't.' Rollo-Smith leered at him, his big demon head feeling like it was looming over him. 'Inspector Quaresma has made me aware of your behaviour out here. Kicking the snot out of anyone who looks down their nose at you.'

'You better watch out, then.'

'Excuse me?' Rollo-Smith shook his head. 'Lance Corporal, you need to leave or Inspector Quaresma shall have you on charges.' He nodded at Chantal. 'I suggest you follow orders for once'

'We're not letting you—'

'Craig...' Chantal seized Hunter's elbow and led him away. 'Come on.'

'No, he needs—'

'Drop it.' She tugged hard at his arm and he let her pull him away from Rollo-Smith.

~

HUNTER STOPPED OUTSIDE THEIR ROOM. 'This is a bloody nightmare.'

'Craig, we need to *go*.' She grabbed his elbow again. 'Come on.'

'We can't—'

'Craig, you've heard what everyone's got to say. We need to get out of here.'

Hunter brushed Chantal off and looked back the way. Rollo-Smith was outside Tulloch's room, almost shouting into his phone. *Prick.*

Going back to Scotland is giving up. Letting Tulloch get away with it.

Leaving poor Anna Crichton tied up on a bed for three days, a bowl of stale water for company, while he went to Blackpool with his mates. Treating her like... That. No one deserved that.

Battering the living shite out of Paisley. After all he'd put her through.

But... What else could they do? There wasn't anything, was there? I can't give up, not yet.

One last futile glare at Rollo-Smith and Hunter went inside. He started chucking his clothes back into his suitcase and looked over at Chantal. 'Here's the thing. Tulloch's ID is gone. What does that mean to you?'

She was mirroring him, throwing her possessions in the case. 'Craig... Come on.'

'I'm serious.' Hunter shoved his washbag into the pouch at the front. 'What does it mean?'

'That he's left the country or is on his way out.'

'Well, maybe. Maybe not.' He shook his head at her. 'What it means is he's been in that room since attacking Finlay.'

She frowned, looking like she wasn't quite following his logic.

'His MOD90 was in the room a couple of hours ago.' Hunter checked his watch. 'It's half six now. Nearer eight hours, but most of that time he was in the police station. His MOD90's gone now...'

Chantal rammed her washbag in the case and stuffed it down. 'So where is he?'

'That's the million-dollar question.' Hunter scanned around the room. Be lucky to get back their deposit. 'Look, Elvis said Quaresma's stopping Tulloch flying out of the country. Which means he's still in Portugal.'

'He could've driven, though.' She zipped up her case. 'Could be in Spain.' She kicked her case over towards the door. 'Or he could've got a boat and be tucking into some Marrakech hash right now.'

Hunter let his head dip. 'I need to find him.'

She tapped on her watch. 'We need to get on that plane, Craig.'

'He can't...'

'Come on.' Chantal wrapped an arm around him. 'It's not our fight anymore. We've got to leave this to Quaresma and Rollo-Smith, okay?'

Can't leave it like this...

Hunter fished out his phone and dialled Quaresma again.

'Craig, what are you doing?'

He went back out to the patio. 'Give me a second.'

Quaresma answered it quickly. 'Constable.' He sighed, clicking his tongue against his teeth. 'Do you need a lift to the airport?'

Hunter leaned back against the wall. 'Have your forensics officers been through Tulloch's room yet?'

'We've not had the chance.' Quaresma paused. Sounded like an engine firing up in the background. 'It's just been a monitoring operation so far.'

'Not a very good one. Tulloch's been in there and taken his ID with him.'

'Shit.' Quaresma hissed into the phone. 'Shit.' The engine noise got louder. 'Why have you been in his room, Constable?'

'I haven't. But I take it you know Captain Rollo-Smith is there now?'

Quaresma hissed again. 'Stay there.'

'I've got to leave the country, I'm afraid.' Hunter killed the call and pocketed his phone.

Chantal got in front of him and blocked him getting past, her nostrils flared. 'Craig... What are you doing now?'

'Causing some mischief.'

'You need to grow up.'

Rain started hammering down, thick stair rods drilling into his shoulders. Like a Tuesday afternoon in Stranraer.

Over the quad, Elena and another two officers stood guard outside Tulloch's apartment. He gave her a nod, got one back.

Gordon Brownlee staggered past her, looking like he'd spent all day hard at it. He stopped by the apartment next to Tulloch's and fumbled some keys out of his pocket.

Hunter barged past Chantal. 'Come on.'

~

THROUGH THE WINDOW, Gordon Brownlee was sitting on a chair in full-on hangover slump, flicking through TV channels.

Hunter tapped on the door and waited, out of view. He smiled at Elena, her eyes narrowing. 'Meeting a friend.'

Elena nodded and looked away.

Chantal got up close and whispered, 'Craig, what the hell are you up to?'

Another knock on the door. 'If this doesn't work, we're getting on that plane. Okay?'

'Craig, come on...'

The door slid open and Hunter wedged his foot in the gap. Gordon Brownlee stood there, giving him the up and down. 'What the hell do you want?'

'Where's Tulloch?'

'What?' Brownlee pushed the door. It dunted off Hunter's toes. 'Piss off.'

Hunter nodded at Chantal, his eyebrows up, then thumped again. 'Where is he?'

Brownlee looked away. 'Not seen him for a while.'

'That's bollocks.'

'Piss off.' Brownlee shoved the door. Hunter caught it with his foot and heaved it back, cracking off Brownlee's nose. Hunter stepped forward and grabbed Brownlee's throat, pushing him inside, pinning him against the wall. 'Where is Tulloch?'

'I've no idea!'

'Tell me where he is.'

'Help!' Brownlee's shout came out as a whisper.

Hunter nodded at the wall. 'Thought you were staying next door?'

'Cops aren't letting me in.' Brownlee sucked in air. 'Matty gave me his keycard.'

'Where is he?'

'No idea, man.' Brownlee grabbed Hunter's hands, trying to pry them away from his throat. 'Not seen Sean since last night.'

'You're lying.' Wriggling bastard was going to alert the cops next door. Hunter pushed him against the wall with a thud. Like that's any better. 'Where is he?'

'He's not been here!'

Hunter tightened his grip on Brownlee's throat. 'You and Keith were with him this afternoon, weren't you?'

'Stop that!' Brownlee pushed Hunter away then rubbed at his throat. 'Sitting, having a few beers. Sean called Matty. Matty ran off. Keith went with him. This was hours ago, man.'

'About five o'clock?'

'Maybe.'

Hunter glanced at the door. No sign of Chantal. 'It was to attack me, wasn't it?'

'No.' Brownlee pushed Hunter back. 'That bird wouldn't—'

The door burst open.

83

CHANTAL

Chantal checked behind her. That female uniformed officer was looking their way. Hunter was about to go all Rambo on Brownlee. *The last thing we bloody need.*

She walked towards her, smiling. 'It's Elena, isn't it?'

She got a narrow-eyed smile in response. 'What's going on in there?'

'One of Craig's friends from his army days.'

Elena frowned. 'He's a soldier?'

'Was.' Chantal leaned against the wall outside the front door. 'Weirdest coincidence, right?'

Elena barked out a laugh. 'I do not like coincidence.'

'Me neither.' Chantal gave her a sisterly grin. 'Did you get to interview Sean Tulloch in the end?'

Another nod, smaller and shorter, but noticeable. 'He is a pig.'

'And, still, your boss let him go?'

'He is not my boss.' Elena made a face like she wanted to spit. 'Craig told me what that *pig* did to those women in your country. Is it true?'

Chantal huffed out a sigh. 'The trouble is getting the victims to confirm it, you know?'

'Is problem we have here. Nobody will speak.'

A thud came from behind them.

Chantal tried to act like it was nothing. 'Do you have any idea where Tulloch is?'

Elena shook her head. 'He is vanished.'

Chantal ran a hand through her hair, still damp from her shower. How much bloody time did he need? She leaned back against the wall. 'It's nice here.'

'Too much sun.'

'Not a thing where I'm from.'

'Where is?'

'Edinburgh.'

'I know that city. Is lovely.' Elena frowned. 'Your skin is not Scottish, though. I mean—' Her radio blasted out static and a wall of guttural Portuguese. She entered Tulloch's room and answered it.

Chantal nodded at the two officers inside with her. Male, more interested in checking her out than stopping Hunter... doing whatever he was doing to Brownlee.

Elena burst out of the room, clutching her radio, and barged past Chantal. 'I need to deal with this.' She unholstered her pistol and kicked the door open. She aimed her gun at Hunter, then shifted it to point at Brownlee. 'Gordon Brownlee, I'm arresting you for the murder of Finlay Sinclair.'

Brownlee raised his hands. 'I've done nothing!'

Hunter got between Elena and Brownlee. 'This is wrong. He didn't push Finlay.'

She glanced at him. 'I have my orders.'

'But it was Matty Ibbetson.'

'You need to take this up with Inspector Quaresma, my friend.' Elena unfolded a pair of handcuffs and slapped them on Brownlee's left wrist. 'I need to read him his rights. If you get in my way one more time, I will—'

'It wasn't him!' Hunter's whole body clenched. His eyes flickered. 'Wait, did you say murder?' He swallowed hard. 'You mean attempted murder, don't you?'

Elena snapped the other cuff on and led Brownlee towards the door. 'You need to speak to the Inspector.'

Hunter stormed out of the room, his eyes like tiny pinpricks. Chantal wanted to grab him, take him away and calm him down.

Quaresma stepped out, shaking his head at Rollo-Smith. 'Here they are, indeed. Very clearly not at Faro airport.'

'What's happened to Finlay?'

Quaresma's head slumped low. 'I'm very sorry. Finlay Sinclair died.'

84

HUNTER

Hunter sucked in breath, bitter and acidic. Snot bubbled in his nose. 'He's... He...'

The bedsprings creaked as Chantal sat next to him. Her hand stroked down his back.

He wrapped an arm around her and held her there. The shitty hotel room spinning, Finlay Sinclair's life dispersing around them, his last breath fizzing out into the air. Nothing of him left, just a pile of skin, flesh and bone. His personality, his annoying habits, his everything, all gone.

Jabroni.

Twat.

She kissed his cheek. 'Do you want me to stay?'

Hunter grabbed her hand, clutching it between both of his. 'Of course I want you to stay.'

'You need to let it out.'

Hunter rubbed his cheeks, swiping the tears away like a windscreen wiper. 'I'll grieve for him later.' He looked over at the door, his eyes narrowing to a thin strip. 'Right now, I want to make sure we get Matty for this.'

A knock on the door.

Quaresma leaning in, pouting. 'Mr Hunter, does Mr Sinclair have a next of kin?'

'His parents are dead.' Hunter brushed away fresh tears. 'He got divorced a few years ago. No kids either.' His forehead creased. 'Do you know what happened?'

Quaresma nodded. 'He cracked rib in his fall, tore something. Bad luck. Mr Sinclair bled out. The paramedics and the doctors tried everything they could, but...'

Hunter got up and paced around the room. The curtains weren't fully shut, letting in light. 'I was speaking to him. He didn't have any blood in his mouth or...'

'I understand. That's what the doctor told me.' Quaresma perched on the dressing table opposite Chantal. 'She assures me there's nothing anyone could have done.'

Hunter stopped next to him and leaned low. 'Nothing we could've done?' He gripped the edge of the table. 'How about arresting Tulloch when we asked? Pick any of the times, go on. I can count at least four of them.'

'Don't play that card, Constable. I'm warning you.'

Hunter stood, blood curdling in his veins. 'You let him go and...'

Quaresma looked down his long nose at Hunter then at Chantal. 'Now, I will escort you to the airport.'

Hunter gritted his teeth. 'You let him murder someone!'

Quaresma jolted upright and jabbed a finger in the air. 'This is my country!' His words rattled round the small room. He rubbed a gob of saliva from his lips. 'You are leaving! Now!'

The door opened behind them. 'I could hear you in France, João.' Hunter didn't even have to look round. Rollo-Smith's syrupy tones. 'Can I have a moment with them, please?'

Quaresma shook his head. 'Anything you want to say, you can say in front of me.'

Rollo-Smith held the door open wide and smiled at Quaresma. 'Two minutes, please.'

'Very well.' Quaresma huffed to his feet and trudged out, keeping a leery glare on Chantal. He slammed the door.

CHANTAL

Rollo-Smith cracked his knuckles, left then right. Sounded like he'd snapped the ligaments. 'Now what the bloody hell is going on here, mm?'

Chantal ran a hand through her hair. *Play it cool. And keep playing it cool.* 'We were obtaining intelligence on—'

'Sergeant.' Rollo-Smith shook his head slowly. 'Sergeant, Sergeant, Sergeant. How about I give you a little bit of friendly advice, mm?' He left a pause, but Chantal wasn't going to fill it. 'Your behaviour and that of your colleague is close to turning this into an international incident. You have to leave.'

Chantal hauled herself to her feet and stepped away from him. 'We need to bring Tulloch and Matty in.'

'Matty? Who?'

'Ibbetson. Another one of your lot. He killed Finlay Sinclair.'

Rollo-Smith clenched his jaw. 'Inspector Quaresma has Gordon Brownlee in custody.'

'He's got the wrong man.'

'Need I remind you that you're on foreign territory and you are expected to extend due courtesy to those officers guiding you, mm?' Rollo-Smith let it rest for a few seconds. 'João is an honest man, doing an honest job here.'

'When did you get on first name terms with him?'

'I'll have your bloody badge, Sergeant.' This is a disgrace.'

'The only disgrace here is how your good friend *João* can aid and abet Sean Tulloch's crimes in this country.'

Rollo-Smith stopped, his breath hissing out. He shut his eyes. 'Do you have any evidence, Sergeant?'

Chantal looked away. 'We've been here since early yesterday and, at every opportunity, he's slowed us down. Or got in our way.'

Hunter pulled away from the window, looking like he was going to kick into some martial arts. 'He—'

'Lance Corporal Hunter, enough.' Rollo-Smith held up a thick paper file. 'João passed me this. Do you know what it pertains to?'

Chantal didn't even have to look at it.

Rollo-Smith shook the file in the air. 'It details the times you have assaulted someone in the very short time you've been here. Now, João is promising to rip this up if you clear off. But you don't seem to want to—'

'He's got the wrong man in custody!'

'Lance Corporal...' Rollo-Smith walked over to Hunter and gripped him by the arm. 'An ex-colleague of yours lies dead because *you* enlisted him in some illicit activities.'

Hunter frowned at him. 'What?'

'Don't think you're dealing with some civilian officer, Hunter. I know what you've been up to.' Rollo-Smith took out a photo showing Hunter getting out of Finlay's car outside the police station. 'You honestly thought the local officers wouldn't notice a red Fiesta in their car park, mm? You had Mr Sinclair tail Tulloch.'

Hunter looked up at him. 'This isn't my fault.'

'It bloody is!' Spittle flew from Rollo-Smith's mouth, landing on Hunter's cheek. 'Believe you me, the MOD takes Private Tulloch's actions very seriously. If there is a shred of evidence that he's been up to anything illegal, then I will frogmarch him back to the UK for a court martial. But you...' He shook his head. 'You have undermined me at every step. You've muddied the waters sufficiently well that nobody knows what the bloody hell's going on. And, because of your actions, Mr Tulloch is nowhere to be seen.'

Hunter wiped at his cheek. 'My actions?'

'Your actions have destroyed any hope of securing a prosecution on Portuguese soil.' Rollo-Smith grabbed his bicep. 'Right, Lance Corporal, let's process you.'

No you don't, you monkey bastard.

'You've no authority over me, here or back home.' Hunter pushed him away. 'I'm not the one you should be arresting.'

'You're not giving me any choice!' Rollo-Smith pulled him outside. 'Come on!'

Thump, thump, thump. Quaresma was ploughing across the quad from the other end. DI Bruce was following him, his face flushed with umpteen pints.

Hunter stopped dead. 'What's happened?'

Bruce swivelled round to him. 'Your mate Tulloch is on a flight to Newcastle.'

HUNTER

Quaresma pulled out into the oncoming lane as they bombed out of Albufeira, blasting past a lorry, the low sun almost blinding.

Hunter sat back, his throat tight. Couldn't feel anything.

Chantal sat next to him, phone clamped to her ear. 'Right, Shaz, I'll see you in Newcastle.' She killed the call and put her mobile away, then gave Hunter a glance. 'They're holding up the plane for us.'

Quaresma swerved past another lorry, the speedo clearing a hundred and twenty. 'You are very lucky.'

Hunter locked eyes with him in the rear-view and gave him a glare. 'If you'd done your job, we'd be taking Tulloch back, not chasing him.'

'Be thankful you have power of arrest in your own country.'

'And what about Finlay Sinclair? Should I be thankful he's dead?'

'It is not my fault, Constable.'

'You've got the wrong man.'

Quaresma gave him a short look. 'The wrong man?'

'Gordon Brownlee didn't kill Finlay. Matty Ibbetson did.'

Quaresma spoke Portuguese at his phone. It started ringing through the stereo and he had a loud conversation with someone in his native tongue.

Hunter slumped back in the seat, starting to rattle through the timeline. A couple of hours were missing, unaccounted for. 'How the hell did Tulloch get on that flight?'

Chantal glowered at him. 'Elvis was supposed to be monitoring flights to Scottish airports and he seems to have forgotten the rest of the UK.'

～

QUARESMA SWERVED off the main road and pulled up in front of the airport. A local squad car was idling by a heavy-duty guard entrance. He swung round and grabbed Hunter's arm. 'These men will take you to the plane. Make sure you follow them.'

'Thanks.' Hunter tried to shrug his grip off, but it wasn't budging any. 'Do you mind?'

'Are you listening to me?' Quaresma narrowed his eyes at them. 'If I ever see you in my country again, I will arrest you. You understand?'

'I won't be back in a hurry.' Hunter got himself free and hefted up his bag. He followed Chantal across the tarmac towards the squad car, her case squeaking as she dragged it behind her.

Another black Audi pulled up. Rollo-Smith eased himself out of the passenger seat and tapped the roof. He glowered at Hunter then shooed him off. 'Hurry up! The plane is waiting for us!'

Bruce got out of the other side, head bowed as he traipsed off.

Hunter caught up with him. 'You're heading back, too?'

'Orders from the top.' Bruce shook his head, stinking of breath mints, his face ruddied with booze. 'Absolute shambles, anyway. We're pissing money away out here. Public money.'

～

HUNTER STARED through the tiny window, the pinging light on the wing the only illumination in the pitch black. In the distance, the yellow gridline of a city passed into view. Could be anywhere in western Spain, France or southern England.

Chantal's head swung over and landed on his shoulder, a dribble catching on his shirt. She mouthed something quiet then her head dipped again, snoring.

Rollo-Smith was over in the other window, his head nodding as he slept, arms folded tight, head bowed, like he was concentrating hard.

Bruce was across the aisle from Chantal, scowling over the top of his Lee Child hardback. 'You'll get him.'

Hunter got a tingle of pins and needles in the arm Chantal was leaning on. He nudged her back into her seat. 'You think?'

'Aye, I think.' Bruce clapped the novel shut and stowed it away in the seat pouch. 'Guy like Tulloch can only be at large for so long.'

'Maybe.' Hunter sighed. 'I used to be like him and his cronies. A stupid squaddie, taking orders, getting rat-arsed. It sickens me.'

'You're not like that now, though.'

'Not for a long time.'

'Chantal said you're a good cop. Do you like it?'

'I like what I'm doing now.' Hunter shrugged again. 'I liked what I was doing before, but then I got shunted down to uniform.'

'Why was that?'

Hunter looked over at him, locking eye contact. 'My face didn't fit.'

'I've seen that a few times.' Bruce cracked his knuckles. 'Sounds like you're onto a good thing in this Sexual Offences Unit...'

'We keep letting the offenders go.' Hunter's spine tingled like a horde of rats were climbing it. 'There's seven women, maybe eight, who've been abused by him in one form or another. He left one girl tied up on a bed while he pissed off to Blackpool. He's got no emotions. I need to stop him doing this. I need to get justice for all his victims.' He shook his head. 'In the army, this guy in my unit... Turns out he'd raped this Iraqi girl, a teenager. Then he killed her. The powers-that-be covered it over. Let it slide. That's what's happening here.'

'Hard to take, isn't it?' Bruce picked up his book again and flipped it open. That was it? That was all he was going to say?

Stupid Geordie bastard. He dug his nail into the dustcover, making it click. 'Listen, I tried having a word with Quaresma about him arresting the wrong suspect.'

'He needs to find Matty Ibbetson.'

Bruce traced a finger down the page of his novel, frowning at the text. 'I don't disagree.' He smiled. 'Finlay Sinclair was your friend, wasn't he?'

'Ex-partner.' Hunter ran his fingers over his palms, knobbly with calluses from the kettlebells. 'I'm not looking forward to breaking the news to Finlay's ex-wife.'

Bruce arched an eyebrow. 'That's very difficult.'

'It'd be easier if I had a story to tell. Like some bent Portuguese officer let his killer go.'

Bruce leaned over the aisle. Chantal stirred in her sleep. 'Do you have anything on Quaresma?'

'Not as such.'

'The old copper's gut instinct, then?'

'Pretty much.'

'Ah, Constable... Whatever will we do with you?'

'Help me catch Sean Tulloch.'

87

CHANTAL

Chantal was still blinking herself awake, gripping Hunter's hand tight.
Newcastle lay below them, yellow and white, like a chalk outline. Could just about make out the Metro Centre next to the shine of the A1 twisting through the series of rivers, other dual carriageways spiralling off from it. The plane swung round towards the runway and plunged down. The wheels hit the tarmac with a squeal and the plane rocked to the side, then pushed her forward.
Brucie Boner didn't even look up from his Jack Reacher, just licked his finger and turned the page.
The plane jerked back, Hunter gasping as Chantal's nails dug into his palm. They wheeled round on the runway and followed the row of lights towards the terminal building in the distance.
The stewardess at the front unbuckled her seatbelt and strolled up the aisle as the plane taxied. She leaned in to Chantal and whispered, 'You can use your phone now.'
'Thanks.' Chantal let go of Hunter's hand and fished out her

mobile, stabbing at the screen. She hit dial and it was answered without ringing. 'Shaz, that's us landed.'

'Good. I've sent a car over to get you.'

Out of the window, a squad car sat a few hundred metres away, the blue lights twinkling, a man standing in front of it.

'Have you got Tulloch?'

Sharon paused. 'Not yet.' Then she sighed. 'He got off the flight and we've bloody lost him.'

88

HUNTER

The cool evening breeze cut through Hunter. Home again. He stepped down the staircase. The tarmac felt solid beneath his feet. 'Christ, you never forget that wind.'

Rollo-Smith was first down. He jogged towards a car and got in. It pulled off.

The squad car's headlights flashed, and Hunter started over towards it. The plane set off again, taxiing to its gate.

A figure got out of the car, hooded by the glow of the squad car's lights. 'Evening, Craig.' Sounded like Elvis. 'Chantal.'

She got in the back seat without a word and sat, arms folded tight across her chest. Bruce got in next to her, grumbling about something or other.

Hunter joined Elvis, his face appearing through the glow. 'What happened?'

Elvis opened the passenger door but stopped Hunter entering. 'You could thank me.'

'What for?'

'I didn't tell her nibs about you and Chantal.' Elvis pushed his index finger through a hole made from his thumb and other index finger. 'Alright?'

'Get in the bloody car, you clown.' Hunter barged past him and got in the back.

Bruce was manspreading, pushing his legs into the door.

A local officer was behind the wheel. He tore off across the tarmac before Hunter had his belt on.

He clicked it in. 'What's been going on here, Paul?'

Elvis was in the front, his seat pushed all the bloody way back. He twisted round and flashed his eyebrows. 'First time in years you've called me Paul.' He held out a hand to Bruce. 'DC Paul Gordon. Pleasure to meet you, sir.'

Bruce fished out his mobile and stabbed at the screen with his thumbs.

Hunter almost laughed. 'I asked if there's been any progress?'

Elvis had huffed back round, like a surly teenager. 'You know the drill. Usual amount of nothing.'

The car rattled to a halt just in front of the terminal. Chantal was out first, racing towards the security guards.

Hunter got out and nodded thanks at the uniformed officer. He scowled at Elvis. 'How the hell did you lose Tulloch?'

Elvis led inside the building as a fresh gust of wind blew through them. He waved a hand at Chantal ahead of them as she caught up with DI McNeill. 'Swear, mate, this lot take forever to do anything.'

'They've got a different agenda.'

'Maybe.' Elvis scratched at his sideburns as he held the door open. 'Mind in CID, we'd get a new case every week, always something to do. Got the blood pumping.'

'Right. Sort of.' Hunter's gaze switched over to Chantal as McNeill shook her head in a fury. *Much rather be over there.*

Elvis gave him a sly look. 'Take it you were banging, aye?'

'Piss off.'

Elvis paced over towards them. 'Nice wee romantic break on the expenses. Good effort.'

'I'm not in the mood.' Hunter grabbed his shoulders. 'How the hell did Tulloch get on that flight without you knowing?'

Elvis wriggled away from him. 'Search me, mate.'

'You're lucky you've not been sacked.'

Elvis scowled at him. 'Bullshit.'

Hunter gripped his shoulders. 'You dropped a clanger, mate. Only monitoring Scottish airports.'

'What?' Elvis shrugged Hunter off and set off down the corridor. 'That's bollocks.' He stopped a few metres from Chantal. 'We had all UK and Irish airports hooked up to our laptops. And the bloody ports, even Rosyth. The north of France, Holland, Belgium, Denmark, you name it, I can see the manifests. Newcastle United flew down to Southampton ahead of tomorrow's match. Doubt they'll stay up this season.'

'I don't give a shite about Newcastle United.' Hunter got a glare off a passing security guard. 'I want to know how a Geordie DI found Tulloch on a flight back to Newcastle and you didn't?'

'No idea, mate.'

Hunter frowned.

That DI with the eyebrows, the twat who was always doing triathlons, stood there, next to Scott bloody Cullen.

Hunter groaned. 'That's all I bloody need.'

DAY 4

*Sunday
15th May*

89

CHANTAL

'We're nowhere, Chantal, and that's the brutal truth.' Sharon looked lost, her eyes blinking slow, her breath slower. 'He's got off that plane, then poof, he's disappeared into thin air.'

Chantal looked around the area. Ten or more security guards lingered around, coupled with some uniformed cops. She felt her shoulders drop. 'How did they let him go?'

'One of those things, I suppose.'

Chantal wanted to grab hold of her and shake her. 'Right, so what are you doing about it?'

'Me? It's not my—'

'Sharon McNeill.' Bruce barged in between them, like James Bond at a cocktail reception, eyes twinkling with mischief and a hint of menace. 'It's been a while.'

'Not long enough, Jon.'

'Charming as ever.' He winked at her. 'You got a minute?'

'Fine.' Sharon followed him away.

Hunter appeared, scowling over at Scott Cullen, skulking around with a couple of DCs. 'What's he doing here?'

Chantal grimaced. 'Sharon's managed to get Colin Methven's team on loan for this. We need help here.'

'More chiefs. Great.' Hunter nodded over at their huddle. 'Have they got anything on Tulloch?'

'That's the thing. He got off the plane before they could lock it down. They think he's still in the airport.'

'Think?'

'Well...' Chantal put her hand on her hip. 'I'm as pissed off as you, believe me. They're interviewing the staff and security to find out what happened.'

'That plane landed hours ago!'

'I know, Craig.'

Cullen walked over, nodding at Hunter. 'Evening.'

Hunter couldn't even look at him. 'How the hell have you let him off that plane?'

'It's not my fault, mate.' Cullen put his hands up. 'Besides, his passport didn't get swiped at the controls.'

Hunter shut his eyes, rubbing his temple. 'He doesn't need to show a passport!'

HUNTER

Hunter raced down the corridor, shaking his head. 'Schoolboy error, Scott.'

'You need to call me sergeant if you're going to be a twat like that.' Cullen pushed open the door and let Hunter go first. 'He's in here.'

DC Simon Buxton sat at a laptop. Cockney wanker and Cullen's right-hand man. He frowned at Hunter, recognition flickering over his forehead. 'Alright, mate? Not seen you in donkeys.'

'Have you got him?'

Buxton nodded at Cullen. 'I've got that property search, Scott. Nothing on either Matty Ibbetson or Sean Tulloch.'

'Neither own property. Right.' Cullen leaned in close. 'Have you got the CCTV of that flight's passengers getting through?'

Buxton tapped on the monitor. 'Here we go.'

Thing was on fast forward, quadruple speed at least. A queue of holidaymakers wound its way up to passport control, still wearing their shorts and summer dresses like they weren't back in northern Britain and could keep the holiday going forever.

Hunter scanned through the crowd, eyes weaving through the

faces. Barely anyone over six foot, let alone— Wait— A hulk stood near the gate.'

'Stop!'

Buxton hit the space bar on the laptop. 'What?'

Hunter drew a circle on the monitor around a big guy, just a grainy collection of pixels. Squint hard enough and it was a squaddie type. Shorts and T-shirts, huge. 'That's him there.' He swallowed. 'That's Tulloch.'

'What?' Buxton squinted at the screen. 'Shit... You sure?'

'Trust me, he's kicked the shit out of me enough times for me to recognise him.' Hunter tapped the display again. 'That is Sean Tulloch.'

Buxton's eyes pleaded with Cullen. 'He didn't show up on the passport database.'

'He wouldn't.' Hunter leaned back in the seat and stared over at Cullen. 'He's used his MOD90.' He reached past Buxton and hit play.

On the screen, Tulloch flashed his card at the guard and had a quick chat, then he headed through to Arrivals.

'See? He waltzed right through...' Hunter looked at Buxton. 'What other CCTV have you got on this?'

The screen flipped to show Tulloch marching through the place like he was on parade. He walked right to the front door and waited in the taxi queue. Another burly squaddie joined him outside, his face hidden by a comedy hat. A third figure appeared, even bigger, his identity lost in a grey hoodie.

Tenner says one of them is Matty Ibbetson.

A car pulled up next to them. The second one took off his hat and leaned in to speak to the driver. It was Big Keith, Tulloch's mate. The one with the knife, the one who was going to gut Hunter. He got in the back of the car.

Hunter tapped the screen, his finger dulling the display over the silver Skoda. 'Find that car!'

~

HUNTER TIGHTENED his grip on the "oh shit" handle above the door as Cullen threw them around another tight bend. 'Your driving hasn't improved any.'

'You love it.' Cullen glanced over, a maniacal grin on his face. 'Have they surrounded the house yet?'

Hunter let go of the handle enough to stick his phone to his ear. 'Elvis, have you got an update on—' Another tight turn pushed him towards the door. Hard to believe they were on a main road. '—on that address in Otterburn?'

'You okay, Craig?'

'Give me an update.'

'Aye, checking now.' Sounded like Elvis cracked his knuckles. 'Sorry, dude, I'll need to get back to you.'

'Right.' Hunter put the phone back on his lap and snatched hold of the grab handle again. 'Useless sod.'

'Elvis?' Cullen's grin was lit up by his Golf's dashboard. 'I warned Sharon about taking him on.'

'And still she took him on, eh?'

'Cheeky bastard.' Cullen gave the tightest shrug as he veered out to overtake a coach. Oncoming headlights blared at them, so he pulled in and hugged the back of it. 'She wants someone who can do all that CCTV analysis in-house.' A car blitzed past. 'You're not exactly great at it, are you?'

'And you are?' Hunter couldn't help his eyebrows shooting up. 'I remember having to show you how to log on more than once.'

'I got there in the end but I'm a sergeant now, so I get you drones to do it for me.'

'Drone, eh?'

'You know what I mean.' Cullen pulled out into the grey blankness of the oncoming carriageway and hurtled towards the front of the bus. Headlights flashed a few hundred metres ahead of them.

Hunter's hands gripped tighter.

Cullen tugged the wheel back in with metres to spare. Worse driving than Chantal. He patted the dashboard. 'The GTI's worth the extra, believe me.'

'Take your word for it.'

'So how much further?'

'Are we nearly there yet?' Hunter picked up his mobile. Still nothing from Elvis. The map app showed five miles. 'Not far.'

'Right, well I'll overtake this lorry, then.' Cullen swerved out and blasted past, straw flaring out both sides. 'Need to keep this from the insurance company.'

'What, that you're driving like an idiot?'
'That I'm driving it at all on police business.'
'No pool cars?'
Cullen's head shake betrayed his disappointment. 'Fat Keith's down to the last Vauxhall.'
'What about the Volvo?'
'Buxton wrote it off last month.'
'Twat.'
Cullen laughed. 'Anyway. You guys have a nice romantic break?'
Don't rise to it...
Hunter looked over. 'What do you mean by that?'
'You and Chantal. Did you have a nice romantic break in the Algarve?'
'Piss off, Scott. The Portuguese cop we were working with kept mugging us off and I got seven shades of shite kicked out of me by a dirty, raping bastard.'
'I'll take that as a yes.'
'You're welcome to.' Hunter flicked up his phone and checked the display. 'So, you busy?'
'Just finished a nightmare case. The worst sort. You know how it is. Too many heroes and not enough villains.'
'I'd ask for more, but I can't be arsed.'
'You'll find out someday, don't you worry.' Cullen shot him a wink. 'When you get your stripes.'
'Again, piss off, Scott.'
'Piss off, Sergeant Cullen.'
'You're a vain idiot.' Hunter shook his head at him. 'You should've known about the MOD90.'
'You should maybe have told us?'
Dozy git.
Hunter's phone blasted out the drill sound and he put it to his ear. 'Elvis?'
'Aye, local uniform have surrounded that house, Craig.'
'You got the name of the owner?'
'Not yet. We've got the warrant, though. The local sergeant has it.'
'Noted. Tell them not to move in until we get there, okay? These guys are dangerous.'

'Aye, noted.' Sounded like Elvis was actually writing it down.

'Have you found that taxi driver yet?'

'Finished speaking to the local uniform up in Morpeth. Sounds like a straight street pick-up. You okay to let him go?'

'Clear it with DI McNeill first.' Hunter spotted the town lights in the valley below them. 'We're almost there. Can you let the local squad know?'

'What did your last slave die of?'

Hunter's mouth went dry. 'That's not very funny.'

～

HUNTER LOOKED up and down the street, concrete blocks of misery lining both sides. The windows were all dark except for one at the other end by the broken streetlights, death metal screaming and grinding blaring out.

Hunter scanned the warrant with his torch. Looked fine. He flashed it twice and waited.

Seconds later, he got a flash from the two units halfway down.

Cullen spoke into his Airwave radio. 'Serial bravo, this is serial alpha. We are moving in. Repeat, moving in. Maintain the perimeter.'

'Roger.'

Cullen took the warrant and waved at Hunter to go first.

He snapped out a borrowed police baton and crept forward, keeping to the height of the breeze-block wall. The bitter northeast air cut at his neck.

The downstairs windows were misted up with condensation, a bare light bulb burning in the living room. A large figure loomed in the dim glow then disappeared again.

Hunter waved forward. 'Right. Let's get in there.' He jumped over the wall and landed on cracked tarmac. He clicked off his torch and left it on the wall then moved towards the house, brandishing the baton.

The two Northumbria police uniforms flanked Elvis as they neared the house. He gestured for them to head round the back. Elvis gave a nod like he knew what he was doing.

Cullen hunkered down next to him, unfolding the warrant. 'You're in charge here, okay?'

'Fine.' A short blast of static on the Airwave and Hunter darted over to the front door. He gave it the policeman's knock.

Nothing.

Then louder. 'Police! Open up!'

A light across the street flicked on. The house door stayed shut.

Hunter leaned over to Cullen. 'Have we got an Enforcer?'

'No.'

Bolts behind the door clicked and rattled. Then it opened to a crack, a shaft of yellow light bled over the grey pavement. An eye peered out at them. 'What?'

Cullen inched Hunter out of the way. 'Mr Brannigan, police. We need a word with you.'

'Go on.'

'Can we do this inside, please, sir?'

'No, you can't.'

Cullen held up the sheet of paper. 'We have a warrant to enter and search these premises.'

'You're not getting in.'

Hunter barged in front of Cullen. 'Is Sean Tulloch there?'

The door slammed against Cullen's toes. 'Ah, shite!'

Hunter lurched forward and rammed his shoulder against the painted wood. Felt like a bull was pushing the other side. Cullen joined in and the door jolted back the way, cracking off the wall.

Big Keith lay on his back, groaning. 'You bastards...' He pushed himself up to a sitting position and reached to the side for something. Steel glinted in the low light.

Hunter smacked his baton off Keith's wrist. Something metallic clanged on the laminate, rattling as it rolled. He pounced, landing on Keith and digging the baton into his throat. 'Where is Tulloch?'

'Piss off, you pig bastard.' Keith reached for the bread knife lying against the maroon skirting. 'I'll gut you!'

'Where. Is. Ibbetson?'

Keith coughed hard as Hunter put more of his weight on the baton. Fingers grabbed at him from behind — Cullen.

Hunter shrugged him off and applied more weight. 'Where are they?'

Keith sputtered something out.

Hunter let the pressure slacken off a touch. 'What was that?'

'Sean's took my bloody car. Thought that was him coming back.'

'Where's he gone?'

'Not telling you that.'

'Who else was with you?'

Keith scowled at him. 'What?'

'Three of you got into that taxi.'

'Piss off.'

Hunter's gut lurched. It was Matty. Had to be him. 'Was it Matty Ibbetson?'

'Piss. Off.'

'You'll tell us now or down the station.'

Keith held out his hands in a cuff gesture, or as close as he could get with a cop sitting on his chest. 'Milk and two while we're waiting for my lawyer.'

∼

BIG KEITH'S shoulders slumped as a pair of uniforms led him over to the idling squad car. A smirk flashed across his lips as he was pushed inside.

Thumps and thuds came from inside the house. The least careful search in the history of modern policing. Not likely to turn up Sean Tulloch or Matty Ibbetson, though.

Hunter slumped back against Cullen's car. *Where the hell is Tulloch?*

Elvis rested his laptop on the car roof. 'Craig, your secret's safe with me.'

'I'm not bothered about that.' Hunter's sigh misted in the air. 'Tell whoever you want.'

'Right. Whatever. Tell you, I'm glad to get out. Been a bloody taxi service all day, ferrying that Presley bird back down to Gala.'

Hunter locked eyes with Elvis. 'Paisley?'

'Aye, her.'

'She's out of hospital?'

'Doc didn't recommend it but couldn't keep her in. Her injuries weren't life threatening.' Elvis coughed. 'Still, double time to drive her home, happy days.'

Paisley was out of hospital.

And Tulloch knew she was blabbering to the cops about him. *Because of them. Because...*
It can't be...
His gut churned at the thought. Policeman's hunch. Not good. But, even so...

He found Paisley's mobile number and dialled it. It went straight to voicemail.

Ah, you stupid bastard. It's in the evidence store in Bathgate. He flicked through her contact details. No house number for her. *Shite.*

Hunter got out his Airwave and called Control. 'This is DC Craig Hunter, I need a unit to attend Paisley Sanderson's address in Galashiels.'

Laughter cut through a mouthful of crisps. 'Aye, good one, son. You know there was an Old Firm match this afternoon, aye? First one in yonks. I've got ten cars on tonight in that area, getting their arses handed to them by fans of bloody Glasgow teams.'

'Right. Can you get me her house number?'

'I'll text it to your Airwave.'

'Thanks.' Hunter killed the call and called Chantal.

She answered slowly. Sounded like she was driving. 'Hey, you got him?'

Hunter locked eyes with Cullen as he left the house. 'Not yet.'

'What does that mean?' McNeill's voice. *On speakerphone. Better watch what I say.*

'Tulloch's taken Big Keith's car.'

'Where?'

'I've got a few ideas, but it's a needle in a haystack job. And there's Old Firm fighting on.' Hunter watched the car rattle off down the road. 'We'll take Keith to Northumbria HQ, might get something out of him there.'

'Well, I've got my fingers and toes crossed.' Chantal huffed down the line. 'We're heading there now. It's going to be a long night.' She sighed. 'I've got to go.'

'Wait. Matty Ibbetson was with them. He was the third man at the airport.'

'Right, that's useful. Speak soon.' Click.

Cullen looked up from his phone. 'Elvis is heading back now.'

'Fine.' Hunter's Airwave chimed. A text from Control. He

tapped on it and put the Airwave to his ear, waiting for an answer, his heart thudding in his chest.

The phone was answered without a voice, just room sound.

'Paisley, it's Craig Hunter. Are you okay?'

Her voice was a whisper. 'He's here.'

'Sean?'

'Aye.' Harsh, distorted, desperate. 'He's—'

A man shouted, 'What the—'

Click.

91

CHANTAL

Chantal got out of the car into the biting wind blasting almost horizontal.

Northumbria Police HQ was lit up in the night, rain streaking past the lights. Stuck between a B&Q and the A19 dual carriageway, heavy trucks spraying rainwater as they headed north. Could be three storeys, could be five, it was all a muddle. Every inch the New Labour PFI, all turquoise glass and breezeblocks.

Bruce got out of the other side and started jogging across the car park. 'Lovely night, isn't it?'

'Wish I'd stayed in Portugal.' Chantal huddled through the revolving door into the station's foyer. Could be a bank or insurance company office.

Bruce signed her in and nodded at the guard. 'Are our guests here yet?'

The guard's sleeves were rolled up, his arms all tattoos and spirally grey hair. 'DI McNeill's in your office. And there's a taxi driver waiting in interview room six.'

CHANTAL STOPPED in the corridor and took a polystyrene cup of what looked like tea but smelled like coffee. 'Thanks for this.'
Sharon sipped her own drink. 'What's with the goggle eyes?'
'Well, Craig and Scott have got Keith Brannigan. They don't know where Tulloch is.' Chantal took a sip. Weak and sour, but warm. She locked eyes with Sharon. 'And Craig reckons Matty was the third man at the airport.'
'That's... interesting.' Sharon opened a door behind her. Looked like an Incident Room, crowded with fifteen or so officers. 'Britpop, have you got the taxi driver?'
DC Simon Buxton twisted round to look at them, his hair shaved almost to the bone. His laptop showed CCTV footage of a deserted street. He frowned at Chantal, blushed, then nodded at Sharon. 'Sorry, what taxi driver?'
'The one at the bloody airport?'
'Right, yeah, sorry.' Buxton shook himself, then thumbed at the door. 'He turned up about two minutes ago. DI Bruce took him into the interview room.'
'Thanks.'
'And Britpop? Really?' Buxton looked disappointed in Sharon. 'You sound like Bain.'
She walked off down the corridor, sipping tea.
Chantal smiled at Buxton. 'Nice to see you, Simon.'
Buxton grimaced at her. 'Yeah, and you.' His accent was softening, bits of Scottish in amongst the Cockney. 'You better hurry.'
Sharon was at the end of the corridor now.
Chantal dashed after her, coffee sloshing in her cup.
Sharon was waiting outside, arms folded. 'What is Brucie Boner doing on our case?'
Chantal finished her coffee and tossed the cup into a bin. 'Thought you okayed it?'
'He's supposed to be finding missing children not leering at us again.' Sharon shook her head and opened the door.
Northumbria Police clearly didn't have the same budget as Police Scotland. The room was scabbier than even the ones in Pilton. Bare concrete blocks, a winking strip light hanging

lopsided from the ceiling, still stained with nicotine ten years after the ban.

Bruce and one of his cops sat opposite a thin man, streaks of grey at his temples almost like wings. Burgundy cardigan and navy Adidas trackies. Comfort wear.

'DI McNeill...' Bruce raised his eyebrows at Sharon. He coughed. 'This is Lee Curtis, the taxi driver.'

'I know who he is.' Sharon took the free space next to Curtis, leaving Chantal to stand. Not that Bruce was gentlemanly enough to get up.

Sharon got out a tattered notebook. 'We understand you had a collection at the airport this evening.'

'That's right, pet.' Curtis scowled at Elvis. 'Though I've spent the last five minutes telling this chump all about it.'

Sharon smiled at him. 'Then it should still be fresh in your memory.'

Curtis sighed, deep as the ocean. 'Right.' He got out a mobile phone, the sort of flashy bling you'd expect from a teenager in their first full-time job, not a middle-aged cabbie. He stabbed at the screen with a stylus and squinted at it. 'Aye, I did.' More stabbing at the display. 'Dropped two lads in Otterburn, just up the A696. Pretty quiet for that time of—'

'Was there another passenger?'

'Aye, took another lad on to Alnwick.' Curtis rested his phone on the desk. 'Otterburn to Alnwick's a long stretch, like. Through Rothbury and up the back there. Bad road in the dark. Did it in less than forty minutes, mind.'

Chantal leaned forward, almost pushing Elvis out of the way. 'Did you get the name of the passenger?'

'Sorry, pet. Lad paid cash.'

Chantal reached into her pocket for her phone and showed him a grainy CCTV photo of Matty Ibbetson. 'Was it him?'

~

'SHARON... GAH.' Chantal eased the pool car down the hill, the engine grumbling. 'I wish you'd stop going on about it.'

Alnwick was lit up below them, half fairy-tale medieval town, half sixties housing disaster. Long rows of yellow street lights bled into white. She turned down a side street, sodium catching a pair of cats in a stand-off. They hissed and separated.

Sharon smirked at her. 'You need to stop denying you're a couple.'

'You need to stop being a cow about it.' Chantal's headlights caught two squad cars at the end of a cul-de-sac, eight dark houses in a tight circle. She pulled up and hauled on the handbrake. 'Think what Craig's going through right now.'

'Right.' Sharon opened her door and let the bitter air in. 'Sorry, I'm just winding you up.'

Chantal buttoned up her jacket. 'This isn't the time for joking.'

Sharon reached over and grabbed her hand. 'Are you denying it?'

'Drop it, okay?' Chantal got out and made her way to the first squad car.

Bruce gave her a wave. 'Evening, ladies.'

Sharon smiled at him. 'Have you got eyes on the suspect?'

'Local lads have him in the back room.' Bruce pointed at a sixties villa, the street lights showing up the mock Tudor features on the front. Could just about make out a light on downstairs. 'We've got a unit out in the lane at the back there. Two lads marking it. And another two cars. He's not getting away.' He unfolded a sheet of paper. 'And here's the warrant, so we're ready to go.'

'Thank God for insomniac judges, eh?' Chantal nodded, then sucked in a breath. 'This guy is very dangerous, okay? Remember that.'

'Murdered an ex-cop, I know.' Bruce pocketed the warrant. 'Howay then, ladies.' He stomped off into the cul-de-sac and headed for the house, speaking into his Airwave.

Chantal followed, Sharon next to her. A pair of burly uniformed lads flanked them. Maybe not quite big enough to pass as fully-fledged Geordies, though, and you could almost understand their accent.

Chantal stopped behind Bruce and blew out a breath into the cold air. 'Let's do this.'

Bruce rapped on the door. 'Mr Ibbetson, this is DI Jon Bruce of Northumbria Police. We have a warrant to enter and search these premises.'

No sign of life. No sounds.

Bruce held up the Airwave. 'Any movement out back?'

Crackle. 'Negative.'

Bruce put his hands round his mouth. 'Mr Ibbetson, this is the police. We are entering your property.' He waited a few seconds then nodded at the uniform to his left. 'Open it up, Doug.'

Doug cracked his knuckles then launched his shoulder at the door.

Then again.

Nothing.

'Right, if at first...' Doug stepped back and kicked the door. The top hinge burst off and Doug wrestled the whole door to the floor.

'Stay here.' Bruce nodded at him then motioned for the other uniform to lead them inside.

Looked like an old person lived there — heavy wallpaper, dark pictures, plastic runners on the green carpet. A navy blue bathroom suite to the left.

Something caught Chantal's nose as she followed Bruce into a living room. The walls were painted white, the floors stripped. Like someone was modernising, room-by-room.

Her nostrils twitched again. Dark and bitter. Like...

No.

Bruce opened a sliding door at the far end. The bitter smell got worse.

Matty Ibbetson stood in the doorway, eyes wide, smoking a cigar.

~

CHANTAL STOOD SHIVERING *in the rain, wiping her hair from out of her eyes. The rugby ground was shut, all the other kids gone home with their parents. Cars streamed past, their headlights burning, but none stopped for her. The wind battered her bare legs, already cut and bruised from the tournament. Touch rugby, my arse.*

She hugged her arms tight. Bloody top was soaked and scratchy and—

Hoooonk!

A silver Mercedes pulled in next to her, the indicator pulsing orange into the twilight. Just a red dot inside. An arm reached across and

opened the door. Uncle Ditinder looked out, puffing on a cigar, the bitter smoke leaking out, coiling around her. 'Sorry, I'm late, Chucka.'
Chantal let out a sigh. 'Is Dad busy again?'
'He had to go to the cash and carry. Asked me to pick you up.'
Chantal blew air up her face. Didn't shift the soggy fringe covering her eyes. 'It better be an emergency...' She got in the passenger seat and tugged her belt on.
'How was the game?' Uncle Ditinder pulled out into the traffic, sucking on the cigar. The whole car stank of it. Horrible, horrible smell. 'You score any goals?'
'They're called tries?'
'Tries, eh?' Ditinder looked at her thighs. Her skin was almost white. He puffed on the cigar, spilling ash onto the tray. 'I'm a cricket man, myself. A much more noble sport.'
'Right.'
Dirty old pervert couldn't take his eyes off her legs. Why didn't Dad just get her the trackies? They weren't expensive, even had them at—
'How old are you now, Chucka?'
'Don't call me that.' She tried to move away from him. 'I'm twelve. Chucka's a little girl's name.'
'You've grown, my little princess.'
'I'm nobody's princess.'
'Right, right.' Ditinder turned left off the road and pulled on his cigar. 'Need to do a wee favour for your father.' He drove down a lane, away from all the traffic, the car rocking with potholes.
Twisted trees on both sides. No streetlights, just the flicker of cars in the distance.
She gripped her seatbelt tight. 'Where are we going?'
Ditinder pulled in and stopped the engine. He sucked on his cigar and flicked more ash into the bucket. Kept looking at her legs. 'You really have grown, Chucka.'
'Don't call me that.'
He put a hand on her thigh, warm against her frozen flesh. 'You're my favourite niece.'
'Don't—'
Ditinder grabbed her mouth and covered it with his stinking hands. He pushed her head back into the seat, his other hand tearing at her shorts, pulling them down. Her seatbelt tightened around her shoulders, pinning her down. His fingers were up her soaking top,

inside her bra, cupping what little breast there was, tugging at her nipple.
She tried biting his fingers, but he let go.
She screamed, but he covered her mouth again.
She kicked, but he pushed her back against the seat.
'This is our secret, Chucka.' His trousers were down, his tiny cock erect and brushing against her knee. He tore her knickers to the side, his knees pushing her legs apart. 'Tell anyone and I will kill you.'
She slapped his back, but he yanked her sports bra over her throat, choking her, silencing her. 'My little Chucka!'
The dirty smell of cigar in her face. Bitter, dark. Holding her down, his pathetic little cock inside her.

∽

CHANTAL BLINKED HARD. *Where the hell am I?*
A living room, leather couches. White walls. Dirty cigar smoke.
DI Bruce staggered backwards. Matty Ibbetson stepped into the room and cracked him on the chin. Bruce tumbled over one of the sofas and fell onto the floor.
Sharon McNeill was slumped in the corner, a hand covering her head. Barely awake. A uniform lay behind her, groaning in a pool of blood.
Matty spotted her. *Murdering bastard.* He took another suck on a cigar and puffed out a cloud of smoke. 'Look who the cat dragged in.'
Chantal snapped out her baton and hefted it in her right hand. Ready to strike. Ready to batter the shite out of him.
He blew a puff of smoke at her. The bitter air went up her nose. 'My little Chucka!'
Clatter. Something struck her feet. She looked down. Her baton.
'My little Chucka!'
Matty grabbed her by the throat and lifted her clean off her feet. He threw her onto the sofa. 'Never had a Paki before.' He straddled her, grabbing her throat again, tight enough to stop her breathing. 'I'm almost salivating at the prospect.' His other hand tore at her skirt, pulling it down to her knees, while he covered her mouth.

She tried biting his fingers, but he let go. His fist wrapped around her throat again.

She screamed, but his fingers filled her mouth.

She kicked, but he pushed her back against the sofa. His weight on her, pushing her down.

Zip. 'Going to take my time enjoying this, I swear.' A hand ran up her thigh, dirty fingers tugging at her knickers, pulling them aside.

92

HUNTER

'Come on, come on, come on.' Hunter held his phone to his ear and listened to the ringing. *Where the hell is she?* 'She's still not answering.' He redialled Control. 'It's DC Craig Hunter. Can I get an update on the units sent to Murchison Grove in Galashiels?'

A cough filled with catarrh rattled the speaker. 'Still blocked on that, son.'

'I just need one squad car to get—'

'Listen, I've got two squad cars in the Borders the night. That's it.' Another cough, sounding like her lungs were going to flow down the phone line. 'You're no' the Chief Constable so you can get off the line and let me do my job.'

Click and she was gone.

'Bloody hell.' Hunter punched the glove box. 'Bloody hell!'

'Watch the car!' Cullen blared past a slow-moving SUV and pulled back into their lane. 'You need to calm down, mate.'

'Calm down?' Hunter shot him a glare. 'How the hell can you expect me to calm down? I've let that psychopath go I don't know how many bloody times now. And he's going to kill her!'

Cullen's face glowed in the pale light from the dashboard lights. 'We don't know it's him.'
'I've got a pretty good idea.' Hunter hit redial. Same result. 'Shite.'
Cullen descended into a valley, the speedo clearing ninety. 'Is there anyone else you can try?'
Was there?
Local cops were blocked. Edinburgh cops were as far from Galashiels as they were now.
Shite.
Hunter tapped another number and let it ring.
'How're ye?' Irish blarney boomed out of the phone. PC Lenny Warner, sounding like he was in a pub.
'You on duty?'
'For my sins, yeah.' Shouting in the background. Rangers songs. 'I'm attending a pitched battle in a Hawick pub. Jaysis!' Glass smashed. 'Shoite!'
'I had a call from Paisley Sanderson. She thinks Tulloch's at her house.'
'She's at home?' Warner's voice went all shrill.
'Can you get round there and check?'
'I doubt I'll get away from—' More smashing. 'Ah, feck this. I'll see what I can do.'

∽

CULLEN SWERVED into Paisley's street.
Dark, just the street lights. No sign of any squad cars. Hunter hissed out a breath. 'Where the hell is Warner?'
Not that that was a bad thing. Tulloch clocking the flashing blue lights wouldn't be ideal.
'Craig, we're here.' Cullen snapped on the handbrake. 'Will you stop having kittens? Like dealing with Bain, I swear...'
'I don't think you under—' Hunter caught himself. *Don't moan. Just get on with it.* 'Come on.' He got out of the car.
Big Keith's Subaru was wedged between two small Fiats, three car lengths from Paisley's flat. A pyramid of sodium yellow bled it from off-white to mustard.

Hunter stared at the house. Pitch black, quiet as the grave. Curtains drawn. *Was Tulloch still in there?*

Headlights arced round the bend from the main drag. A squad Volvo parked next to the Subaru, shrouded in darkness. Lenny Warner got out of the passenger side and pulled his hat on. 'Got here as fast as I could.'

'Right.' Hunter started off across the street. He pointed at Warner's partner, a female officer with short hair and tired eyes. 'You two take the back.'

'Thanks would've been nice.' Warner shot him a wink. 'Come on.' He led his partner towards the lane.

'I don't know where you find them, mate...' Cullen marched up to the door. 'We've not got a warrant, but we've got probable cause, right?'

'Oh, hell yeah.'

Cullen thumped the door. 'This is the police! Open up!'

Nothing.

Hunter stepped round the front to the living room window, sticking his ear to the glass.

Muffled screams, like someone's mouth was taped. Could be TV, but not bloody likely.

Cullen thumped the door again. 'Open up! This is the police!'

'Who the hell's that, eh?' A male voice. 'You *have* been talking to the police, you stupid bitch!'

Tulloch. *Shite.*

Another muffled scream.

'We need to get in there!' Hunter ran back to the door and launched himself at it, shoulder-first. He bounced off it. Another go and it didn't even budge. 'Shite, there's no way that's opening.'

A louder scream bled out.

Cullen tried kicking the door. 'What's going on in there?'

'He's... Shite, I don't know what he's doing to her.'

Maybe better luck round the back.

Or...

Hunter snapped out his baton as he jogged back round to the front. He touched the baton against the centre of the window pane, then swung back. And lashed out.

A huge pattern of cracks splintered out from the corners. Glass hit the ground, tinkling. A pair of shards fell out onto the street.

Hunter swept the glass away from the frame and tugged the curtains open.

Tulloch was inside the window, his white T-shirt soaked through.

Paisley sat on a chair, arms behind her back. Silver tape covered her mouth, curling away at the edges. Her face was a black-and-blue mess, her eyes puffed up even worse than a few days ago.

Tulloch swivelled around, his face leering in the dim glow from the side lights. 'Shite!' He wrapped his left arm around Paisley's throat, his right holding a spitting iron in front of her face. 'Any movement from you and I'll burn this bitch!'

'Sean, it's over.' Hunter held his baton in a neutral position. 'Drop the iron and let her go.'

'Nae danger!' Tulloch pressed the iron into Paisley's cheek.

Fat sizzled in her face, steam hissing. She screamed against the tape.

The smoked-bacon stink of burning human flesh hit Hunter's nose...

~

'AND YET HERE WE ARE AGAIN.' *Captain Morecambe's office looked the same in Iraq as it did in Afghanistan, but the giant desk and filing cabinets were squashed into a room less than half the size. The plate on his desk had two rolls, flabby slices of bacon poking out of the sides. He picked a roll up and bit into it, tomato ketchup splattering the plate like blood patterns from a knife frenzy.* 'The good news, Lance Corporal, is that Corporal Terence Saunders wasn't under investigation by the RMP.'

Hunter couldn't prise his eyes off the bacon roll. The smell coiled around him, forcing itself up his nostrils. Could almost taste it.

Like when Terry—

He tried to slow his breathing, keep his eyes shut.

'Lance Corporal, are you okay?'

Hunter opened his eyes again. Morecambe's roll was resting against the plate. Fat slid out the side, into a pool in the middle. 'I'm fine.'

'Yes, well, as I was saying, Corporal Saunders wasn't—'

'I plan to tender my resignation.'

Morecambe dropped the roll onto the plate. 'I see.' *He rubbed his hands together then wiped his thumb across his pathetic moustache.*

'Well, Lance Corporal, we are actively investigating you.'

'Well, fill your boots, because I'm leaving.'

'We don't want you to leave.'

'But you don't want me to stay, either. You just want to do me because a bunch of cretins with stripes dropped a massive bollock over that operation and you're looking for a patsy.'

Morecambe picked up the roll and narrowed his eyes at Hunter.

'We've been over your medical record and you're not fit to serve, are you?'

'Fine, invalid me out. I don't care.'

Morecambe opened the lid on his roll and let the reek seep out. 'Very well.'

〜

SEAN TULLOCH SWUNG the iron around.

Heat seared the air in front of Hunter's face. He braced himself against the smashed window, catching his palm on the broken glass. Pain burnt up his arm as he tumbled backwards.

Paisley screamed, loud enough to hear outside the flat, despite her mouth being taped. Then nothing.

Cullen hopped over the windowsill into the house. He thumped into the curtains and collapsed off to the side.

Hunter pushed himself up to standing and peered inside.

Tulloch lurched towards Cullen, brandishing the iron. 'I am going to kill you, you pig bastard!'

Cullen jumped forward and lashed out with his baton.

Tulloch stepped aside and punched with the iron. He missed. Cullen slapped Tulloch in the face. He laughed then cracked his fist into Cullen's cheek. He tumbled onto the coffee table, two legs snapping off as it collapsed under his weight.

Hunter still had his baton in his right hand. Blood dripped down his wrist.

Tulloch held the iron over Cullen's face. 'Now, you little cu—'

Hunter jumped through the window and snapped his baton at Tulloch's right arm.

The iron thudded to the floor.

Hunter swung out again.

And caught thin air.

Tulloch danced around the blow and kicked out, his army boot cracking off Hunter's right wrist.

He dropped the baton with a yelp.

Tulloch reached out and pinched Hunter's shoulders, squeezing like a vice. Hunter squealed as the pain bit into his shoulder.

He couldn't block, tried to push his arms wide. Just... couldn't.

Tulloch grabbed his throat, curling his fingers around his flesh, and squeezed tight.

Hunter's throat closed up. He couldn't breathe. 'Kuh, kuh, kuh.'

Tulloch squeezed and squeezed, wrapping his meaty fingers tight. 'How do you like that, you faggot?'

93

CHANTAL

Dirty fingers scratched at Chantal's legs as she kicked and screamed, tearing and fumbling at her.
Her focus darted around the room, switching to anything she could find.
Matty pressed his hand into her throat, crushing her windpipe.
The cigar lay on the leather, smouldering away.
She reached a finger over as something hard pressed into her thigh. Matty's micropenis. Cigar breath lashed her face.
'My little Chucka!'
She touched the cigar, grabbed hold of it, felt the heat in her fingers. Then swung it over and jammed it into Matty's eye, letting it sizzle the flesh.
He screamed and his hands reached for his eyes.
She pushed him back and pressed the cigar onto his arm. Then lashed out with her left foot, cracking him on the chest.
Matty staggered backwards, one hand against his eye. His trousers were by his knees, his pathetic half-erect half-cock an acorn lost in a moss of pubic hair.

Nothing to worry about at all. Something to laugh about. Something to kick.

She lashed out and smashed the top of her foot into his balls, like she was converting a try.

Matty squealed.

Again. Trying to get the ball to sail over the upright.

Matty sank to his knees, clutching his balls.

Chantal grabbed his hair and kicked his balls again. Two points on top of the try. 'Piss off!'

Matty rolled back on the floorboards, trying to curl into a ball. His pathetic little cock shrivelled away, lost inside his body.

'Piss off, Ditinder!'

His shorts were turning red.

'Piss off, Ditinder!'

Crunch. Squeal.

Crunch. Squeal. 'No!'

An arm wrapped around Chantal's shoulders and pulled her back. 'Stop!' Sharon.

Chantal stopped, her chest heaving.

Bitter cigar smell filled the air.

'Piss off, Ditinder...' Chantal collapsed against the sofa, sucking in deep breaths, trying to ignore the cigar smoke. 'Piss off, Ditinder...'

Matty lay on the floor, coiled up and screaming. Blood poured from his scrotum.

Two uniformed officers burst in the back door. The first one spotted Matty and squatted next to him, trying to inspect his wounds.

'Cuff him.' Sharon was standing over the sofa, rubbing at a cut on her temple. She waited until the handcuffs clicked before sitting beside Chantal. She rested a hand on her knee. 'Who's Ditinder?'

He put a hand on her thigh, warm against her frozen flesh. 'You're my favourite niece, Chucka.'

Chantal rubbed her damp hair out of her face. 'He's nobody.'

∽

CHANTAL LIFTED up her head and let the paramedic get a look. 'I told you I'm fine.' She covered a hand over her throat.

The paramedic pushed the hand away. 'If you don't stop, I'm going to sedate you.'

Chantal clasped her hands and let the paramedic work. 'I'm fine...'

Fingers prodded at her throat. 'Just a bit of bruising.'

'Like I told you.' Chantal stood up and pulled her coat on. 'So can I go?'

The paramedic was already looking at the next patient. Sharon.

Chantal hopped out of the ambulance, the street now filled with squad cars and two ambulances.

DI Bruce stood between two unmarked cars, smoking.

Chantal walked over and smiled at him. 'You okay?'

'I'll live.' Bruce sucked on his cigarette. 'What about you?'

'Same.' She rubbed her throat. 'Just bruising.'

'He tried raping you.'

'Did he?' Chantal stuffed her hands deep in her coat pockets. 'Half an inch at the most. Doesn't really count, does it?'

'You think you're cool, but what he tried to do to you?' Bruce exhaled slowly, sweet cigarette smoke spraying out of the side. 'It's serious.'

'I know, Jon, it's... This is how I cope.'

'With what?'

She shrugged. 'Never mind.'

He took another drag, eyeing her with suspicion. 'What happened to you?'

'What do you mean?'

'You froze while that prick started battering us.'

'Don't know what happened.' Chantal rubbed at the back of her head. Felt like the wound from the car had reopened. 'I...'

Had a flashback. To my uncle raping me.

Sharon stepped down from the ambulance and grabbed a hold of Chantal's shoulder. 'I don't feel so good.'

'What did they say?'

'Can't remember.'

Bruce tossed his cigarette butt to the ground and stamped on it. 'You going to get back to Edinburgh, okay?'

Sharon frowned. 'We've got to find Tulloch.'

Bruce reached into his jacket pocket for a packet of B&H. 'You're welcome to stay at mine.'

Sharon stared at him for a few seconds then waved over at the house. 'What's going on over there?'

A squad of cops thundered in the front door of Matty's house, thudding up the stairs.

'We've got a warrant.' Bruce shrugged. 'Might as well use it.'

A uniform jogged out of the front door and waved at them. 'Sir, you want to see this!'

∼

CHANTAL FOLLOWED the uniform up the stairs, clomping against tired carpet.

At the top, two uniforms stood in a hallway, arms folded, looking bemused. Thumps came from the other doors.

The first officer banged his fist off a door. 'Open up!'

'What's going on?' Bruce looked around, eyebrows pushed high on his head. 'Eh?'

'Can't get in that room, sir.'

Bruce barged him out of the way and kicked the door. The panel splintered.

An eye looked out of the crack, switching between them.

'What the hell?' Bruce knelt low and grabbed at the wood. 'Open the door!'

'No!'

Bruce hacked a big chunk off and reached his arm inside. 'What's your name?'

'Go away! Matty will be back!'

'Matty isn't here.'

The door clicked and Bruce yanked it open.

Chantal barged past him into the room. She had to vault over a bed propped against the door. A door on the far wall.

A woman stood by the bed, almost skeletally thin. Deep bags under her eyes, fading bruises on her forearm. 'Get out!'

'Jesus Christ.' Bruce stopped dead next to her. 'Petra?'

She frowned at him. 'Have you found my boy?'

Bruce pushed past her and waved a hand behind him. 'Take her down to the nick, please.'

She lashed out at him, clawing her nails into his arm. 'Get out!'

Bruce picked her up like she didn't weigh anything and passed her to the nearest uniform. 'Get her out of my sight!'

Chantal hauled him back. 'What's going on?'

'That's Petra Oliveira.' Bruce snorted at her. 'Harry Jack's mother.'

'What?' Chantal turned and watched as Petra was carried away. 'What's she doing here?'

'That's what I want to know.'

Chantal walked over and opened the door. She flicked on the light. A small room, barely a box room, but with a window looking out across the back yard.

A small boy lay on a bed, his face twisted as he blinked against the light. 'Mummy?'

Harry Jack.

94

HUNTER

Tulloch's grip tightened on Hunter's throat. 'I'm going to kill you!'

Hunter punched his fists into Tulloch's elbows, bending his arms down. Crunch. He pushed into Tulloch, side-on, and smacked his right fist off his windpipe.

Tulloch hit the deck, groaning, grabbing at his neck.

Hunter sucked in breath, deep gulps like he was downing pints of water in Iraq.

Cullen was out cold, lying on his side, mouth hanging open like a panting dog.

Tulloch stirred, his head twitching.

Hunter swung out with his boot and caught Tulloch square in the bollocks.

Tulloch pulled into a ball and screamed.

Hunter rubbed at his throat, trying to get some feeling back. 'Sco—' He coughed, blood welling up in his throat. 'Scott, are you—'

Tulloch's boot swept out and caught the back of Hunter's left knee. He rocked forward and toppled to the floor. A boot hit him on the side. Then another one.

Pause. And another.

Tulloch lashed out and Hunter rolled away, making Tulloch swing at air. He stumbled and righted himself against the wall.

Tulloch's boot smacked Hunter in the side again. Then it stopped.

The muffled screaming started up again.

Hunter opened his eyes.

Tulloch stood over Paisley, fists clamped to her throat. Her skin was turning blue.

Hunter hauled himself to his feet and charged over.

Tulloch let go of Paisley and pushed forward with his left fist, smashing into Hunter's temple. He toppled over, landing on Cullen.

Tulloch booted him in the side again. 'Stay down till I've finished, eh?'

Hunter rolled over onto his side. Pain speared up from his ribs. He blinked hard as he tried to open his eyes again.

Tulloch was strangling her, his face twisted with effort, her hands clawing at his, not making any difference.

Smoke smells came from behind Hunter. The iron sizzled against the carpet, face down, dark clouds pluming up. He grabbed the handle then pushed himself up to standing.

Tulloch's eyes shut as he squeezed his hands around Paisley's throat. She was half in the air, kicking against the ground, eyes bulging.

Hunter pressed the iron against Tulloch's bare arm. Hair singed, skin burned. Bacon stink filled the room.

Fight it!

Come on, fight through it!

'You bastard!'

Paisley dropped back down to the seat and tumbled off the side.

Tulloch was staring at the dark red burn on his arm.

Hunter snatched up the cord and swung the iron around. He let go and it thudded into Tulloch's temple, digging into his skull. He staggered backward, fighting against his failing footing, and hit the wall.

Hunter grabbed him under the chin and pushed him back. He seized a fistful of Tulloch's hair and smacked his head against the wall, denting the plasterboard. Again, the dent widening. Another go and he broke a hole in it.

Arms grabbed Hunter from behind. 'Woah, woah, he's had enough.'

Cullen, pulling him back from the abyss.

Hunter let go and Tulloch flopped into a heap on the floor.

∽

HUNTER SLUMPED FORWARD in the passenger seat of Cullen's Golf.

The interior swam around in front of his eyes, the rear-view looking like it was attached to the gearstick. Sick, like flu. Ribs were even worse than before. Kneecap felt like it stuck on the outside of his knee. Wrist like it'd bent so far the wrong way it became the right way again.

Blue lights from the ambulance and other police cars bounced off the buildings. Most windows had rubbernecking faces pressed up to the glass.

Paisley's house's side door opened, and the paramedics pulled a gurney out between them. The figure on the bed's face was swaddled in bandages, difficult to make out if they were male or female, dead or alive.

Hunter wobbled backwards, blinking hard as a giant paper cut seared up his shoulder blades.

Cullen walked back from the house, mobile to his ear. 'Might want to rest for a bit, He-Man.' He stabbed a finger on his phone and pocketed it. 'Sharon's got Matty, by the sounds of things.' He clapped Hunter's shoulder in the only part that didn't ache. 'And Paisley's heading back to hospital.'

'How is she?' Talking felt like it could knock teeth out.

'She'll live.' Cullen let out a sigh. Deep, like he used to do back in the day. 'Tulloch went to town on her, though.'

Hunter eased himself up. Felt like a rib was poking through his heart.

Cullen clapped him on the shoulder, right where it hurt. 'Just like old times, mate.' He got out his car keys then seemed to think twice about something. He grabbed Hunter's arm. 'Craig, when you were hitting Tulloch... Are you all right?'

Hunter shrugged off his grip and started off towards the car. 'I just wanted him to stop. He deserved it.'

'Not saying he didn't.' Cullen shook his head. 'I've never seen anything like that. You brutalised him.'

'You can thank me, you know?'

'What?'

'He was going to press the iron on your face.'

'Shite.' Cullen swallowed. 'I didn't know.'

Hunter brushed away some dried blood from his forehead. 'I got lucky when I twonked him with that iron.'

Cullen put his hands in his pockets. 'Well, the paramedics are in there. They reckon they can patch Tulloch up enough to get the okay from the duty doctor at Leith Walk.'

'Tonight?'

'As long as he can speak...' Cullen shrugged. 'Either way, his lawyer's on the way there.'

'Think he'll sue?'

'All depends on the lawyer, Craig.'

~

CULLEN'S CAR was the last in a long motorcade through the streets of sleeping Edinburgh, the flashing blue lights of the squad cars ahead of them.

They hit Portobello Road, filled with taxis and Ubers ferrying tanked-up clubbers into town and wasted boozers back home.

Hunter stretched out his knuckles. *Going to have to lay off the kettlebells for a week or so at this rate.* Could still feel the iron's cord between his fingers, slipping away as he sconed it off Tulloch's head.

They ploughed along London Road and Hunter's phone lit up. A text from Chantal:

HEARD WHAT HAPPENED. WELL DONE. X

He stabbed out a reply:

FEEL PRETTY BROKEN. HOW YOU?

A young couple staggered underneath a speed camera, both as pissed as each other. His phone flashed up again:

EVEN BROKER. I'LL KISS YR BRUISES BETTER LATER. X

WHAT'S HAPPENED? WHY ARE YOU BROKEN? X

He stared at the string of messages, going back months. Xs on most lines. Work stuff in amongst their chat. Christ, some of it was rancid. And God knows what McNeill would think if she saw any of it.

Cullen was more interested in Hunter's phone than the road. 'What's that?'

Hunter pocketed the mobile. 'Just checking in with the boss.'

'Boss, my arse.' Cullen set off across the London Road traffic lights, guided through by uniformed officers, then turned right onto Leith Walk. 'You're seeing her, aren't you?'

'No comment, Sergeant.'

Cullen grinned at him. 'Wanker.'

Hunter couldn't help but share the grin. 'Twat.'

Cullen barked out a laugh as he followed the ambulance down into the bowels of the police station. 'Chantal worked for me, remember?' He pulled up in one of the free spaces, next to a purple Jag. 'Moving her on was for the best.'

'I'll pass that on.' Hunter tried to get out, but his legs were locked. Bruises and lactic acid burned up the back of his thighs.

Cullen got out of the car and helped Hunter out his side. 'You old bastard.'

Felt like he was three hundred years old. 'So, are we getting to dance with Tulloch tonight, then?'

A car door thunked open behind them, echoing round the car park.

Cullen shrugged. 'Depends on which scum-sucking lawyer Tulloch's got.'

'The scum-sucking lawyer representing Mr Tulloch is here.' Dead eyes hid behind rimless specs. Brylcreemed white hair swept back to hide a good chunk of baldness. The sort of Morningside accent you only heard in jokes. Hamish Williams of McLintock, Williams & Partners.'

'My commiserations.' Cullen did up his suit jacket and helped Hunter to his feet. 'Bit odd for a big-shot like you to represent a raping scumbag like Tulloch.' Then he frowned. 'Oh hang on, it's what you do every day.'

Hunter started off across the garage, limping like an old man, every step feeling like a mile.

Williams got between them, blocking their path to the ambulance as Tulloch's lumbering shape was helped out. 'My client has been violently assaulted and requires urgent medical assistance. I would greatly appreciate it if you could see your way to releasing him from custody forthwith.'

Hunter got in his face and grinned as wide as his aching face would let him. 'Not going to happen.'

'Then I must insist that any interview is postponed until tomorrow morning.'

Cullen shrugged at Hunter. 'I'll process him, you go home and get yourself some shut-eye.'

95

CHANTAL

Chantal leaned against the wall in the corridor, her fingers numb around the mobile. 'An iron?'
'That's what I said.' Hunter's voice sounded like it was thousands of miles away, not just over a hundred. 'He...'
Chantal felt sick. Acid burned in her gut. 'But you got him?'
'Right. We got him.' Hunter let out a deep sigh. 'He's not in a good way. He's a bit too... injured to interview.'
'What did you do?'
'Arrested him. Ish.' Hunter sucked in air. 'You okay?'
'I don't think they've invented a swearword strong enough for how bad this is.'
Hunter laughed. 'I need to use that swearword when you've invented it.'
'That bad?'
'It's shite. Anyway. You okay?'
'No, I'm not. I'm just... Glad you caught him.'
'Me too.'
Chantal swapped the phone to her other hand. 'Look, Craig,

I'll be here another few hours interviewing and...' She yawned into her free hand. Felt like her jaw was going to slice open.

'Right, well, I'm back at my flat. The cats haven't killed each other, so it's looking positive.'

She cry-laughed, a lump catching in her throat.

Hunter's yawn rattled the speaker.

Chantal swallowed down bile. 'Look, Sharon told me they're charging Gordon Brownlee with Finlay's death.'

'Two days of hell in the Algarve and God knows how many PTSD flashbacks just so Matty Ibbetson and Keith Brannigan can walk free?'

'Tell me about it.' Footsteps rang off the metal from below as some cops climbed the stairs. Chantal moved over to look down. DI Colin "Crystal" Methven and a local uniform. 'Look, I've got to go. I'll let myself in.'

~

BRUCE WAS WAITING outside the interview room. 'That's some good work back there.'

'It's not over yet.' Chantal sucked in a deep breath. 'We need to put them away for what they've done.'

'Oh, we will.' Bruce glanced round at Chantal. 'Can't believe Petra's been lying to us for this long.' He huffed out a sigh. 'Under our bloody noses, Chantal. My mother lives down the road from that house.'

'We've got them now, Jon. That's what matters.'

'What matters is putting that pig bastard away.' Bruce stabbed a finger at the door, clattering against the wood. He straightened up and did up the buttons on his suit jacket. 'Your boss and I had a conference call with our friend Quaresma.'

'And?'

'He wants extradition.'

'You going to give him it?'

'Maybe. Not my decision. But he was gambling, started showing us his cards too soon.'

'Such as?'

Bruce thumbed at the interview room door. 'Petra in there? Her sister is none other than Luisa Oliveira.'

'What?' Chantal tried to process it, her brain struggling under lack of sleep and too much booze. 'So that's why Matty was speaking to her?'

'Correct.' Bruce entered the room and kicked off the interview recording.

Chantal checked her watch. Half two. Two hour drive back to Edinburgh, as well. She blinked away her tiredness and pushed into the interview room.

Matty Ibbetson slouched on the other side of the table, rocking from side to side, eyes shut. His face was puffed up, thick and purple. His right eye was bandaged, the left focused on the table top. He kept clenching his jaw then letting go. Didn't look up as Chantal sat opposite him.

His lawyer gave her a glance. An old Indian man, by the looks of things. Skin much darker than hers, so not from Pakistan, anyway. Tamil or Sri Lanka, maybe. He didn't say anything, just jotted something on his notepad.

Chantal sat back. The seat was warm, but the legs were cold against her bare skin. She stared at Matty, trying to look through his one open eye, dead as it was, trying to look deep into his soul. Nothing there, just emptiness, not even evil.

Murdering bastard.

Raping bastard.

Bruce jostled her elbow. 'DS Jain?'

'Right.' Chantal cleared her throat. Still no reaction from Matty. 'Mr Ibbetson, we need you to outline your movements yesterday evening.'

Matty's good eye peered around the room, homing in on Chantal. 'You can go to hell.'

'We're going nowhere.'

'You smashed my balls!' Matty reached under the table and grabbed something. 'It hurts like you wouldn't believe.' A tear slid down from the side of his eye, like a weeping wound rather than any emotion. He jabbed a finger towards his bandaged eye. 'You stabbed me in the eye with a cigar!'

'I was defending myself from you raping me.'

'Piss off I was.'

'You almost penetrated me.' Chantal drummed her thumbs on

the table. 'It'd be a very different story if you had a normal-sized cock.'

Matty rubbed at the bandage, wincing. Eyes shut, rocking. Like he had headphones in.

'We've got a tough decision to make, matey boy.' Bruce got to his feet and walked around the room, tugging on his suit jacket like a Victorian schoolmaster. 'We're going to extradite you to Portugal where you'll face a murder charge. Portuguese prisons are worse than British ones. You won't get Sky or an Xbox over there.' He flashed a grin. 'The decision comes down to whether we extradite you after you've faced justice for attempting to rape DS Jain. And, of course, the other thing.' Bruce kept his silence until Matty opened his good eye. 'I mean. Harry. We found him. Him and Petra in your spare room. Fancy that.'

Matty folded his arms. 'You're wasting your time here.'

'Who would've thought Harry is safe and well in sunny Alnwick. Not in the Algarve.' Bruce shrugged his shoulders and sat down again. 'Was it Luisa who called in the sightings?'

Matty's eye bulged. He glanced over at his lawyer. 'No comment.'

'We know that she's your soon-to-be sister-in-law.'

'He wasn't raping her!'

'So, what's it to be — the rape and murder charge in Portugal first, or the rape and child abduction here?' Bruce was nodding his head slowly, trying to match Matty's tempo. 'You get to choose, son. Any time you're ready to—'

Matty held up his fingers, covered in blood. 'I'm bleeding again!'

The lawyer helped Matty to his feet. 'We need to get him urgent medical attention!'

Bruce hit the recorder and reached over to grab Matty by the wrists. 'You're not getting out of this.'

'Piss off!'

'You're going to prison for a very long time, sonny.'

'When I get out, mate, I'm going to hunt you down and mess you up.'

CHANTAL

'You lied to me, Petra.' Bruce was opposite Petra Jack. He glanced over, his face twisted into rage. 'You lied to the whole world.'

Chantal stood. Hurt too much to sit.

Petra stared at the table.

'All that time, he was in Alnwick. Petra, you sat in this very room, telling us how you hadn't seen your boy for days. You lied your face off to us. "No, officer, I don't know where my son is. When you find the people who did this, I will kill them myself." Yadda, yadda, yadda. Well, we've found the people who took your boy, so are you going to kill yourself and Matthew Ibbetson?'

Nothing from her.

'Didn't think so.' Bruce reached into his pocket for his cigarette packet and rested it on the table. Petra's gaze swarmed all over it. 'Here's what happened. Someone abducted Harry on his walk home from school. That was Matty Ibbetson, your lover, wasn't it? Then he took him to his house and hid him there. Meanwhile you pretended to be the distraught mother.'

Petra rubbed her hands together.

'And, of course, you needed some misdirection, so you got your sister to call in a couple of sightings in Portugal, didn't you?'

Petra looked over at her lawyer.

'My client doesn't have to say anything.' Fresh out of law school, not yet tarnished with years of representing scumbags. Short with mousy hair, her over-tight blouse seemed to squish her torso. 'I suggest you allow her to leave and we can maybe reconvene when you have something concrete to put to her.'

'I don't think you realise how serious this case is.' Bruce drilled his nastiest glare into the lawyer. Didn't seem to have any impact. 'Ms Oliveira, Mrs Jack, whatever your name is this week, you kidnapped your son. You were party to it.'

'That remains to be proven.'

'What? We found them together.'

'Coincidence.'

Chantal stared around the dirty walls of the room. This wasn't working. She eased herself into the spare seat and smiled at Petra. 'You love Matty, don't you?'

Petra's eyes closed to narrow slits.

'You know that Matty is a murderer, don't you?'

Petra's eyes bulged. 'He is my man.'

Chantal got out a photo and slid it across the table. 'This is Finlay Sinclair. He was a police officer in Edinburgh.' She waited until Petra focused on the gurning face, sunshine glinting off his bald head. 'Matty murdered him today. Pushed him off a rock. He broke a rib and died from his injuries.'

Petra nudged the photo away.

'Matty pushed Finlay. Deliberately.'

'That happened in Portugal, not here.' The lawyer waved her hands around. 'I don't see anyone from the Portuguese police here, do you?'

Chantal narrowed her eyes at Petra. 'He pushed him off a cliff. Then he ran to the airport. Finlay died just as the plane took off. That's very cowardly for a big man like him.'

Petra huffed back in her seat, arms tight around her torso.

Another dead end. What other cards do we have left?

Chantal gritted her teeth. 'Do you know what I was doing in Portugal? How I came in contact with Mr Ibbetson?'

A shrug.

'I work for Police Scotland's Sexual Offences Unit. We're investigating one of Matty's best friends. Private Sean Tulloch of the 3rd Battalion of the Royal Regiment of Scotland. We've got five cases of domestic abuse against him over the last five years, all involving serious sexual assaults.'

Another shrug.

'Sean Tulloch meets damaged women, charms them, moves in with them, then he exploits them. Beats them up. Rapes them. Treats them like a slave.' She let it hang in the air. The lawyer's eyes bulged. 'Five women. So far.'

'I don't believe this.' Petra blinked hard. 'Sean is a nice man.'

'So you know him?'

Petra shrugged again.

'Mr Tulloch's latest victim is a woman called Paisley Sanderson. She lives in Galashiels, not too far from here. Before he flew out to Portugal, Mr Tulloch put her in hospital.'

Petra couldn't look anyone in the eye, just focused on her fingers.

'Then tonight, Sean Tulloch came back here and put an iron to her face.' She let it hang again. The lawyer looked like she was going to be sick. 'Paisley's back in hospital. I suspect she'll be deformed for life. All because she decided to talk to us about what Mr Tulloch has put her through.'

Petra reached over and picked up her cup of water. It splashed out of the sides as she sipped it.

Chantal wanted to reach across and...

She sighed. 'Mr Tulloch raped two women in Portugal. Heather Latimer. Nice Irish girl. On a hen weekend with her pals and family. Then she gets her drinks spiked. Next thing she knows, she wakes up with Tulloch on top of her. Gordon Brownlee was watching. Another of Matty's friends.'

'Shut up.'

'And, of course, the other rape. . . Mr Tulloch took Luisa Oliveira upstairs at the bar and raped her.'

Petra made eye contact. 'That wasn't rape.'

Chantal sighed. 'What?'

'Nothing.'

'We know she's your sister.'

'I am not saying anything.'

'You should speak to us, Petra. We might be able to have a word with our colleagues over in Portugal. See what they can do about your... Nah, you're screwed. Matty's going away for a very long time.'

Petra folded her arms. 'She loves Sean.'

Bingo...

Chantal leaned low, managing to lock eyes with Petra. 'How do you know this?'

'Luisa called me this morning. She was upset. Police broke down door in her apartment.' Petra huffed out a sigh, then shrugged. 'This is what she tell me. These men came in to the bar with Matty. They had breakfast. Then Sean started chatting to Luisa. She had a drink with them.'

'And then?'

'Then she asked him if he wanted to go to her place. Her shift was over, so she was free.'

'And he raped her there?'

'He didn't rape her!' Petra smacked a fist off the table. 'Don't you understand? Matty introduced Sean to Luisa. She liked him. Get over it.'

'Was it like you and Matty?'

'What?'

'Did you meet him in a bar?'

'I met him at Catterick when he was based there. I worked as a cleaner. Matty was different from the rest of them.' Petra patted her cheek, almost like a lover's caress. 'We started sleeping together.'

'But you got divorced?'

Petra nodded, little trails of tears sliding down both cheeks. 'My husband found out. He tried to get custody of Harry.' Her face twisted up. 'The judge, this *pig*, he gave him temporary custody! He took Harry away from me! My own son!'

'So you and Matty decided the best thing was to kidnap your son?'

Petra inspected her nails. 'It's just until my divorce comes through. Then we can be together as a family.'

'So you abducted Harry?'

'Harry should be with his mother!' Another thump on the table. 'Do you know why I love Matty? Because my husband, the pig, he used to hit me. He beat me up. Every night. I told Matty and... Matty took me away from him. But he left Harry! There was nothing we could do.'

'You could've spoken to the police.'

'The police wouldn't believe me.'

'You could've tried. Instead, you've got this situation.'

'Matty saved Harry from that bastard!' Petra banged the table again, tipping her water over. 'You should give him a medal!'

The lawyer snorted at Chantal, then stared back at Bruce. 'My client was in a desperate situation. I expect some leniency here.'

'She's going away for a long time.' Bruce nodded at her then leaned over to Chantal. 'That's nailed it, pet. Do you want to get yourself home?'

HUNTER

Hunter stared out of the kitchen window while the coffee maker whistled on the stove. Leith was in full flow, Sunday morning traffic turning Commercial Street into a car park as people headed to Ocean Terminal.

He stretched out, touching his palms to the floor. His thighs ached, burning up the back. Dark bruises dotted his side. Even looking at it hurt.

Hunter went over and took the coffee off the hob. He got two mugs out of the cupboard and poured the thick syrupy liquid in. Beautiful. Dark and musty, smelled like truffle oil. He poured in the hot milk and tried to feather off Chantal's.

What a bloody mess.

He grabbed the handles and walked through the flat towards the bedroom. Muffin shot out, scuttling along the laminate. Bubble followed him, managing to run on three legs at the same time as punching his arse.

'There's my girl.' Hunter pushed the door open.

Chantal lay in the darkness and let out a groan. She flicked on the bedside light and blinked with one eye, the other shut. 'Fell asleep again.'

Hunter put the coffees down on his side of the bed. 'When did you get in?'

She stared right through him, like understanding speech was beyond her. 'Half four.' She lay back and yawned. 'Sharon was still there when I left.'

A thump came from the hall.

Hunter pushed himself up. 'That'll be the paper.'

'You're such an old man.'

Hunter padded through, feeling like an old man. Muffin stood over *The Sunday Argus*, looking like he was going to piss on it. 'Don't you bloody dare.' He shooed him off and picked up the paper.

HARRY: COPS FIND MISSING CHILD IN ALNWICK RAID

The photo below showed Chantal and Bruce leading the mother into a police station somewhere. Newcastle, probably.

Jesus Christ.

Hunter went back through and threw the paper on the bed. 'You're famous.'

'I'll try and not let it go to my head.' She picked it up and stared at it. 'I look terrible.'

'You wish you *could* look terrible.' Hunter perched on the edge of the bed. 'You didn't tell me you found him.'

'Well, I couldn't think of anything after you told me about Tulloch.' She grabbed her coffee and slurped at it. 'This is good.'

'I know.' Hunter sipped at his own coffee. 'Smells like cigars.'

She froze, the mug against her lip. 'What?'

'I said it smelled like cigars.'

She put down her mug. 'Last night, when we arrested Matty. Before I went... Before I went medieval on him. He was smoking a cigar. My uncle used to smoke cigars. Maybe the same brand, maybe not...'

'Shite, I should've thought.'

She grabbed his wrist. 'Craig, I had a flashback to when I was playing rugby. I was twelve and he... He picked me up. Dad had to go somewhere. He took me down a country lane and... That was the first time.'

Hunter sat on the edge of the bed and stroked her arm. 'I didn't know.'

'That fat bastard and his cigars.'

'Do you want to talk about it?'

'I don't want to stop.' Her jaw clenched tight. 'I went ballistic on Ibbetson. I kicked his balls so hard they bled. I couldn't stop. Just kept on kicking. All because...' She broke off, shaking her head. 'All because of what Ditinder did to me.'

'I'm so sorry.'

'It's not your fault. It's... It's deep in the past. He can't do what he did to me again.'

'He won't.' Hunter smiled at her. *If I had a time machine...* 'What did Sharon say about it?'

'She's going to cover it over. It's all part of the arrest record now.' She picked up her coffee again. 'Matty tried to rape me.'

Hunter's blood went from boiling point to ice. 'He what?'

'He tried to rape me.' Chantal ran a hand through her hair. 'I stabbed him in the eye with the cigar. Then I beat the shit out of him.'

'I wish I'd been there to stop it.'

'To protect me?'

'Maybe.' Hunter tasted sick at the back of his throat. 'Him and Tulloch, they won't do it to anyone ever again.' He swallowed hard, trying to get rid of the taste. 'Only goes to show that, no matter where you're from, a scumbag is a scumbag. We're all the same underneath, it's what we do that makes a difference.'

~

HUNTER DROVE into the car park in Bathgate station, taking it as slowly as his battered hands would allow. He parked in the first of a row of three empty bays. 'Wouldn't get this on a Monday morning.'

Chantal glanced over at him, frowning. 'Right.'

Hunter opened his door and let it hang there. 'You okay?'

'Not really.' She stuffed her phone away and let her seatbelt flop to her lap. 'I need like a year's sleep. I'm worried we're going to mess it up.'

'Not going to happen.'

'Craig, we need hard evidence on Tulloch. We need to...'

'It's okay.' Hunter grabbed her hand and held it tight. 'Look, you maybe shouldn't be working today.'

'Tulloch has to... I've got to make sure he—'

Something clunked off his window. DI McNeill stood there, her pencil-thin eyebrows standing to attention. She jabbed a finger at Chantal then at Hunter.

Chantal snatched her hand away from his. 'Shite on a lamppost.' She opened the door with a breezy smile. 'Shaz, good morning. We—'

'You lying cow.'

'What?'

'Don't think I didn't see that.' Sharon pointed at Hunter as he got out of the car. 'You pair must think we're all idiots. Chantal, my office, now.' She turned and clattered away.

Chantal ran after her.

This is all we need...

Cullen was leaning against his Golf, parked next to them, yawning into a fist. 'Morning, Craig.'

'Morning.' Hunter huffed out a sigh. 'Any news?'

'Other than you two getting here at the same time?'

'There's nothing—'

'Save it, mate. Not my battle.' Cullen plipped his car's locks. 'Look, Sharon wants you and me to interview Tulloch, okay? I'll see you inside.'

'Fine.' Hunter watched him go, slumping back to rest on his car, arms folded.

Bollocks.

Playing with fire for far too long and—

'Alright?' Elvis was skulking around a couple of cars over. Didn't look himself, his mouth hanging open.

Hunter pushed off from the car and joined him. 'You okay, mate?'

Elvis blew out a sigh. 'I feel emaciated.'

'What?'

'When Chantal and Sharon took out that Matty guy last night, they left me looking through CCTV.'

Hunter almost laughed. 'You mean emasculated, right?'

'Whatever, still a load of shite, mate.' Elvis hauled his laptop bag up his shoulder. 'They were running a big dunt in Alnwick and they didn't want me there. How's that supposed to make me feel?'

'Like you've got other uses?'

'I can kick a door down with the best of them.' Elvis started walking over to the back entrance. 'Starting to wish I'd never come here.'

98

Tulloch sat back in his seat, arms folded across his chest. His face was bandaged up, broken red skin outlining the sunburnt white. 'I'm saying nothing.'

Hunter still ached all over, but he couldn't sit down. He paced around the interview room and stopped behind Cullen's chair. 'Mr Tulloch, can you outline your movements on the night of Thursday the twelfth of May 2016?'

Tulloch shrugged both shoulders. 'When you tried to assault me at Waverley?'

Hunter leaned forward to rest against Cullen's chair. 'How did you know we'd be there?'

'Eyes and ears everywhere, my sweet prince.'

'Name your source.'

'Piss off.'

There's something there, something to push and prod. What, though? 'Okay, so after Waverley?'

'I went to the airport.'

'Aye? How did you get there?'

Tulloch sniffed. 'Can't remember.'

'You didn't steal a car, did you?'

'No I never.' Tulloch licked his lips. 'Look, I flew out to Portugal. There's no law against that, far as I'm aware.'

'And what did you do there?'

'Met some boys from the squad and we went for a few drinks.'
'Do any karaoke?'
Tulloch smirked. 'A bit, aye.'
'Did you speak to any women?'
'Might've done.'
'So that'll be when you raped Heather Latimer?'
Tulloch snarled at Williams's latest attempt to elbow him. 'Like I told that Portuguese wanker yesterday, that bird was so pissed I doubt she even remembered her name.'
'So how could she give her consent?'
'Because she said she wanted my monster cock inside her.' Tulloch grinned and grabbed at his groin. 'Here, do you fancy a portion?'
Hunter held his gaze until he looked away. 'What about Luisa Oliveira?'
'Nice girl.'
'Who you raped.'
'Asked and answered, buddy. Consent given.' Tulloch leaned over to whisper into Williams's ear, loud enough for the microphone to pick up. 'See, Hamish, this boy burst in on us at it. He's after my cock, isn't he? Big poof.'
Williams gritted his teeth.
Hunter waited for Tulloch to look at him. 'You raped Luisa, didn't you?'
Tulloch paused for a few seconds. 'Move. On.'
'Later on, you were trying to get back in to Luisa's flat. Why?'
'No comment.'
'Worried she was going to tell us you had actually raped her?'
'You find it hard to believe that a girl like that would be into a boy like me?'
'Kind of. Aside from your penis, what's her interest?'
'Can't it just be my knob and my rugged charm?'
Hunter stared at him. 'And your date rape drugs?'
'Piss off. You've no evidence of anything, have you?'
'Matty introduced you to her, right?'
Tulloch looked away. 'It's his bird's sister.' He shrugged, like it was a normal thing. 'We had a few drinks. She liked me, invited me back to hers.'
Hunter's gut burned. All the guilt and rage simmered away,

biting at his gullet, gnawing at his stomach. He switched to another sheet of paper. 'Next, you were complicit in the murder of Finlay Sinclair.'

Tulloch shrugged his left shoulder. 'Don't recall it.'

'He was pushed off a cliff yesterday afternoon. He punctured a lung and died later that day. You deny being there?'

'Yup.'

Hunter stopped. 'We have evidence of you at the crime scene in Albufeira.'

'Wasn't there.'

'So who did it?'

'No idea.'

'Matty?'

'No idea, mate. Move on.'

'Gordon Brownlee.'

'Hardly. Prick wasn't even there.' Tulloch clicked his finger a few times. 'You're screwing that Paki, aren't you?'

'You assisted Matthew Ibbetson in the murder of—'

'You satisfy her, do you?' Tulloch made a little hook with his pinky. 'That how big you are, eh? Little maggot. When I get out of here, how about I give her a real portion of cock?'

Hunter slumped back in his chair, shaking his head. Everything hurt that little bit worse. 'Mr Tulloch, we have been running a case against you for over a year now.' He hefted up a paper file and dropped it on the desk, the thud echoing round the small room. 'This is the evidence we've so far obtained.'

'Whilst I certainly do appreciate early sight of this...' Williams looked over the top of his glasses. 'Perhaps we are jumping the gun here, slightly?'

'Of course.' Hunter pushed the file across to the other side of the desk, just in front of Cullen, scratching at his chin again. 'We've only got started with this. We'll need a few more files by the time this goes to trial. But I wanted to ask you a few questions about Paisley Sanderson.'

'Piss off.'

Williams jostled Tulloch's arm. 'My client denies any involvement.'

'You deny assaulting her?'

'No comment.'

'You deny pressing a hot iron against her face?'

'Move on.'

'No, I won't move on.' Hunter leaned forward, narrowing his eyes. 'You tortured her, tried to kill her. Are you denying that?'

'No comment.'

'Of course, you'd already threatened to kill her, hadn't you?'

'No comment.'

'This is a text message you sent on Wednesday night.' Hunter held up a print-out. 'Do you want me to read it out?' He waited for a reply. Didn't get one. 'It says, "Know who you spoke to. You are dead, bitch."' He put the sheet down in front of the lawyer. 'I am, of course, translating the text speak.'

Tulloch snorted. 'I didn't send that.'

'It came from your phone.'

'Must be one of the lads in my mess.' Tulloch folded his arms tight around his torso. 'Must've left it on the table when I went for a slash.'

'You didn't lock it?'

Tulloch's lips curled up at the sides. 'Foible of mine.'

'None of your ex-partners received similar messages.' Hunter tapped the file. 'I should say victims, of course. You only threatened Paisley. Why is that?'

'Like I said, pal. Can't help you.' Tulloch smiled at him then winced. 'Someone messed about with my phone. Gogs Brownlee, I'd say.'

'So you deny sending these messages?'

'Have you got any proof that my client typed them and then sent them? No. So move on.' Williams flourished a gesture up and down Tulloch's body. 'As you can see, my client is still in need of medical attention, so time is of the essence.'

'Your client has spent a night in hospital and the duty doctor has approved him for interview.'

'Move on, Constable.'

'You sent her a text threatening her, then you went round to her house and tried to follow through on the threat.'

'That right, eh?' Tulloch winked at his lawyer and nodded over at Hunter. 'Tell you a tale, Hamish. This boy assaulted me on the Strip in Albufeira. Then he attacked me when I was slipping a bird a length. So, I'm thinking he wants a portion of my dong, eh?'

Hunter jolted up to his feet again, leaning on his hands. 'I arrested you when you were pressing an iron into—'

'Piss off!' Tulloch almost snarled at him. '*You* assaulted *me* with an *iron* when I was *speaking* to Paisley.' He pointed to a white bandage on his arm, red splotches leaking through. 'You burnt my arm, you prick! Then you threw it at me!' He rubbed at some stitches in his temple. 'Do you know how much this hurts?'

You deserve everything you get.

Hunter raised his eyebrows. 'You were pressing the iron into Paisley's flesh.'

'Assaulted me, man. Police brutality.'

'You were torturing her.'

'I wasn't.'

'So you deny torturing Ms Sanderson?'

'Aren't you listening to me? I've done nothing.'

Williams sucked a deep breath through his nostrils. 'My client wishes you to move on.'

'What I don't get is how you found out that Paisley was talking to us.'

'When you pricks start talking to my squad mates about me, you honestly think they're *not* going to tell me that someone's been blabbing?'

'What? Who spoke to them?'

'You're a stupid prick.' Tulloch laughed, scratching his wounds. A stream of blood trickled down his forehead.

Williams rubbed a finger on Tulloch's temple, smearing it. 'My client requires urgent medical assistance. This interview is terminated.'

CHANTAL

Chantal walked across the empty office, her heart thundering in her chest. She stopped short and...
Shite. This is it. Caught.
This is where she breaks us up and...
She pushed at Sharon's door and peered in. 'Sharon.'
She was on the phone, nodding her head. A Thornton's chocolate box sat on the desk. 'Okay, I'll speak to you later. Bye.' She put the phone down and fixed a glare on Chantal. 'You going to start telling me the truth?'
'Okay.' Chantal glanced at the door behind her and sucked in a deep breath. 'Me and Craig are an item.'
'I know.' A grin crept over Sharon's face. 'You lying cow.'
'It's not like you thought. We—'
'Don't even think about saying "oh, we got together in Portugal for reals".' Sharon reached into the chocolate box and took one out. 'You've been shagging him for months, so don't try it.'
'It's the—'
'Chantal. Stop. Back in August, I popped round to your flat when I was passing. Your neighbour let me into the stairwell. I was

going to knock on the door but I heard you. "Oh, Craig! Oh, Craig!" Sound familiar?'

'Right.' Chantal rubbed at her cheek, not all the heat from the tan top-up. 'So, are you going to separate us?'

'I've not got a choice.' Sharon took another chocolate from the box, the paper rustling. 'Look, Scott and I did that for a month when we started going out, remember? It's not a good idea. We've got to be cleaner than clean.'

'I know, it's just…'

'Look, I'll cover it over, but I need you to stop lying to me, okay?'

'Fine.'

'Right. Good.' She took another chocolate. Didn't look like she was going to offer any. She finished chewing and picked up another. 'So, what's going to happen is, once I've filled the new DS position I've got approval for—' Her eyebrows flashed up. 'Craig's nowhere near ready.' She took another chocolate, looked like a toffee from the way she chewed it. 'Once this new DS is in, Craig will report to them, okay?' She winked at Chantal. 'Try not to shag them, aye?'

'Fine.' Chantal yawned into her fist. 'Sorry. Look, I've acted like a cow about this. You don't deserve it, and—'

'That was the Procurator Fiscal on the phone.' Sharon stretched out. 'She thinks we've got more than enough to prosecute and we've barely done any detailed interviews.' She pulled out a notepad and started flicking through. 'Of course, you'll be working with Elvis on it. I'll have to pair Hunter up with Jenny or Jim. He might be able to show them how it's done?'

The door rattled open and Rollo-Smith stormed in. 'Inspector.' He glowered at Chantal. 'Sergeant.'

'How can we help, Brian?'

Rollo-Smith bristled, probably at being addressed by his first name for the first time since boarding school. 'I have spoken to my superiors.'

'And are you going to try and help us?'

'Excuse me?'

'You've been a hindrance to us all throughout this case.'

'And yet you still don't have solid evidence against Private Tulloch, do you?'

'The Procurator Fiscal's pressed the button on the prosecution. We'll be charging Tulloch as soon as DC Hunter and DS Cullen are finished with him.'

'This might help.' Rollo-Smith extended a mobile phone like it was a bugle.

Chantal frowned at it. 'What's that?'

Rollo-Smith fiddled with the screen. 'This is gold dust, Sergeant.' He showed her the display, a video playing.

Paisley Sanderson, tied up on a bed, screaming while Tulloch thrust away at her. She looked into the camera, terror in her eyes. 'You love my cock, don't you?'

Rollo-Smith paused it, tears streaming down Paisley's cheek. 'It would appear that Mr Tulloch sent videos of him torturing the women to a few friends.'

Chantal reached for the phone.

Rollo-Smith pulled it away. 'Not so fast.'

'We need that locked up in evidence. Where did you get it?'

'DI Bruce obtained it from Matty Ibbetson. I spoke to him this morning.' Rollo-Smith cleared his throat. 'I shall hold onto this. But, the evidence we have obtained will be at your disposal.'

Chantal put a hand on her hip. 'Give.'

'Excuse me?'

'That's our case.' She nodded at the handset. 'Give me the mobile. Now.'

'I won't take orders from a *Sergeant*.'

She snatched it from his hand. 'This is going in our evidence store.'

'Detective Inspector McNeill, I refuse to be subjected to insubordination like this. I demand that.'

Sharon smiled at him. 'Get out of here.'

Rollo-Smith barked out a laugh. 'I beg your pardon?'

'You heard.'

'Very well.' Rollo-Smith put his left hand into his blazer pocket and walked over to the door. 'I shall be in touch with DCI Fletcher.' He left them to it.

'First name terms.' Chantal slumped into the chair opposite Sharon. 'You're getting on like a house on fire.'

'He's an idiot.' Sharon reached into her box of Thornton's

chocolates. 'Brucie Boner sent these through. There's flowers in the kitchen and three bottles of Prosecco in the fridge.'

'That's good of him.'

'You stupid bastard!' Shouting came from out in the office. 'You could've got her killed!'

Chantal rushed out, Sharon following her.

Hunter had Rollo-Smith by the lapels, pushed up against the wall. 'It's your bloody fault!'

Rollo-Smith wriggled against him. 'Let me go!'

Chantal raced over and pulled Hunter back. 'Craig, what the hell are you doing?'

Hunter let Rollo-Smith go with a final smack. 'This craven little worm leaked it to Tulloch's mates. Told them we were speaking to Paisley.'

Chantal stared at Rollo-Smith. 'Is this true?'

He brushed the shoulders of his jacket. 'My officers have been interviewing Tulloch's cohort off the record.'

'Wait, your officers have interviewed him?'

Rollo-Smith nodded. 'Naturally.'

'Did you speak to Tulloch?'

'Naturally.'

Chantal glared at Rollo-Smith. 'You did leak it, didn't you?'

'Excuse me?'

'You told a bunch of his mates that we were speaking to Paisley.' Her turn to grab Rollo-Smith and pull him close. 'Tulloch tried to kill Paisley because of what you did!'

'This isn't my fault!' Rollo-Smith pushed away from her. 'We were carrying out an investigation in support of yours!'

'Her injuries are a direct consequence of you blabbing. I'll see what I can charge you with.'

Rollo-Smith laughed. 'I'd love to see it.'

'You're an arsehole.' Chantal narrowed her eyes at him. 'Tell me. Inspector Quaresma. Your mate João. Was he really inept or had you two come to an understanding? Cover over what one of your officers was up to?'

'This isn't the end of the matter.' Rollo-Smith turned on his heels and marched off, pressing a mobile to his ear.

'Right, well, that's the end of that, then.' Sharon snatched the phone from Chantal. 'Time you two were out of here.'

HUNTER

Hunter held the door open for Chantal. The hospital corridor stank of cleaning chemicals and boiled cabbage. 'So we're out of the closet, then?'
'We are. You've got what you wanted.'
'So, where does that leave us?'
'You tell me, Craig.'
'I meant about us at work.'
'Wait and see. Shaz's got approval for another DS.'
'So no more uniform?'
'Correct.'
'It's for the best. You know that, right?'
She leaned over and kissed him on the cheek. 'I know.' Then she sped off down the corridor towards the ward.

Hunter followed Chantal. His new trousers were far too tight.

Dr Yule was chatting to PC Lenny Warner. She nodded at Hunter. 'Well, I might as well tell you both...' She left a long enough pause that made Hunter think that Paisley was dead. 'She's not in a critical condition. Ms Sanderson will, however, require skin grafts. She's suffered some very serious injuries.' She narrowed her eyes at Hunter. 'I wish you'd caught the barbarian who did this to her.'

Chantal nodded. 'We have.'

'I meant in time. Before he did this.'

'So do I. So do I.'

Warner beamed at Yule, his grin seeming to dilute the bile pouring out of the doctor. 'I think they need a few moments with her, is that alright?'

Hunter folded his arms. Bloody shirt was too tight as well. 'A couple of minutes, at the very most.'

'Very well.' Yule paced over and opened a door.

Paisley lay on the bed, the left half of her face covered in a bandage. She made eye contact with Hunter and looked away.

Hunter stood over her, keeping a decent distance. 'How are you doing?'

'I'm buggered. Thanks to you. My skin's burnt. I need grafts. Who's going to want me after that, eh?'

'Paisley, we've charged Mr Tulloch with both assaults on you, as well as a series of domestic abuse charges.'

'So I've got to go through it all again in court? With him standing there? His mates will kill me!'

'It's all going to be taken care of, Paisley.'

'That's bullshit. You're going to mess it up and let him go!'

'I know it's difficult to process and you're thinking of all the bad things that can happen, but once he's away, the army will court martial him. Then he'll face charges in Portugal relating to a rape he committed there.'

'A rape?'

'He's not going to get out of prison for a very long time, if ever.'

'What did he do over there? He raped someone?'

'A Northern Irish woman. He spiked her drink and raped her in his hotel room.'

'That's not what he did with me.'

'Or with his victims. He changed his MO and...' Chantal broke off. 'Look, he's going away for a long time. It's not going to be easy, but we'll have to take detailed statements over the next few weeks from you. When you're better.'

'Do you have any idea what this feels like? Having my life torn apart like this?'

Chantal nodded slowly. 'I do.' She fiddled with her blouse collar. 'I was abused when I was a girl. By my uncle. It took me a long time, but I spoke out about it. I remember the police coming around to our house. I spoke to them, told them everything. My uncle died in prison. I don't regret it.'

Paisley started crying. Didn't look like she was going to stop any time soon.

The next Police Scotland book is out now!

"HEROES AND VILLAINS"
Starring DS Scott Cullen

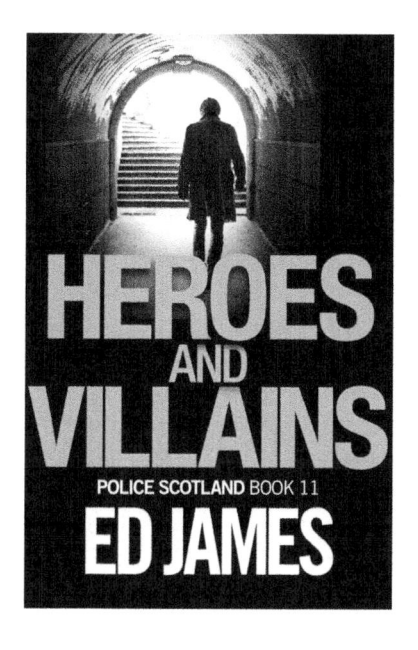

Get it now!

If you would like to be kept up to date with new releases from Ed James and access free novellas, please join the Ed James Readers' Club.

ABOUT THE AUTHOR

Ed James is the author of the bestselling DI Simon Fenchurch novels, Seattle-based FBI thrillers starring Max Carter, and the self-published Detective Scott Cullen series and its Craig Hunter spin-off books.

During his time in IT project management, Ed spent every moment he could writing and has now traded in his weekly commute to London in order to write full-time. He lives in the Scottish Borders with far too many rescued animals.

If you would like to be kept up to date with new releases from Ed James, please join the Ed James Readers Club.

Connect with Ed online:

Amazon Author page

Website

OTHER BOOKS BY ED JAMES

DI ROB MARSHALL

Ed's first new police procedural series in six years, focusing on DI Rob Marshall, a criminal profiler turned detective. London-based, an old case brings him back home to the Scottish Borders and the dark past he fled as a teenager.

1. THE TURNING OF OUR BONES
2. WHERE THE BODIES LIE (May 2023)

Also available is FALSE START, a prequel novella starring DS Rakesh Siyal, is available for **free** to subscribers of Ed's newsletter or on Amazon. Sign up at https://geni.us/EJLCFS

POLICE SCOTLAND

Precinct novels featuring detectives covering Edinburgh and its surrounding counties, and further across Scotland: Scott Cullen, eager to climb the career ladder; Craig Hunter, an ex-squaddie struggling with PTSD; Brian Bain, the centre of his own universe and everyone else's. Previously published as SCOTT CULLEN MYSTERIES, CRAIG HUNTER POLICE THRILLERS and CULLEN & BAIN SERIES.

1. DEAD IN THE WATER
2. GHOST IN THE MACHINE
3. DEVIL IN THE DETAIL
4. FIRE IN THE BLOOD
5. STAB IN THE DARK
6. COPS & ROBBERS
7. LIARS & THIEVES
8. COWBOYS & INDIANS
9. THE MISSING
10. THE HUNTED
11. HEROES & VILLAINS
12. THE BLACK ISLE
13. THE COLD TRUTH

14. THE DEAD END

DS VICKY DODDS

Gritty crime novels set in Dundee and Tayside, featuring a DS juggling being a cop and a single mother.

1. BLOOD & GUTS
2. TOOTH & CLAW
3. FLESH & BLOOD
4. SKIN & BONE
5. GUILT TRIP

DI SIMON FENCHURCH

Set in East London, will Fenchurch ever find what happened to his daughter, missing for the last ten years?

1. THE HOPE THAT KILLS
2. WORTH KILLING FOR
3. WHAT DOESN'T KILL YOU
4. IN FOR THE KILL
5. KILL WITH KINDNESS
6. KILL THE MESSENGER
7. DEAD MAN'S SHOES
8. A HILL TO DIE ON
9. THE LAST THING TO DIE

Other Books

Other crime novels, with Lost Cause set in Scotland and Senseless set in southern England, and the other three set in Seattle, Washington.

- LOST CAUSE
- SENSELESS
- TELL ME LIES
- GONE IN SECONDS
- BEFORE SHE WAKES

HEROES AND VILLAINS
PROLOGUE

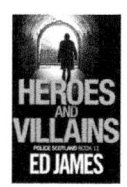

Detective Sergeant Scott Cullen kept his gaze on the silver Range Rover three cars ahead as they followed it past the Scottish Parliament, which still looked like a municipal swimming baths from provincial Scotland, just with some Catalan window dressing stapled on. Showed where the country was these days.

DC Paul 'Elvis' Gordon was behind the pool car's wheel, giving off the vibe of his namesake's final hours in Vegas, rather than his Hollywood pomp. He scratched at his massive sideburns, keeping the car a steady thirty as they passed through two roundabouts and two sweeping bends along the busy road from the city's political heart to its social armpit, Dumbiedykes. He stopped to wait for an old man to cross, drumming his thumbs off the wheel, then headed into the former council estate. The high-rise blocks still seemed like a junkie haven, even though the flats were mostly leased to MSPs and bankers, and filled with designer furniture and bespoke kitchens. Mostly.

The Range Rover pulled up outside a beige-and-grey tower block, the blacked-out windows hiding the driver.

Cullen gestured for Elvis to drive on by the target – no slowing down, no turned heads, no suspicious behaviour. As they passed, Cullen angled the wing mirror.

Dean Vardy hopped out of his pimp ride, his disco muscles

and skin-tight T-shirt a cocky challenge to the afternoon's fourteen degrees, the Edinburgh wind lowering the temperature. He strutted up to the front door like he owned the place. Not far off the truth – his legal businesses owned twenty flats inside. God knows how many his illegal ones did.

Elvis cruised around the turning point at the end, doubled back to the neighbouring block and slowed to a halt at the side of the street. He killed the ignition and yawned, releasing a blast of coffee breath. 'Hope you're pleased I haven't made a joke about you being the dumb guy in Dumbiedykes?'

'Very pleased.' Cullen reached for his Airwave radio and put it to his ear. 'Suspect has entered premises at Holyrood Court, Dumbiedykes. Want us to follow him in?'

'Negative, Sundance.' DS Brian Bain's Glasgow rasp hissed out. 'We've got eyes on you from up here, so sit tight. Your front-left headlight is buggered, by the way.'

'Look, she's in that flat alone.' Cullen tightened his grip on the 'oh-shit' handle even though they weren't moving. 'We're just letting Vardy walk up there?'

'It's called a plan for a reason, Sundance. Boss's orders. Now you make sure he doesn't leave without us knowing.'

Bloody hell.

Cullen ended the call and slid the Airwave back into the sleeve pocket of his battered green bomber jacket.

Across the street, by the entrance, some neds were playing football – none of them looking any older than ten.

Nothing else happening.

Elvis was stroking his lamb chops, a look of puzzled constipation stuck on his face, like the King of Rock 'n' Roll on his resting toilet. 'So we're just to sit here?'

'Those are the orders, aye.'

'Tell you, this undercover stakeout's been dragging on longer than one of Wilko's morning briefings.' Elvis shook his head. 'Here we are, sitting on our arses, while that Vardy bastard runs around like he owns the place, raping and killing. And I'm only here because you pissed off the boss.'

'You don't need to remind me.' Cullen gave him a glare, hoping it would warn him that a constable should watch what he says to a sergeant. Elvis looked the other way. 'Fine, I'll say it if it makes you happy. You're here because I messed up Wilko's case, but I did solve a murder in the process. And, for my troubles, I got a secondment to Operation Venus. Along with the rest of the Special Needs class.'

'Very funny.' Elvis chuckled despite himself. 'Just saying, that's all.'

'You could put in for a transfer, you know.'

'How did you…?' Elvis settled even deeper into his seat, blushing. Something groaned. Could've been the back rest, could've been his stomach. 'Sorry, Sarge. Might want to open a window.'

Cullen held his breath as he got out into the blustery wind and leaned against the car.

The sky looked like it had been in a fight. Hard winds from the North Sea pummelled grey clouds across the horizon. One seemed beaten up, a lumbering purple mass like a bloody bruise.

Edinburgh in August. Got to love it.

The car rocked as Elvis got out. He stepped around and settled his bulk on the bonnet, upwind of Cullen. 'Look on the bright side, though. You've got me for company. Dragged me into this unexpected career development opportunity and I haven't resented you for one moment. Must be my sunny deposition.'

'You mean disposition.' Cullen stuck his hands into his jeans pockets. 'And you don't mind this new gig because it means you're not gawping at CCTV all day.'

Elvis pushed himself off the bonnet and puffed up his chest. 'Hold on a—'

'Alright, Scotty?' A big guy in a shiny blue muscle-shirt slapped Cullen's shoulder with one hand, holding a two-litre plastic bottle with the other. 'Alright, my man?'

'Aye, just walking the daftie here. What's up?'

'Your daftie looks fair exhausted, Scotty.' Big Rob grinned at Elvis, killing any attempt at a witty comeback with a confused wink. 'You boys doing interval sprints?'

Elvis rolled his eyes. 'Aye, that's what we're doing out here.'

'Good effort, my man.' Big Rob waved the bottle around, splashing water on the pavement. 'Been working hard myself all morning. Today's target is ten litres.' He flexed a pair of bulging biceps. 'Need to hydrate these bad boys.'

'Ten litres?' Cullen smirked at him. 'Isn't that going to dehydrate you?'

'Science.' Big Rob tapped his nose and wandered off.

Elvis watched him go. 'That your ex-boyfriend?'

'Just some old CHIS.'

Elvis did that particular frown, his features squishing up like a used chip wrapper. Usually meant he was thinking of something funny. 'There's nothing covert, human or intelligent about him, is there?'

Cullen glanced at the heavy clouds pressing down on the tower blocks. 'Elvis, you'll need to drive me to A&E, I think I've split my sides.'

'Come on, mate. That was funny. Got to admit.' Elvis crossed his arms and did his best impression of a petulant toddler, huffing and puffing.

Cullen closed his eyes, wondering what he'd done to deserve this. Then he remembered, in exact detail. When he opened them again, the dreich weather made him sigh for the four hundredth time that day.

'Looks like a right cloudburst's on the way.' Elvis elbowed Cullen in the ribs. 'Bet you've pulled yourself off so much in the shower, you get a hard-on every time it rains.'

Cullen couldn't even muster the energy to turn the radio back up. *I need out of here. Or to get shot of this clown.* 'Me and Craig Hunter busted a steroid ring in a gym a few years back.'

'Sounds like a great excuse for you pair to hang around with a load of naked blokes.'

'That's Craig's thing, not mine.' The first raindrops battered off the pavement, so he got back in the car and scanned the radio. Had to settle for *TalkSport*. Even though the caller sounded off his head, it was better than listening to *Elvis in the Afternoon*.

Elvis got behind the wheel again, stroking his sideburns as he turned off the radio. 'Load of pish.'

In one of the towers, Dean Vardy was meeting a young woman. Unprotected, unguarded, and alone. With *his* record.

It didn't feel right.

Elvis cleared his throat and spat out of the open window. 'I was reading this article in the New Yorker by this boy called Art Oscar. Heard of him?' He took Cullen's silence as an instruction to keep talking. 'Said the war on drugs was a political ploy cooked up by Nixon to take out people who weren't going to vote for him. You know, blacks and anti-war lefties. Think that's true?'

Cullen cocked an eyebrow. 'I didn't know that.'

'Said it was heroin and marijuana at the start. Makes you wonder what this war on drugs is all for, eh?'

Cullen paused. 'I mean, I didn't know you could read.'

Elvis rolled his eyes.

Sod this for a game of soldiers.

Cullen opened the door and pointed at Elvis. 'Stay here and wait for Vardy. I'm going upstairs.'

~

CULLEN KNOCKED on the door three times, the secret signal that was about as subtle as a brick in the balls. Or one of Elvis's jokes.

The door cracked open and half a face appeared in the gap: round suedehead, receding hairline, deep frown, squinty eyes, and a limp moustache. DS Brian Bain. 'Sundance, I *told* you to wait downstairs, you tube.'

'You did.' Cullen looked down at him, letting Bain feel his height disadvantage. 'How about you go and babysit Elvis?'

'How about you piss off?'

Cullen stared at him, then lowered his eyes and unzipped his jacket to give his hands something to do other than punch the little bastard. 'I need to speak to the boss. Move.'

'You could ask nicely.'

'You wouldn't understand nicely.'

Bain stared at him, an uneasy smile twitching under his moist moustache. He recovered his cool, stepped back and swung the door open. 'You charming bastard.'

Cullen walked straight past him into the flat. Boarded-up windows, grotty old furniture, cold strip lighting making the place feel as inviting as a mortuary. Must be the last place in the tower block that hadn't been turned into an IKEA showroom.

In the kitchen, an Armed Response Unit loitered with intent. Four men, two women, dressed head to toe in black tactical gear, handguns strapped to their thighs, semi-automatic rifles slung tightly over their chests, index fingers resting idly on the trigger guards. The sight alone made Cullen twitchy.

DI Paul Wilkinson sat at the kitchen table, fussing over some recording equipment. Well, one of his hands was. The other was busy stuffing his mouth with chocolate raisins. A pong of stale sweat radiated off him. He caught sight of Cullen and dropped the smudgy paw to give his balls a good scratch. The guy seemed to gain at least a stone of flab every week, his manboobs straining at his latest checked farmer's shirt. 'Well done, Cullen. You found us all the way up here.' His Yorkshire accent was hiding behind an acquired Scottish one, just a few syllables off here and there. He gathered another handful of raisins and hoovered his wee sweeties up with a wet sucking noise. 'Despite being told to stay down there.' He chewed open-mouthed, a mess of brown and pink and purple.

'I'm worried about Amy Forrest, sir.' Cullen looked away from his jowly face. 'More specifically, about Vardy murdering her.'

Wilkinson stared at him for a few seconds. 'We're sticking to the plan. End of.' He popped another chocolate raisin in his gob.

Cullen glanced at the men and women standing to attention. 'Come on, you've got this lot hanging around with their thumbs up their arses, while Vardy's downstairs, right below our feet. With *her*. She's alone. With *him*. We know where he is, what he's capable of, and what he'll do if we don't stop him.'

Wilkinson snorted, then rolled his eyes at the figures in black. 'I said no.'

'Come on, let's just get in there. We can pick him up for the assault charge and collect evidence on the murder allegations while he's in custody.'

'Cullen...' Wilkinson took another mouthful and chewed slowly, really taking his time with it, like he was provoking Cullen to do something rash. And get himself kicked off another case. 'This isn't a simple murder investigation, the sort you're used to. You're in the drugs squad now and you need a bit more of this.' He tapped his temple, repeatedly, then kept his finger there.

Even the ARU cops became so restless they started running unnecessary checks of their equipment, rustling in the awkward silence.

'You need strategic thinking in this game.' Wilkinson

dropped his hand and leaned back on his chair. 'That girl is risking her life for this operation, seducing Vardy into some dirty pillow talk, while we record it. You want to do him for some assault that'll get him, what? Five years? Out in two? I want him bragging about his drug deals, I want him off the streets for life.' He gave Cullen a stern look, then reached for his raisins and popped another load into his mouth. 'That little enterprise nets him seven million quid a year, right? And you want him inside on assault charges. Leave the thinking to the big boys, yeah?'

Cullen stared at him. *Playing power games while an untrained mark lured a violent misogynist into a honey trap.* He flexed his fingers and zipped up his bomber jacket. 'Understood. Sir.' He turned away and stepped over to the wall to await orders.

I know all about your kind of 'strategic thinking'. Throw bait to a shark, then wash your hands of any responsibility if the shark kills the bait, just as long as you catch the predator.

The audio recorder on the table burst into noise. A door creaking, followed by a female voice: 'Why... why don't we slow things down a wee bit, eh?'

'Slow down? *Slow down?*' Vardy's voice, guttural and deep. 'You having a laugh? Thought this was a booty call.'

'Sure, but I want to get to know you first, Dean. I see you at the club all the time, but you're my boss. You're so distant. I mean you're cool and that, but I want to get to know you. What you're thinking.'

'Right now, I'm thinking that I want to smash your back doors in before I get back to work. How about you get to work on this rager, eh?'

'Okay, then. But I've got a wee surprise for you.' Amy Forrest's voice was close to the mic. Sounded like a door opening.

'Now we're talking!' Bed springs creaked, followed by some slobbery noises. 'Aye, that's the game. Cup the balls, nice and hard. Work the shaft. Just like that. Oooh. Bite it. Aye, you too.'

Cullen left Wilko glued to his recorder and stepped out of the flat into the dank corridor.

'Here, Sundance.' The door closed behind Bain. 'What a farce.'

'We need to stop it. Right now.' Cullen powered over to the stairwell. One floor down, Vardy was in a flat with Amy Forrest.

'We've got way more than enough on Vardy. We should be arresting him.'

'Wilko's having a laugh if he thinks that wee lassie will get Vardy to incriminate himself.' Bain was up close, moaning into his ear. 'I should still be running this. Load of—'

A gun shot, echoing up the stairwell. Cullen froze. Felt the pressure in his chest, took a sharp breath, glanced around, tried to—

Another shot.

Down there.

And another.

Shite, Amy's flat.

Cullen sprinted down the stairs, a rush of blood like static in his ears, disembodied voices shouting, then along Amy's floor, combat boots hammering along the corridor behind him, the door rushing towards him, his shoulder crashing through it, the force carrying him several paces into the flat before he stumbled to a halt. He jerked his head around to get his bearings.

There – bedroom door wide open, Dean Vardy's back framed by the doorway, motionless, head bowed, arms loose by his sides, trousers round his ankles, a gun dangling from his right hand.

Cullen felt like he was staring at a picture – a perfectly composed still life.

Then Vardy spun around. His eyes shot to Cullen, fury flashing. But, just like that, it was over. He dropped the gun, grinning. 'I found her like that.'

Cullen charged at him just as the first ARU cops piled into the flat, their shouts deafening in the confined space. He flew through the bedroom doorway, pushing Vardy sprawling onto the floor.

But Cullen's gaze was drawn to the bed.

A woman lay tangled in the blood-soaked sheets, naked but for her torn underwear. It felt wrong to look at her exposed body, even more wrong that her chest was burst open by a gunshot wound. Her head was like some overripe piece of fruit used for shooting practice.

Amy Forrest.

Cullen's mark.

Cullen's fault.

He grabbed Vardy's T-shirt and yanked him up. Fist poised,

ready to strike – but didn't. It took all his strength to stop himself from smacking that smug, smug face. 'You're going away for a long time.'

Vardy glanced around to make sure no one else was looking at him. Then he winked at Cullen, whispering, 'Sure, sweetheart, you keep telling yourself that.'

~

THE NEXT POLICE SCOTLAND BOOK, HEROES AND VILLAINS, is out now. You can get a copy at Amazon.

If you would like to be kept up to date with new releases from Ed James, please join the Ed James Readers Club.

Printed in Great Britain
by Amazon

48768045R00239